PALO DURO MUSTANGS

⤚THE WILL & BUCK SERIES: BOOK III⤚

BY

ALICE V. BROCK

Pen-L Publishing
Fayetteville, Arkansas
Pen-L.com

BOOKS BY ALICE V. BROCK

~ The Will & Buck Series ~

The River of Cattle, Book One

Mystery on the Pecos, Book Two

Palo Duro Mustangs, Book Three

PALO DURO
MUSTANGS

ISBN: 978-1-68313-251-6

Pen-L Publishing
Fayetteville, Arkansas
www.Pen-L.com

First Edition
Printed and bound in the USA

Cover and interior design by Kelsey Rice
Cover art by June Dudley

DEDICATION

This book is dedicated to the real Will—Will Nevill, a true cowboy, and his sweet wife, Logan.

Acknowledgments

A special thank you to June Dudley, western artist extraordinaire, who painted the beautiful cover artwork, Mustangs in Palo Duro Canyon. You can view her amazing work at www.junedudley.com. Also, to Teresa Galliher of Mustang Meadows for allowing us to photograph and use her Spanish Mustangs in the painting.

A heartfelt thank you to my sister, Sherrill Nilson, author of the Adalta Series—Karda, Hunter, and Falling. Her encouragement and constant support are what keeps me writing.

A very special thank you to Victoria Sherrow with the Institute of Children's Literature. This book would not have happened without her.

And, as always, a special thank you to the folks at Pen-L Publishing for their patience and for not giving up on me.

Blizzard: February 1869

Each step of Gray Wolf's hooves crushed the snow's crust and broke the muffled silence. Two Feathers squinted through the wind-swirled snow that burned his cheeks and stung his eyes. Ahead of him, a dark blur faded in and out of bare-branched cottonwoods along the snow-filled dry stream bed, sending a tingle up the back of his neck. Was that blur his missing bull? No, he was almost sure he'd seen the upright shape of a man. Yellow Hawk? Thoughts of that Comanche warrior sent a sick flutter through his empty stomach. How much longer would Yellow Hawk stalk him?

Forcing thoughts of his uncle, who had more sense than to be out in this weather, aside, Two Feathers pushed on. All day he'd looked for the bull but found no sign. *One of our bulls is dead, and now the other is missing. No bulls mean no calves, and no calves mean no Pecos River Ranch.* Those words had been the mantra Will Whitaker, his adopted brother, had been repeating since Big Tom had gone missing. Two Feathers shook his head, trying to throw off the weight of those words.

Dull gray clouds hung low, removing any sense of time. Instead of coming straight down, the high desert snow rode sideways on wind cold enough to snap bones. Two Feathers shuddered. Gray Wolf, his grullo horse, stopped and cocked his ears back toward Two Feathers. Stroking his neck, Two Feathers searched the falling snow around him. "I know, my friend. I do not like it either. I do not want to spend the night with floating shapes in the dark."

The horse stamped his hooves and tugged on the reins. Two Feathers strained to see as far as the storm would allow, but nothing showed but a bleak wall of gray clouds blending into the white snow. Snowflakes covered horse and rider, increasing his worries. If he didn't find Big Tom soon, he wouldn't make it back to the house before night, and the storm would swallow him in its icy grip. He had to find that bull, so quitting was not an option.

No tracks broke the white surface. The wind blurred his vision. Turning Gray Wolf, so their backs were to the wind, he sat for a few minutes and wiped at his tearing eyes and running nose. "You want to know something?" The horse turned back one ear. "It is dumb to be out here. Even the jackrabbits are safe and warm under the bushes. They have more sense than we do."

Cold seeped through his buffalo hair-lined moccasins and bit his toes. His thick wool socks and long johns usually kept him warm, but the temperature was dropping even lower as night approached. Humping his broad shoulders, he tightened the collar of his heavy wool coat around his neck and loosened its pull on his long braids.

Gray Wolf shook his head and rattled his bit when Two Feathers nudged him into the storm. "I know, my friend, but we have to find Big Tom. He is either in trouble—or dead—since he hasn't come up for hay in three days."

Two Feathers headed for a narrow gully he knew branched off a larger arroyo. Maybe Big Tom had found shelter there. As he descended, the banks grew taller and blocked the sharp blasts of wind. Several tracks, now faint and filling, showed on a trail heading into the gully.

Gray Wolf stopped and turned his head toward the rim.

Movement caught Two Feathers' eye. A vague shape floated for a second and then was gone. "Did you see that? What was it?" Gray Wolf shook his head.

Two Feathers squinted and shielded his eyes from the heavy falling flakes but saw nothing. He tapped the horse to start him moving. "We must find Big Tom and soon. We are starting to see things that are not there." He attempted a laugh, wondering if Gray Wolf believed that any more than he did.

A sharp gust of wind dumped snow from the pinyons and junipers along the rim above him, flattening his hat and spreading its cold, wet fingers down his collar. Two Feathers yanked his hat off and beat it against his leg.

"I have had enough of this snow. I saw tracks here, and now they are covered." He tied his bandana over his mouth, nose, and ears, slapped his hat back on and jerked it tight.

Gray Wolf plowed his way through the deepening snow. Up ahead, Two Feathers spotted a dark bulk... at last. Big Tom! His head turned in their direction as though waiting for them.

"There you are." An explosion of frosty breath and a sudden slump of shoulders released the hours of held-in tension. "Do you know how much trouble you are?"

With his rope stiff from the cold, Two Feathers struggled to loosen it enough to build a loop, twirl it over his head, and throw it over Big Tom's wide horns. The Longhorn bull didn't flinch. He lifted his left front hoof and moaned. Dallying the rope around the saddle horn, Two Feathers, his movements jerky from the cold, dismounted and followed his lariat through the deepening snow to Big Tom.

"Easy. What trouble are you in now?"

Even though the bull was gentle, Two Feathers approached him with caution. He'd learned the hard way that gentleness didn't always guarantee protection from harm. Snow crusted the bull's face and nostrils, so Two Feathers brushed away what he could from his nose to the curly hair between the massive widespread horns and scratched behind his ears. "Easy, ol' boy. Does that feel good?" Only then did he run his hand down the left foreleg. He lifted the big hoof, brushed away the snow, and found a mesquite thorn embedded in the tender flesh of the bull's foot. He pulled it out with his knife. A bellow, a wild swing of horns—Two Feathers ducked—and a gush of greenish pus followed the long thorn.

"Hey!" Two Feathers barked as he stood and brushed snow off his pants. "Be careful how you sling your head." He cleaned his knife in the snow, dried it on his coat, and shoved it down into the scabbard. "How long have you been carrying that thorn? Your foot is swollen and hot as a bed of coals. We need to get you to the barn so Will can fix it."

Testing his weight, Big Tom took a timid step—then two. With the bull limping and rumbling a low moan with every step, they headed home.

Once again, a dim form took shape in the distance and disappeared into the snowy blur so fast Two Feathers wasn't sure he'd seen anything. Who would be out in such dangerous weather? Why did they hang back? Was it wolves hungry enough to leave their dens? That thought set his nerves humming and sharpened his senses.

He nudged Gray Wolf to keep him moving. When they turned into the larger arroyo, the wind slammed into them again, and the drifts grew larger. Gray Wolf and Big Tom floundered in their depth. Two Feathers decided they wouldn't reach the house by nighttime. He remembered an undercut cave in the windward wall he'd seen on the way into the arroyo. It was deep enough for him and Gray Wolf. After a short time of floundering in the snow drifts, he spotted the tangled jumble of driftwood that marked the entrance to the cave. He closed off the opening using the larger branches to support his ground cloth. He wondered what he wanted more, a fire to warm him or a means to keep the strange shadows away.

When he hobbled Big Tom to keep him from drifting before the storm, he ran his hand up the infected leg. He felt the warmth of fever halfway to the knee. He didn't like that foot's feel, look, or smell. He packed snow as high as he could on the leg but knew Big Tom wouldn't stand still long enough for it to help.

A small fire spread its weak warmth toward Two Feather's cold hands. He wondered what Will and the ranch hands were eating for supper back at the Pecos River Ranch. He scooped snow into his tin cup with a piece of venison jerky and let it simmer at the edge of his fire. Soon, he sipped the warm broth and chewed the softened meat with relief. Wrapped in wool blankets from his bedroll, a large stack of stout sticks beside him, and his feet resting on warmed rocks, he packed his worries into the back of his mind and settled in for a long, cold night. Gray Wolf snuffled at the last bits of grain piled on a flat rock in the back of their shelter.

Before sleep got a firm grip, the crunch of footsteps and the soft nicker of a horse startled Two Feathers. A voice spoke to him in Comanche. The familiar low tone stole his breath and most of his courage. Scrambling into the deepest corner of the undercut cave, he held his knife in one hand, his rifle in the other. The ground cloth lifted, and a man, squatting low, slipped into the shelter.

Dark leathery skin covered sharp cheekbones. The man's broad face was framed with long thick braids wrapped with hairy buffalo hide that hung to his waist. Hawk feathers, fastened with a tight leather band around his forehead, hung with them. His chin thrust forward, almost to a point.

Yellow Hawk!

His uncle hunkered down on his haunches, stretched his

hands to the fire's warmth, and stared at Two Feathers. His eyes, as always, were flint-hard and black, like deep pits. Hatred flared in those eyes, then faded to something that had always left Two Feathers anxious and shaking. Something he didn't understand. Something that made his hackles rise.

"I have followed you since the sun rose. You did not conceal yourself. Your decision to live with the white man made you forget the ways of the Comanche." His voice was hard and sharp as slate.

He continued to stare at Two Feathers for a long time. A slight twitch pulled at the corners of the slash that was his mouth. The voice deepened even more. "You are easy to find." The words dripped like venom.

Two Feathers couldn't answer. His uncle's words tightened his shoulders and pulled his elbows against his ribs. He pressed his back into the hard rocks of the cave wall. *Kee*. No, *Kee, Kee*, echoed over and over in his head like a pounding drum. Fear of his uncle had plagued him since he was small, before the Day of Death when the soldiers killed his Comanche mother and Yellow Hawk killed his white father.

He sucked in a shaky breath and the cold air lit a flicker of courage in Two Feathers. He returned to the fire and slid his knife into its scabbard but held his rifle ready in his lap.

"I reject you as my uncle. I am not a son to you." He tried to put force into his words, but it was not there.

Yellow Hawk snorted. "I do not want you for a son." He spoke through bared teeth. "You are. . . *white*." The last word slithered past the snarl on his lips.

The stones of the cave hung heavy over them, dark and foreboding, and for a moment, it felt as if it would all crash down on Two Feathers. "Do you not remember teaching me, when I was small, about the dogwood trees? How to find the best trees to make arrows? I remember your hand on my shoulder as we walked through the woods."

Yellow Hawk said nothing.

"Now, I remember that day three years ago before I ran from your village, your hands around my neck squeezing the breath of life out of me. I remember seeing hatred and death in your eyes." Two Feathers drew in another sharp breath, until the roaring in his ears stopped and he could force the words past his anger. "Morning Dove, your sister, was my mother. John Randall was my father." He leaned forward and drove his gaze to meet Yellow Hawk's. "You cannot change that. I *AM* Comanche. I *AM* your blood." The force of his words surprised Two Feathers. Never in his life had he spoken so forcefully to Yellow Hawk. It felt good.

For a long time, Yellow Hawk sat still. Two Feathers watched his eyes. He wanted to see something good there. He wanted to see—family. What he saw instead were flat raven-black eyes that simmered with hate.

The warrior's look never shifted. He slid his arm from under his buffalo robe, picked up a bent, gnarled chunk of cedar driftwood about the size of his hand, and pointed it at Two Feathers. He rolled it over in his hand. His gaze shifted from the boy to the wood he held.

"Yes, you are my sister's child. She wanted me to give you a strong horse." Again, those dark eyes latched onto his. "I never did."

Yellow Hawk drew a short knife from his belt and started carving the chunk of cedar. Two Feathers had forgotten that his uncle liked carving animals. Cedar was his wood of choice. Two Feathers watched the knife change the chunk's shape and wondered what it would become. He looked away to hide the smirk that showed up on his face, sometimes it was hard to figure out what animal he'd carved.

"The storm blows, and the wind freezes everything it touches. I ask for shelter. Tonight, I would be your guest, not your enemy." Yellow Hawk's words filled the air between them and hung there.

Two Feathers wanted to shake his head. *He hates me. He wants me dead Why give him shelter?* Outrage rose in Two Feathers. He opened his mouth to refuse him when he heard the soft whisper of Weeping Woman, *that is not the Comanche way. That is not the way I taught you.* His aunt, who'd loved him when no one else had, who'd cared for him and protected him from the rage of Yellow Hawk. This was her husband, she loved him. Instead, he forced his head down and back up.

At Two Feathers' faint nod, Yellow Hawk pulled back the ground cloth and brought his horse inside.

The hours crawled through the night. Two Feathers kept the fire burning and fought against sleep—his knife ready, his rifle on his lap—watching the bitter smirk on the lips of the man his aunt and his mother had loved. He tried to see what they saw. But he failed. He saw only hate in the hollow core of his eyes, in the hard line of his jaw, and in the dull sheen of his knife.

Yellow Hawk

In the dim light of the fire, Two Feathers studied the hard face of his uncle. The slight crackle of the flames as they released only weak heat left the shelter in deep cold. It worked its way into his bones as he watched Yellow Hawk whittle away cedar chips. As the hours passed, the body of a horse took shape.

Two Feathers fed sticks to the flames and pulled his blankets tighter around him. The heat from the fire warmed only his front. His back felt the cold drafts coming in around the ground cloth covering the opening. He couldn't decide which was colder, the temperature or Yellow Hawk's eyes.

A bit later—he was unsure how long, Two Feathers jerked awake. He couldn't believe he had fallen asleep. The fire was still burning, but a dim light slipped around the ground cloth and into the cave. Yellow Hawk rose and stretched, the knife still in his hand.

One long step brought him around the fire. Two Feathers gaze climbed up the fur-lined moccasins that stood over him and stopped at the knife. It seemed to belong in that hard, scarred hand—like one twitch would send it flying.

Two Feathers couldn't take his eyes from that knife. He felt frozen to the ground. Neither his legs, arms, nor mind would move.

Stepping back, Yellow Hawk returned the knife to its scabbard. He pointed to the crudely finished horse on a rock by the fire.

"I carved this horse because your mother asked me to." Picking it up, he shoved the legs and then the tail into the ashes and rubbed them black with soot.

"This is the only horse I will give you. It is a gift from your mother." He dropped it in Two Feathers' lap.

Jumping up, Two Feathers spilled it onto the ground and stepped away.

"This is not a gift from you or my mother. It is a warning."

Yellow Hawk stopped at the cave opening. "The dunnia is mine. I will have the yellow-horse-with-black-mane-and-tail."

The corners of his mouth twitched into a crooked smirk. "You cannot stop me. You are *not* Comanche." He disappeared into the thin morning light.

Two Feathers stood too stunned to move. The cave opening held him, and he couldn't pull his eyes away. He waited, knowing his uncle would come back, knowing he would kill him.

But he didn't. The cold wrapped its icy arms around him, and he shivered. The fire died down to ash-covered coals. He found several small twigs and got it going again. Picking up the carved horse, he turned it over and over in his hands. Puzzled, he wondered why Yellow Hawk had carved it. It wasn't a good job. In fact, it was ugly. His mouth twisted into a lopsided grimace. A gift from Yellow Hawk had to mean something evil. He started to throw it into the fire. Then, he remembered Yellow Hawk saying his mother had asked him to give her son a strong horse. The figure was stout, with thick legs and a long, muscled neck. He rubbed his fingers over the mane, tail, and legs stained black. He knew it was Buck, the dunnia, the beloved horse that belonged to his brother, Will. Clenching his fist around the carving, he understood. The message was clear. Yellow Hawk wanted him to never forget—he was coming.

He slumped, turned the figure around, and studied it through narrow eyes. This didn't make sense.

Morning Dove slipped into his thoughts. Maybe Yellow Hawk was keeping his promise to Two Feathers' mother. Maybe in some twisted way, he was giving her son a strong horse.

He sat close to the fire, braided his hair, and stared at the horse. Picking up the carving, he held it at arm's length. From a distance, it wasn't so bad. He dropped it in the medicine bag that hung from his belt. Maybe it would be best to consider it a gift from his mother.

Big Tom's sore foot made for slow going, so the trip to the warmth of the barn took most of the day. When Two Feathers pulled Gray Wolf to a stop across the creek from the ranch house and barn, he hollered, "Hello, the house." He knew Will, Jake, or Tony would be on the lookout. To be mistaken for an enemy and shot wasn't how he wanted to end this cold trip. He stepped Gray Wolf down the creek bank and into the water crusted with ice. Big Tom balked and refused to put his sore foot on the rocky creek bottom. Two Feathers screwed his face into a scowl.

"I do not blame you for not wanting to step in the creek, but this is the only way to get to the barn. I am cold. Gray Wolf is cold. You are cold." Impatience made his words brittle. "So, come on." He clicked his tongue several times, tugged firmly on the rope, and Big Tom crossed the creek with a loud bellow.

Will Whitaker met Two Feathers at the cave they used as a barn.

"I'm sure glad to see you and Big Tom. I worried last night when that storm hit."

Two Feathers was too cold to do anything but nod. He turned Big Tom into the corral next to the barn and dismounted. Leading Gray Wolf into his stall, he watched the dunnia, Will's big buckskin stallion, greet the grullo. At seventeen hands, Buck towered over Gray Wolf. They nuzzled each other and nickered their hellos. He decided he would never get over wishing Buck was his. Then, he immediately felt guilty. Gray Wolf was the perfect horse for him, both fast and strong. He could run all day if needed.

Will took the saddle and settled it over the top rail of the stall. He spread the saddle blanket next to it. After throwing some hay into the troughs for the horses, he scooped grain into their feed bin and, breaking the ice in the barrel, filled their water buckets.

Two Feathers leaned against the end post dividing the stalls and watched Will. How much should he tell him about the night with Yellow Hawk? The carving was from his mother. That's what he wanted to believe. He brushed the hair on Gray Wolf's back until it lay smooth. His body was heavy, and weariness made his movements stiff and awkward. The cold had seeped so deep inside him he was afraid if he tried to wiggle his toes, they would break off.

He felt Will watching him. "Stop staring at me. I am not hurt."

"I know you saw him. Worry lines are all over your face, and I see fear in your eyes."

Two Feathers watched his brother. The bulkiness of Will's heavy coat and chaps made him look stouter than he was.

Will had grown taller this past year, but Two Feathers knew he wasn't as tall as he wanted to be at thirteen. His tanned face was almost as dark as Two Feathers' own, except for the white band between his hat line and hairline that showed when Will cocked his hat to the back.

He shook himself and pushed away from the post. "I will tell you what happened when we go to the house to eat. Big Tom's foot is hurt. You need to treat it."

"What's wrong with it?"

"A mesquite thorn stuck deep. I think it has festered."

Will took the turpentine can and pine tar pail from a shelf built into the cave wall and handed the pail to Two Feathers. "Put this on the stove in the house to soften, so I can spread it."

Jake and Tony rode into the ranch yard from behind the adobe house. The twin ranch hands were impossible to tell apart with their faces covered by woolen neck scarves wound around their heads and their hats pulled low. Two Feathers waved the lanky pair toward the corral on his way to the house. He stoked the fire, and while waiting for the pitch to warm, he ran back to the corral and jumped onto the rails to watch.

Will opened the corral gate, and the twins rode in. Keeping a watchful eye on Big Tom, they circled wide.

"What's going on?" said one, his voice muffled in the scarf.

"Need help?" mumbled the other.

"Big Tom picked up a mesquite thorn." Two Feathers hooked one leg over the top rail.

"Jake, get a rope on his right forefoot," said Will, setting the turpentine can on the ground. "Tony, rope his back leg and stretch him out. He's gonna jump around some when the turpentine hits that foot. When I slap on the pine tar, hold him. Don't let go right away."

He looked toward the house. "Two Feathers, that tar ought to be 'bout ready."

Two Feathers ran across the yard. Holding the wire handle with a rag, he quickly gulped down a warm cup of coffee, then hurried back, letting the door slam, and set the pail next to the turpentine.

The twins started their loops twirling in the air, and before Big Tom knew it, he was stretched out on the ground.

"Watch those horns, Will. He likes to throw his head." Two Feathers shimmied through the bars.

Will dodged the horns and soaked the bottom of the hoof with turpentine. The bull bellowed, and the giant horns swung. Hunkered low, Two Feathers swapped the can for the pitch pail, and Will smeared on the warm tar, one eye on the foot and the other on the horns. When Will finished, both boys ran and jumped to the top rail.

"Hold his foot up, Jake." Will hollered over Big Tom's loud roar.

After a few minutes, the cold hardened the tar, and the twins released their ropes. Big Tom snorted his displeasure at his rough treatment, then limped to the hay piled in a corner where the barn blocked the north wind and lay down.

"Maybe the snow helped keep the infection down. Maybe we'll only have to treat him this once." Will's voice held a little hope and a lot of worry.

They watched the bull for a few minutes. Two Feathers didn't like what he saw. "Will, why did he not eat?"

Will joined him. "I wondered the same thing. You know he's hungry. I'm more worried about that runny nose. He's got snot all over his face. We'll have to watch him for the next few days."

After Jake and Tony settled their horses in the barn, they went to the other side of the cave to their living quarters and fired up the stove. Will and Two Feathers followed the twins. Every few minutes, Will went to check on Big Tom. Each time he returned, Two Feathers saw more worry lines on his face.

With his hands warming on his coffee cup and his feet thawing on the sides of the potbellied stove, Two Feathers struggled to keep his eyes open. When it was too dark to see Big Tom, they finished their coffee and headed toward the adobe house and a pot of warm lamb stew.

Later that night, after supper, Will, Two Feathers, Jake, and Tony sat around the table in the kitchen. The hot cookstove warmed the room, and the moon's glow cast a dim light through the window over the sink. Two Feathers had eaten very little and sat absorbed in his worries of how much to tell Will.

"Two Feathers? What happened?" Will asked.

Jake leaned forward over his cup. "Come on, boy. I can tell by your face you saw Yellow Hawk. Tell us what he did." The words came out as a command, not a request.

"I saw no tracks all day and decided to check that deep arroyo to see if Big Tom had gone there to get out of the wind. I found him and started for home, but his sore foot slowed us down. The storm worsened, and I decided to make a shelter. After nightfall, I heard a horse coming and the voice of Yellow Hawk."

Will gasped, gripping his cup so hard he spilled his coffee onto the table. "What'd he say?"

"He wanted to come in out of the storm."

"Did you let him?" Tony asked.

Two Feathers cocked his head to the side and gave Tony a how-was-I-going-to-stop-him look.

"Yes, I let him in."

Will jumped to his feet. "He could've killed you." His voice rose to a choking squeak. "Are you stupid? Why'd you do that?"

"He was gone by morning."

"He's been tormenting us for two years but didn't do anything to you when he had the chance. Why?" Will's words slammed together in a tight croak.

"Sit down, Will," said Tony. "Take a deep breath."

Will sat.

"Two Feathers?" Tony reached across the table and gently squeezed the boy's arm. "What happened?"

"After the shock of seeing him passed, I knew he would not harm me. I was safe as long as he was a guest in my shelter. But I kept my knife and rifle in my lap." A shudder shook his body. "I told him he was no longer my uncle. Hate had always been in his eyes when he looked at me, but this time it was more. One time, when I was little, I was playing in the rocks near the creek where we camped, sliding on my belly, pretending to be sneaking up on an enemy. A rattlesnake was coiled under a narrow rock shelf, and I did not see him until I heard his rattle. We stared at each other for a long time. The eyes were an ugly flat tan with a slit in the middle that was dark black. They were scary, but there was no hate. Yellow Hawk's eyes were blacker than the snake's and looked wild. Those eyes scared me more than the snake's."

Silence filled the room. Two Feathers sucked in a shuddered breath and sat up straight. "We thought he would not come in the winter. We thought we would be safe."

Will stood, took the coffee pot off the stove, and filled all their cups. "We were wrong."

Yes, we were wrong. I will never understand Yellow Hawk. Two Feathers' thoughts were sluggish with fatigue, and his head hurt. *Why does he hate me so? What did I do?*

Early the next morning, Two Feathers put on two pairs of woolen socks before stomping into his boots. It was a tight fit, but the boots were warmer than his moccasins. After building a fire in the cook stove, Will followed him outside. The wind had calmed overnight, but the air was cold. Two Feathers, Will, Jake, and Tony, went about their usual morning chores even though a quiet hung over the Pecos River Ranch that made Two Feathers jump at any unusual sound. The creak of a tree branch as it sagged under the weight of the snow. . . the crunch of men's boots breaking through the thin layer of ice covering the snowy ground . . . the splash of Jake's ax chopping holes in the frozen creek. . . . all these prompted a quick search for any movement in the trees.

While Two Feathers fed the horses, Will poured buckets of water Jake had brought up from the creek into their water pails. When the morning chores were done and breakfast over, all four lingered in the kitchen's warmth.

Will poured the last of the coffee into their cups. "Tony, you and Jake stay here and look sharp. Take turns manning the lookout behind the barn. Jake, the woodpile's low. This would be a good day to cut those logs we dragged up from the creek. We'll be back by noon or early afternoon at the latest. And keep a watch on Big Tom. See if he's eating. Be sure he has water."

Two Feathers piled their cups in the sink and followed Jake and Tony outside. The door slammed, and Will crossed the porch, pulling on his gloves.

Two Feathers stood beside his partner, his eyes roaming over the snow-covered ranch yard. It shimmered in the sun. Suddenly, Two Feathers was tired of worrying. He decided to change things. He nudged Will. "Watch this." A grin tugged at his lips.

Two Feathers waited until Tony was in the barn, then he scooped a handful of snow from the hitching rail, packed a tight snowball, and smacked Jake between his shoulder blades. Jake whooped and grabbed up a handful of snow. Two Feathers and Will scrambled for cover behind the woodpile, leaving Jake in the open.

"We got you now," Will yelled. "There's no place to hide."

Tony, with Buck following, burst through the barn door, throwing snowballs as fast as he could make them.

Two Feathers dodged a well-aimed throw from Tony. "Bad shot. You missed me."

Jake blasted him high on the shoulder. Cold exploded over his neck and cheek and hung up in his coat collar. He hit the ground as though wounded but came up with three snowballs he rapid-fired at the twins.

When the snow on the woodpile was used up, Will stepped out into the open and sailed one over Jake's head. Buck scrambled back and forth between the teams, managing to escape the flying missiles, but mashing the snow into brown slush.

Tony nailed Two Feathers in the chest. "Now, who's a bad shot?"

Two Feathers hollered a loud whoop and sent a big one flying hard and fast that caught Tony on the rump as he bent over to pack more ammunition. Tony yelled, "Hey, that ain't fair." He fired one back that caught Two Feathers in the belly. The fight lasted until one of Will's snowballs whacked Buck on the hip. With a loud snort, he trotted back across the yard and into the barn.

"Well, I guess he told us it's time to get to work." Will stepped onto the porch and peeled off his wet gloves. "It may take a handful of corn dodgers to get Buck to forgive me."

With his mood lightened, Two Feathers was eager to start the day's chores. The morning air was crisp, and the wind had stopped blowing. Two Feathers followed Will and Buck toward the Pecos River, searching for wayward cattle to haze back toward the ranch. Tomorrow was hay feeding day. He figured if they pushed the cattle closer to home today, tomorrow's efforts wouldn't take so long.

The trail led upriver along the sandy banks until the canyon walls narrowed to the river's edge, where it wound its way up the steep banks to the desert above. Two Feathers searched for tracks of the black gelding Yellow Hawk was riding but saw none. There were no fresh cattle tracks either. After about an hour, Will stopped and pointed to the ground—sheep tracks. They scouted around and found the tracks of Tomas, the youngest son of Mateo, their friend and closest neighbor.

"What is Tomas doing this far from home?" Two Feathers kicked Gray Wolf into a lope. "We need to find him before Yellow Hawk does."

An hour later, the sound of bleating sheep filled the desert, and they rode up to Tomas. Sheep scattered, dogs barked, and Tomas hollered out his welcome.

Dismounting, Will smiled, pulled off the boy's wool cap, and ruffled his black hair.

"Welcome." Tomas' gaze hopped from face to face, delighted to see them.

Two Feathers put his hands on the slight shoulders and gave him a gentle shake so the boy would know he was serious. "Tomas, you must take your sheep and your dogs and go home. Yellow Hawk is near." At the sound of the dreaded name, the young boy's face paled.

Two Feathers' spirits sank. *Why does it have to be my uncle's name that brings that look to Tomas' face?*

Will picked up the supplies and shoved them into packs. "What are you doing here? The snow covers any grass."

"Sheep dig under the snow. The wind has died. Papa says it's safe to come. Comanche are far away in the winter. They don't come when it snows."

Will huffed. "Well, there's one here now. Go home as fast as you can and stay there. Tell your Papa Two Feathers has seen Yellow Hawk."

Tomas slung his packs over his shoulder and called orders to his dogs to head the sheep toward the Pecos River.

Later that afternoon, after they had pushed the cattle on the east side of the Pecos across the river and onto their range, Two Feathers lagged behind Will as they headed further north. He let Will push any bunches that had drifted with the storm back toward home, where he wished he was going. He was cold and hungry. His lunch was so long gone his stomach didn't even remember it.

Will stopped and let Two Feathers catch up. "I haven't seen any sign of Yellow Hawk's tracks. He must have headed back to Palo Duro Canyon. Let's make a pass through the Red

Mesa country and head to Mateo's." Will pulled his chin out from the tall collar of his coat so he could be heard. "I could use some of Alma's good cooking and warm kitchen fire. How Mateo ended up with a wife as good a cook as Alma, I don't know."

A low chuckle rumbled from the depth of Two Feathers' wool muffler wrapped around his mouth and ears and over his head. "Lucky for us, he did."

Red Mesa rose from the snow-covered desert floor in the distance. The ground was rocky, and the horses picked their way with care. A low rise topped with jumbled rocks blown clear of snow stood before them. Just as Two Feathers turned Gray Wolf to ride around it, a shot rang out and pinged off a large rock to his left. The horses bolted toward a clump of juniper they had just passed. Bailing out of his saddle, Two Feathers hit the ground and rolled into the middle of a cluster of rocks and trees.

Will hit the ground beside him. "Buck, hide!" he yelled. The horses galloped back the way they had come. "Did you see where the shot came from?"

"No."

Two Feathers lay still under the bushes, his carbine in hand. The cold seeped through his pants and chilled his already cold legs.

Neither boy spoke. Neither boy moved. Both boys waited.

"*Two Feathers!*" The harsh bellow of Yellow Hawk's voice startled Two Feathers.

Will laid his arm across his brother's back. "Don't move. I'm not sure he knows exactly where we are."

"He knows!"

Two Feathers heard the click of hoof on stone and knew Gray Wolf and Buck weren't far away. He glanced back to be sure they were behind cover.

"*Two Feathers.*" The Comanche called again. "*I will get*

you and your white brother. I will have the dunnia and kill the grullo you ride. You could never pick a good horse."

"Look! There he is." Will gasped and grabbed Two Feathers' arm.

Yellow Hawk stood on the top of the low rise and raised his rifle. He screamed his war cry, and the sound was as cold as the snow they lay on.

Will jerked up his rifle, aimed, and was about to fire when Two Feathers put his hand over the hammer. "Do not waste your bullet. He has moved out of range."

Yellow Hawk disappeared from the top of the rise. Two Feathers lay still for a long time, one hand on Will's shoulder. Assured there was no movement, he stood. They mounted their horses and headed for Mateo's. Two Feathers scanned the ground as they rode, looking for tracks—unshod horse, cattle, or sheep. He saw none. Where was Tomas?

A Dog

Two Feathers and Will reached Mateo's house at dusk. A loud chorus of happy barks from Tomas' dogs greeted them, and the bleats of the sheep in a corral behind the barn told Two Feathers the boy had made it home. When several other dogs appeared from the barn and added their voices to the confusion, Gray Wolf's skittish movements threatened their safety. It took Two Feathers a few minutes to settle him enough to dismount. He grabbed Buck's reins at the bit to keep him from rearing. Will spoke to the big stallion and stroked his neck. Buck calmed some, and Will dismounted, but when a smart-aleck older pup got too close, one powerful kick sent him rolling like a yipping snowball.

The dogs soon lost interest and retreated to the warmth of the barn by way of a hole dug under a corner. Will and Two Feathers, opening half of the wide double door, led their horses to the one empty stall. They stripped off the saddles and blankets and settled the gear on racks along the side wall, saddle blankets on top to dry.

"I hope Buck behaves and doesn't beat up on Gray Wolf since they are crowded in here." Will's light chuckle made Two Feathers glance at him.

"Humph!" Two Feathers grunted. "Do not fret. Gray Wolf will keep Buck quiet. He always does." He poured water into their tub, and Will scooped grain from a bin and dumped it into the feed trough.

Mateo, his short, stout figure wrapped in a sheepskin coat, came in behind them with an affectionate greeting that included giant hugs and a firm pounding on the back.

"Welcome, muchachos. Ven a mi casa. Come to my house. Alma saw you ride in and stirred the fire in the stove. You'll have hot food soon."

The boys followed their host to the low-roofed adobe house, hung their coats and hats on hooks by the door, and headed for the roaring fire in the open fireplace. Stretching his cold, stiff hands to the heat, Two Feathers rubbed them back and forth and flexed his fingers to loosen them. He roasted his front side for a while before turning to roast his backside. Beside him, Will's slow circles matched his brother's and brought a giggle from Elana, Mateo's oldest daughter.

With a bright smile, like the one Tomas often wore, she called her Papa to the table. Her long, brownish-black hair hung in a single fat braid down her back, and her dark eyes sparkled in the firelight. Two Feathers chose to ignore his brother's help-me look when she peppered Will with question after question about Jake and Tony. She had more questions than Will had answers. Two Feathers grinned and headed for the big table in the center of the room.

The topic on everyone's mind was left unspoken during supper. After the dishes were cleared and the young children sent to bed, the food that had tasted so good during their meal's laughter and happy talk now sat like a lump in Two Feathers' stomach. Each face he looked at was grim. He hated that look. Why was Yellow Hawk so filled with hate that it spilled out on everyone else?

At one end of the table, Mateo wore a stern expression mirrored by César, his oldest son, at the other end. Alma, who usually fussed over the boys, constantly shoving food at them, now sat still next to her husband and gripped his hand. Elena leaned against her mother, her eyes wide and her teeth nibbling her lip.

Two Feathers sat across from the women at the long table, Will beside him. In the warmth of the kitchen stove, he drank his coffee in the silence. Finally, Mateo uttered the dreaded name. "Tell us about Yellow Hawk."

Two Feathers' hands twitched, and he locked eyes with Mateo. He described seeing the shadows in the snow and how his uncle entered his shelter. "At first, all I saw in his eyes was anger. That I have always seen. But then, his face changed. It looked like it was carved from stone. Then the look was gone."

"What kind of look? What are you talking about?" Will asked.

Two Feathers stared at his hands folded on the table. Finally, he looked up. "What I saw on his face scared me more than he ever has before. It was like something evil was trapped there."

"The children must stay close to the house," said Alma. The quiver in her voice saddened Two Feathers.

"At Mass," her voice was almost a whisper, "the priest told of a Comanche raiding in this area. He's often alone. He steals horses, kills cattle and sheep, and... people. Halcón Amarillo!"

"Yellow Hawk." Two Feathers translated.

Alma looked at Elena. "Do you understand this?"

"Si, Mama," her words barely loud enough to be heard.

Mateo's calm tone soothed Two Feathers' raw nerves. "We must be careful. Here and at your ranch we must always be on guard. Never go anywhere alone. Always watch."

"But" César interrupted his father, "we can't let this Comanche make us afraid. We go on. We work our ranches. We live our lives."

Will looked at Two Feathers. "We will fight this together."

He looked at the scar on the palm of his hand left there when Pa, shot by Yellow Hawk and dying, cut his and Two Feathers' hands and smeared their blood together, making them blood brothers. He picked up Two Feathers' hand and put the scars together. "We are brothers."

Two Feathers' hand gripped Will's with a comforting firmness. "Brothers."

Two Feathers shifted away from Will and looked at Mateo. "We need a dog."

A smile brightened Will's glum face. "Hey. That's a great idea! A dog would warn us when someone was near the house. Like this morning. The dogs made so much noise half of New Mexico heard them."

Mateo rose from the table. "We need sleep. Tomorrow Tomas will give you one of his sheepdogs. We have too many." He walked away from the table mumbling Demasiados perros, too many dogs. Alma followed, dragging Elena behind her.

The next morning after breakfast, Tomas bundled up in his warm coat and knit cap and left to feed his dogs and put out hay for his sheep. Two Feathers followed him to look at the pups Tomas had locked up for the night in a slat-sided, grass-roofed hut behind the barn.

"I will help you feed, and then we can look at the dogs," Two Feathers said and plucked off Tomas' cap and tousled the thick-cropped hair.

"No, señor. Let the pups out. They will be hungry. You can watch them run and pick the one you want."

Two Feathers untied the rope holding the door and was nearly run over by the rush of puppies that leaped, jumped, and flew out in their mad dash for the back door of Alma's kitchen. Mateo, Will, César, and Estevan, one year younger than César but several inches taller, sidestepped and let the pups rush by. Two Feathers watched the last of the pack pass but didn't see one big enough for their needs. He wanted an older, smarter dog, one with experience. He followed the others to the barn.

There was none of the usual teasing among the four boys and Mateo. Silence hung like a black cloud in the barn. While Buck and Gray Wolf munched their oats, Two Feathers and Will helped muck out the barn, feed the milk cow and the other horses.

Two Feathers shot a quick glance at Will when they finished and dipped his head toward Mateo. Will nodded, layered his hands on the scoop handle he was using to clean the droppings, and rested his chin on top. "Mateo, we have more troubles with the ranch than Yellow Hawk."

"¿Qué?, what?"

César and Estevan left to do their outside chores, letting in a cold draft through the quickly opened door. Mateo hung his pitchfork on the tool rack, put his hands on his hips, and looked back and forth between the boys. "You'll learn on a ranch, there's always trouble. Mucha molestia. Much trouble."

Will brushed Buck's back and smoothed the saddle blanket before he spoke. "We lost too many cattle this winter. The storms have been bad, and cattle drifted. We got most of them back, but our losses were still severe. Two bulls died, and Big Tom has an infected foot. We've fewer steers to send with Mr. Goodnight when he comes. We've decided to buy two new bulls from John Chisum at Bosque Grande below Fort Sumner."

"Sí. That's a good plan. Charlie Goodnight's a good man. Let him get the bulls."

"He won't be here till late summer or early fall, and we need them now."

Two Feathers spread fresh straw in the stall. He walked up beside Will. Once again, he heard the worry in Will's voice. It had crept in little by little after Yellow Hawk raided the ranch and killed Pa last year. It now lived there, keeping his words tight like the drawstring around a medicine bag.

"In early summer," said Will, "when you shear the sheep, we'll sell our half of the wool from the flock we have together. But for now, it will take all the ranch money to buy the bulls. Charlie won't bring our money for last year's steers till he comes by here with a herd headed north in July or August. We need money sooner for our supplies. Pa never ran a tab at any store. If things don't change, I'll be forced to do what Pa never did."

Two Feathers watched Mateo, hoping to see understanding. He wanted to help Will persuade Mateo to help them, but the English words wouldn't come to him, only the Comanche words. He finished saddling Gray Wolf.

Mateo said nothing.

Will slung Buck's saddle onto the tall horse, settled it on the blanket, then reached under his belly for the cinch.

"Jake and Tony will buy the bulls. They're good cattlemen. I know they'll pick good ones. We need César to help us with the ranch while they're gone. Two Feathers has an idea to raise quick money. When they return, he and I will go catch wild horses, and they will need César. We will be gone for a while."

There was silence in the barn. Mateo leaned against a support pole and chewed on a straw. Finally, he looked at Two Feathers. "Do you know where to find caballos salvajes?"

"Sí."

"Where?"

"Palo Duro Canyon."

Mateo pushed himself away from the pole. He shuddered and whispered the dreaded word, "Comancheria, the land of the Comanche."

He looked from Two Feathers to Will and back.

"You've been there?"

"Sí." Two Feathers answered. "I have been there many times."

"What will you do with the horses?"

Will answered. "We'll rough break them and sell them to a horse trader I know in Las Vegas."

The boys led their horses from the relative warmth of the barn into the snowy cold and mounted. Puffs of air steamed from their horse's nostrils, as well as their own mouths.

"I'll send César and Estaban to help. They must bring in hay from the stacks before they come. When the snow stops, the coyotes and wolves will hunt. We'll keep the sheep close to the house. César and Estavan will come in. . . one week. When you ride to the Comancheria, watch with eyes that see what shouldn't be there. Smell the wind. Listen. Ride with your thoughts on the trail."

Mateo focused on Two Feathers. Those sharp brown eyes pierced through him as though they could search out what was hidden. His breath caught until a slight smile softened Mateo's gaze, and a callused hand patted his leg. "You lead."

Two Feathers breathed a sigh of relief when those invading eyes shifted to Will. "You follow Two Feathers. He's Comanche. You aren't. He knows things you'll never learn. Do what he tells you, and don't question. Goodbye, my friends."

The boys nodded. Will's eyes grew round and large and glistened in the cold air. Two Feathers felt a lump rise in his throat. He had to swallow hard to breathe around it.

When Mateo reached the house, he stopped with his hand on the door handle and called out, "Chicos, vuelvan a casa con muchos caballos. Boys, come home with lots of horses." He stepped inside and closed the door.

Tomas ran up, dragging a brown, battle-scarred dog on a long rope. He started to hand the rope to Will but took one look at Buck and gave it to Two Feathers. "Ten cuidado. Es un perro muy malo!"

He backed away from the dog and toward the house. "Will,

Papa said to take Oso. His name means bear. He's a good watchdog. He barks loud and doesn't like people. . . except me. And he's good at hunting cows." He spun around and ran for the house, wiping his eyes.

"That boy hates to give up any of his dogs," said Will.

Two Feathers wrapped the rope around the saddle horn, and they headed toward home. Since the dog either dragged on his haunches or jerked on the line, Two Feathers kept a little distance between Gray Wolf and Buck. He didn't want the dog to upset the stallion. Buck hadn't been around dogs much. After an hour of riding, Oso settled down and moved up beside Gray Wolf, his trot keeping pace with the horses.

"What did Tomas say when we left?" Will asked.

"He said to be careful. Oso is a mean dog."

Will twisted in the saddle and watched the dog following Gray Wolf, his long tongue lolling out the side of his mouth, panting. "He doesn't look mean to me."

The day warmed as they rode. The clouds drifted away, and the wind settled down. The snow glistened and sparkled in the sunlight. The sun felt good on Two Feathers' face. He unbuttoned his wool coat and enjoyed the brisk air that had lost its fierce cold bite.

"Two Feathers," said Will, "we need to talk."

The anxious tone in his brother's voice made Two Feathers turn toward him.

"Do you know how to catch wild horses? I don't even know where to start. How are we going to get them?"

Will's words brought a slight smile to Two Feathers' face. Never in the five years he'd lived in the camp of his uncle, Yellow Hawk, had any of the Comanche boys asked him for advice on anything. They only teased and mocked him. They'd picked at him about his horse, Old Pony, the last gift from his father because he was way past his good years. They'd tormented him when he went into the woods with Weeping Woman, his aunt and wife of Yellow Hawk, to learn the lessons of the plants and animals. Now, his white brother was asking him how to catch wild horses. And he knew! Even though Yellow Hawk hadn't taught him what a Comanche boy should know, the other men sometimes did. And he'd watched. He'd listened. He'd learned.

"Yes, Will. I know where they are and how to catch them." He ignored the little niggle of doubt in the back of his head.

During the trip home, the boys scanned the countryside, close in and far out. Two Feathers squinted against the glare from the sun and watched for anything unusual. He paid close attention to what was ahead of them and what was off to the side. He knew a quick movement would grab the eye faster than something stationary. Two Feathers had been teaching Will how to track, and he was getting pretty good. Whenever they came across an animal track, Will identified it.

Nearing the ranch, Will pulled Buck up short when several shadows swept over the snow in front of the horses. He pointed to the sky. "Buzzards. I hope we haven't lost more stock." He tapped Buck, and the big buckskin picked up his pace.

Two Feathers gave the rope a yank, and Gray Wolf matched Buck's gait. "Come on, dog."

They found bloodstained, churned snow about a mile from the ranch house and slowed their horses. The crunch of horses' steps took on a sinister sound as they followed the bloody drag marks that wiped out any animal or horse tracks. Buck snorted, pranced around, and jerked the reins, not liking the smell of blood.

Thoughts of Yellow Hawk flashed through Two Feathers' mind. His shoulders tightened, and his stomach lurched toward his backbone. A quick glance at Will showed white knuckles on the hand holding Buck's reins, and the other rubbed his belly. His eyes, however, never left the trail. It led into the grove of cottonwoods where Will had been run over by a bobcat the year before.

"Two Feathers," Will whispered, "this is no bobcat."

"No. It is Yellow Hawk. Look." Two Feathers pulled up Gray Wolf. A dead cow lay near the base of a tree with buzzards perched on the carcass. With their wings beating the air and grunting in protest at being disturbed, they took flight. The cow's calf was pinned to the tree with an arrow through its neck.

Will dismounted and tied Buck to a scraggly oak away from the slaughtered animals. He walked over to examine the pair. His head drooped, and Two Feathers watched his body go limp as though all his energy had leaked out. Bracing himself against the tree above the dead calf, Will's eyes were unswerving as they met Two Feathers'. "Do you recognize this calf?" Will's voice smoldered. "He's the one we were so proud of."

"We were going to keep him for a bull." The last word barely slipped through Two Feathers' clenched teeth. He studied the grove of trees, every bush, every shadow, and the surrounding ground. Was Yellow Hawk still around here? Or did he just leave his latest message and go?

"Maybe it wasn't him. Maybe it was some Apache."

"No! They would have taken the meat." Two Feathers stepped off Gray Wolf. Three long strides took him to the calf, and he tried to yank the arrow from its neck, but the arrowhead was embedded in the tree trunk. He looked at the thick crimson blood staining his hands that curled into tight fists and drove his nails into his palms. His mind swelled to bursting with hatred. *Yellow Hawk!*

With stiff, jerky movements, he pulled his rifle from the scabbard and slammed the butt down on the arrow, snapping it. Shoving his rifle into Will's hands, he grabbed the calf under its jaw and ripped it from the arrow's shaft. Released from the tree, the calf crumpled to the ground.

"This is Yellow Hawk's arrow." He forced his words past stiff lips. Taking his knife, he dug the arrowhead and remaining shaft from the tree. He held the two halves of the bloody arrow outstretched in his fist. His voice growled low, "I watched him make many arrows, just like this one. I gathered feathers for him from birds he shot." He slung the pieces to the ground. Scooping up snow, he scrubbed his hands clean, never feeling the snow's cold burn. Rising back up, every muscle strained and quivered. His gaze followed Yellow Hawk's tracks that led away from the tree. He knew they would disappear as though the earth had swallowed his uncle. *Where are you? Why did you do this? What will you do now?* "Come on, Will. We need to get home. I fear for Jake and Tony."

Trading Bulls

Later that night, after they finished their chores and dinner, Will asked Jake and Tony to stay a while.

"I couldn't talk about this earlier today, but you need to know. We found another dead cow down the creek about halfway to the river. Yellow Hawk killed her and her calf. That reddish-speckled one with a solid red face. The one we wanted for a bull."

Jake slammed his fist on the table, making their cups jump and slosh coffee. "That blasted Comanche is gonna ruin us if the army don't do something."

Tony wiped up the mess and glowered at his twin. "Sit down, Jake. Gettin' mad and spilling coffee everywhere ain't doin' any good."

"No, it isn't, and neither is the army." Will huffed out a huge sigh. "They've done nothing except accuse us of stealing their supplies. We spent all last year getting that straightened out. And had to catch the thieves ourselves. Since Fort Sumner closed after the Navajo left, there's no army around to ask for help."

"That may be a good thing," Two Feathers mumbled.

But Will heard it. "How can you say that?"

Two Feathers stood from the table. "The army started all this with Yellow Hawk when they killed my mother."

Will huffed again. "There's not a thing we can do about that."

"Sit down, boys," said Tony. "We need to figure out what we're going to do about all this."

Two Feathers sat down and folded his arms on the table. "Sit, Will. Maybe Yellow Hawk will leave us alone for a while. Tell Jake and Tony what we planned."

"You're right. All we can do about Yellow Hawk now is to keep our eyes open and our weapons ready. Two Feathers and I have a plan to improve the ranch. We talked to Mateo, and he's sending César and Estevan to help us."

Will repeated what he'd told Mateo about going to John Chisum's Jinglebob ranch to buy two bulls. "We need young bulls. About two years old. I thought you'd leave in the morning and return as soon as possible. You'll be gone about a week, give or take a day or two. What do you think?"

Jake leaned toward Will, his expression solemn. "That'll take a lot of money to get good bulls."

"It'll take all you have left." Tony was all business. "Are you sure you want to do that now? I think you need to wait for Mr. Goodnight."

"Two Feathers and I have been talking. We have an idea to make enough money to get us through until Goodnight brings our cash from the steers we sent north with him last summer."

"What kind of plan?" asked Tony. "My feeling is that this isn't good. You have to admit, the plans you come up with often mean trouble and—danger."

Two Feathers slid his hand over his mouth to hide his grin.

Will's face crumpled at Tony's remark. "All we're gonna do is trap some wild mustangs and green break them for that horse trader I met last year."

Silence.

The twins looked at each other. "Where are you going to find these wild horses?" asked Tony, with raised eyebrows.

"In Palo Duro Canyon," Two Feathers answered.

More silence.

The twins stared at Two Feathers, then Will. Tony picked up the coffee pot and filled his cup but didn't drink it. "I don't even know where that is."

"I heard about it one time," said Jake. "It's somewhere off the Staked Plains, right in the middle of Comanche and Kiowa country. Why do you want to go there? Don't we have enough Comanche trouble here?"

"We camped there many times when I was younger. There are horses," said Two Feathers, "and the Comanche are my people."

Tony tilted his chair onto its back legs. "And one of them is Yellow Hawk. Do you think he's gonna let you boys prance around in the middle of his canyon and take his horses?" Rubbing his hands over his face, he dropped his chair with a loud thud on the wooden floor. "If Mr. Goodnight were here, he wouldn't let you go."

Two Feathers twisted his head to look out the window. "Tony is right. Yellow Hawk will not want us to have horses. We will have to stay far away from his camp."

He watched the moon break through the cloud layer that had brought the snow. Its cold light stretched long finger-like shadows over the ranch yard from the bare, leafless trees along the frozen creek. A shudder ran down his back. He blinked and turned his head to look at Tony.

Breaking the silence, he said, "The buffalo will be moving back north soon. Maybe he will be gone on a hunt."

Tony's slow, exaggerated back-and-forth head shake and cocked eyebrows left no doubt about what he thought of this idea. "Charlie Goodnight told you to stay put. Not go traipsing off anywhere."

Will sat down. "Well, Mr. Goodnight isn't here, and we have to do something, or we're goin' broke. . . if Yellow Hawk doesn't get us first."

The door shut with a firm clunk as the twins faced the cold night air and trudged their way to their quarters. Will drank his coffee and dumped the grounds into a bucket to be tossed into the kitchen garden.

Two Feathers sat still at the table. Yellow Hawk wouldn't have come here except for him. The trouble was his fault.

Will stopped at the kitchen door. "Are you going to bed? Don't forget to blow out the lamp."

Two Feathers didn't answer.

"What's wrong?"

"It is all my fault."

Will returned to his chair. "What is?"

"All the trouble with Yellow Hawk."

"Oh? How do you figure that?"

"If I had not wanted Buck so much, Yellow Hawk would not have hunted him. He would not have captured you or killed Pa."

"You can't control what other people do."

"He kills our bulls, our cows. The ranch will not work without bulls."

"We'll get more."

"We have so little of what you call money. The Comanche does not need money. But you cannot make a ranch work without it."

"Pa and I lived on less."

"I have seen you with your pencil and paper adding up long rows of numbers, then wadding up the paper and throwing it into the fire."

Will's finger drew circles on the tabletop. "I don't know the answers." He looked at Two Feathers. "I don't know much about how to run a ranch. But we have Jake, Tony, Mateo, and Mr. Goodnight to help us. Even though they aren't here, we aren't alone. You—aren't alone."

Two Feathers sat with his hands folded in his lap and his back slumped.

Will squeezed his brother's shoulder. "I've lost almost everything. First, my mother when I was little, just like you. Then, my home in Texas, just like you. My Pa, just like yours, was killed by Yellow Hawk. All I have left are Buck and you."

Two Feathers lifted his head and sat straight in his chair. "And all I have are Gray Wolf and you."

Will smiled. "We're partners. We have this ranch, and together we will make this our home. It's my idea to buy good bulls. It's your idea to capture wild horses. Together we can do this."

Early the following day, Two Feathers set four plates of eggs, strips of salt pork, and tall flakey biscuits around the table. Will filled coffee cups. Jake and Tony tied their horses and a loaded packhorse to the hitching rail in front of the house, then joined the boys inside for breakfast.

Tony picked up a biscuit and slipped a fat slice of butter inside it. "Will, you've mastered the art of making biscuits." He pushed the entire biscuit into his mouth.

Two Feathers' mouth was too full of biscuits to comment. He grinned and picked up another one.

With breakfast over, Will handed Tony a leather pouch bound with a rawhide strip. "Here's the money for the bulls. Pick out two good young ones. We'll see you in a week or ten days. Be careful and keep a watchful eye."

Two Feathers and Will watched the twins cross the creek and ride out of sight. Emptiness spread over the yard and house without their laughter and teasing.

Will gave Two Feathers a light slap on the back. "Let's get our coats and check on Big Tom. Then we need to put out hay today. I know the cattle are hungry."

On the way, Two Feathers stopped to give Oso some breakfast scraps and a good scratch behind his ears. The dog wagged his tail so hard his whole back end wiggled with it. It hadn't taken long for Will to win the affection of the grumpy bear of a dog. Big Tom was still in the corner of the corral next to the barn where they'd left him the afternoon before. Only this morning, he was stretched out on his side. Yellow snot bubbled from his nose with every panting breath, and his tongue lolled out the side of his mouth.

Will laid his head on the heaving side, listened for a moment, and then sat up. "This is bad. His lungs rattle like Cookie's pots hanging in the cook wagon."

"What are you going to do?"

"I don't think there is anything we can do." Will stood and chewed his bottom lip. "But let's try to make him get up."

Will pulled, and Two Feathers pushed, but Big Tom didn't move. Two Feathers strained to pull on his horns while Will twisted his tail and pushed with all his strength, but the bull wouldn't even lift his head. The boys sat back on their heels and glared at the downed animal.

"Blast it, Big Tom," fussed Will, "you walk all the way from Texas just to die the second winter you're here. I thought you had more sense than that."

"That thorn in his foot made him sick, and he could not fight the breathing sickness." *Is this also my fault?* "I guess walking him back in the storm made him worse."

"Do you think it might help if I drenched him with that willow bark and dandelion root tea you made me drink last fall when I got sick?" A small flicker of hope flashed across Will's face.

"I do not think we can do that. But we can try to steam him with camphor. If he breathes better, maybe he will get up." Hope lightened Two Feathers' sour mood. "If we can get him on his feet, we can put the medicine in his water."

At the house, Will grabbed a bucket and hurried to the creek for water. Two Feathers added wood to the fire in the stove, grabbed a blanket, and tossed it on the table with a small bottle of camphor oil. When the water was steaming, they headed back. Big Tom hadn't moved. He wheezed with every breath. Will picked up three stout sticks from the wood-pile, and they set up a teepee over the bull's head, set the steaming bucket laced with camphor inside, and stepped back. The sharp smell of the medicine wafted from under the blanket and made Two Feathers' eyes water.

They waited for about ten minutes before Big Tom's tail twitched. Rumbling noises came from beneath the tent. The big horns wiggled, the tent flew one way, and the bucket went the other. Big Tom lunged forward...once...twice...three times. His back end rose. He stood, took three steps, and fell over—dead.

Shocked, the boys walked to the bull lying in the middle of the corral.

"Tom?" said Will. He pushed the animal's shoulder with his boot. There was no rumble, no rattle, no wheezing breath.

Two Feathers stared at Big Tom. *How can that bull be dead? He walked back here just yesterday.* "Now, what are we going to do?"

Will didn't answer. He stood looking down at Big Tom and kicked the dirt. Rubbing his hands up and down his arms, he stepped away from the bull and kicked the dust again. Finally, he grunted out a giant sigh, stepped forward, and kicked Big Tom—hard. "Well. . . let's get some coffee. We can't do anything else here."

That afternoon, Two Feathers sat slumped on one of the mules. Will, long faced, sat beside him on the other mule. Two Feathers couldn't think of anything to say that would ease the trouble losing Big Tom caused. He cast his loop over the wide horns. Will cast his. Together, they pulled Big Tom from the corral. They dragged the carcass south of the ranch house for several miles and left him for the wolves, coyotes, and buzzards. It was a grim job, and neither boy spoke all the way there or back.

Cesar and Estevan finally came. Two Feathers didn't know who was happier to see them, he or Will. The next morning, Two Feathers followed Will onto the hay wagon. It was their turn to feed hay. Will drove the wagon while Two Feathers pitched the hay to the cattle. When the last fork was tossed, they sat on the tailgate, watching the cattle. "Take a look at these calves," said Will. "Most of these are Big Tom's babies."

Two Feathers pointed to a small calf staggering on wobbly legs trying to suckle his momma. She kept pushing him away to grab a mouthful of hay. "Look at that little bull calf over there. It looks just like Tom. I think we have more calves this year than we thought."

"I think you're right." Will's next words slid out with a hefty huff and a dose of sarcasm, "Despite Yellow Hawk's efforts to ruin us."

"We're going to miss Big Tom. I hope Jake and Tony have good luck at Chisum's."

The boys, with Cesar and Estavan, kept busy with chores around the ranch and tried not to worry about Jake and Tony or the new bulls. By the week's end, Two Feathers and Will drove the hay wagon into the barn and unloaded the last stack of hay into the loft. "You know what I do not like about this time of year?" Two Feathers didn't wait for Will to answer. "The wind cannot make up its mind. In the morning, it blows with the bite of winter, so you dress for the cold. But, by afternoon, it blows warm and laughs at you for being all bundled up."

Will crinkled his eyes at Two Feathers. "What are you talking about? With all the snowstorms we had this winter,

I'd think you'd be happy. Spring's on its way." Two Feathers shook his head and followed Will to the house.

The following day, Two Feathers couldn't keep his mind from fretting about Jake and Tony. He wondered if they worried this much about him and Will when they were gone. Every time he and Will rode away from the ranch house, he studied the ground watching for tracks of unshod ponies. He watched for Yellow Hawk. He watched for Jake and Tony.

The days stretched into the second week and still, there was no sign of the loyal ranch hands. Two Feathers climbed to his favorite spot on a rock ledge behind the barn. This was his thinking place and a good lookout. Today he was watching for any movement on the Llano Estacado. As he settled in, he spotted a dark shape moving along the bank on the other side of the Pecos River. It was too big to be one person. He stood to see better. The shape turned where the bank leveled its slope at their crossing and moved down to the water, then separated into more than one form. . . Jake and Tony! With two bulls! He spotted Will coming out of the barn. He hollered and pointed north, then scrambled down.

By the time Jake and Tony splashed across the creek, Will had put hay in the corral trough and filled the water tank. Two Feathers tied Oso to a tree behind the house so he wouldn't spook the bulls. Will swung the gate wide open, and the Jinglebob bulls made themselves at home. The twins dismounted and led their horses into the barn. César and Estevan joined the Pecos River Ranch cowboys on the top rails of the corral and gave the bulls a good looking over.

The bull with his nose buried in the water tank had horns that spread wide and straight out from his head, with the ends angling up. He was red in color, with large white areas covered in red spots of various sizes and shapes. His head between the horns was white, and his nose was red. The second bull was mostly white, with red on his neck and shoulders and spots radiating down his back. His horns were set higher, and their upward slant began almost at his head. Both animals were stout and strong.

With a promise to return in a few days, Estevan and César left. Will slipped down from the rails. Making a wide circle around the bulls, he studied first one, then the other. Two Feathers jumped down and joined him. "What do you think?"

Will circled again.

Tony and Jake came from the barn. "That Jinglebob Ranch had plenty of bulls," said Jake. "We looked at quite a few."

"Mr. Chisum's foreman showed us around," said Tony. "We told him what we were looking for, and he showed us these two. I liked them right away."

Jake grinned at Will. "The thing I liked best is they're gentle. They walked along real easy behind the horses. They kept pace and never stumbled or slowed."

"See how their hips and hind legs are well muscled—how they stand square and solid on their feet." Tony pointed to their hips. Will and Two Feathers followed him as he circled the animals. "They've been out on the ranch, not been penned in a corral, so they're range ready."

"Do you like them?" asked Will, glancing at Two Feathers.

Two Feathers grinned.

Will shook Jake's, then Tony's hands. "Thanks. You did a good job. They look strong and healthy. Leave them in the corral for a week to lose their desire to return to their home range, then take them to the meadow behind the house and turn them loose with the heifers. We'll see what they can do."

Tony handed him the leather pouch and grinned. "Glad you're happy with 'em. Here's the leftover money. It's not much, but Chisum said if he didn't give you a bargain, Charlie Goodnight would have his hide."

Will counted the money. The look on his face told Two

Feathers they were better off than expected. For supper, Will made the twins' favorite dessert to celebrate, a dried apple pie.

Later that evening, after no one could hold more pie or coffee, they cleared the table, and Will called a strategy meeting.

"I've been thinking about those wild mustangs. We'll go to Las Vegas and see if I can line up a buyer. That's my part. If I do, we'll stay in the canyon long enough to rough break the horses there. That's Two Feathers' part. Then, we'll drive them to town. I'll meet up with the buyer and sell them. That's my second part."

A beaming smile spread across Will's face. "Well, what do you think? It's gonna be easy."

The twins didn't say a word, and Will's smile became strained. "What's the matter?" He looked at Two Feathers. "You can handle the middle part, right?"

"Yes, I can handle my part." Two Feathers' words were matter of fact. "But you make it sound like we will be home in a week. It is not going to be an easy job."

"Will." Jake's words came out spaced and slow. "You have a good plan, one I think will work. But do you realize how long that will take? Don't you think Tony and I should go after the horses? You'll be gone for at least two months, if not more. Breaking horses is rough work."

"No, Jake, no!" Two Feathers' words rang with authority. "This will only work if I go and let Running Wolf know I am there. He is like an uncle. He will let me hunt horses—but not you. You would never survive the Comanche."

TRADING HORSES

The stiff winds of March died down and April found the boys approaching the Gallinas River outside of Las Vegas. Two Feathers headed upstream toward their old campsite. He and Will wound their way through the cottonwood trees and willows until they found the spot where large slabs of rock layered down to the river like giant stair steps. They set up camp in a cottonwood grove and watered the stock.

By early afternoon, Two Feathers was stretched out, dozing with his head on his saddle, when Will interrupted his nap.

"Why don't we stash our stuff under that deadfall over there, and you come into town with me?" Will propped himself up on his elbow and poked at Two Feathers. "There are sights in that town you won't believe. There's one building that seems as tall as a mountain."

"I will not go to town. The people there would not be happy to see a Comanche."

"Put your braids under your hat. Take off your moccasins and buckskins and wear your trousers and boots. It won't hurt you to be John Randall for a day. That is your name."

Two Feathers didn't answer him for a while. Go or stay? White or Comanche? Two Feathers, the name his mother gave him, or John Randall, named after his father? Who was he? He wondered if those questions would always haunt him.

"Come on, Two Feathers, I might need you. You know

about wild horses, and I don't. We are partners, remember?"

Two Feathers glared at Will. "I was planning on a nap."

"You can sleep tonight." Will nudged his brother with his foot.

Two Feathers dug into a pack and pulled out his boots. "We will go to the river and wash. A Comanche always cleans up and wears his best clothes to trade horses."

"A bath? I wasn't counting on taking a bath just to trade horses." Will's voice squeaked.

"Do you want me to go?"

"Yes."

He tossed Will's saddlebags to him. "Then take a bath."

An hour and a half later, they rode into Las Vegas. Buck and Gray Wolf drew attention as they rode down the main street of town. Will had brushed his big buckskin until his golden coat shone in the late afternoon sun. Gray Wolf's unusual grullo color glistened, and Two Feathers, now John Randall, rode ramrod straight in the saddle.

Will stopped a passerby. "Where's the sheriff's office?"

The man pointed down the street about a block.

"By the way, what's his name?"

"Crook."

"What?"

"His name is Crook?"

Will laughed out loud, and Two Feathers turned his head to hide his grin.

Will looked back down at the man. "The sheriff is a crook. Now, that's funny."

"I wouldn't say that to him if I were you. He doesn't think it's a bit funny."

When they dismounted in front of the jail, Two Feathers was no longer laughing, but Will was still chuckling.

Two Feathers scowled at him. "You better hide that grin

before we go in. I do not want him mad before we even get started."

Will and Two Feathers stepped into a midsized room with a big desk sitting catty-corner opposite the door. Light entered the room through wide-spaced iron bars on the large windows on either side of the door. In the back wall near the desk was a stout oak door with heavy iron bands. Two Feathers stopped in the middle of the room when he saw jail cells through a small, barred window near the top of the door.

He couldn't take his eyes off that door. Wishing he was anywhere but here, he remembered the cell he and Will were locked in at Fort Sumner when Captain Stanaway arrested them last year. They had spent a night in jail, accused of killing a soldier and stealing army supplies. Thoughts of that cell sent sweat rolling down his back and from under his arms, and he couldn't swallow.

"Hello, boys. What can I do for you?"

Will grabbed Two Feathers' arm and squeezed it as tight as he could.

"It's okay," he whispered. "He's not going to arrest us. We'll leave in a few minutes."

The boots on Two Feathers' feet wouldn't move. Will pushed him toward the desk.

"Sir," said Will, "we need a horse buyer for some rough-broke wild horses. We thought maybe you could recommend someone who wouldn't cheat us."

The man leaned over the desk and took a closer look at Will. "Do I know you?"

"Yes, sir. We met last year when I got my buckskin horse back from Mr. Porter."

"I remember now. You were the boy who bet his ranch he could ride that buckin' buckskin. And gave me a good laugh that lasted for a month or more when you beat ol' Porter. Especially since he treated your horse so bad."

He came around the desk and reached out his hand. Will shook it and gave Two Feathers a sharp nudge when the sheriff stuck his hand in his direction. Two Feathers snapped out of his frozen state and shook the man's hand.

"This must be your brother. The one who owns the grullo you also took from Porter."

"Yes, sir. This is John Randall."

Two Feathers nodded at the man.

"So, you got mustangs to sell? Do you need 'em sold quick?" Suspicion flickered across his face.

"No, sir. We got 'em tucked away safe," Will lied, "but we have to get 'em rough broke. They'll bring more money if they're broke some. They'll be ready in a couple of months."

The sheriff leaned against his desk and rubbed his chin.

"Well, the army is in town, but they already bought their quota and will be heading back to Fort Union in the morning." He thought for a minute. "The only man left in town buying horses is ol' Porter."

"Sheriff? Can you wait a minute while my brother and I talk outside? We'll be right back."

"Go ahead. I'm not going anywhere."

Will grabbed Two Feathers' arm and pulled him outside. "What's the matter with you? Your face is white as snow. Get a grip on yourself. We don't want him to think we're robbers or something."

"I cannot go back in there. I know there are jails back there. I am sick."

"No, you aren't. You're just scared." Will took Two Feathers to Gray Wolf. "Do you think we should trade with Mr. Porter?"

Sitting on Gray Wolf made Two Feathers feel better. He

looked down at Will. "If he is the only trader in town, we do not have much choice. Find out where he is so we can go away from here."

Will patted Gray Wolf's neck. "I'll be right back."

Waiting outside, Two Feathers sat still and wished Will would hurry. He glanced around him at the people on the sidewalk and on the street. No one was staring at him, only a few were even looking at him. He pulled his hat down low on his forehead. Relief swarmed over him, and for the first time, since he walked into the sheriff's office, he took a deep breath.

He watched the flow of people. Everyone seemed so busy. Some hurried up the street, and some hurried down the street. Where could they all be going? There were buildings along both sides of the churned-up, rutted, muddy road. Horses and wagons were everywhere, some tied to hitching posts and rails. He couldn't understand why Will wanted him to come here. It was dirty and muddy, and it stunk. When the Comanche's village camping spot became dirty, they packed up and moved. He wanted to go to a clean place.

Will came out the door and mounted Buck. "He said Mr. Porter has an office at the livery stable on the other end of town." They headed that way. Buck pranced and sidestepped as though he didn't like the muddy street or the confusion of the town any more than Two Feathers did. Will had his hands full controlling him. Gray Wolf wasn't much better. As they reached the livery barn, the crowd thinned out, and both horses settled down. Two Feathers breathed a sigh of relief.

Before Two Feathers dismounted, he took his hat off and recoiled his braids on top of his head, pulling his hat down tight to hold them. They walked into the barn and stopped just inside the wide-open double doors. It was the biggest barn Two Feathers had ever seen. A long wide aisle ran down the middle of the building with ten stalls on each side. Some held horses or mules, and some held sacks of grain or big piles of hay. Over their heads was a loft with hay spilling over the edge. About halfway down the aisle, a ladder rose to the loft with a huge fork leaning against it. On the posts between the stalls hung all sorts of horse tack—bridles, halters, feed bags, and other things Two Feathers had never seen before.

It smelled of horses, and Two Feathers liked it. He raised his head, closed his eyes, and sniffed. There was the scent of hay, and of manure, and of sweat, and of grain. The smell of horses.

Then a not-so-pleasant smell of sour sweat and body odor assaulted his nose. He opened his eyes to see a pot-bellied man in baggy pants that drooped over his boot tops walking toward them. The man's bright red vest was stained and streaked with he didn't know what.

"Howdy, boys. What can I do for you this af—" He stopped, stepped around Will, and headed for Buck. He didn't get far.

"Don't go near him," Will warned. "He has a good memory. He'll kick you into the next county."

Porter stopped and backed up beside Will.

Two Feathers stepped away about three paces so he could breathe. Studying the man, he didn't like what he saw. Weeping Woman had told him about such white men. She said that some white men weren't important enough to even think about. He decided Porter was such a man. According to what Will had told him, the man could never be trusted because he was a cheat and a louse.

"What are you doing here? Did you decide to sell me that buckskin? I can use him. And the grullo."

Two Feathers snorted.

Porter spun around. "Is this your brother?"

"Yes," said Two Feathers.

The man's mouth spread, showing brown tobacco-stained teeth. "Well, ain't this nice. Come on in the office, and we'll talk business."

As he and Will exchanged quick glances, Two Feathers rolled his eyes and jerked his head toward the office.

"Mr. Porter." Will yanked his hat off and ran his hands through his hair. "We're not here to sell these horses."

The man cocked one eyebrow and scowled at Will. "What do you want? Make it snappy. I ain't got time for a mouthy kid." The smarmy tone was gone.

Will's face turned a shade of red Two Feathers knew meant trouble. He stepped in front of Will.

"Sir, we will soon have around twenty head of rough broke horses for sale." He worked to make his tone sound confident, like Will's. "We would like to sell them to you. Sheriff Crook said you were just the man we should talk to." He neglected to mention the sheriff had said he was the only horse trader in town.

Two Feathers stayed in front of Will until he heard him suck in a long breath of air, hold it, and blow it out. Only then did he move.

Will stepped up. "We'd like to do business with you."

Porter jerked his pants over his belly and smoothed the greasy vest. The pinched look on his face faded, and his voice returned to the smarmy smoothness. "Come in. Come in. We'll see what we can do."

A few minutes later, Will and Two Feathers stomped out of the office, mounted their horses, fought their way back up the muddy street, and stormed out of town. Neither said a word.

Two Feathers' angry thoughts filled the hour's ride back to camp. His frustration festered. *I do not understand some white men—they lie and cheat. They try to take from their own people what is not theirs.*

When he and Will arrived back in camp, long familiarity with caring for Gray Wolf kept Two Feathers' hands busy, allowing his mind to let go of his thoughts. He shook his head, grabbed his bow and quiver of arrows, and stalked off upriver to hunt for their supper. His luck was good, his aim was okay, and in a short time, he returned with a skinny rabbit.

It didn't take long for a cast iron pot to be simmering on the fire with beef jerky added to stretch what little meat was on the rabbit. Will tossed in a few potatoes they'd brought from home, salt for seasoning, and a dab of flour for thickening. Some corn pone filled the empty spots in their bellies the "skinny rabbit" stew had left.

Dark found the boys settled in their bedrolls as close to the fire ring as they could get with a hot rock in their bedroll to warm their feet. A large pile of driftwood was stacked within reach. Knowing how far sound carries at night, Two Feathers spoke barely above a whisper.

"Will, what are we going to do about a buyer? Porter is not offering a fair price."

"I've been thinking about that all afternoon." Will squirmed and wiggled until his blankets were tangled. He jerked them up, snapped them straight, and flopped back down on his bedroll. "I'm going back to town in the morning and smash my fist in his nose."

"That sounds like a great way to make him buy our horses." Each word came out louder than the one before until a flame burned in the center of Two Feathers chest. He sat up and yelled, "GO AHEAD! RUIN EVERYTHING!"

LAS VEGAS, NEW MEXICO

At daybreak, Will and Two Feathers rode down the main street of Las Vegas leading both pack horses. They stopped at the sheriff's office on the way to Grzelachowski's store.

"Maybe Sheriff Crook will have an idea of what we should do about Mr. Porter," said Will as he dismounted.

At the door, Two Feathers looked back to see what was holding Will, who stood calming Buck. The horse had been a little too frisky on the ride into town, and Will had spoken harshly to him. Two Feathers turned to enter the office when Sheriff Crook stepped out. He smacked into the big man.

"Whoa, boy, watch where you're going." The heavy-set man grabbed Two Feathers' arm to steady him. "I ain't had my coffee yet, and you're trying to knock me down."

The authoritative tone riled Two Feathers until he saw the grin that put crinkles at the corners of the man's eyes. His face, bronze from the sun, was strong and pleasant, with curly gray sideburns below his wide-brimmed hat.

"Sorry, sir." Two Feathers jumped back like he'd touched a hot stove.

Will stepped onto the boardwalk beside Two Feathers. "I was checking on Buck. He's a bit frisky this morning. I was making sure he was gonna behave himself."

Sheriff Crook looked back and forth between Will and

Buck. "I still can't believe that big horse belongs to a runt boy like you."

Anger, already simmering inside Two Feathers from the day before, threatened to blow until the man patted Will on the back. "I don't mean no disrespect to you, but you have to admit he's mighty big, and you ain't."

The sheriff walked down the street, his hand still on Will's back. "Have you boys had coffee this mornin'?"

"No, sir. We left camp before breakfast."

"I'm headed to the cafe. How about I set you up with a hot cup of coffee and a tall stack of flapjacks?"

"Pancakes? Yes, sir." Will's face lit up like a noonday sun.

Two Feathers didn't answer, but his mouth watered at the thought of sweet syrup. A half hour later, his belt squeezed and pinched his stomach. Two Feathers pushed his empty plate away and sipped his hot coffee.

"Well, boys. You haven't said a word about making a deal with ol' Porter."

Will set his cup on the table and narrowed his eyes. "Sir, that man is a thief. I said it last year when he had Buck, and I'll repeat it now. He wanted us to do all the work, but he wasn't willing to give us a fair price. Surely there is someone else around that will buy horses."

Slipping one elbow over the back of his chair, the sheriff studied first Will, then Two Feathers, then Will again. "You're not serious about going out on the Llano Estacado to hunt wild horses, are you? I don't want to have a report come across my desk about the bodies of two young boys found shot and scalped by the Comanche or Kiowas." All the teasing and fun faded from the lawman's voice. His eyes lost their twinkle.

Two Feathers sat tall in his chair. "Yes sir. We are serious."

"We need the money," said Will.

The noise of the other people in the room faded away. Two

Feathers watched as determination firmed Will's face and strengthened his voice.

"Sir," said Will. "We're on our own. We need to make our ranch work. We'll do whatever it takes to get the job done. Being alone on the Llano Estacado isn't new to us. We're a team. John can follow any trail. I can travel by the stars."

The lawman's face didn't change. His eyes didn't soften.

"We will find wild horses." Two Feathers looked Sheriff Crook in the eye. "We will catch them, and rough break them."

"If we can't find a buyer in Las Vegas," said Will, "we'll drive them to Fort Union and sell them to the army. We've no other choice."

Sheriff Crook leaned forward on the table. "Okay. If you're that serious, here's what you need to do. Always remember, Silas Porter ain't got an honest bone in his body. As a matter of fact, he's so crooked he could swallow nails and spit out screws. Don't tell ol' Porter I told you this but go back to him and tell him the price you want. If he balks again, tell him you're considering driving them south and selling them to the Comancheros."

"Sir?" Will's eyes and mouth flew open. "The Comancheros?" He gulped, swallowed, and almost choked. He'd heard Pa and Mr. Goodnight talk about the notorious traders and their thieving, corrupt, deceitful ways.

Two Feathers grinned.

"Silas Porter hates the Comancheros worse than anyone I've ever heard. There was a time when he was wealthy, and the Comancheros raided and wiped him out. He'll give you just about anything to be sure they don't get your horses. Make him write it out when you settle on a price, and you both sign it." He studied Will for a minute. "Can you read?"

"Yes, sir. My Ma taught me. After she died, Pa made me read every book he could find and do all my sums. He taught John to sign his name."

"Good. Make three copies. After the papers are signed, he will keep one, you will keep one, and bring one to my office. I'll lock it in my safe. That way, he can't wriggle out of the deal."

The sheriff asked the waitress to bring paper, a pot of ink, and a quill pen. Sheriff Crook wrote out a contract and had Will and John sign it. He made a space for Porter to sign. Will copied it two more times.

"Thank you, sir. We appreciate your help. I'll bring it back as soon as he signs it."

An hour later, Will and Two Feathers walked into the sheriff's office and handed him the signed promise-to-buy paper.

Sheriff Crook took it and read it carefully.

"Will Whitaker, I don't think I'll ever underestimate you again. Last year you managed to find your horse after it'd been stolen by the Comanche and rescue him from ol' Porter by betting your ranch. Then, you and John managed to flummox that old chiseler and sell him a herd of wild half-broke broncs he ain't even seen for a darn good price."

The muscles in Two Feathers' cheeks pulled tight with the size of his grin. "We do not have those broncs yet. That is going take some doing."

Sheriff Crook grinned and shot Will a quick glance. "How long did Silas give you to bring them in?"

Two Feathers' grin shrank. "Eight weeks."

Sheriff Crook's eyebrows shot up, and his whistle ended with a long slow downslide.

"You boys better hit the trail. Even if you catch those horses, gettin' them green-broke is a tall order."

"Thank you, Sheriff Crook," said Will. "We appreciate your help. We'll be back for Mr. Porter's paper in two months." He shook the man's hand, mounted Buck, and led the pack horses down the street to Grzelachowski's Mercantile. Two Feathers managed a quick handshake, then raced after Will.

The clump of Two Feathers' boots sounded loud as he walked down the wide space between the rows of goods piled on tables and shelves. Clothing, boots, pots, and other household items filled one side. Barrels, bins, buckets, and bags of all kinds of food filled the floor and shelves on the other side. Clusters of red chili peppers and bunches of onions hung from the ceiling, and colorful tins of herbs and spices decorated the shelves behind the counter. Big glass jars on the far end away from the cash register caught Two Feathers' attention. One held a rainbow of colored chunks of hard rock candy, and the other was about half full of stick candy.

"Will." Two Feathers grabbed Will's arm and dragged him to the big jars. "Look at that!"

"We don't have money for candy. If we did buy some, you know what you'd do."

"What?"

"You'd eat every piece before we got back to camp."

Two Feathers pulled himself to his full height and looked down at Will. "Do you dare insult a Comanche?"

Will's eyes sparkled and laugh lines crinkled at the corners. "Right now, you aren't Two Feathers. You are John Randall, so I'm not insulting a Comanche."

They stood face to face, toe to toe. Two Feathers held onto his determination not to be the first to break down into laughter.

Finally, Will's stubborn streak broke, and he stepped back. Their laughter drew the attention of the store clerk. "We need supplies for a long trip," said Will. "I've got pack horses out front." Two Feathers dropped one handful of peppermint, clove, horehound, and molasses candy sticks on the counter. The other hand dropped its load of lemon, cinnamon, and sassafras.

"Bring the horses behind the store. Mr. Grzelachowski's back there."

Will and Two Feathers found the storekeeper helping a freight driver unload a wagon. Jumping down from the loading dock, he grabbed Will's hand and gave it a vigorous shake.

"It's you? The boy with the big yellow horse?"

Two Feathers grinned at the happy uptick at the end of Grzelachowski's sentences.

"Yes, sir. I'm back." Will followed the big, bearded man into the store. "I need supplies for two months."

Grzelachowski grabbed his not-so-white apron and tied it around his not-so-small belly. The humor slid from his face, and a no-nonsense look replaced it. "Two months?" The happy uptick was missing.

Will handed him the lengthy list he, Two Feathers, and the twins had made out before they left the ranch.

Studying the list, Grzelachowski scratched his beard. After what seemed like forever, he put it on the counter.

"This's a lot of goods. Can you pay?"

Will frowned and shuffled his feet. He told the man their plans for the wild horses. "I can pay for half of our supplies now and the other half when we bring the horses back. Mr. Porter has promised to buy them."

"Silas Porter?" The uptick was back, but not with the same happy lilt. "Oszust!" He spat the word out.

"Sir?"

"Cheater. Oszust!"

"He will pay us. I've his promise to pay on a paper in the sheriff's office. We have a deal. You can ask Sheriff Crook."

"Margaret Mary," he bellowed.

A freckle-faced girl popped up from behind the nearest rack of dresses.

"Get the sheriff."

She grabbed her coat and headscarf, flashed Will a big smile, and bolted out the door, slamming it behind her.

When the sheriff arrived, Will asked him to explain his and Two Feathers' deal with Silas Porter about the horses. When Crook finished talking, Grzelachowski looked back and forth between Will and the lawman. Two Feathers followed every twist of the man's head.

"This is true?" There was the happy uptick.

Two Feathers let out a breath he'd been holding since the sheriff stopped talking.

"You have such a paper?"

Sheriff Crook's face turned a funny color of purple. He nodded.

"With his signature? Silas Porter's signature?" The store-keeper's face was turning the same color as the sheriff's. The uptick was kind of choked.

Both men burst out loud, deep rumbling horselaughs that filled the store and brought the men from around the stove running to see what was up. They struggled to have enough breath to tell the crowd the story of Will, John, and Silas Porter.

Will backed away through all those laughing men whose slaps on each other's backs and fists slamming the store counter threatened to land on him. Two Feathers followed. Will spotted Margaret Mary, and she motioned them over. They replaced the men at the stove.

"What's so funny?" Will asked.

She unwound the scarf from her head and unbuttoned her coat. "Silas Porter's known around these parts as a hard-nosed trader and, when he can get away with it, a cheat."

"What's that got to do with us?"

The smile twisted into a frown of disbelief. "Don't you know?"

"Know what?" Will looked from the fire to Two Feathers and back.

"You're the only person who has beaten Silas Porter two times. If you bring this deal off, you'll be famous."

"I don't understand. What'd I do that was so funny? It's just a horse deal."

Margaret Mary pulled Will down onto one of the chairs and Two Feathers to another. She pulled up a chair for herself close to Will's. "You've made that cheater promise to pay for wild horses from the Staked Plains—sight unseen. No matter what they look like or how good they are. He has never done that before. He always makes the wranglers bring the horses in first, and then he does his best to cheat them by threatening to not buy them." She sat back in her chair and blinked her blue eyes at him. "When you bring the horses in, you must be careful of that smelly ol' rascal. He'll still try to cheat you by figuring how to get around that paper he signed. Be sure to take Sheriff Crook with you when you talk to him."

"Margaret Mary!" boomed throughout the store. She jumped up and ran to the counter.

"Hey, boy." An old man picked up the back of Will's chair and dumped him on the floor. "Just because you outfoxed ol' Porter don't mean you can sit in my chair. Get those goods and head on out of here. We'll be waitin' to see if you boys make it back here in two months." He held out his hand to Will and pulled him off the floor. "You better make it back. I done bet a whole dollar you will."

A short while later, with the pack horses loaded, Two Feathers headed toward the edge of town. For once, the people, animals, wagons, and noise level held no fascination for him. He didn't see, hear, or feel the excitement. Will had signed an I.O.U. for half the supplies. When they rode away from the store, Will explained what that meant. I Owe U (You). Those three letters burned in his head.

"Two Feathers, we had to do this." Will fiddled with the

reins, twisting them in his hands. "Did I do the right thing? I've done something Pa told me never to do. If you can't pay for it, you don't need it. That's what he always said." Will pulled Buck to a stop. "What if we don't find horses? What if we can't break them in time? What if we can't get them back in time?"

Will's what if. . . what if. . . what if roared through Two Feathers' head. He didn't know what to say. They rode about a block when he heard someone holler. It jerked him from his worries.

"Will Whitaker. John Randall." Sergeant Baker stepped off the boardwalk and headed toward them.

Will and Two Feathers dismounted and tied their horses.

"Boys, it's mighty good to see you. How's that ranch of yours farin'?" The tall soldier pounded them on the back. "Let me look at you." He shoved Will back a few steps and looked him up and down. Then did the same to Two Feathers. "You've grown some since the last time I saw you at Fort Sumner."

"Sergeant Baker, it's good to see you too." Will grabbed the man's hand and gave it a vigorous shake. "Aren't you stationed at Fort Union? What are you doing in town?"

"I had a few days leave, so I rode into town with the supplies Captain Stanaway sent Grzelachowski to freight to the other forts in the area. You're a goodly way from the ranch. What are *you* two doing here?"

Will dug into his pocket and pulled out a couple of dollars. "It's a long story. I've enough left from buying all these supplies to get us some lunch. Where's a good place to eat?"

Finding a table in a quiet restaurant on a side street, they ordered antelope stew and coffee. Will and Two Feathers took turns telling the sergeant about their troubles getting through the long cold winter.

"I did my best to remember all Pa had us do last winter." Will blew on his coffee to cool it enough to drink. "We cut and stacked what I thought would be enough hay, but if we get one more cold norther, I don't know if it will last."

Two Feathers dipped a bread crust into his stew and let it soak up the gravy. "We cleared ice from water holes. Every day we moved cattle that had drifted before the cold wind back toward the ranch. We worked hard."

"Tony and Jake made a difference," continued Will. "They're good cattlemen, and their advice is usually sound. We wouldn't have made it without them. Our losses this winter were severe, and our bulls took the biggest hit. Jake and Tony went down to the Jinglebob to pick up two more. They chose good ones. We're hoping Charlie Goodnight will have good bulls when he comes through this summer to take our calf crop north."

"I'm a soldier, not a cattleman." The sympathy in Sergeant Baker's look and words made Two Feathers feel there was at least one soldier he could trust. "But it sounds like you're doing a good job. All ranchers have losses during the winter."

"I know they do," said Will. "It's not the number of cattle lost to the cold that worries me. I expected that. It's the stock Yellow Hawk killed. Just recently, he killed a cow and her calf. It was a great calf. We were planning on keeping him for a bull. We can't afford losses like that."

The waiter collected their dishes. He brought them thick slices of bread pudding covered in butter sauce and freshened their coffee. Two Feathers closed his eyes and lost himself in the sweetness.

"Why are you boys in Las Vegas? I've a feeling it's not only for supplies."

With his finger, Will chased the last bit of sauce around his plate before licking it. "Sergeant," he shot a quick glance at Two Feathers, who nodded, "we've a plan to get us through until Mr. Goodnight brings our money."

Sergeant Baker sat up straight. "What kind of plan?" He looked back and forth between the brothers. "I've seen your plans in action before. I don't think I'm going to like this."

"We're going to Palo Duro Canyon. . . " said Will.

"To trap and rough break wild mustangs," finished Two Feathers.

Sergeant Baker had his cup of coffee halfway to his lips when it stopped in mid-air. He slowly set it back onto the table. "I've one question concerning this new plan of yours. How will you keep Yellow Hawk from taking Buck and killing you?"

PALO DURO CANYON

Sergeant Baker rode with Two Feathers and Will. During the hour it took them to reach the Gallinas River, he argued against their "crazy plan."

When they reached their campsite, Will and Two Feathers stretched a taut rope between two trees and tied the horses. Will unpacked the coffee pot. Sergeant Baker sat quietly while the coffee brewed. Two Feathers began to wonder what was happening inside his head. During the ride from town, he'd pointed out every possible problem the boys might face, and suddenly he had nothing to say. It made Two Feathers apprehensive.

When Will filled their cups a second time, the sergeant picked up a stick and drew an X in the dirt. "If I can't talk you out of the idea, then maybe I can help you survive it. We will leave shortly and meet the army supply wagons heading back to Fort Union." He tapped the X, drew a line southeast from the first mark, and put another X. "A supply train is set to leave in the next day or two for Fort Bascom, and you will go with them." He tapped the second X and drew a wiggly line. "You will follow the Canadian River into Texas. It goes on into the Nations," he turned his line downward, "but at West Amarillo Creek, you'll turn south and should reach the canyon in a few days."

Two Feathers' face lit up. He took Baker's stick and continued the wiggly line east past the downturn. "I know this river. We followed it when we traveled from the Nations. We made this turn to use the creek to take us to our winter camp."

He pushed at Will's shoulder and laughed. "Good plan, brother. This is a good plan."

For ten days—the first seven traveling at the slow rumbling pace of supply wagons—questions swirled in Two Feathers' mind. Though their plan looked good and could help them stay safe, it wasn't foolproof. Could he find the canyon? Could he find wild horses? Could he catch them? How would they tame them to be ridden—and in time? Was Weeping Woman camped there? Was Red Wing? Thoughts of her brought an ache to his heart. He wanted to walk with her in the woods again and talk to her. She'd always eased his fears, even when they were little. She was there with him after the soldiers rode away on the day of death. She'd always been there, and she always made him feel better.

But the closer they got to the canyon, the more his thoughts of Yellow Hawk broke loose from the locked place in his mind. His body reeled and made him grab the saddle horn. He was relieved Will had ridden ahead and didn't see him. The last thing he wanted was to endure Will's teasing about a Comanche falling off his horse.

Will stopped Buck and stood in the stirrups. Two Feathers rode up beside him. In awed silence, his sight stretched to distances beyond his ability to imagine. As far as he could see, all the way to the distant purple blur of the horizon, was a land split open with steep walls ending in a broad valley. It curved its way around and between flat-topped mesas that seemed endless. The valley floor showed signs of green, while slices of snow remained in the shaded crevices.

The walls held hues of red from pale pink to the bright red

of iron-laced rock and sand. Some places were striped with shades of tan layered within the wide red bands. Against the walls, towers of light sandstone slab rocks rose to the sky, looking as if some ancient force had purposely stacked them there. Twisted shrubs and short stubby trees grew within the cracks, dotting the walls with all shades of green. Some of the trees grew upright, while others clung to the walls with trunks and limbs that leaned out into the abyss held by roots anchored in the rocks. The gnarled, twisted limbs deformed by the wind and rain reminded Two Feathers of the knobby, weathed hands of the old ones in his village.

Will tapped Buck, but the big stallion would only go two steps forward. He shook his head and stepped back next to Gray Wolf. "Two Feathers? What is this place?" Will's words sounded hollow and seemed to get lost in the vastness of the open space before them.

"This is Palo Duro Canyon." Two Feathers sucked hard and filled his lungs with clean, sharp air till they ached. "The home of the Comanche."

They searched for a trail off the rim for the rest of the afternoon. The river below pooled in places and narrowed in others as it wove its way through the wide valley. Sweeping curves left bright red sand and gravel bars. In places, the water slowed to work its way through the scrub brush that grew along the banks. Further downstream, graceful willows trailed their long draping branches in the sluggish water backed by tall bud covered cottonwoods.

"Deer tracks." Will pointed to the ground. Two Feathers leaned from his saddle and studied the trail ahead. They followed the delicate hoofprints until they turned toward the rim and disappeared.

"Come on, Will. Looks like we found our way down. Wait until I am about halfway down before you start. I do not want

Buck to run over us." Two Feathers studied the trail as far ahead as he could see. It veered to the left and zigzagged its way to the bottom. Scattered rocks dotted the few short flat sections with juniper trees hugging the edge. He didn't like the look of it but decided not to waste time looking for another. He loosened Gray Wolf's reins, and the daredevil horse went over the rim.

Two Feathers' leg muscles gripped hard. He leaned back to keep from pitching forward over Gary Wolf's ears, pushed hard against the stirrups, and trusted his horse to get him down. Rocks kicked loose by the horse's hooves bounded down the trail ahead of them. They skipped the twists and turns and sailed off into nothingness. Two Feathers gasped. His stomach lurched each time Gray Wolf stumbled as the stones slid under his feet.

Behind him, Buck snorted and pawed the ground. Two Feathers risked a quick backward glance at Buck. Will, holding tight to the saddle horn and leaning back as far as he could, rode Buck off the rim. The rattle of rocks tumbling behind him and the grunts and huffs of air from the horse let him know they were coming. Gray Wolf rushed the last few feet and raced onto the canyon floor to get out of Buck's way.

At the bottom, Will slid off Buck, bent over with his hands on his knees, and sucked in great streams of air. "I don't believe I took one breath all the way down." He heaved in more air. "That's about the scariest thing I've ever done. Promise me we'll find another way out of here."

Two Feathers didn't answer.

Will shot a quick look his way. "You all right?"

Two Feathers stood with his head against Gray Wolf's shoulder and held up one hand. "Wait," he gasped. "I have to. . . catch. . . my. . . breath."

The boys stood for several minutes until their legs could

move normally again, then walked the horses to the river. Gray Wolf and Buck stood in the water and drank.

Will groaned. "If that's the only way out, I'll have to take up residence right on this spot because I'm not going back up that trail. That was a deer trail, and we ain't ridin' deer!"

Two Feathers chuckled. "There are many ways in and out. I did not want to waste time looking. Come on. We need to find a camping spot."

By daybreak the next morning, they'd finished their coffee and packed up camp. They headed upstream to find a place suitable for holding horses. But each branch they found that led off from the main canyon lacked one or more needed features: a wide-open area for grazing, a water source, and a narrow opening they could close.

Later that afternoon, they settled the horses and themselves on a sandbar at a curve in the river under a cottonwood tree where a creek teased their ears with a tinkling trickle of water. Two Feathers stretched out with his head propped against a small log for a quick nap, trusting the horses to warn him of any danger. Will flopped down beside him.

After a time, something tugged at Two Feathers' mind, and he awoke about halfway. Listening to determine what was pulling him from sleep, he heard a turkey in the brushy woods behind him. Turkey would be a welcome change from jerky for supper! Rolling over and grabbing his bow and quiver, he inched his way up the narrow creek. About fifteen minutes later, his arrow caught the turkey while his eyes caught the sun's reflection on a pool of water behind a mud and stick dam. He stepped out from the cover of the trees. An open area of about twenty-five acres surrounded by high red and tan walls stretched before him. A creek tumbled down a waterfall about fifteen feet high between smooth round boulders and then angled across one corner. He recognized this place as a catch corral for horses made by some Comanche in the past.

The dam leaked in a few places but still held water. The wide band of dried, cracked sand and gravel around the pool told Two Feathers it had once been bigger. The rotted logs and brush used to close the opening where the creek flowed to the river lay scattered.

Two Feathers returned to get Will. He poked him with his foot. "Wake up. I think I have found the place we need. Come on. I want to look it over."

They spent the next three days tracing the little creek to where it fell off the canyon rim and cleaned out as much debris as possible to allow more water flow. They patched and strengthened the dam. After cutting small logs and branches, they lashed them together with rope making a gate that secured the opening into their new brush corral.

Now that they'd found their holding pen, the next step was to take Will to Yellow Hawk's camp. That wouldn't be easy, but they'd no time to waste.

Two Feathers led Gray Wolf and Buck to the fire ring, picked up his saddle blanket, and smoothed it out. "I need to find Yellow Hawk's camp."

"What? Why?" Buck grunted when Will jerked too hard on the cinch. "Are you crazy? We can't go there."

"You do not have to go. You can stay here."

"What? Why?" Will's face turned white under his tan.

"The brush corral is not tight enough. We have not checked it all the way around. There might be places the horses could get out. And I want to see Weeping Woman and Red Wing."

"A girl? Is that all you think about?" Will swung his leg over the saddle. "I'm not staying here. We don't have time to look for girls." He sat on Buck but didn't move.

Two Feathers sat still as well. Both horses swished their tails and shook their heads in impatience.

Two Feathers searched Will's face. "If your mother could be near, would you go find her? Weeping Woman is my aunt, but she is also the mother I remember."

Will slumped in the saddle, took off his hat, and ran his fingers through his hair. He wiped a splotch of red dirt off the hat's brim. He put his hat back on, looked at Two Feathers, and gathered his reins. "Yes, I would. I'm going with you. I won't stay here. We can check the walls when we get back." Will held Buck still.

Two Feathers waited for Will to work through the struggle with his fear. He kept silent. The inner battle was all over his brother's face. Two Feathers knew Will would go, but he had to win the battle alone.

Finally, Will nodded at Two Feathers. "Let's go."

They rode to the river and turned east to head deeper into the canyon—the home of Yellow Hawk.

COMANCHE CAMP

Two Feathers followed a sandbar smoothed by high water where the river curved. "Watch for tracks along the river. The horses will come to drink." He stepped Gray Wolf into the water, and Will followed. At dusk, they made camp. By first light, they were in the saddle. Two Feathers scanned the sky for the smoke of cooking fires. Will searched for trails and tracks. Night fell, and neither had found anything.

They searched the following day, and by afternoon they spotted a dust cloud in the air ahead of them. Two Feathers and Will slipped behind a grove of willows and waited to see what was coming. Will slid off Buck and held his head to keep him quiet.

Two Feathers handed Will Gray Wolf's reins. "Stay here. Do not move. Keep the horses still." He faded away through the hanging branches, moving from rock to rock, leaving no tracks until he heard the soft murmur of voices. A long line of travoises pulled behind horses moved along the riverbank. Two Comanche girls walked in the water, splashing and kicking at each other, carrying their moccasins.

Two Feathers gasped. Red Wing! He watched her as she played with her friend. He stepped out and walked to the water's edge. "Red Wing."

She stopped still in the water and stared at him, then took a couple of steps and stopped.

"Two Feathers?" Shoving her moccasins at her friend, she waded across the shallow water. "Where did you come from?"

"I was hunting for you. I wanted to see you and Weeping Woman." He took her hand and helped her step onto a sandstone slab.

She didn't speak, but her gaze searched every inch of his face. She gripped his hand hard.

Looking at the people watching them from across the river, he walked with her toward them. Running Wolf and Barks Like Coyote met him. He told them he wanted to see Weeping Woman. Running Wolf nodded to Red Wing. She ran to get her, taking her moccasins from her friend.

Most of the people continued on their way. A few greeted Two Feathers. Weeping Woman arrived on a strong bay horse with Red Wing riding behind her. When she saw Two Feathers, she slid off, ran to him, wrapped her arms around him, and hung on for a long time.

She tugged one of his braids, stepped back, and looked him up and down. "It is good to see you. You have grown tall and strong. You are taller than Yellow Hawk."

Two Feathers looked around. "Is he here?"

"No, he does not stay here anymore. Sometimes he comes to visit and to bring me meat, but then he goes again." She looked around at the people passing her on the trail. "I am afraid of him. We are all afraid of him."

Slipping his arm around her shoulders and taking Red Wing's hand, he walked to Running Wolf. "My brother and I have come to hunt wild horses. We will not bother any horses of the Comanche."

"We are not far from our night camp. Stay with us and eat. We will talk." Running Wolf mounted and rode toward the head of the line.

Barks Like Coyote stared at Two Feathers and Red Wing

as they walked by. His eyes held the same simmering look that had always been there when Red Wing was with Two Feathers.

Two Feathers met his eyes, then turned away from his childhood enemy and took Red Wing's hand. "Go with Weeping Woman to the night camp. I will be there in a while."

Reaching the willows, he whistled a bird call. When the answering call came, he grinned, trying to decide what kind of bird it was supposed to be. He found Will and the horses behind a cluster of large boulders. A trickle of water formed a small pool that spilled between the rocks to join the Prairie Dog Town Fork of the Red River. Buck and Gray Wolf drank the clear water.

"I found her. I found Weeping Woman."

"So I see from the look on your face. I'm glad for you. Now can we start looking for horses?"

"No, not yet. I want to go to Running Wolf's night camp and talk to him. Get the horses and come on."

"What? Are you kidding? I'm not going to a Comanche camp."

"Yes, it is okay. Yellow Hawk is not here. It is safe."

"I'm still not going."

"Will. Nothing will happen to you. You have been to Running Wolf's camp before."

"Yes, but there were only two Comanche, not a whole village. I'm not going. I'll camp here."

"They are my family, my friends. I trusted you and Pa when you took me into the soldier's fort. We went many times. I never said I would not go. Even though I did not trust the soldiers, I went because you went with me."

"You're sure Yellow Hawk is gone? Who told you?"

"Weeping Woman."

"Well, I guess she would know."

Two Feathers mounted Gray Wolf. Will stuck one foot in

the stirrup but didn't mount. He stood that way until Buck turned his head back to look at him.

"Will, I think Buck wants to know if you are going mount up or just stand there on one foot."

Swinging himself into the saddle, Will glared at Two Feathers. "If I get scalped, I'll be really mad at you."

The boys crossed the river and followed the last of the Comanche. At their night camp, the people stared at Will as they rode past. His hands twitched and moved up and down on the reins, and he sat ramrod stiff in the saddle. Sweat beaded on his forehead and top lip. Two Feathers kept Gray Wolf next to Buck. The big buckskin sidestepped and threw his head, his eyes rolled, and his ears turned in every direc-tion. If anyone got too close, they laid back against his head. Will stroked the muscled neck. Two Feathers wondered if he was trying to calm the horse or himself.

"He remembers being in Yellow Hawk's camp," said Will. "He doesn't like to be here anymore than I do."

"I know. I can see it in you and in Buck. But you are my guest. You will be safe, I promise you. Think, Will. Would I bring you here if there was danger? Buck is not going to calm down until you do."

As the sun set, Running Wolf, Barks Like Coyote, Two Feathers, and Will sat around a low fire. Will stayed close to Two Feathers, following every move he made. Two Feathers knew the night ahead would be long and sleepless. He knew Will's memories of captivity in Yellow Hawk's camp and of Running Wolf's face painted for war would not let him sleep.

The low murmur of voices around the fire felt good to Two Feathers. He remembered sitting curled in his father's lap listening to the Comanche men talking of their days, making plans for a buffalo hunt. His father was a good shot, bringing down many animals with his rifle.

"Two Feathers," Will spoke just above a whisper, "If Yellow Hawk isn't here, where is he? Do you think they know?"

"No, Weeping Woman would have told me. They do not want him here."

"Me neither."

Laughter from somewhere in the camp pulled Two Feathers' thoughts away from the dangers of his uncle. "I will ask Running Wolf and Barks Like Coyote to help us hunt and break the horses."

Will jerked straight up. "What? We don't need their help. We can do it by ourselves."

"No, we cannot. We cannot capture, break, and deliver the horses in the short time we have without help. I can convince Running Wolf if we promise him his choice of the horses and two steers for payment."

Two Feathers could see Will's shoulders stiffen even in the low glow of the fire's coals. He started to get up, but Two Feathers held him in his spot.

"Think, Will. The only horse you have ever trained is Buck."

"I did a pretty good job with him. There's no better horse in this country."

"Yes, you did a good job. But he was never wild, and you started when he was a colt. These horses have always been wild, or at least for several years." Two Feathers let that idea soak in Will's head for a few minutes. "Running Wolf has been capturing and training wild horses his whole life. I know only a little compared to him, and you know nothing."

Both boys sat silent. A moment later, Will huffed. "I see your point." More silence. Another huff. "But why didn't you tell me this earlier?"

"Because I knew you would not agree unless you saw the canyon yourself."

A third huff. "You said you could do it."

"I can. But not like Running Wolf. And Barks Like Coyote is like a son to him. They work as a team."

Two Feathers felt comfortable and at ease. But Will wouldn't sit still. Two Feathers could almost feel his brother's nerves humming in his uneasiness. *Why doesn't he relax? I've told him he is safe here.*

Watching Will, Two Feathers remembered the soldiers. He remembered how he felt whenever he went to a fort. How he could not stay inside a building. How he felt trapped. How the uniforms brought back memories of the day of death, the day the soldiers killed his mother.

Remembering these things, he understood Will's fear. His brother had his own set of memories. Two Feathers knew the sight of the Comanche brought back memories of Will's capture—the brutal ride for days without stopping, his mistreatment. He wouldn't leave Will alone.

"Two Feathers?" Running Wolf pulled a rock out of the fire ring and rested his feet against its warmth. "Do you know where there are horses?"

"No, but you do." He fed a handful of wood to the fire. The light showed Running Wolf's stern face soften into a slight smile. "You were always more of an uncle to me than Yellow Hawk. You taught me much. I need your help."

The flames faded back to coals. Two Feathers waited. Will started to speak, but his brother shoved his elbow into his ribs, cutting off his words. "My brother offers you two steers and your pick of the horses for your help."

Running Wolf cocked an eyebrow at Will.

Two Feathers hurried to finish the offer before Will did or said something to ruin it. "Help us catch, rough break, and drive them close to Las Vegas."

Running Wolf rose to his feet and looked at Barks Like Coyote, who nodded. The chief smiled at Two Feathers. "We will go tomorrow. Tell your brother to leave the dunnia here. He may be big, but a wild stallion would kill him."

Two Feathers' smile faded at the man's last words. *Will won't leave Buck in a Comanche camp and Running Wolf does not like to be disobeyed.*

WEEPING WOMAN

"That's NOT going to happen!" Will spat the words out in a hoarse whisper just loud enough for Two Feathers to hear. His gaze shot across the glowing coals of Running Wolf's fire and locked on the older man. "I won't leave Buck in a Comanche camp. He goes with me. He always goes with me."

"I know. I was not going to ask." Two Feathers watched Will swing his gaze from Running Wolf to Barks Like Coyote and back. "You are learning more Comanche than I thought."

Two Feathers shifted his position to look at his brother. "Will, look at me." He waited until Will turned. "I want to talk to Weeping Woman. I want you to know her. It will be warmer in her teepee, and we can sleep there. If you give her a chance, you will like her."

They left Running Wolf's fire to go to Weeping Woman but Will immediately returned to the older man. He stood by the fire, staring at Running Wolf, then said something in Comanche, but Two Feathers couldn't hear it. After jogging several steps, Will caught up.

"What did you say to Running Wolf?"

"I told him Buck was mine, always had been, and always would be."

"What did he say?"

"He just laughed."

Two Feather started walking, but Will pulled his arm, stopping him.

"Can't we make our own camp and come back in the morning? We don't have to stay. . . ."

Frustration coursed through Two Feathers, and he stopped listening. *It is Will's turn to be in the camp of his enemy.* Two Feathers clenched his fists. *I trusted Pa and Will when we went to Fort Sumner. Will should trust me now.* He felt his anger rising, but a quick glance back toward Running Wolf made him swallow it. This wasn't the time or the place to fight with Will.

"Two Feathers?" The high squeak in Will's voice brought Two Feathers out of his thoughts. He hung his head when he saw the rigid muscles in his brother's face and his bulging jaw. Two Feathers knew that look. He'd seen it when he rescued Will from Yellow Hawk's camp two years ago and again last year when Pa was killed. He thought of it as Will's brave face. It always showed when times were tough. Two Feathers wondered if he showed his brave face when they went to the soldiers' fort.

Two Feathers gazed around at the familiar scene of his people setting up camp. He was happy to be there. It felt comfortable. "Will, remember the first time I went to Fort Sumner with you and Pa and Mr. Goodnight? When we brought the herd of cattle from Texas? Remember how scared of the soldiers I was? You told me you would not leave me. That I would be safe, and I trusted you and Pa. Now, it is time to trust me. You will be safe. No one will harm you in the teepee of Weeping Woman."

Will's grip relaxed on his brother's arm. After a long study of Two Feathers' face, he nodded.

Weeping Woman and Red Wing were waiting when they reached her teepee. Two Feathers, followed by Will, lifted the flap over the opening and entered his childhood home. A small fire burned low in the middle of the floor and warmed the interior, giving off the comforting, slightly pungent smell of sage. A pot of meat and vegetables simmered over the fire. He savored its familiar aroma. His stomach growled.

Buffalo hides covered the floor. Two Feathers found the burned spot in one where he'd dropped a hot cinder when he was small. He'd tried to cover the damage with a pile of kindling. Several pallets of hides covered with brightly colored blankets lay against the walls. Various sized bags stuffed with dried food, utensils, and clothing hung from the support poles that held up the buffalo hide walls. He remembered the bag Weeping Woman used to store dried leaves for tea.

His aunt sat by the fire, cutting up tubers and adding them to the pot. "Come," she said, "sit here." She patted the floor beside her.

How many times had he seen her sitting like this? She was a little heavier than when he had seen her last. Her hair was cut below her ears and, as usual, unruly. But now it was streaked with gray.

Along with the stew's aroma, Two Feathers breathed in other familiar smells. He remembered the feel of a warm rock wrapped in a soft deerskin nestled against his cold feet, the smoky smell of the fire when it hissed as rain fell through the smoke hole. He searched for the bag of pemmican that always hung near Weeping Woman's bed. When he was a child, she could hear the softest step when he tried to snitch a piece and had quickly sent him scampering through the flap, giggling when he managed to steal a bite.

Jerking Will down with him, Two Feathers sat beside Weeping Woman. Red Wing hid behind his aunt and would not come out. He watched this girl who'd been his childhood friend peek at him but glare at Will. How much she'd changed! She no longer looked at him with the eyes of a trusting play-mate. She was different. Her look at him was different. There were tawny flecks in her eyes. Had he seen them before? He couldn't remember, but now, he wouldn't forget.

Finally, Weeping Woman spoke to her and patted a spot beside her. Red Wing sat as far from Will as she could but watched his every move. Two Feathers watched his two good friends—Will with his stiff back and Red Wing with her frightened glare. Would they ever come to understand each other?

Red Wing handed wooden bowls to Weeping Woman, who filled them with stew. Passing the first one to Will, Red Wing wore a stone face, but it softened when she handed the second to Two Feathers. He grinned at her, and her eyes dropped, but the corners of her mouth twitched into a quick smile, a smile that made his face burn.

Two Feathers showed Will how to scoop the food into his mouth with his fingers. "Eat. It has been a long day and I am hungry."

"What is it?" whispered Will, not looking at Weeping Woman.

"It is stew. Kind of like Cookie makes."

Will dipped in the tip of one finger and licked it. "Is it rude to ask for seconds?" he whispered.

When the pot and the bowls were empty, Red Wing collected them. Her gaze lingered on Two Feathers. The teepee seemed empty when she disappeared into the night. Pulling his look away from the flap as it closed the opening behind her, Two Feathers noticed that the crinkles decorating Weeping Woman's cheeks met the lines radiating from her eyes. He'd always thought of them as happy lines because they appeared when she teased him. At her soft chuckle, he gave her a lopsided grin.

"Where is Red Wing going?" Will asked.

"She will clean the bowls and pot and then go to the teepee of her mother."

"I thought she lived with Weeping Woman."

"She does. Just not tonight. Not with us here."

Weeping Woman spoke to Two Feathers and pointed toward two of the blanket piles along the wall.

"Here is your bed for tonight," Two Feathers nodded toward one of the bundles, "and mine is next to yours. It is late, and we have a full day tomorrow. You will sleep warm."

Will's eyes lingered on the older woman's face. He smiled at her. Using his halting Comanche, told her the food was good and thanked her for her hospitality.

He started to stand, but she spoke, and Two Feathers pulled him back down.

"She wants to talk with you. Speak to her in Comanche. If you do not know her words, I will translate."

Will looked at her. "What do you want to know?"

"I want to know who you are. . . what you are. . . and why my son chooses to live in your world."

Will studied her face for a while. Then, glancing at Two Feathers, he started speaking in Comanche. "Two Feathers tried to take my horse many times when my father and I traveled to Fort Sumner with a cattle herd." He shot a quick side-glance at his brother. "My father captured him, and even though we were enemies at first, in time, he decided to stay with us on the ranch we built there."

"How did that happen? What did you do that made him choose to stay?" Her voice drooped with her shoulders. Two Feathers started to interrupt but decided to let Will speak. He was happy they were talking.

Will turned to him and spoke in English. "What do you want me to tell her?"

"Tell her the truth."

The coals grayed with ash, and Two Feathers added some sticks. A flame blazed up, adding more light. Will scrubbed at his face, then pulled at his chin as though he had a beard. "As time passed, we learned more about each other, and Pa. . . " Will stopped and looked at Two Feathers, "How do I say you and Pa took a shine to each other?"

Two Feathers spoke around his big grin and told Weeping Woman what Will wanted to say.

Weeping Woman leaned her head to the side and studied Will. "Do you want to make him white?"

Puzzled, Will looked to his brother. "Did she ask if you want to be white?"

"No, she asked if you want me to be white."

Will shook his head. "It's not for me to say what Two Feathers wants. He is himself. He wanted to learn the white man's ways—his father's ways—so we taught him. Yellow Hawk attacked our ranch. Pa was shot. Before he died, he cut our hands, squeezed them together, and mixed our blood, making us brothers. What Two Feathers does with that is up to him." He showed her his scar.

Picking up both their hands, she rubbed her fingers over their scars, looked into Will's eyes, and then into Two Feathers'. She looked so hard Two Feathers thought she was going to crawl inside him. Then, she let go of Two Feathers' hand but held onto Will's.

"Two Feathers is half white. Do you want to be half Comanche so that you will truly be brothers?"

Will's eyes popped wide. He stared at the Comanche boy he'd known for more than two years. Two Feathers watched the surprise fade from his eyes and wariness take its place.

"Yes. Two Feathers is my brother. What do I have to do to be his?"

"You must learn his ways, the ways of the Comanche. You need to trust him. He has to trust you. When you can do that, you are both Comanche and both white. Will, you have taught Two Feathers the white man's way."

She looked toward her son. "Now, Two Feathers, you must teach Will the way of the Comanche."

She let go of Will's hand. "Two Feathers has told me of your dunnia, the yellow-horse-with-black-mane-and-tail, of your love for the tall horse. And his for you. Your Comanche name will be Tall Horse."

What his aunt said surprised Two Feathers. He felt her eyes on him and looked up. He wondered why she'd asked Will what he wanted and didn't ask him.

"You are the son of my friend and now my son. That will never change." Her voice held the same soft crooning tone he remembered when he would get his feelings hurt as a child. He had learned long ago that whatever Weeping Woman said was how things went. Pa had made them white brothers. Now, Weeping Woman had sealed it by making them Comanche brothers. There would be no changing that fact.

With a huskiness in his voice that surprised Two Feathers, Will announced, "I'm going to check on Buck."

Two Feathers followed him out. Gray Wolf was staked next to Buck beside the teepee. Both munched on dried grass some younger boys had cut for them. The air smelled clean. The bright moon cast shadows that hid an owl who called in the distance. It was good to be here. He'd been away too long.

Will walked over to Buck and stroked the golden neck. He slid his hand under Buck's forelock and scratched his favorite spot. "Hey, ol' boy. You doin' okay?" He pulled a pair of hobbles from his back pocket. "I know you don't like to be hobbled, but I'm a little nervous about where we are. We both know a stake won't stop you if you decide to wander off, so don't fight me this time." Buck stood easy while Will secured the hobbles, then lowered his head. Another mouthful of dried grass disappeared. Will pulled his fingers through the black mane. "I don't know how you get so many tangles. You're a mess."

Will stroked Buck until Two Feathers wondered if he would stay outside with him all night. At the ranch, he often found Will sleeping in Buck's stall. He decided to stay with Gray Wolf a little longer and give Will more time.

Will pulled Buck's head up and stroked the long nose. He brushed the forelock away. "Buck, listen to me. You don't need to worry." Buck snorted and shook his head. "I know. We're in a Comanche camp . . . " he looked at Two Feathers, "but . . . Two Feathers says we'll be safe." He scratched Buck's happy spot again. "We trust him. And I guess I'm half Comanche now. So. . . we'll be fine."

He pointed to the teepee. "I'll be right there. You'll know where I am. I'll see you in the morning." He stepped away but suddenly turned back. Grabbing Buck's head, he pulled it up again. "You stay close and listen. You keep your ears perked up and listen for Yellow Hawk. Okay?" He gave Buck's head a gentle shake. "You hear me? You warn me if he comes."

Will's nervousness about Yellow Hawk had settled some-what inside the teepee, but here—outside—in the dark—Two Feathers saw it drape itself all over Will. Even with plenty of moonlight, Will was spooked. And his fear seeped into Two Feathers.

Without speaking, Two Feathers followed Will back inside. He closed the teepee flap and fastened it so the wind wouldn't blow it open. Will stretched out on his pallet. Even with the fire's flickering dim light, Two Feathers knew Will's eyes stared at him. In the silence, he heard a slow whoosh of air that could only come from the release of long-held tension.

Will pulled a blanket over himself. "Remember what I told you. I'm gonna be mad at you if I get killed."

Two Feathers chuckled. "That will worry me all night." He

meant it as a joke but wondered how well he would sleep. Feeling restless, Two Feathers went back to sit beside Weeping Woman. He didn't look at her but was aware of every move she made. This woman had always been a presence in his life. Even before the day of death, he would run to Weeping Woman when he was hurt or sick. She always had what he needed. As he grew older, he asked questions, but she wouldn't answer. Why didn't she give him what he needed now? He waited several minutes for Weeping Woman to speak. When she didn't, he decided to wait no longer.

"Weeping Woman, you are the only mother I have. You have been good to me and taught me well. I would not have survived without the time you spent in the woods, teaching me how to find and use the plants' gifts of food and medicine and to hunt small animals. I thank you. But there is one more thing I need to learn from you."

He watched her face. The happy crinkles he'd seen moments ago faded away. In their place settled a deep sadness. What had she suffered? What had happened that brought her such pain?

"I know. I hoped you would never have to learn what Yellow Hawk has always been and what he has become." Her voice was soft but firm and steady.

"He is a danger to me, Will, and Buck. He will not leave us alone."

"When he is here, his hate for you and the white boy and his longing for the dunnia are all he talks about. His mind is bent."

"Why is he gone from you so much? Why does he not take care of you?"

For a long time, Weeping Woman remained silent. Two Feathers wondered if he'd asked the wrong questions. Had he offended her? Was she angry?

Her eyes looked far away as though she'd gone to another

place, another time. When she spoke, she didn't look at him. "He has always been difficult to live with. Even when we were young, he was full of anger. Only Morning Dove, your mother, could handle him. When she was born, he was almost a grown man. Her name, Morning Dove, was his choice, not her mother's. He watched over that child all the time except when hunting or off on a raid."

"If he loved her so much, why does he hate me?"

She gave no answer. She was still far away and continued as though he'd never spoken.

"Your mother and I were friends, even though I was older. I was always afraid of Yellow Hawk, but he was a great warrior and a hunter. He became a war chief when still young because he feared nothing and was fierce in battle. It was a great honor to be his wife."

Each word she spoke pulled at his already stinging nerves. Each time she evaded his question, he felt squeezed from the inside. All he wanted to know was why. The thought slid through his lips as though exhaled from his heart.

"But why does he hate me?"

Still, she didn't answer. "Yellow Hawk never let any young men come around Morning Dove. He threatened all of them, and they stayed away. She tried to talk to him, but he wouldn't listen. Once, he was gone for a long hunting trip with many men from our village. We traveled with the elders north across the Red River into the Nations. At a trading post, Morning Dove met your father."

A slow smile spread across her face. She turned toward Two Feathers. Taking his hand in hers, she stroked it gently. She faded even deeper into her memories.

"He was selling cattle to the Indian Agent there. We camped near the post for nearly a moon and traded for many things we needed. That was a fun time. Yellow Hawk was gone.

Morning Dove was happier than I had ever seen her. Before we left the agency, John Randall took her for his wife. She went to live with him."

Two Feathers pushed for more answers. "What happened when Yellow Hawk found out?"

She sat unmoving for a while. Then shivers shook her body, and her eyes squeezed shut. When they opened, she smiled. "I am tired. You and your brother have a long day tomorrow. You must sleep." She went to her pallet and lay down, turning her back to Two Feathers.

"But, Weeping Woman, what happened when Yellow Hawk discovered she was gone?"

Weeping Woman's only answer was silence.

Two Feathers stared at her. He wanted to shake her shoulder and make her talk to him. But he didn't disturb her. Thoughts swirled in his head like a stream tumbling over rocks. He had so many unanswered questions. For as long as he could remember, those questions had clouded his life. Why would no one talk to him?

"I feel like a battlefield, sometimes fighting in the thick of battle, and sometimes I am the quiet after the battle. Will I survive, or will Yellow Hawk?" His words fell on sleeping ears.

Wild Mustangs

About mid-morning the next day on the canyon rim, Two Feathers and Will watched a herd of fifty horses grazing in a branch off the main canyon. Five young stallions stood together, separate from the main herd. Three mares drank from a willow-lined creek that merged with the river only a short distance ahead. When they raised their heads, water dripped from their muzzles and sparkled in the sunlight. Two more young stallions watched from a sandbar. An Appaloosa with a short, scraggly mane and tail lifted his head and sniffed the air.

Two Feathers could barely hold his excitement. He forced himself to lie still. All his life, he had wanted to hunt horses with the men of his village. Yellow Hawk never let him. Now he was doing it! Will was twitching and wiggling all over the place. Two Feathers grabbed Will's bandana, jerked him close, and exploded a loud whisper in his ear. "If you are not still, you will spook those horses, and I will bust you a good one on the nose."

Never taking his eyes off the herd, Will jerked his head in a quick nod.

Running Wolf had sent Barks Like Coyote and two men ahead to turn the horses into the catch pen. He rode up with two additional men. They dismounted far enough back to avoid being seen by the horses below. Hunkering down beside the boys, they watched the herd. Now, it was Two Feathers who could not keep still. At the sight of the Comanche in their buckskins, Will stopped wiggling.

Running Wolf pointed to a curve toward the upper end of the offshoot. "We will go off the rim around that bend and come up behind the horses. Do not make a move until I signal. Men are blocking the downriver trail, so the herd will turn upriver toward Barks Like Coyote. We will move slow. Tell Will to keep his stallion behind the men. I do not want the lead stallion to see Buck. If the herd stallion feels challenged, he will fight. I do not think the boy can hold that big horse."

"Do not worry about Will and Buck."

Cocking his head to one side, Running Wolf looked at Two Feathers. With a hefty huff, he arched his eyebrows. Motioning for his men to follow, he mounted his horse.

Two Feathers leaned toward Will and whispered in his ear. "You better control Buck when he sees the stallion or Running Wolf will be mad at both of us. That is not something you want to experience."

They rode single file down the trail off the rim, then spread across the narrow neck of the offshoot. As they came around the bend and into the canyon, the lead mare, a black with white stockings, spotted them. Alarmed, she snorted and laid her ears back against her head. Running Wolf stopped his horse on a wide sandbar at the water's edge and held his horse still. His men did the same.

Two Feathers' heart raced. Feeling his excitement, Gray Wolf pranced around and wouldn't stay still. Two Feathers watched Will pull his hat tight and grip hard on Buck's reins. They waited for the signal.

Running Wolf stepped his horse forward. The men followed. The boys eased their horses in behind, still holding the reins tight, controlling their nervous mounts. The line moved at a steady pace toward the herd.

Shaking her head, the mare moved away from the men. Following her, the herd showed their distress and trotted away from the approaching danger. A piebald stallion jerked his head up when the horses started moving. He headed toward the approaching men. With one quick look, he spun around, driving the herd forward with a few well-placed nips. The lead mare broke into a racing gallop, throwing up dust clouds. Gray Wolf and Buck bolted after the warriors. The race was on.

At the junction of the offshoot and the main canyon, the Comanche men turned the herd upriver, following the winding riverbed and sending wet spray high into the air. Through the water curtains, Two Feathers watched the men driving the herd hard with Running Wolf coming behind them. Manes and tails sailed through the air like wings. The mares' high-pitched squeals and the young stallions' loud screams spoke the herd's alarm. The men spread out, flanking the horses and keeping them together. Gray Wolf raced like he'd never run before. Two Feathers couldn't feel Gray Wolf's hooves striking the ground. He and his horse became one and flew like a red-tailed hawk. The canyon walls and the trees flashed by in a red and green blur.

Each man led a spare horse. When their mount tired and while still running at full gallop, they sprang from the tired horse to the fresh one. The horses never broke their stride, and the men never lost their balance. The wild mustangs and the riders chasing behind them soon outdistanced Running Wolf, who caught the tired mounts.

Two Feathers and Will rode through the herd's dust and the fading sounds of their pounding hooves. When they caught up, the Comanche had turned them into the catch pen. Not wanting to miss the action, Two Feathers and Will dismounted and walked Gray Wolf and a nervous Buck back and forth in front of the gate to cool them down.

"You were right, Two Feathers," said Will, panting and

grabbing at a breath between words. "I've never seen... anything like that... in my whole life... Wow! What a ride!"

Eyes wide and with a giant grin, Two Feathers watched the wild horses racing around the catch pen, searching for a way out. The herd charged the front gate again and again, sending a dusty haze over the catch pen. The warriors held their ground, turning them away until they bunched against the far back wall behind the slight swell of a hill and out of sight of the men. Standing guard on the hill between his herd and the enemy, the piebald stallion reared and screamed his challenge.

Buck reared. His answer echoed against the canyon walls, sending fear through Two Feathers like a bolt of lightning and seared his feet to the ground. The reins jerked from Will's hands. Buck gathered himself to sail over the gate and meet the stallion's challenge when Running Wolf on his bay slammed into him, knocking him off balance. The Comanche grabbed the dangling reins, turned Buck away from the gate, and at full gallop, man and horse drug the angry buckskin away from the fight.

Two Feathers leaped onto Gray Wolf, grabbed Will's arm, and swung him up behind. They raced after Running Wolf. Reaching the river, the Comanche didn't slow down. Water exploded from the bay and Buck's hooves as they raced to a gravel bar about a quarter of a mile upriver.

When Two Feathers reached them, he slowed Gray Wolf to a walk. Will slid off the horse's wet rump and walked up to Buck. Two Feathers stayed on his horse. He'd never seen Will's face without any color in it. He looked sick. Will stood between Buck and the angry Comanche.

Buck was wet with sweat and river water. He pranced around until Will stroked his neck and spoke to him. Then, like magic, the big horse settled and lowered his head. Will rubbed his nose while cooing into his ears.

Running Wolf handed Buck's reins to Will. He spoke in Comanche to Two Feathers. "I told you not to bring that stallion. You and Tall Horse will stay in camp like children who do not listen to their elders until I tell you to come."

Two Feathers hung his head, avoiding Running Wolf's gaze.

Neither he nor Will moved after Running Wolf rode away. Two Feathers didn't know if he was angrier at himself for letting Will bring Buck or at Will for not controlling him.

Finally, Will mounted and walked next to Gray Wolf. "I guess we really messed up."

"I guess we did."

"I got some of what he said, but not all."

"He said to stay in camp like children."

Will's forehead crinkled. His lips tightened until the bottom one disappeared.

"Will?" Two Feathers' voice held a warning. "Do not get angry at Running Wolf. He told us to leave Buck behind. We decided not to."

Will sat still and stared at the running water while Buck drank. When he released his breath, it hissed like steam from a kettle. "I guess you're right. He told us." He looked at Two Feathers, his eyes begging for understanding. "But Buck has never acted like that before."

"He has never been around a wild stallion."

Will's head drooped. "That's true."

They walked the horses back to camp. Two Feathers dreaded facing Running Wolf, so he set a slow pace. He knew the older man would get over being mad at him and Will but thought it best to stay out of his way for a few days. Arriving in camp, they removed the heavy saddles, brushed Gray Wolf and Buck until they shined, then hobbled the horses in good grass.

"Let them graze," said Two Feathers. "They have had a busy morning."

Each morning for the next three days, Two Feathers waited for Running Wolf to signal that he and Will could join the men working the horses in the catch pen, but no signal came. Two Feathers cut a mountain of wood for the cook fire, while Will cooked pot after pot of stew. Each afternoon, Running Wolf let them come to the catch pen—but not to work with the horses. The brothers cut and dragged brush to tighten the enclosure.

"Two Feathers, do you want to know what I think?" Will sunk the blade of his hatchet into a tree, sat on the ground, and leaned against the trunk. Rubbing his hands, he counted his blisters. "Pa and Running Wolf are no different. Pa had us spending weeks cutting brush for the brush corral back home. Now we're doing it again for Running Wolf."

Two Feathers showed Will a particularly puffy blister. "I have blisters on top of blisters." A shadow fell across Two Feathers. His gaze climbed up a pair of tall moccasins to the stern face of Running Wolf with two warriors standing behind him.

"We are hungry."

Will stiffened. Two Feathers rammed his elbow into his brother's ribs. Scrambling to their feet, Two Feathers pushed Will ahead of him back to the cook fire. "Come on. This will not last forever. Running Wolf will give in soon."

Because the Comanche men stayed to help with the horses, there were four extra mouths to feed. While the boys were cooking another big pot of whatever they could find, Will fussed. "We're going to run out of food if we keep those extra men around. They're your friends. You need to tell them to go."

"What?" Two Feathers looked up from the deer he'd shot that morning. "Are you serious? The horses are already calming and getting used to us. I know we are short on time before we have to be in Las Vegas. But we would never have made it this far without them, and you know it. Quit whining and lift the lid off the pot so I can put this meat in."

Will scowled at the meat as Two Feathers raked it off a flat piece of bark into the half-cooked beans. Tying the rest of the deer carcass in a tarp, he hoisted it off the ground and left it hanging away from predators.

"Come on, Running Wolf is going to work on the piebald stallion this afternoon. This is something you do not want to miss."

Will banked the glowing coals around the pot's base. "I thought he said we had to stay in camp except to cut brush."

"He did." Grinning at Will, Two Feathers scooped coals onto the pot's lid. "But I heard him telling Barks Like Coyote about working that piebald, and I am not going to miss seeing this. You coming?" They took off to watch the action.

The piebald and four mares ran loose in the catch pen, staying on the far side of the grass-covered swell away from the men. The warriors held the remaining horses in a rope corral on the opposite side of the enclosure where the creek spilled over the canyon wall. The black and white stallion, a tough, scarred fighter, was smart and wary and stayed out of sight behind the hill. No one had attempted to get a rope on him until today.

Running Wolf motioned for Two Feathers and Will to follow him. He put them on two of the Comanches' mustangs. "Go over the rise and start the piebald running. Run him without stopping. There is enough land to run him until the sun crosses the sky. Do not let him stop. Do not let him eat. Do not let him drink. When your horse tires, come get a fresh mount. Keep him running until he can run no more."

Two Feathers, with Will beside him, kicked his mustang into a lope. They stopped at the top of the rise and searched for the horses.

Will sat for a minute, and then his entire face grinned. "I can't believe I'm chasing wild horses on a Comanche mustang."

He yelled a wild whoopee and slapped his heels to the horse. The horse jumped into a gallop. Two Feathers let out a wild whoop of his own and bolted after him.

They raced off the rise, bent forward with their horses' manes whipping in their faces. Two Feathers spotted the stallion and mares in a cluster of cottonwood trees in the corner of the enclosure. "Will?" he shouted over the pounding hooves and pointed toward the trees. They turned their mustangs in that direction. The piebald burst from the east side of the grove and took off across the open ground, the mares keeping pace close behind. Two Feathers and Will raced after the stallion, dodging yucca plants and boulders, jumping over creosote bushes, and kicking up clouds of red sandy dirt.

Soon, they settled into a steady pace. When Two Feathers' sweat-lathered mustang slowed, he turned toward Running Wolf and a fresh horse. He and Will, also on a fresh mount, kept the piebald running. They changed horses several times as the sun climbed higher, and their shadows shrank. When the mares could no longer follow the stallion, Two Feathers, riding wide around them, let them slow to a stop. When the stallion veered in one direction, Two Feathers was there to push him on, if he turned in another direction, Will was there. Dust filled the air and sifted over the stallion until the white foam on his coat turned a crusty red.

The stallion staggered, and the boys finally allowed him to stop. Frothy sweat streaked his heaving, dirt-covered sides, his head hung low to the ground. Two Feathers and Will blocked any desperate move he made to escape.

Running Wolf rode up on the bay, a lasso in one hand and the loop in the other. His rope settled over the piebald's head, and he pulled it tight. The horse bucked and jerked against the rope, but the lasso choked off his wind until he fell to the ground, gasping for air. Keeping the rope tight around his neck, Running Wolf advanced, hand over hand, to the horse's head and hobbled his forefeet. Kneeling on the stallion's neck, he loosened the lasso, then fastened a noose around its lower jaw. He slowly released the pressure of the choking rope, stood, and backed away, taking the hobbles with him. The horse lunged to his feet, snorted, and bucked like a maddened beast. The bucking went on and on until the grass was scraped away, and clods of dirt flew from his hooves. White froth soaked the body of the enraged horse. Finally, once again exhausted, he calmed and stood with his front legs spread wide, his head hanging low.

Running Wolf advanced hand over hand toward the stallion.

The piebald fought against the rope, but now with less fervor. The man stood his ground with the rope braced against his hips. The lasso was taut and pulled the animal's head low to the ground. Running Wolf held the piebald until exhaustion stilled the animal. Placing one hand over the quivering nostrils, he rubbed his hand over the nose and eyes, murmuring softly. The trembling horse and the steady man stood together for a long time. Then, Running Wolf leaned forward, cupped his hands over the horse's nose, and breathed into his nostrils with long slow breaths. The piebald relaxed, and Running Wolf led the exhausted animal, covered in sweat, around in a wide circle.

Two Feathers followed the man and horse in quiet admiration of the man's skills. Every move Running Wolf had made was locked in his memory. When he was young, he'd watched the Comanche men from a distance working with their horses, but never up close because Yellow Hawk didn't want him nearby. Someday, he would capture his own wild stallion and raise his own horses.

Later that night, two men faded into the night to guard the

horses. The others rolled into their blankets until their turn. Two Feathers settled in his bedroll. The bright moonlight cast long shadows. Even though the day had warmed, the night was cold. Two Feathers followed Running Wolf's example and pulled a rock from the fire ring, resting his feet against its warmth. Though tired and sore from the day's work, he felt comfortable. The camp settled into the quiet of the night. The soft fluttering sound of bat wings as they swept overhead hunting for insects, the deep hoot of a horned owl sailing through the crisp air, and the rattle of budding branches in the breeze welcomed Two Feathers back to the land of the Comanche.

Yellow Hawk crept into his thoughts uninvited. He'd put off talking to Running Wolf about the man while the work with the horses filled their days, but time was running out. They would be returning to Las Vegas soon. Maybe he would know how to deal with his uncle. Sucking in a shuddering breath, he glanced at the older man propped against a log. He rose and sat next to him. "I need help. Yellow Hawk fights against me all the time. He threatens my life."

"I know."

"What can I do to stop him?"

"That, I do not know."

Two Feathers' shoulders sagged, and his arms dropped into his lap. His hands felt too heavy to lift. "So. . . I just wait for him to kill me. . . and Will."

Running Wolf's face took on a distracted expression as though he'd gone to another place and time. "When Yellow Hawk and I were young, we were friends. We hunted together. As we got older, we went on raids together. We captured many horses. He is a strong warrior."

"Why did he change?"

"I do not know. He is not the same man. He is mean. He rides with other Comanche and Kiowa who have been put out of their villages. They have declared war on all whites. We told him he could not ride with us. He could not stay in our camps. We all want the whites to leave our land, but you and I know that will not happen. Someday we will have to give up our ways."

"What does that have to do with his hatred for me?"

"When Yellow Hawk does come, he talks of killing you and your white brother and taking the dunnia."

"That makes no sense. One Comanche does not kill another." His head hurt. . . this problem had been a part of him forever. *Maybe I should go far away. Go where Yellow Hawk cannot find me. But where?* There was no place to go that would be far enough. Thoughts of Weeping Woman entered his mind. He could not go far from Weeping Woman and Red Wing.

"No, it does not," said Running Wolf. "You are not at fault. A bad spirit twisted him until he lost his own spirit, his puha. There is nothing to guide him."

"What can I do?"

"Stay away from him. Guard yourself against him at all times."

"We are trying to do that now."

Running Wolf stared into the night. "He has gone into a world that is not Comanche, not Kiowa, not anyplace I know of. I am afraid he will not stop until he is dead. He has gone to a dark place and cannot get back."

They sat together in silence for a long time. Two Feathers' sadness ran so deep no thoughts could escape it. His head felt heavy and empty at the same time.

Running Wolf stood. "Go to sleep. Your time to guard the horses will come soon."

Two Feathers rolled in his blankets near Will. Too tired for his worries to linger, he slept. Hours later, Will shook his shoulder. "Wake up. It's your shift. I saddled Gray Wolf for you." It was so cold that Will's teeth chattered, making his words choppy. "Barks Like Coyote's with the herd on the far side. You take the near side. You shouldn't have any trouble. Take your blanket. The wind's cold." He rolled into his blankets as close to the fire as he could get.

Rubbing the sleep from his eyes, Two Feathers walked to where their horses were tied. He mounted Gray Wolf and headed for the herd. The heaviness in his head eased, but his thoughts whirled in circles. He thought about what Weeping Woman and Running Wolf had told him. Why would Yellow Hawk hate him for being born?

Then a new thought hit him. It didn't matter who he was. It wouldn't have mattered if he'd been born a girl or some other boy. Yellow Hawk would hate any person born from his sister and a white man just as he hated him. Running Wolf was right—he'd done nothing against Yellow Hawk—it wasn't his fault.

The cramps in Two Feathers' shoulders eased. He felt better and wished morning would come so he could tell Will. But what difference did this new thought make? Understanding Yellow Hawk changed nothing. His uncle still wanted Buck, still wanted Will dead, still wanted him dead. He stopped Gray Wolf and studied the night around him, watching for anything moving, anything out of the ordinary, any shadows where shadows shouldn't be.

A week later, in the cool evening air, Two Feathers, Will, Running Wolf, and Barks Like Coyote sat around the campfire alone. The other Comanche men, taking twelve horses, had left that afternoon. Two Feathers glanced at Will.

"Did you get over being mad? You did not think those men helped us because they liked you."

"I didn't think they would take all those horses and the two steers."

"Will, stop thinking like a white man. The Comanche trade in horses, not steers. Steers have no value except food. A Comanche is what you call rich when he has horses."

Will jabbed at the fire with a stick until sparks flared into flames. "But white men think they're rich when they have cattle."

He heard soft laughter from Running Wolf and looked up.

"You're a good white boy," he spoke in English.

Startled, Will's eyes popped open. "You speak English?"

Lifting his thumb and forefinger, Running Wolf indicated a small space. "A little."

Speaking once again in Comanche, Running Wolf and Two Feathers talked for several minutes.

"Will, Barks Like Coyote is taking his and Running Wolf's horses in the morning. Running Wolf has agreed to go with us to the Gallinas River. We will cross the Llano Estacado. That will shorten our trip by nearly a week."

"That sounds good to me. Tell him I appreciate his help."

"But he is taking the piebald stallion."

"Oh, no. No! That's the best horse in the whole bunch. I was planning on breeding him to our mares."

"That is what he is going to do."

"No!"

"Will, stop, and think. We would have failed without his help. We have twenty good horses to sell at a good price. And because of him, we are taking four good mares back to the ranch."

Will opened his mouth as if to say something but shut it again. He huffed a big sigh. "That's true."

"Tell him the stallion is a gift for his help."

With his face scrunched up and his eyes squeezed shut, Will nodded.

Two Feathers hid his grin. "That is good. Besides, he would have taken him anyway."

With his eyes still shut tight, Will nodded again. "I know."

Two Feathers settled into his blankets. "All we have to do now is not get cheated by Silas Porter."

Horses For Sale

Late in the afternoon a week later, Two Feathers slid off Gray Wolf in the spot where they'd camped earlier on the Gallinas River. Taking his grullo and six mustangs through the willows, he led them down the slabs of flat rocks to the river to drink. He bellied down, brushed away the water beetles, and drank his fill. The clear water tasted good, much better than the stagnant pools Running Wolf managed to find as they crossed the Llano Estacado. When done, he led his animals to a grassy patch in a cluster of cottonwoods and tied them with enough slack to allow them to graze.

Will took his place at the rocks with his string of six horses and Buck. Running Wolf followed with his two strings of six and his bay. After the horses drank their fill, they hobbled them in a rope corral. The week on the trail had settled the horses enough that they peacefully cropped the grass within their reach.

Before Two Feathers and Will finished cooking supper, the evening sky turned from orange to a scattering of wispy, red-fringed clouds. Backstrap from an antelope Running Wolf shot earlier in the day sizzled in the skillet and set Two Feathers' stomach growling.

After eating and with just enough light to see by, Will scoured the skillet with sand at the river's edge. Two Feathers stretched out on his blankets away from the fire and studied the mustangs. Traveling slowly left the horses in good condition, well-muscled with shiny coats. Running Wolf stopped a few hours before dark each day to allow the three of them to work with the horses. When they reached the Gallinas River, the animals accepted their rope halters and a saddle, some allowed a rider. Two Feathers' pride in the fact they could be mounted without too much difficulty felt good.

He watched the four mares he'd picked out. Two were bays, one with a white blaze down her face and the other with four white stockings. One was a gray roan. The fourth was brown with a black mane and tail and a perfect white star between her eyes. The memory of Running Wolf's cocked eyebrows and pat on the back when Two Feathers showed him his choices wouldn't be forgotten. Any praise from Running Wolf was hard won.

Will's digging in his pack pulled Two Feathers' attention from the horses. With a clean shirt, socks, and pants in hand, Will called out, "I'm going to take a bath. I can't stand the way I smell any longer. Don't wait up for me. I plan on soaking for a long time." Taking a few steps toward the river, he turned back toward Two Feathers, "Why don't you come on? There's enough soap for two, and it's a big river."

"What for? I do not need a bath."

"You don't? Well, that's news to me." He headed toward the river.

Two Feathers moved next to Running Wolf. The older man lifted his nose, sniffed, and frowned. He spoke in Comanche, "Do you smell a skunk in the wind?"

Two Feathers lifted his elbow and sniffed. He crinkled his nose. "I will wash in the morning. You have learned more of the white man's words than you want Will to know." He untied a small pouch hanging from his belt and opened it. "I have something to show you." He handed over the horse figure Yellow Hawk carved.

Running Wolf sat up straight. "Where did you get this?"

"Yellow Hawk gave it to me."

"I thought so. He likes to carve things but is not very good." He rolled the crude figure around in his hand. "Do not be fooled by what you think is a gift from him."

"He said my mother asked him to give me a strong horse when I was little, but he never did. So, he carved this when he asked for shelter last winter during a snowstorm."

Running Wolf turned to sit cross-legged, facing the boy. "Two Feathers, know what I say to be the truth. He did not give you a gift. That is not why he did this. It is a warning. I know this man."

"I know, Running Wolf. It is the dunnia. I know he gave it to me because he wants Buck. He wants me to know this is the only buckskin Will and I will be able to keep."

"Do you? Do you really understand? He no longer thinks like a man. He is twisted."

Two Feathers didn't answer. He stroked the small figure and turned it over and over in his hands. Then, he gently slipped it back into the bag and tied it to his belt.

"It is a gift from my mother, even though it came to me through Yellow Hawk. That is why I chose to keep it."

Running Wolf cocked his head. "Is that all?"

Two Feathers didn't answer.

"What else happened that night?"

"I did not see it at the time. But when I think back, he changed. When he handed me the horse, for just a minute, his eyes were like they used to be. . . before the day of death. When I was little, once in a while, he would forget to hate me. That is what I saw that night. For just a second, he forgot to hate me."

The noise Will made as he came back into camp stopped their conversation.

Rubbing his hair dry, Will rolled out his ground cloth and blankets as close to the fire as he dared. "That water has a cold bite to it. I'll see you in the morning." He stuck a warm rock in his bedroll and crawled in after it.

Before first light the following day, Running Wolf mounted to head back to Palo Duro Canyon. A lump grew in Two Feathers' throat. It seemed he was always telling the Comanche side of himself goodbye, and he didn't like it.

Sitting tall and straight on his horse, the man looked down at Two Feathers with sadness. "I watched you with the horses. You have a way with them. They trust you." He studied the boy's face, shot a quick glance at Will, then a longer one in the direction of town. "This is what you want? To live with white men? You do not want to be Comanche?"

"I am Comanche." Two Feathers gripped the older man's wrist as tight as he could squeeze. "I. Am. Comanche!"

Running Wolf covered Two Feathers' hand with his and massaged the corded muscles until they relaxed. "Yes, you are. Do not forget it."

Two Feathers saw love in the man's eyes, love for a half-white Comanche boy. Why wasn't this man his uncle? Why did his uncle have to be Yellow Hawk?

Two Feathers watched as Running Wolf faded into the weakening darkness. How many times had that man filled a hole Yellow Hawk had torn in Two Feathers' heart? He didn't want him to go. He watched as Running Wolf grew smaller the further he traveled, until he disappeared. Two Feathers shaded his eyes from the stabbing rays and watched the empty desert. Empty like he was. Waiting. . . for what? He didn't know. The sun made his head hurt.

He pulled his thoughts out of the Comanche world where

he'd spent the recent weeks. He dug in his packs to find his cowboy clothes. At the river, the buckskins slid off, and after a quick wash in the cold water, the tan pants, the faded blue shirt, socks, boots, and handkerchief pulled him back into the white man's world. He braided his long hair, tied the ends with thin rawhide strips, and tucked them under his hat. The feathers he usually secured within the braids were safely rolled in his blankets. Why couldn't his heart change between worlds as easily as his clothes?

"Will?" he called. "You ready?"

Will tightened the cinch on Buck's saddle. "We need to sell these horses and get back to the ranch. We haven't seen any sign of Yellow Hawk. That worries me."

Each took two strings of six animals and a packhorse. A steady lope with walking breaks ate up the miles and brought them to the outskirts of Las Vegas in an hour. A farmer with a loaded wagon of supplies directed them to a side road that, to Two Feathers' relief, took them to the stables without leading the skittish horses down the main street.

Once the horses were settled in the pens, the boys removed the mustangs' ropes, coiled them, and secured them to their saddles. Will stood beside Buck with his head resting on the golden, muscled shoulder.

"Will? You okay?"

There was no answer.

"What is wrong?"

Will lifted his head.

Two Feathers studied Will's face hoping for even a hint of confidence. All he saw was a nervous tongue licking twitching lips.

Will heaved a shaky sigh. "Come on. Let's get this over with."

They went in search of Silas Porter. He sat in his chair

behind his cluttered desk, wearing the same stained vest and baggy pants.

"Well, well, well. Look who's here." The pudgy face wasn't a welcome sight. Nor was the smart-aleck tone that made Two Feathers clench his fists. The man stood, walked around the desk, and out the barn door. "I'm guessin' you brought me some horses. How many did you catch? How sorry are they?"

The insult stung Two Feathers. Spotting Will's clenched fists, he relaxed his own and pulled his brother to a stop.

"I'm okay, Two Feathers. I'll handle this." Sucking in a deep breath, Will closed his eyes and shook his fingers, releasing his tension. "I can do this."

They reached the pens behind Porter, who managed to hoist his considerable bulk onto the corral rails to look at the animals. The horses milled around, stirring up the dust. They either rubbed against or nudged one another while nickering softly. Some found the trough and drank the not-too-fresh water. For what seemed like forever, the old man studied the horses. At last, he stepped to the ground.

"Come inside. We'll talk."

Will shot Two Feathers a triumphant look. Both boys followed him into the cluttered dim office. His chair squawked in protest as he settled his greasy bulk behind his desk.

"Boys, I never thought you could do it." His eyes shifted back and forth between the mess of papers scattered across his desk and Will's strained face.

Two Feathers' skin prickled. He slid to the edge of his chair. Would he stay with his earlier offer? Would it be enough?

"We have twenty-four horses in your pen." Will stood and stepped behind his chair. His hands gripped the top chair rail. "Four…" His voice cracked. Clearing his throat, he continued, "mares are still tied together. They're not for sale. The rest of the mares are yours. Any stallions we caught were gelded and are now healed."

Mr. Porter continued to fumble with the papers on his desk and shot quick glances at Will, ignoring Two Feathers.

"I hate to tell you boys, but my buyer ain't showed up. I can't find that paper you made me sign when we agreed to this deal. So. . . " He flattened his hands on the messy pile and stood. "I ain't gonna buy no horses from you."

Two Feathers forgot to breathe.

Will froze. His knuckles turned white on the chair rail.

The door to the office squeaked slightly and then shut with a soft click. Two Feathers couldn't pull his eyes from Will's face to see if anyone had come in.

Mr. Porter took a deep breath. "Since my buyer ain't showed up, I got no need for your mustangs. I can't sell them to the army. Mustangs ain't big enough for them soldiers."

Will blew a soft low whistle between his lips.

Two Feathers took a breath.

"That's true," said Will. "But many ranches and farms around here will want range-savvy horses. And—there are the Comancheros."

Curling his grimy hands into fists, Porter sank back into his chair. His face paled, but his eyes hardened. "You've no contact with the Comancheros, the filthy thieves."

"That's true. I don't." Will's head lowered just a bit. He gave Silas Porter a knowing smirk. "But my brother does."

Two Feathers snapped his head toward Will.

Will's hand dropped from the chairback where Porter couldn't see and slammed his fingers and thumb together, signaling his brother to keep his mouth shut.

Two Feathers pulled his hat off, allowing his long braids to tumble to his waist. Squinting his eyes into what he hoped were mean narrow slits, he did his best to copy Running Wolf's angry look.

Will glared at the old horse trader. "My brother has two names. In town, he is John Randall, a white rancher. On the Llano Estacado, he is Two Feathers, a Comanche warrior."

A slight scratching sounded at the door. Two Feathers shot a quick glance that way but didn't see anything.

The heavy man wiggled in his chair. It groaned in protest. "Well. . . uh. . . " His gaze wavered between Two Feathers' long braids and Will. Despite the rolls of fat that layered around Porter's neck, Two Feathers could see the man's Adam's apple bob up and down as he swallowed repeatedly. "What do you want me to do? I don't have a buyer."

"The paper you signed didn't say anything about needing a buyer. It said you would buy twenty horses at a price we both agreed on. Do I need to send for the sheriff to get his copy from his safe?"

"This is a business matter. The sheriff has no say in private business."

Two Feathers kept his shoulders from slumping. He forced his back to stay straight. He didn't like the way white men traded horses. He decided the Comanche way was better. If a Comanche wanted horses, he talked it over with the horses' owner and traded goods or other horses. Everyone got what they wanted. They had no need for the white man's money.

Come on, Will. Make him pay. The words rattled around and around in his head. Were those weeks of hard work for nothing? They couldn't fail. *Hurry, Will.* They'd been away from the ranch too long. Where was Yellow Hawk?

The office door rattled again. A rangy, sun-browned, long-legged man in a dust-covered suit stood in the doorway beside Sheriff Crook.

"Hello, Porter," boomed the sheriff. "Look who I found getting off the morning stage. Boys, meet Clarence Hampton, the horse buyer." Crook pulled the signed contract from his shirt pocket and handed it to Will.

An hour later, Two Feathers leaned against the counter in Grzelachowski's store with his elbows on the scarred surface and his chin resting in his hands. He studied the big jars full of candy and grinned at the lively tone of Will's voice. The creased worry lines on Will's forehead disappeared when he paid for a large supply order to take back to the ranch and the other half of the supplies he'd bought on credit. Two Feathers added two small brown bags of stick candy.

Outside the store, they pulled Gray Wolf's and Buck's reins from the hitching post.

"It's gonna take a while for Grzelachowski to get everything loaded on the pack horses," said Will. "Let's go see Sheriff Crook. He said he wanted to talk to us before we left."

Two Feathers' candy turned sour. "I do not want to go into the white man's jail." He spat his candy back into the bag.

"I know you don't. But Sheriff Crook acted like it was important, so we should go. I promise we won't stay long. I'll stand between you and the jail. You'll be safe."

They mounted and walked the horses down Main Street. Two Feathers sat tall on Gray Wolf with his eyes focused straight ahead. He watched the people he passed. Some paid him no attention, but others stopped to stare in disbelief. He could see their faces turn from anger to fear. He knew where their fear came from. It came from the same place as his. . . their days of death.

As they rode, the sheriff's office seemed to grow farther away and the street more crowded with white men. His stomach burned. Sweat rolled down his back. He was glad when they reached the office but wondered which was worse, going inside where the jail was or staying outside with the angry people. His sour stomach made the decision. He went inside.

The sheriff's face lit up when they walked in, but his tone was serious. "Howdy, boys, Come in. Sit down. I've got some news you need to know."

They sat in front of the desk. No matter how hard Two Feathers tried, he couldn't keep his eyes from glancing toward the jail door. The harder he tried not to look, the more he looked.

"You did a good job with those mustangs. I don't know how you managed, and," Crook glanced at Two Feathers, "I don't want to know. I do know that Will is making quite a name for himself around here."

"What do you mean, sir? I haven't done anything."

The alarm in Will's voice cranked up the burn in Two Feathers' stomach. The jail door once again filled the room. "Will?" slipped out in a hoarse whisper.

Will squeezed his forearm.

"Now, don't get in a tizzy. Course you ain't done nothin' wrong. But you've done a bunch of things right."

A quiet sigh escaped from Two Feathers. Will let go of his arm.

"I went to Fort Union last week and ran into Sergeant Baker. We got to talking, and he asked about you. He told me about the stolen army supplies last year and how you figured out who the thief was. Then I told him how Will's big buckskin stallion was took by a Comanche and how you trailed him on the Llano Estacado. After I told him you bluffed that old skinflint, Porter, he made me follow him to the Quartermaster's office. I told it all over again to Captain Stanaway. The captain deals with Porter and was still laughing when I left."

"Well, sir. Me and Two. . . uh. . . John," Will shot Two Feathers a quick glance. "We just did what we had to do. My Pa always told me if something's worth doin', it's worth doin' right."

The sheriff's face lost its amused expression and took on a more serious demeanor. "I learned some news from Sergeant Baker that's both good and bad for both of you."

Two Feathers didn't like the sound of that. He glanced at Will, but there were no clues in his expression.

"What news?" Will asked.

"Rumors are flying all around Fort Union that the army's building a new fort in Indian Territory. They'll be moving several tribes, including the Comanche and the Kiowa, to a reservation there. They may have already started." He looked from John to Will and back. "The Comanche aren't going to go easy. There will be war. Maybe the army will capture Yellow Hawk."

No one spoke. It took all Two Feathers' strength to stay upright. The silence bore down on him with a weight heavy enough to slide him out of his chair and onto the floor. The word "reservation" swelled in his head until it filled his skull with throbbing pain. He could see Will and Sheriff Crook talking, but he heard no sound.

Will stood to leave. Not seeing or hearing, Two Feathers rode after him. His head filled with images of the Navajo he'd seen the year before at Fort Sumner. Their thin bodies, vacant eyes, and defeated expressions raced back and forth inside his head.

The afternoon wore on. Somehow Two Feathers managed to stay in the saddle. Will handled the packhorses and the four mustang mares they'd picked up from Porter's corral. They made good time. After several hours, Will stopped in a grove of cottonwood trees along a narrow creek and made coffee. He dug in a pack and pulled out the pemmican Weeping Woman gave them.

"Here," Will put a cup in Two Feathers' hand and food in the other, "drink some coffee. Eat. We'll talk about this when you're ready."

Thoughts of Weeping Woman and Red Wing swirled in Two Feathers' head. He could neither eat nor drink.

"They will not live on a reservation." He sucked in a shaky breath. "They will not end up like the Navajo."

"I know. We'll talk about this when we get home. We'll decide what to do. But, for now, eat. Drink your coffee. You can't help them if you're sick."

Two Feathers took a sip of the warm coffee.

At dusk, the following day, they rode into Mateo's yard. The barking dogs were their only welcome. At the barn, they were hurried inside by one of the younger boys. He slammed the doors behind them and dropped the bar, locking them in. He helped them unload the packs. All their horses were in their stalls, so they knew Mateo's family was home.

"What's happened?" Will asked. "Something must be wrong. It's way too quiet around here."

While they fed and watered the horses, the boy told them about the Comanche and Kiowa attacks. With their horses settled, they walked to the house. The sky lost most of its color, and shadows filled the corners.

"Look, Will. Unshod horse tracks." Two Feathers scouted the yard. "It looks like five or six horses." His nerves started humming, sending his gaze into every possible hiding place.

They carried their rifles ready. The dogs disappeared back into the barn.

At the porch, Will tried to open the door, but it wouldn't move. "Mateo, it's Will and Two Feathers. Let us in."

"Si, Will." The door opened. Hands grabbed both boys, yanking them into the room. The door slammed with a bang behind them. The heavy thud of the bar falling into its place across the door startled Will making him jump and holler. Two Feathers stumbled over someone's feet and sprawled across the floor.

"What's goin' on here?" Will staggered to the table. "You folks scared the heck out of me." He collapsed into a chair and laid his rifle on the table.

Two Feathers grabbed César's hand and was pulled to his

feet. He straightened his buckskin shirt and checked to be sure the hawk feathers in his braids weren't broken. "The doors and shutters are closed and barred. Has Yellow Hawk attacked?"

"Si, he sent you a message. He found Tomas out with his sheep. He shot him with an arrow and killed his dog."

Will shot up from his chair. "Tomas? Is he. . . is he. . . ?"

"No, Will. He isn't dead. He's wounded and sleeping. You can see him later."

Two Feathers slid into a chair next to Will. His usually straight back slumped. The anger in Will's eyes matched the anger building inside Two Feathers. He turned to Mateo. "What was the message?"

"He spoke to Tomas in Spanish, so he understood every word. He said you cannot take the yellow horse with the black mane and tail far enough away that he won't find him. He said he WILL have the stallion . . . and you . . . and your white brother."

Mateo choked. His face turned a purplish brown. Engorged with blood, veins bulged across his forehead and down his temples.

His words came out in a low growl. "And he left Tomas bleeding in the dirt."

Back at the Ranch

As the night approached, the shadows in the corners of Mateo's living room deepened and spread, leaving the burning candles on the heavy oak dining table an island of light. Mateo, César, Will, and Two Feathers, drew close to the comfort of their glow. Mateo's pain-filled eyes sent guilt deep into Two Feathers. Once again, his uncle, his flesh and blood, had done something terrible.

"I am sorry we have brought this trouble to your door. I am sorry Tomas was hurt." The air in the closed room felt too thick for Two Feathers to breathe.

"No!" Mateo banged his fist on the table. "Don't say that. You didn't do this. It was Yellow Hawk."

"Mateo," said Will, "when'd this happen?"

"Tres days ago." He held up three fingers.

"Have you been closed up like this for three days?"

"Sí. César came home today to check on us. Estevan's still at your ranch."

"Has Yellow Hawk attacked the ranch?"

"No. But he attacked many around here. Farmers have been hit. Livestock killed. People killed."

Two Feathers paced the length of the room, stopping beside Will. Even in the dim light, he could see all color had drained from his brother's face. His gaze stayed fixed on Will as he spoke to him in Comanche. "We cannot control what

Yellow Hawk does. It is not our fault people were killed." He spoke slowly. Even though Will's command of the Comanche language was improving, he wanted to be sure Will understood what he was saying. "Running Wolf and Weeping Woman told us that."

Will's gaze met his brother's. He nodded.

Two Feathers shifted his attention to Mateo.

"Our sheep?" asked Two Feathers. He didn't know how many more of Yellow Hawk's attacks the ranch could withstand.

"How many did he kill?" Will's voice still held a slight quaver.

"We were lucky," said Mateo. "I split the flock into small bunches and grazed only a few at a time. So, he killed only eight ewes out of that bunch. I'd sent three dogs with Tomas. The two guard dogs attacked the horses, but Yellow Hawk shot an arrow into Tomas before they rode off. Tomas told the herd dog to take the sheep home. He brought them in on the run. The guard dogs stayed with Tomas."

"How many rode with Yellow Hawk?" asked Will.

Dreading the answer, Two Feathers massaged his temples to relieve the growing headache above his eyes.

He raised three fingers again. "Tres. . . Kiowa. Their faces painted."

César slammed his hands on the table and thrust himself up. "Where's the army? Why can't they do something? We can't survive out here without protection."

Mateo's firm grip pulled César back down into his chair. "Calm down. Anger solves nothing. Our family has lived on this land for many years. We'll survive."

Alma came in from the back of the house with a blanket wrapped around her shoulders over her nightgown. Her long hair hung in a single braid down her back. "It's late. You can't solve this tonight. Go to bed. You'll think better in the morning."

No one moved.

Her hands slammed together with a loud pop. "Now!"

Two Feathers led the stampede out of the room.

The following afternoon, Two Feathers and Will crossed the creek at the Pecos River Ranch.

"Hello, the house," Will hollered.

Two Feathers heard the front door bang. The answering whoops and frenzied barking from Oso welcomed them home. His feet barely hit the ground before the happy pounding on his back knocked the breath out of him.

"It's about time you two showed up," said a grinning Tony.

"We 'bout gave up on you." Jake and Tony tied the horses to the hitching rail.

"It's mighty good to be here," said Will. He tightened his grip on the lead rope of the two mares, who decided they didn't like the noise of the happy greeting and jerked and pulled on their ropes.

Two Feathers eased his way up his rope and spoke quietly to his two mares. "Will, we need to take them to the corral so they will calm down. It will take a while for them to get used to being here."

Jake and Tony followed them across the yard studying the four mares. Once released from their lead ropes, the mares circled the lot with heads high, sniffing the air.

"You got some good mares here, boys," said Jake.

"Did you find 'em in that huge hole in the ground you told us about?" asked Tony.

Two Feathers' heart couldn't hold his pride. He felt it spread all over his face.

Will headed back to the house with Tony and Jake in tow. Two Feathers brought up the rear and listened to Will tell the twins about the mustangs. "We managed to catch a good-sized herd and cull out the bottom half. We rough broke what we kept, then took them to Las Vegas and sold them to that flea-bag of a horse trader."

"How'd you catch them?" asked Tony.

"Where'd you find 'em?" asked Jake.

"How'd you keep them from getting loose?" asked Tony.

Two Feathers interrupted the volley of questions. "Do not believe half of what he says. He did not do everything by himself. I did manage to help a little. . . and. . . we had some outside help."

At the twins' surprised expressions, Will grinned and raised his hand, palm out. "Don't ask. You won't believe the answer." Laughter filled the ranch yard and flowed into the house with each pack of supplies they carried into the kitchen.

Two Feathers left Will and the twins unloading the last supplies while he took the pack horses, one still loaded with the sacks of grain, to the barn. Buck and Gray Wolf followed him into their stalls. "I do not know who is happier to be home, me or you two."

Pulling one of the grain sacks off the packhorse, he stopped short. "Home." He said it aloud and didn't move until the sack became too heavy. He poured the contents into the grain bin. He couldn't remember using that word when think-ing about the Pecos River Ranch. It belonged to him and Will, but he was unsure he understood what that meant. The ranch was where he lived with Will and with Pa before Yellow Hawk killed him. But home had been with Weeping Woman and the Comanche. It had never been a place. He thought of it as the people he knew and loved. Thinking of the ranch as home was new. It stuck in his mind. He wasn't sure what to do with it.

Walking back to the house, he watched Estevan ride into the yard and hurried toward him. "Do not get down. You need to go. Yellow Hawk attacked the sheep and wounded Tomas, but he is alive. If you leave now and ride hard, you can get there by dark."

Estevan turned his horse around without a word and raced back across the creek. Two Feathers stared at the place where the boy had disappeared through the trees. He was about Red Wing's age. He hoped she was safe. Could he ever make her think of this place as home?

Two Feathers stirred from a light groggy sleep, half awake—half asleep, listening. He blinked and lifted his head, straining to hear what had awakened him. They'd seen no sign of Yellow Hawk during the few days since their return, and he'd started to relax just a little.

There it was, a low growl outside his window. The air was still and hot. Moonlight streamed into the room. He silently slipped from his bed.

Staying out of the moonlight, he made his way to the window. He could see Oso standing in the shadows at the corner of the house. His body was stiff, and his attention was on the barn. Oso sniffed the air. A shadow appeared for an instant in the trees beyond the corral—then vanished.

He eased over to Will's bed and shook him. "Will," he whispered. "Something is near the barn. Come on."

Will wiped his eyes, slid on his moccasins, and grabbed his carbine. Carrying his own weapon, Two Feathers led the way out the back kitchen door and around the house. When they reached Oso, he quieted the dog and hunkered down to study the corral. The mustangs stood bunched in the center with their ears pricked forward and their heads turned toward the creek. The shadow appeared again near a corner post. Will raised his carbine, but Two Feathers pushed the barrel down. He whispered low, "You might hit one of the horses. Wait for a better shot. We do not know where Jake and Tony are."

The mustangs moved away from the center toward the barn but shied away and raced across the corral. A dark figure appeared in the moonlight. Yellow Hawk! The barn door groaned. Will and Two Feathers raised their carbines and fired at the same time. The shots sent Oso into a barking frenzy. Two Feathers raced toward the creek where the shadow had vanished. Will ran to the barn door calling for Tony and Jake. Two Feathers rounded the end of the corral and came to the barn. Will tried to open the door, but it wouldn't budge. He pounded on it with his fists. Two Feathers heard a thud from behind the door, and it flew open. Jake and Tony stood with rifles pointed out the door. The mustangs milled around in the corner of the corral as far from the confusion as they could get.

"He's gone, Will. We cannot track him in the dark." Two Feathers walked to Gray Wolf and stroked him. "Whoa, boy. Easy."

"Why wouldn't the barn door open?" asked Will, his voice taut.

Will walked into Buck's stall and rubbed the nervous horse's neck. A few soothing words along with more rubs and pats eased the horse and the buckskin's head settled between the boy's outstretched arms. Two Feathers didn't know if this habit of behavior between Will and Buck was to calm the horse or Will.

The twins looked at each other. "We got to worryin' that if Yellow Hawk got into the barn, he could climb over the dividing wall and into our part," said Jake.

"So, we set a heavy bar across the door to keep everything out," finished Tony.

"What about your door to the house part?" asked Will.

"It has one, too," said Tony. "I ain't riskin' gettin' killed."

Two Feathers picked up the heavy bar and dropped it into its supports. "That is a good idea. But what happens when we are gone. You cannot drop this bar in place if you are outside."

"We found a back way out," said Tony, "just like a prairie dog's backdoor."

"A backdoor? I thought there was no way out of here. How did you find it?"

"Estevan found it. He was on guard duty up on your thinking ledge using your field glasses when he spotted a rat comin' out of the rocks with a biscuit in his mouth."

"Biscuit?" Will's eyes popped wide. His mouth twitched into a ha-ha grin. "How'd he find a biscuit in the barn?"

"Somebody snuck some in for a late-night snack." Tony scowled at Jake. "We enlarged the hole and the trail the rat followed to get out. We now have an escape route if needed. It's big enough for a man to crawl out but not big enough for the horses."

A cool breeze followed them to the house and helped blow away some of the tension. Oso's tail beat a rhythm on the porch step when they reached him.

Two Feathers knelt beside him and scratched his ears. "Good boy, Oso. You did your job."

Will brought a biscuit from the kitchen and fed it to the dog. "You earned your keep tonight, ol' boy."

The following morning broke hot and clear. The mid-summer sky was a pale blue with thin wisps of ragged clouds scattered over its vast expanse. After finishing the last cup of coffee, Two Feathers and Will mounted their horses and headed across the creek. Turning away from the Pecos River, Two Feathers rode beside Will north toward Red Mesa. The mon-soon season had turned the usual red sandy desert into a checke-board of green rabbitbrush and bunchgrass.

"It feels like forever since we've seen the cattle." Will's eagerness to check the herd's condition spilled onto Two Feathers.

He smiled. "We were gone nearly all of spring. It is good to be home." There was that word again. He wondered if it would ever sound natural.

As they rode in silence, Two Feathers heard only the clop-clop of hooves in the dust and the creak of saddle leather. His thoughts drifted over the sagebrush and yucca. They floated with the wind that fluttered the hawk feathers in his hair and rippled over grama grasses blowing in the wind. He felt no need for words.

Will pulled up Buck. "This is July. That means Charlie Goodnight will be coming soon. We need to start hazing cattle back this way toward the brush corral."

Two Feathers kept going. "And talk to Mateo about help-ing with the branding."

A short ride brought them to the first dam across the creek. It was supposed to be a low dam that backed the water into a shallow pool. But now there was no dam and no pool. The creek rippled over the debris that remained from their work.

Will dismounted and pulled a trapped log from the jumble.

Two Feathers scouted the area on both sides of the creek. "Plenty of cattle tracks, small animals, and some coyote. No moccasins. No unshod horses."

Will tossed the log onto the bank. "Do you think Yellow Hawk did this?"

Two Feathers cocked his head, arched one brow, and gave him an are-you-kidding? look.

Will ignored the look. "Let's check the catch basins in the arroyo where you sat out that blizzard."

The horses' mile-eating lope brought them to the arroyo before noon. When they found bunches of grazing cattle along the way, they started them moving south.

After heading a large bunch back toward the ranch, the boys neared the arroyo. Two Feathers stopped to let Gray Wolf catch his breath. Will stopped beside him.

"What do you think?" Will's questioning eyes lit a little flame of pride inside Two Feathers. Two years ago, Will hated nearly everything about him. Now he was asking for advice about cattle. Two Feathers opened his canteen, took a deep swig of water, and handed it to Will.

"I think they look better than we hoped."

They rode into the arroyo. The deeper they went, the higher the walls rose around them. A nervous tingle crawled up Two Feathers' spine. He sniffed the air. A faint scent of smoke teased his nose. Will shifted in the saddle and started to speak, but Two Feathers silenced him with a firm grip on his arm. Two Feathers dismounted and handed him Gray Wolf's reins. An upheld palm and a finger across his lips signaled Will to stay put and be quiet. With his carbine in hand, Two Feathers eased his way toward the gully that branched off from the arroyo. He knew this place. The memory wasn't a pleasant one.

A curve in the gully and an outcrop of jumbled rock slabs gave him cover to risk a quick peek ahead. His quick jerk back caused a small spattering of pebbles to roll out from under his feet with a noise that sounded as loud as thunder. He caught his breath, then let it slide on a long, slow exhale. He took another, more careful, look. Someone had built a wall that closed half of the cut bank opening where he and Yellow Hawk had taken shelter from the blizzard. He watched for a few minutes. There was no movement or sound. With his finger on the trigger of his carbine, he eased around the corner, searching every possible hiding place. Seeing nothing, he approached the blackened fire ring in front of the small cave. The ashes were cool but not packed by the weather. So, it'd been a short time since someone had been there. The cave was empty except for a pile of blankets and a buffalo hide he recognized as the one Yellow Hawk wrapped himself in during the blizzard.

They left the camp and headed up the arroyo to the catch basins. They hadn't been disturbed. All held water. At the last one, they filled their canteens and, keeping their carbines handy, let the horses graze and rest.

Will pulled a burlap sack of food from his saddlebag. They chewed on biscuits, and the tough strips of dried venison in silence, then washed it down with water. "We should head back to the ranch and get Jake and Tony," said Will. "Then go to Mateo's for him and César. The six of us can watch that cave until Yellow Hawk returns, capture him, and take him to the army."

Two Feathers didn't answer for a while. He stood with his hand on the saddle horn. "That will not work. When we get back, he will be gone. He will know we were here."

"Maybe that's so, but we need to do something. We have to try."

The boys mounted their horses and turned back toward Yellow Hawk's camp. No matter how hard he tried not to let the fear of his uncle rule his thinking, it was always there, threatening to freeze him in place. Now, that fear changed to anger, flaring into a hot flame. He rode Gray Wolf into the camp and through the fire ring leaving ashes and tracks everywhere. He dismounted and walked into the cave. Pulling his knife, he slashed the blankets and the buffalo hide.

"Follow me. Leave Buck's tracks where he can see them. The trail out of here widens up ahead. When we get there, move up beside me. Leave deep plain tracks in the sand. I want him to see Buck's tracks and Gray Wolf's. I want him to know we were here."

Will's eyes widened in alarm. He chewed on his lip. "What'd you just do? Are you sure this is smart? He's going to be really mad."

"Good!" His voice snarled like an angry wolf. "He cannot get any worse."

"I'm not so sure about that." Will pulled Buck's pace enough to slip in behind Gray Wolf.

The arroyo leveled out onto the desert floor. Two Feathers kicked the grullo into a gallop. Buck caught up, and they kept that pace for a while.

"Two Feathers," Will shouted. "Slow down. We need to talk."

After a few more minutes, Gray Wolf slowed, and they stopped. Both boys dismounted. They walked their horses to cool them after the hard run.

"Why'd you do that? It's only going to make things worse."

"No, it is not. It cannot get any worse. I am tired of being afraid of Yellow Hawk. I want him to know I am not afraid anymore."

Will pulled his bandana off and dampened it with water from his canteen. He wiped the dust from Buck's nostrils and mouth. Two Feathers did the same for Gray Wolf.

The hot sun beat down. Will wet his bandana again, wiped his face, and tied the damp cloth around his neck. "I think we should go to Mateo's and at least talk to him. Maybe he'll have an answer."

"We have talked to him before. He did not have any answers then. Why do you think he will have answers now?"

Two Feathers stood staring toward Red Mesa in the distance. His thoughts skittered back and forth between going to Mateo's for help or trying to track Yellow Hawk alone. But he knew Will wouldn't stay behind. The idea of Yellow Hawk getting Will—he shook his head. That was unthinkable. There was a time when he knew his uncle would never hurt Buck, but now he wasn't so sure. He couldn't figure out what the man was thinking. There was no doubt Yellow Hawk would hurt Will.

He mounted Gray Wolf. "Come on. You are right. We need to talk to Mateo."

They rode away from Red Mesa and headed toward the Pecos River. As the miles fell behind, Two Feathers shut out all thoughts of Yellow Hawk. Instead, he thought about their four Palo Duro mares. They brought a smile to his face.

A chorus of barking dogs met them as they rode into the yard. The hitching rail held three horses, so they took Buck and Gray Wolf to the barn. A pup followed Buck too closely. The big stallion scored a kick, sending it howling out of the barn.

"Buck," Will scolded, "you're gettin' a pretty good aim with that hind foot." He slipped a feedbag with a double handful of grain in the bottom over the buckskin's head. "Be careful. You don't want to hurt those pups. Tomas will need them to work our sheep."

With both horses settled, Two Feathers and Will stood in the barn's open door and watched the house.

"I wonder what's going on. I hope Tomas is okay." Will headed in that direction. Two Feathers didn't follow.

"Are you coming?" asked Will.

"Go ahead. I will wait here." He picked up one of his braids and twisted the end.

"No, you come, too. We both need to know."

Mateo and three men came out of the house. "Muchachos," he called and motioned the boys to come.

Two Feathers shifted his eyes away from the house and didn't move.

Will stood beside him. "You need to hear why these men are here. I've a bad feeling about this." Will jerked his head toward the house. "Come on."

"At least they are not soldiers." Two Feathers followed Will.

The rapid Spanish between Mateo and the other men was too much for Two Feathers to understand. It stopped when the boys reached the porch. Mateo switched to English.

"Boys, this is Raul Baca. He ranches not too far from the Fort Sumner site." A short, stocky man stood off to one side away from the others, his feet widespread, his thumbs tucked in his belt. His jaw muscles bulged under the thick black mustache on his stern face. A wide black hat with a braided rawhide hatband covered long hair slicked back in a ponytail that hung down his back. He nodded only to Will. Two Feathers' nerves flared, and goosebumps raced down his arms.

Mateo continued, "This is Lupe Sanches. His place is north of me, about ten miles."

"Hola, boys. I met your father once in Puerto de Luna. I was sorry to hear of his death. He was a good man. Let your heart rest easy. He's with God now."

His eyes were gentle like his smile, but when he shook Two Feathers' hand, his grip was firm. The man was so thin Two Feathers decided a strong wind would blow him away.

"This is Joaquin Peña. He also ranches near the Fort Sumner site." Two Feathers heard Peña's voice but not his words. The hatred in Baca's eyes sucked him into their black depth and wouldn't release its grip on him. Under the hum in his ears, he heard the faint voice of Will.

"John. . . John."

Two Feathers' arm jerked.

"Listen." A harsh whisper exploded in his ear, and Will yanked on his arm. "What's the matter with you?"

Two Feathers turned to Mateo. He wouldn't look at Baca again.

"Boys, Yellow Hawk has been raiding up and down the Pecos. These men came today to form a posse to go after him. They want me to ride with them."

"You'll never catch him." Will looked at Two Feathers and squeezed his arm. "Tell them, John."

Baca shoved himself in front of Mateo. "I won't listen to these boys. I won't ride with a Comanche to catch a Comanche." Scorn dripped off each word. "We'd all be killed."

Red surged up Will's neck to his hairline.

"Wait a minute, boys." Mateo moved between Baca and the boys. "Let's all take it easy here." He looked at Baca. "This is my home. I want no trouble here. These boys are my guests. Just like you."

"Back off, Raul," said Sanches from behind the bigger man, his voice low and calm. "We need someone to go to Fort Union to talk to the army. Why don't the boys go? We can hunt Yellow Hawk down when we get a posse together."

Baca held Two Feathers with his dark eyes that never blinked.

Peña mounted his horse. "There are more people to talk to farther north and in Puerto de Luna." Sanches and Peña followed Baca out of the yard, their dust clouds trailing behind them.

Two Feathers stayed on the porch after Mateo and Will went inside the house. He watched the three men ride away. The same question—where do I belong?—hit him. Would he ever feel at ease in the white man's world? Certainly not with men like Baca. So, that man didn't want to ride with him? Well, he wouldn't ride anywhere with that man at his back.

A breeze kicked up and blew away the dust left by the riders. Two Feathers stood on the porch until the air blew clean against his face and took his anger with it.

THE ROUNDUP

"Two Feathers," called Will from the house, "if you want any hojarascas, you better get in here before they're all gone."

Two Feathers sniffed, yanked the door open, and let it bang shut behind him. Will sat at the table with a cinnamon cookie in each hand and his mouth busy chewing a third. Elena handed Two Feathers a plate piled with warm, fresh-from-the-oven circles of pure deliciousness. He washed them down with the cool water from the olla, the clay pot that hung in the shade on the porch.

When the plate held only crumbs, Mateo handed over a letter from Charlie Goodnight he'd picked up in Puerto de Luna. The envelope was tattered and showed it had traveled far and taken a while to reach them. César came in time to hear Will read it aloud.

10 June 1869

Dear Will and John,

All is well here. I hope all is well with you. Curtis is bringing the herd from Texas. He'll collect your steers in mid-August and bring them to my ranch in Colorado on the Arkansas River. I've arranged for buyers to come here. Be sure everything is branded and ready to go.

I understand you're still having trouble with that Comanche, Yellow Hawk. I've heard the army started a campaign to capture all the Comanche and put them on a reservation in Indian Territory. That should solve your problem.

News is beginning to drift north about the Pecos River Ranch and the two young boys that run it. I've heard some stories. Keep up the good work. I hope to see you sometime before winter sets in.

Your Guardian,
Charles Goodnight

Two Feathers' thoughts stuck on the word *reservation*. It was like a deep crack in the road you couldn't drive a wagon over. His thoughts of the Comanche in such a place kept piling up against it.

César exploded a big puff of air, jerked his chair from the table, and plopped down, almost turning it over.

"I don't know where Goodnight gets his news, but we haven't seen any sign of the army capturing the Comanche around here."

"We must watch for Yellow Hawk, but we need to focus on the Pecos River Ranch." Will folded the letter and put it in his pocket. "This year's calves need our full attention, or we won't have a ranch to worry about."

"César, Estevan, and I will be there in about a week to help with the branding." Mateo stood to walk with the boys to the barn.

When they were leaving, Elena ran out with a bag of cookies. "These are for Jake and Tony. You've had yours." Her face blushed red as she shoved them into Two Feathers hands. "Don't eat them."

The rest of the afternoon lagged long and slow. Two Feathers worked with Will pushing south any bunches of cattle they rounded up. He couldn't tear his mind away from the thoughts of Weeping Woman and Red Wing having to live on a reservation. The picture of that long line of Navajo women outside the adobe supply office last year at Fort Sumner with their small bags of flour stuck in his head. No matter how hard he tried, he couldn't force his thoughts away from those gaunt, desperate faces.

Each day for the next week, Two Feathers and Will scoured the ranch for cattle and watched for the dust clouds that would herald the arrival of Charlie Goodnight's herd. The four cowboys of the Pecos River Ranch worked from first light to total darkness when they staggered to their beds. One search of the ranch from north to south wasn't enough. They spent long days in the saddle, covering the same territory over and over, making sure they'd found every critter. But another search would uncover new bunches of cattle hiding in shallow gullies and deep arroyos.

The cattle they rounded up were sleek and fat, their condition better than expected. Some cows came out from their hiding places easily enough, but others had to be roped and dragged out, bawling and kicking with every step. Their long, sharp horns were slung in every direction with anger-driven force. Two Feathers decided the work to haze them back toward the brush corral south of the house was endless.

On a windy afternoon later that week, the boys split up to search for the trail of a good-sized bunch of cattle they'd been tracking. Before they left the ranch house, Two Feathers decided to release Oso from his rope and take him along. The hot wind had erased any trace of the cattle. He hoped the dog could find their trail. They made a broad sweep toward the ranch's western boundary when Oso picked up a trail leading into a maze of narrow washes and ravines.

Around a bend in one of the gullies, Two Feathers came to a mound of tumbleweeds piled against a rockslide that filled the end of a steep-walled ravine. Will and Buck had arrived first and faced a bunch of cows and calves they'd trapped there.

Two Feathers stopped Gray Wolf a distance behind him. "Will, you need some help?"

"That would be nice. These cows and me been dancing around this ditch for a while." The light tone of his voice changed to frustration. "They've backed themselves into this corner. I can't get around 'em to drive them out."

A slight tap on Gray Wolf eased the grullo next to Buck. Oso growled. "Silencio!" the boys commanded in unison. The growling stopped. The dog settled on the ground, his eyes fixed on the angry cattle. The lead cow shook her long, pointed horns and bellowed a warning. She raked the ground and grunted.

"That lead cow is worked up," Will said in a hoarse whisper. "Keep your eyes on her. Back off and give her some room."

The horses, with Oso following, backed away from the trapped cattle and stopped just inside a shallow offshoot giving them room to run. Suspicious, the lead cow lowered her head, shook her heavy horns, grunted—but held her ground. The others stirred and bawled behind her, sending dust into the still air where it hung like the quiet before a storm. Knowing what those horns could do, Two Feathers never took his eyes off the cattle.

Oso whined, his body quivering with excitement. "Oso!" commanded Two Feathers. "Get 'em." A brown blur raced to meet the lead cow. The cow charged with maddened fury. Oso circled behind the cow, dodging her sharp horns and the power in her kicking hooves. Moving with quick leaps, sharp turns, and well-placed bites to the cows' heels, he started the herd moving and disappeared into the thick dust. Only his barks, growls, and the moving cattle gave evidence of his work.

Waving his lasso over his head, Two Feathers hollered and raced after them. Will popped his coiled rope against his chaps, and they all exploded out the mouth of the ravine onto the desert floor. The cattle spread out. Will and Buck turned them south toward the brush corral.

The slower pace allowed the boys and their animals to catch their breath. Stopping Gray Wolf, Two Feathers let the reins drop around the saddle horn. Relieved no one was hurt, he took a long drink from his canteen.

Will wet his bandana and wiped the dust off his face and neck. He slid off Buck and wiped the stallion's mouth. "You want to know what I think?"

"What?" Two Feathers dismounted. Oso trotted up to get a good ear scratching.

"I think we would still be back there fighting to get those cows out if Oso hadn't helped. He's a pretty good dog."

"Yes, he is. Mateo trained him well. He is a good guard dog and a good cow dog."

Later that night, after the horses and Oso were fed and watered, Two Feathers joined Will in their room. He peeled off his dusty clothes and washed his face and hands. Settling himself in his bed, he announced. "Tomorrow, I will return to live with my people. The Comanche knows not to make the buffalo go where they do not want to go. White men have no sense. They work hard to make cows with long sharp horns go where they do not want to go." A heavy sigh erupted from his bed, followed by a moan.

"You say that every time we work cattle," Will mumbled

from under his quilt. "Go to sleep. You'll feel better in the morning."

Two Feathers pushed himself up on one elbow and looked at Will. "Humph," he snorted. He didn't think he would feel better any time soon. He hurt all over. His arms ached from endlessly swinging and throwing his lasso. His back and legs hurt from the pressure the stubborn cattle put on his rope as he dragged them out of thickets and choked gullies. Making cattle go where they don't want to go was punishing work.

He wasn't sure, but he thought he heard a low murmur from the lump under Will's quilt that sounded something like, "I just might go with you."

The following day, heavy gray clouds drizzled rain, sometimes light, sometimes heavy. Mateo, with César and Estevan, arrived to help with the branding. They set up camp inside the gate to the brush corral. The box canyon's red and gray stone walls had held the Pecos River Ranch cattle since Pa, Will, and Two Feathers had driven the animals from Texas two years ago. The three of them had spent many hours and built blisters on top of calluses filling every small opening with brush to be sure no animal escaped. After all their hard work, Will had decided to call this holding pasture the brush corral.

Mateo set up two tarps on poles, one to cover their supplies and bedrolls and the other to keep the rain off their fire. His boys unloaded the supplies from the wagon. Soon the smell of coffee boiling in the pot brought everyone to the fire with cups in their hands.

The rest of the day, they sorted cattle. By nightfall, the corral held yearlings big enough to be sold and bawling calves ready to be weaned. Outside the gate, their mamas bellowed the discomfort of their engorged udders without youngsters to provide relief. The noise was deafening.

After supper, Two Feathers didn't fall asleep until after the moon rose to shine its faint light through the clouds, and his nap was short. The bawling cows and calves, some of whose cries had become hoarse squeaks, kept him awake. He lay in his blankets on the damp ground and wished he were in his bunk at the house. Rolling over onto his back, he watched the occasional blinks of the few stars that happened to find a small break in the clouds.

"Will? Are you awake?"

The pile of blankets moved. Will stuck his head out. "Are you kidding? I don't know which is worse, the bellowing cattle or Mateo's snoring. Any idea how long till daylight? I'm ready to finish this job and get back to the house."

"Me, too. I was thinking about Yellow Hawk—"

"Oh, great! That's just what I want to hear," Will interrupted.

"And," Two Feathers continued, "maybe this weather is keeping him in camp. Maybe he went away."

"We can hope so." Will pulled the covers back over his head. "Try to sleep. Tomorrow will be another rough day, and one of us has guard duty soon."

Two Feathers sat by the fire the next morning, holding a cup of hot coffee and coughing. His eyes watered from the thick smoke caused by the wet wood and captured under the tarp. Mateo limped around the fire but kept it going, and the branding irons hot, all the while complaining. He told anyone who would listen he'd given up working cattle from horseback because the wet weather had unleashed the demon that lived in his hip joints.

Last year, Two Feathers recalled, the branding was fun and exciting. This year it was soggy, sodden, and soaked. He didn't know which was worse, choking on the smoke under the tarp, listening to Mateo's grumpy mumbling, or dragging calves through the rain and mud to be branded.

Raindrops sizzled on the glowing red P~R for Pecos River Ranch branding iron as Two Feathers hurried to the calf Jake and Tony had stretched out on the ground. He slapped the hot metal to the animal's hip with grim determination. It bellowed. The rank odor of burning wet hair and hide was a smell he would never get used to. He rammed more branding irons into the fire and wondered, *Will I ever get that stink out of my nose?*

The day passed slowly. Two Feathers and Will took turns manning the branding irons and gathering wood. Jake and Tony made one roping team, César and Estevan made the other. Mateo kept the coffee hot and a bubbling pot of lamb stew simmering.

By early evening, the rain stopped, and the sun tried to break through the few holes in the clouds. The last calf bellowed his discomfort from the hot irons and ran to join his brothers and sisters on the far side of the spring-fed lake that filled the center of the brush corral.

César coiled his rope, secured it to his saddle, and dismounted. "You boys got some good steers and calves here. Mr. Goodnight will be pleased when he sees them."

"Let's break camp and head home." Will took the hot branding irons to the lake to cool them off. Mateo and his boys packed up and left.

"Jake, Tony, Two Feathers, come here before you saddle up. We need to talk."

They gathered around the cooking fire. Will filled each of their cups with the last of the coffee. "I've been thinkin'."

Tony laughed. "Uh-oh, that's not good."

"Last year, when we finished the roundup and branding, we left the cattle here and checked on them a couple of times a day until Charlie's herd came through. They were safe here. I'm not so sure that's true this year."

"You talkin' 'bout Yellow Hawk?" Tony's words held an anxious bite.

"Yes, I am. The cattle need to be guarded and. . . " Will's sentence trailed off. He looked at Tony, "you and Jake will have to do it alone."

The four of them stood around the dying fire holding empty coffee cups. Nobody spoke. Their silence became uncomfortable.

"O. . . kay," Jake said. "What's goin' on in that head of yours?"

"I think it would be best if you and Tony stayed with the cattle without Two Feathers and me. Yellow Hawk follows us, not you. He hasn't come here yet, and I don't want him to. We need to stay away, and you two don't need to be here together. One stands guard, and the other gets sleepin' time in your own beds."

Tony lifted his cup to take a drink, then realized it was empty, and so was the pot. He balanced them on rocks from the fire ring. "Okay, I see your point. I think you're right."

"Good." The word fell out on a huff of air. "Jake, what about you?"

Jake nodded.

"Two Feathers?"

"Yes."

Will picked up a skinny stick, broke it, then turned away. He faced the twins and held his hand out. "Short stick stays here tonight."

Tony stepped up and drew. It was short.

Grinning, Jake pounded him on his back. "I'll bring you some biscuits in the morning."

Before following Will and Jake toward the house, Two Feathers led Gray Wolf over to Tony.

"Stay alert. If Yellow Hawk comes, he will not come by the

gate. He will come over the walls. Find a place high up in the rocks. Do not use the same spot more than once. Stay still. Movement catches the eye. He will see you. Stay quiet. Sound carries far, especially at night. Will and I will stay at the house, so maybe he will not come here. Maybe he will stay where we are. I hope he has gone to the canyon for the rainy season and will stay there."

"Don't worry 'bout me. I can take care of myself." Tony shook Two Feathers' hand. "Jake and I have lived in wild country all our lives. I'll be fine."

Two Feathers rode through the gate Tony held open. He kicked Gray Wolf into a gallop to catch up with Jake and Will. At the house, they entered the yard and stopped. No one dismounted. Not a sound came from the barn, yard, or house. Silence greeted them. Silence that roared of danger.

Oso

Two Feathers scanned the yard. There was no sign of Oso. No barking or yelping a happy welcome. The dog had accepted the Pecos River Ranch as his new home and knew his duties. He ran free in the yard and the land around the house.

"Maybe he's off chasing a rabbit or a coon." Will dismounted at the house. Two Feathers followed Jake toward the barn.

"Two Feathers! Jake!" Will yelled. "Come look!"

Two Feathers shoved Gray Wolf's reins into Jake's hands, "Here." He ran to the porch, where Will stood, staring at three arrows embedded in the door.

"Yellow Hawk's?"

Two Feathers yanked one out and ran his fingers down the long shaft and over the feathers attached to the end. "Yes."

"Where's Oso?" Will scanned the trees near the creek. "He never goes far. Why isn't he here?" He whistled for the dog. They listened, but no answering bark sounded.

"Will!" Jake called. He walked back out of the barn leading the horses, still saddled, and turned them into the corral. "I found Oso."

Something in his tone made Two Feathers' heart falter.

Both boys ran to the barn door. Jake pointed to Buck's stall. On the floor, in a pool of blood, lay Oso. An arrow through his neck cocked his head at an awkward angle as if puzzled by what had happened.

Oso," sighed Will. The word hung in the air. Dropping to his knees, Will snapped the protruding arrow and laid the animal's head in a more natural position.

Two Feathers stroked the still-warm body, smoothing the ruffled fur.

With his rifle in hand, Jake stood in the doorway. The setting sun made a black silhouette of his body as though he were a sentinel guarding the entry.

"Do you see him?" Two Feathers asked.

"No. Only a few tracks between here and the corral."

"I did not think you would. Yellow Hawk is gone. He may watch us for a while, but I do not think he will come back tonight."

"Yes, you're right," said Will, his tone bleak. "He's had his fun."

Two Feathers sank beside his brother, still holding the arrow he'd pulled from the door. He wrapped his arms around his knees and rested his head. *It's just a dog,* he told himself. *Nothing special. Just a dog.* If he said it often enough, maybe he would believe it. He felt as if he were sinking into the ground. Maybe he would slide down and live with the worms and beetles. Then he wouldn't have to think about Oso—or Yellow Hawk.

That thought jerked him straight, and he stood. The arrow he held burned in his hand. He wondered how it got there. That tiny angry flame that was a constant presence in his belly roared hot. Holding the arrow in both hands, he snapped it into as many pieces as possible, then threw them on the ground.

"I'll dig Oso's grave near the creek where he chased rabbits." Jake jerked a shovel from the tools leaning in the corner, sending the rest tumbling to the ground with a loud clatter. He walked stiff-legged toward the creek with a shovel in one hand and rifle in the other.

Will walked over to an old tack box and dug through the contents until he found a frayed quilt. He took it outside and shook off the clinging dust. Back inside, he spread it on the floor of Buck's stall.

"Wait." Two Feathers ran out of the barn, and in a few minutes, he returned with a bucket of water, Oso's favorite chew bone, and a knotted piece of rope he loved to throw into the air and catch.

Using a strip from the edge of the quilt, the boys washed the blood away and dried their friend with clean handfuls of hay. Two Feathers laid Oso on the quilt. They folded his legs under him, curled him into a ball, and laid his head on his paws, then nestled his favorite things against him. Wrapping him gently in the quilt, they bound it with a piece of rope they found in the trunk.

Will started to pick Oso up, but Two Feathers stopped him.

"Let me. I caused this." His words squeezed around the lump in his throat.

"Okay, you carry him, but you didn't cause this. You aren't to blame. We've talked about how you can't control what Yellow Hawk does. Even Running Wolf doesn't blame you for what that man does."

Two Feathers sat still with his hand resting on the quilt. "Will, there is something more we need to talk about."

"I know. Yellow Hawk left Oso in Buck's stall for a reason."

"It is a message to you. Not to me, like the figure of Buck he carved, but to you. He wants you to know he is still coming after Buck. He wants you to know he would have had Buck today if he had been in this stall."

"I know!" Will jumped to his feet and paced in a circle inside the stall. "I know. I know!" He twisted his hands together, rammed them in his pockets, and jerked them out again. "We have to do something more than we are. We can't just wait for him to get Buck or one of us. We have Jake and Tony to think about, and Mateo and his family." He threw himself down beside Two Feathers. "I don't know how to stop Yellow Hawk."

The brothers sat side by side, each with a hand on their dog's wrapped body. Two Feathers tried to hold back his tears. But when he saw Will's dripping off his chin, he let them roll.

"Come on," Will said, "Jake should have the grave ready by now."

Supper that night was light—cornmeal mush and salt pork. Like Jake and Will, Two Feathers stirred his food around on his plate without eating much. Words between the three were as scarce as the number of bites they swallowed. Two Feathers finally gave up, raked his leftover food into the garbage bucket, and put his dishes in the sink. Jake washed the dishes and Will dried.

When the chores were done, Jake went to the back door. "I'll relieve Tony before first light. He'll be hungry. Be sure to leave him plenty of breakfast. I'll see you when my guard duty is over."

"Wait," said Will. "Can you stay a minute and talk? We need your advice."

"Okay. I don't know what my advice is worth, but let's hear it." He and Two Feathers sat back down at the table.

"We have to stop Yellow Hawk. He killed Oso today and Pa last year. We can't just sit here and let him get us." Will's voice trembled. He cleared his throat. "We don't know what to do."

"That's the problem," said Two Feathers.

"What about that posse at Mateo's?" Jake asked." Maybe they caught him. Have you heard anything about that?"

"Mateo didn't go with them. He told me they searched the Llano Estacado for several days but found no tracks," Will answered. "They had to come back because they ran out of water and couldn't find any."

"They could not catch their tail," Two Feathers scoffed in a low mumble.

"What about you, Two Feathers?" Jake asked. "Could you talk to Running Wolf? Isn't he chief now? Could he talk to Yellow Hawk and make him stop?"

Two Feathers shook his head at Jake. "Running Wolf and Weeping Woman know Yellow Hawk is loco. They know his thinking is scattered like the wind. Running Wolf will not interfere between Yellow Hawk and me. Besides, the Comanche are at war against the white man, and Yellow Hawk is a strong warrior. Stories of his battles are told around the Kiowa and the Comanche council fires."

Will heaved a huge sigh and scrubbed his tired face with his hands. "The only other place to go for help is the army. Maybe the soldiers will catch him."

Soldiers. . . Army. . . pinpricks exploded throughout Two Feathers' body and soured his stomach. How could he go to his enemy for help? Whenever he went to the soldiers with Will, he feared what they might do to him. Why would they help a Comanche? He took a deep breath to calm himself. *What about Sergeant Baker? He's always been around when I'm at a fort. He's our friend and has always helped Will and me. But what if we go to the fort and he isn't there? What if Will cannot protect me?*

"No, I will not go to the fort. I will not ask the soldiers for help."

"Why?" A red flush crept up Will's neck. "You've been to forts before." He ran his hand down his mouth and chin. "You'll be fine." The last word snapped short.

"What if Sergeant Baker is not there? You can go without me. I will stay here to help Jake and Tony guard the ranch."

Jake stood and headed for the door. "You boys work this out. I'm going to bed."

The brothers sat at the table. Neither spoke for several minutes.

"I thought we agreed to not go anywhere alone." The red flush spread up Will's neck to his ears. His words stabbed at Two Feathers. "We never know when Yellow Hawk will strike."

Two Feathers hung his head and didn't speak.

Will's voice took on a flat, solemn tone. "I'd be alone on the trail. We decided against that. You agreed."

Two Feathers didn't answer. He couldn't lift his head or look at Will.

Will stood and pushed his chair under the table but didn't move.

Two Feathers could feel his brother's eyes boring right through him.

When Will finally spoke, his words were calm. "Remember when we were in the canyon and went to Running Wolf's camp? You convinced me I'd be safe. You promised me nothing would happen. Because you were there with me, I was safe."

"Yes," said Two Feathers.

"You know I wouldn't put you in danger. We'll look for Sergeant Baker. He's helped us before. We'll go straight to him."

Two Feathers lifted his head, and his eyes met Will's. "We talked to him in Las Vegas. He said the army would not deal with one Comanche. They want all the Comanche."

"Maybe it's different now. Yellow Hawk has been raiding other ranchers. Maybe the army will capture him and put him in jail."

Two Feathers followed Will toward the bedroom. "And maybe not."

They settled into their beds with things still unresolved.

No matter how hard Two Feathers tried, sleep wouldn't come. He missed the sound of Oso settling in his spot under their window. He watched the moon make its appearance and cast black shadows. The *peent, peent* of a nighthawk made him get up and sit at the window. He watched the yard. The trees swayed slightly in the breeze, waving shadows over the ground. He listened to the nighthawk and thought about his puha, a red-tailed hawk that became his spirit animal on his vision quest the previous year. It had come to him when he needed help. He hoped it would come to him again.

Soldiers. . . Yellow Hawk. . . his fear of one was as strong as his fear of the other. He wished he could forget them both. He thought about the soldiers he and Will had traveled with on the way to the canyon. How could the *likes* of them ever outwit Yellow Hawk? They had made no attempt to hide their trail. They were loud, and any Comanche in their vicinity could've attacked them. Even young Comanche children knew how to hide their trail. How could soldiers expect to find a warrior on the Llano Estacado?

Listening to the frogs' croaking in the creek, Two Feathers thought again about Yellow Hawk. Why did Yellow Hawk hate him? He had only bits and pieces of the answer. Nothing that made sense.

But there was one thing he did understand—Will wanting the army to capture Yellow Hawk wouldn't work. The man was a Comanche war chief. If the army tracked him, he would play with them for a while. First, he would leave a trail going one way. Then, he would leave a trail going another. When he tired of the game, he would disappear, leaving no trail in a place with no water. Or maybe attack and kill them. The soldiers would be lucky if they made it back to the fort.

Two Feathers huffed. After Curtis picked up their cattle, he would go to Fort Union with Will. The big question was— where would Yellow Hawk be?

DISCORD AND DANGER

The sun's bright light poked at Two Feathers' eyes and pulled him from sleep. The hot air made him feel sticky, so he kicked off his blanket and sat up. His shirt from yesterday was stiff and stinky with sweat. It needed to be washed, but not today. It'd been a long week since they buried Oso, and no one was in the mood to do the things that needed doing. He grabbed his last clean shirt from the shelf over his bed.

He heard the back door slam. . . loudly. Then it slammed again. . . even louder. Pots and pans banged from the kitchen. What was going on with Will?

Two Feathers didn't want to see Will, Jake, or Tony. Worry for them had become his constant companion, and he was tired of it. He didn't know what to do about Yellow Hawk, so he refused to talk about him. *If only he would just go away.*

Jake and Tony hadn't been around much this past week because they were busy guarding the cattle, and Will stomped around in sullen silence. But no matter how hard he tried, Two Feathers couldn't stop the feeling of crawling ants swarming all over him every time anyone spoke to him. When Will did start talking, it sounded like Tomas' snapping dogs. Lately, Two Fea-thers felt like a simmering kettle with a tight lid.

The smell of bacon triggered his legs, sending him to the kitchen. The sharp slam of the oven door signaled a sour, grumpy Will—something he didn't want to deal with today.

But he might consider forgiving Will's cranky mood if he made biscuits.

"Mornin'," Will barked. He dumped a handful of coffee grounds in the coffee pot. The lid slammed down. "We're checkin' water holes again today."

The snarly tone halted Two Feathers in mid-step. He stood still for a minute, then narrowed his eyes and mashed his lips together. Taking plates and cups from the shelf, he glared at Will. There were no biscuits. What was the matter with him this time?

"Go saddle the horses." Will still hadn't looked at him.

Two Feathers' simmering bubbles grew bigger. He got the forks and knives and dumped everything in the middle of the table. He walked out of the kitchen. The back door banged behind him.

When he passed the window to their bedroom, he stopped. At the corner of the house was the piece of old saddle blanket Will had laid out for Oso. He picked it up, shook out most of the dirt, and carried it to the barn. On the way, he passed Tony heading for breakfast, leading his horse.

"Go easy in there."

Tony lifted a hand and walked on by, his face weary.

In the barn, Gray Wolf and Buck greeted Two Feathers with whinnies. After dumping grain into their feedbags, he filled water buckets. With the roundup finished, he'd taken the mustang mares, Rojo, and the mules to the enclosed meadow behind his lookout hoping Yellow Hawk wouldn't find them. Their absence made the morning chores pass quickly. Leading his and Will's mounts, he headed back toward the house.

Will met him at the back door of the kitchen. He took Buck's reins and mounted. "Come on. We've lots of ground to cover."

Two Feathers flipped Gray Wolf's reins over the hitching

rail. "No! I am hungry. I will eat my breakfast. Then we will go."

"You should've gotten up earlier. I don't want breakfast. I'm not waitin' all day." Will jerked Buck's head. The big horse's tail lashed hard, and he crow-hopped a time or two. Will loosened the reins, stroked his neck, and crooned a soft, "Sorry, big boy."

Buck settled, but Will didn't. He sat astride the tall stallion and glared down at his brother.

Two Feathers waited to see if Will's neck would turn red from his shirt collar to his ears. It did.

"You figure this out," Will said, his eyes hard and his tone sharp. "I'm tired of worrying about Yellow Hawk. He's your uncle. You handle it. Just fix this. Do you hear me? Fix it!"

The simmering bubbles in Two Feathers' belly boiled over with a heat that blocked all sound and all thought. His blood roared in his ears.

"I have had enough of you." His words erupted like a bursting hot spring. Vaulting himself at Will, he caught him around the waist and pulled him to the ground. They landed with enough force to knock out not only their last breath but any remaining sense of reason.

Two Feathers swung a solid punch that struck Will's cheekbone and slid into his eye. Will hollered and scrambled to his feet.

Leaping up, Two Feathers sucked in a huge breath and roared, "You been acting like a bull buffalo with a sore foot. I am sick of it!" He dove into Will, knocking him back into the hitching rail with a whoosh of air.

Will shoved him away, landing a solid punch in Two Feathers' stomach that doubled him over and left him gasping.

Will pulled back his fist for another punch. Tony stepped out of the backdoor in time to grab it and swing him around.

He stuck out his free arm, and Two Feathers stopped before he ran into the man's hard fist.

"Stop it!" Tony bellowed. Letting go of Will's wrist, he shoved Two Feathers away. "Stop it right now!"

Two Feathers leaned over the hitching rail, trying to suck air back into his lungs.

Will charged again. Tony's strong arms caught him, spun him around, and gripped both elbows from behind. "I said stop it! What's got into you? Don't we have enough trouble around here without you two trying to kill each other?"

Leaning on the hitching rail, Two Feathers watched Will. The eye he'd punched was already swelling and turning red. When Tony let him go, Will stood still. Two Feathers dropped his head. He tried to pull in air without making his stomach muscles scream.

"Sit," roared Tony. Both boys sat.

Tony paced in front of the pair sitting on the back step, their heads hanging. He watched them for a minute, then heaved a disgusted sigh. "We got more trouble than a sinner's got sins, and you two decide to beat each other to a pulp."

Bracing his fists against his hip bones, Tony glared at them. "I'm goin' back to finish my breakfast and then relieve Jake. I'm sure he's wondering where I am. We're not working this hard to have the whole ranch fall apart because you two, the ranch owners, decide to solve your problems with your fists."

Two Feathers couldn't meet his eye.

"If you don't work things out, your Pa's plan for a ranch will fall apart. Is that what you want?" Tony looked from one to the other. Neither spoke. "Jake and I have decided to make this our home. We want to be a part of the ranch. So, work it out!"

The last words were said with such force that Two Feathers shuddered under their weight. He dropped his head to his knees and covered it with his arms. The tips of his braids dragged through the dirt. *What have I done? Fighting with my brother solves nothing.*

Tony headed back into the house.

A few minutes later, Two Feathers heard the rattle of breakfast dishes. He sat still for several minutes more, trying to decide if his sore stomach could handle food.

"You want to know something?" asked Will. The belligerent tone was gone.

"What?" Two Feathers snuck a peek under his elbow at Will's eye and winced.

"Tony acts like he runs this ranch, and we work for him."

"Maybe that is the way it should be."

"Maybe so." Will held his hand to his swollen eye.

Two Feathers sat up and rubbed his sore stomach. "I think I can handle breakfast. How about you?"

"You want some biscuits?"

An hour later, Two Feathers rode beside Will to check the catch basins and the low water dam on the creek. He frowned when Will touched his bruised cheekbone and eye. "I am sorry for punching you."

Will's one good eye popped wide when he turned to him. "Why are you sorry? I'm the one that blew up." Everything about Will went limp. "I woke up in the middle of the night. All I could think about was Pa. What would he do if he was here?"

Two Feathers had no answer.

"I'll tell you what he would do," said Will. "He'd go after Yellow Hawk. He wouldn't let things get this bad. But. . . " His voice dropped so low Two Feathers could barely hear him. "I know Yellow Hawk can kill us. I'm afraid."

Two Feathers pulled Gray Wolf to a stop. He sat still in the saddle until the horse swung his head around as though questioning why they'd stopped. Finally, he dismounted. Pulling the top off his canteen, he took a swig, swished the water around in his mouth, and then swallowed.

"Will, we both fear Yellow Hawk. And now it is worse. Pa is not here. We have to solve this without him."

"He would go to the army for help."

When Will said the word "army," Two Feathers stiffened. "I do not want to talk about the army. I have already agreed to go to Fort Union after Curtis picks up the cattle." His words came out crisp and sharp.

Two Feathers mounted and headed toward the arroyo. Will followed.

Approaching the low water dam, Two Feathers stopped before it came into view and studied the ground. There were no unshod horse tracks.

"It doesn't look like he's been here," said Will. "Let's go on. We need to check the hay meadows. I need to know what they look like, how much hay we'll have to cut for next winter."

Two Feathers ignored Will's request to move on and kept his eyes glued to the ground. "Just because there are no tracks does not mean he has not been here." He pulled his carbine from its boot.

Will pulled his.

Two Feathers led out at a slow walk. He searched every bush, every rock, every inch of ground for anything out of place. The closer they came to the creek, the louder the rush of water sounded. He stopped Will when the broken dam came into view. The logs and branches were scattered on the banks again. Rocks from the dam's center tumbled down the creek, making a hole in the base. Two Feathers stepped off Gray Wolf and moved cautiously toward the bank.

In the sand at the water's edge was an upside-down drawing of a male stick figure with its head beside the heel of a full moccasin print. Within the track was a crude picture of a hawk.

Will dismounted and came up behind Two Feathers. He gasped. "What does that mean?"

"The upside-down man means death."

They stood rigid, staring at the drawing etched in the sand.

Two Feathers tightened his grip on his carbine so it wouldn't slip from his sweat-soaked hand. A low moan slid through Will's lips.

Two Feathers put his hand on Will's shoulder.

"It's like he's taunting us." Will picked up a corner of his neckerchief and chewed on it. "I don't understand why he's doing this. What does he want?"

"We both know what he wants." With a swipe of his boot, the drawing disappeared. He turned Gray Wolf away from the creek and the tumbled dam. "Come on. I want to be gone from here."

Anger. . . fear. Fear. . . anger. Two Feathers tried to shut off both emotions, but they were like two demons racing down a dark trail. First, one led the race, then the other took the lead. He wanted to slam the door on both of them.

Through the afternoon, he and Will rode in silence. Working together, they put the rest of the creeks and catch basins in good shape without trouble. On the way home, they stopped again at the first dam.

Wading in the water to repair the damage cooled Two Feathers off. He sat beside Will while their feet dried and chewed on some jerky. "I think we are letting Yellow Hawk win this battle we are fighting."

"What do you mean? I don't see anyone winning anything."

"He wins when our fear of him rules how we think."

Will picked up his socks and pulled them on. "You're right. He wins when we fight each other because of him."

Two Feathers stomped into his boots. "We need to work harder to not let him win."

Knowing they were going home, Buck and Gray Wolf headed east with a steady lope. Their long black silhouettes raced over the ground in front of them as though they were chasing evil spirits they could never catch.

At the creek near home, Will pulled Buck to a stop. "Hello, the house," he hollered.

"Come ahead, slow and easy." The voice was neither Jake's nor Tony's.

Uneasy at the strange voice, Two Feathers dismounted. He hung back within the branches of a willow, carbine in hand, and waited.

Will stepped Buck across the creek. Gray Wolf followed Buck.

A short, stocky man stood leaning against the porch support pole wearing a battered hat that looked as if it might once have been tan in color. His shirt was missing a few buttons, and his boot heels were run down.

Will flew off Buck and raced to grab the outstretched hand.

"Curtis!" He pumped his friend's hand like a stubborn well handle.

"Boy, am I glad to see you. Is Mr. Goodnight in the house?"

"Howdy, Will-boy." He managed to pull his hand free before Will jerked it off his arm.

Two Feathers walked out of the trees and up to the house. He searched the front yard for more visitors.

Curtis pulled one of the long braids. "You boys have growed since I seen you last. Two Feathers, you're gonna be as tall as Charlie Goodnight if you keep goin'."

Jake stuck his head out the door. "Supper's on the table. Come and get it 'fore I throw it out."

Both boys hurried their horses to the barn, where they were fed, watered, and bedded down for the night in record time. They dashed for the house and reached the door at the same time, pushing and shoving to get in first.

Two Feathers took his place.

Will plopped down at the table. "Jake, if you're gonna talk like Cookie, you better have one of his dried apple pecan pies for dessert."

"I never said anything 'bout baking pie. Cookie's the best trail drive cook in Texas or New Mexico. I couldn't begin to beat him."

Between bites, Will asked about a million questions, the last being, "Curtis, where's Mr. Goodnight? I was hoping he'd change his mind and be on the drive?"

"No, this time I'm the trail boss. Charlie's busy settin' up his new ranch in Colorado. He has Smokey scouting everywhere looking for cattle."

Disappointment washed over Two Feathers like a bucket of cold water. He'd hoped to see Smokey, his scraggly, bushy-faced old family friend. If only he'd been able to talk to him about how to handle Yellow Hawk! But—not this time.

"Mr. Goodnight told me to bring your money from the last calf crop, pick up this year's crop, and see how things are goin'. He said he'd try to make it down next spring."

Two Feathers listened to the laughter and talk between good friends. Even though he knew the people and the stories, he was lonely for his family. He laughed at the teasing and joking but added nothing. With dinner and dishes done, a serious mood settled over the kitchen. Two Feathers remembered sitting around the fire listening to the Comanche men making plans for their people. Each man had a turn to say what was on his mind, and the people listened. Now it was his turn. He decided staying silent wasn't the way to solve their problems.

"We have had a tough time this past year." Two Feathers spoke his first words of the evening.

"That's what I hear," said Curtis. "Jake and I talked a while before you came in. It sounds like Yellow Hawk's as savage as a meat ax and has more than one screw loose."

Puzzled, Two Feathers glanced at Will with raised eyebrows.

"That means he's mean as a snake and crazy, you know, loco."

Two Feathers faced Curtis. "We do not know what to do. He has attacked Will and me and killed stock. The low water dams have been busted open. The horses are always in danger of being taken, especially Buck. Today he left us a death threat."

"What?" Jake said. "Where?"

"At the low water dam. He broke it open again," said Will.

"What are you doing about it?" asked Curtis.

"The best we can. We don't go anywhere alone." Will glanced at Jake. "Except for Jake and Tony taking turns guarding the cattle in the brush corral."

Two Feathers interrupted, "We use binoculars to search the surrounding area from the lookout spot behind the barn."

Curtis looked back and forth between Will, Two Feathers, and Jake. "Is that it?"

"We got a guard dog." Two Feathers' voice shrank, "He killed it."

"We talked to other ranchers in the area about a posse going after him," Will said.

Two Feathers kept his face blank at the talk about the posse, but he couldn't forget the hatred on that rancher's face. Baca, that was his name. The thought made him uneasy.

Curtis's eyebrows shot up. He chuckled. "How'd that go?"

"Not so good. One man didn't want Two Feathers along, so we didn't go."

"They found nothing," said Two Feathers and rolled his eyes.

"Well, I'm not surprised. The Comanche know how to live in the desert. I don't want to try to track one."

Jake spoke up. "The talk among the other ranchers is that Yellow Hawk rides with a band of Kiowa. They've raided all up and down the Pecos. We've only seen him or his tracks. No Kiowa."

"What about the army? Have you talked to them?" Curtis's gaze lingered on each face, but no one spoke.

The silence stretched as Two Feathers and Will traded sharp looks.

Will caved in first. "We talked to Sheriff Crook in Las Vegas and Sergeant Baker about Yellow Hawk."

"They said the same thing," said Two Feathers. "Let the army handle Yellow Hawk."

"The army," said Jake, "seems to be patrolling farther north. We see more of Yellow Hawk than we do of the army."

"We're going to Fort Union." Will looked at his brother, but Two Feathers refused to meet his gaze. "We'll ask them for help." Will's words faded away like wind-blown tracks from a dry trail.

Two Feathers rose from the table and walked outside into the dark night. He followed the worn path to the large boulder near Pa's grave. He heaved himself up to his spot, sat, and wrapped his arms around his knees.

He thought about Pa. He was Will's Pa by birth but also his father by adoption. He'd known Pa nearly three years.

Thoughts of Running Wolf slipped in beside those of Pa. He and Pa were so much alike—kind, patient, gentle, but firm. Both were strong and full of the knowledge of life. He wished they were here for him to talk to. He chuckled when he thought of them being together, coming from different worlds, yet so much alike. They would have liked each other.

As always, Yellow Hawk wormed his way into his thoughts, making his heart heavy with feelings of betrayal. How could he go to the army—the enemy of his people?

His gaze brushed across the grave. Pa's words seemed to fly at him. *Go to Fort Union or stay away. It won't change anything. They'll never find one Comanche on the vast Llano Estacado.*

STAMPEDE

Two days later, Two Feathers shut the brush corral gate after the last steer passed through on its way to join Goodnight's herd. The cattle were in good shape. Will was learning to be a good cowman. He. . . he, too, was learning to be a good cowman—a Comanche cowman. A chuckle bubbled up at that thought.

He watched Will push a wandering steer back into their herd. Then a small bunch decided to turn around and head back for the green grass of the brush corral. Gray Wolf's sudden jump after them nearly unseated Two Feathers. He settled himself more securely in his saddle, realizing he wasn't the only one who'd learned to trail cattle. Those pesky critters kept him busy changing their minds about the direction they were supposed to be going. Finally, they crossed the Pecos and joined the larger herd on the far bank.

Riding out of the river, he found Curtis waiting in the shade of a cluster of cottonwoods. Will rode up behind him.

"I got your cattle count entered in the tally book," Curtis said. "We're gonna rest here a day or two before we head out."

The last night in camp, Two Feathers joined Will and the drovers around the cook fire. Cookie had a huge pot bubbling over the fire—beef chunks in savory brown gravy seasoned with onions and potatoes from Jake and Tony's garden. Golden biscuits to sop up the gravy filled one Dutch oven. The aroma set Two Feathers' nose twitching. But a second larger Dutch oven full of dried-apple pecan cobbler made his belly growl and rumble.

When the stew was gone, Cookie lifted the lid from the pie. The aroma brought Will and Two Feathers to the front of the line. Will sucked in a noisy sniff. "Mmmmm. I've been dreaming about your cobbler for a year, Cookie. Pile it high, so I have to use two hands to carry my plate."

Two Feathers brought his loaded plate and sat beside Will on the ground. He filled his spoon, blew to cool it, and eased it into his mouth. The deliciousness soaked in. When he swallowed, he nudged Will with his elbow. "You are pretty good at making Cookie's biscuits. Now, you need to learn to make this."

Will's cheeks bulged with the load in his mouth, but his head bobbed up and down.

Two Feathers finished eating and stretched out to relieve the pressure on his full belly.

After dropping the plates in the wash bucket, Will joined him. He loosened his belt a notch and rubbed his stomach.

"Curtis asked us to ride with the herd a ways. What do you think?"

Propping himself up on one elbow, Two Feathers watched the men gathered around the fire. Gill and Rory had trailed with Mr. Goodnight for several years. He felt comfortable with them, but new men were on this drive. Some of them made him nervous. He didn't like the looks he was getting from those few.

"Why? Does he need help to get our cattle trail broke?"

"No, I don't think so, but I'd like to go. It'll be a year before another of Mr. Goodnight's herds comes back this way, and Curtis' visit was short."

"For how long?"

"I don't think we can give up more than a day. Our cattle

will slow the herd, so they won't get too far from the ranch. September's not far off. We need to have the hay cut and stacked before then."

"What about Jake and Tony?"

"I'll ask them, but as tired as they are from guarding the cattle, I doubt they'll want to ride anywhere."

"If they stay at the ranch, I will go with you."

The next morning, with color fading from the clouds, the cowboys filled up on biscuits with speckled gravy and bacon. They let the cattle graze for a time. About mid-morning, Ol' Blue, Mr. Goodnight's lead steer, took his place at the head of the herd and pointed his long horns toward Colorado. Two Feathers watched as the drovers busied themselves pushing a herd of twenty-five hundred head of cattle away from night camp.

"Ho, cattle. Ho, ho," Two Feathers called. He slapped his coiled lariat against his leg, making a popping sound the trail-hardened cattle knew meant to get up and move. Will worked about fifty yards behind him. Soon the herd was ambling along, grabbing a mouthful of grass when the opportunity allowed.

The morning moved at the slow pace of the cattle. Two Feathers had forgotten the gritty, sweaty heat of a trail drive. He and Will moved around the herd, spending time with each cowboy they knew. Two Feathers liked these men. It was good to see familiar faces. He was greeted with a handshake or a slap on the back but always with a happy smile. As usual, Will had to protect his hat from their attempts to flip it off his head.

By late afternoon, Two Feathers decided he would never be a drover. It was hot, dirty, dusty work, and he was ready to leave. Earlier, he'd seen Will riding with Rory and Gill on the far side of the herd. He worked his way through a break in the moving cattle toward them. He pulled up beside Will, letting the cowboys pass on.

"You ready to head back?" Will asked.

Before Two Feathers could answer, he heard the pop of rifle shots. The terrifying war cry of the Comanche sent every horse into a full gallop. Two Feathers strained to see what was happening, but the cattle burst into a frantic stampede. Billowing clouds of dust blocked his view. More shots boomed. His momentary confusion passed, and Two Feathers slammed his heels into Gray Wolf, who exploded into a racing gallop to keep pace with the stampeding cattle. "Kee! No!" Two Feathers screamed. "It cannot be! Not here."

He and Will ran with the herd, working to keep cattle from spreading everywhere. Again, rifle shots popped. They blended with the roiling dust, spreading confusion and fear over both man and animal. Long sharp horns bobbed up and down as the animals plunged ahead. Two Feathers' heart raced at the speed of the running cattle. He strained his eyes to see where the shots were coming from. A figure appeared through the clouds of dust.

"Will, look!" Two Feathers screamed to be heard above the roar and pointed his arm ahead.

Yellow Hawk, painted for war, rode a well-muscled bay at full gallop. His legs gripped the racing animal. With his bow in one hand and three arrows in the other, he shot faster than Two Feathers could count. One—two—three arrows flew on their deadly mission!

Two cowboys hit the ground. Bending low over the flying mane, Two Feathers raced toward the first man before the cattle reached him. Hanging tight to Gray Wolf, Two Feathers leaned down and grabbed the fallen man by his raised arms. The cowboy hung on with a grip of pure panic. Every muscle screamed in protest as Two Feathers strained to swing the drover up behind him. Moving away from the danger of pounding hooves, Two Feathers eased his load to the ground and dropped beside him to check his condition. The man, now safe, was one of the men who'd been sending Two Feathers dirty looks earlier. Now, his look was grateful. He sent Two Feathers back toward the raging river of cattle that burst its banks and destroyed everything in its path.

Once again, Two Feathers, racing alongside the stampeding cattle, looked for Will but didn't see him. Fear for his brother filled him like dust filled the air. He spotted three raiders pushing about twenty head off from the herd. A lone cowboy raced his horse close to the stolen cattle to drive them back. Curtis!

And behind him came Yellow Hawk. The distance was too great for Two Feathers to recognize his uncle, but he knew him. Clinging to the racing Gray Wolf, Two Feathers pictured his uncle's broad face with his sharp cheekbones, the black in his eyes, and his thick body painted for war, one side yellow, one side black. He knew the man's braids were wrapped in buffalo hide with their hawk feathers tied tight. That picture was forever burned in his memory.

Yellow Hawk broke away from the rest of the raiders. He rode straight for the trail boss, nocked an arrow, and sent it on its deadly flight. Curtis slammed onto the ground, bounced hard, and tumbled, arms and legs flying, into a crumpled heap.

Two Feathers raised his rifle, took aim at his uncle, and squeezed the trigger. His shot went wild when Gray Wolf leaped over a small boulder. Racing past Curtis lying on the ground, he saw Will and another drover drop from their horses and run to the wounded man.

His eyes focused on Yellow Hawk's back. Holding his rifle in his tight fist, he leaned against Gray Wolf's neck. A tap with his heels urged the animal to find even more speed. The horse gave all he had. Gaining on the bunch of running cattle and the painted warrior who raced beside them, he decided to end it.

Two Feathers raised his rifle, but Yellow Hawk slowed the

·162·

bay. He spun the animal around and faced Two Feathers, who pulled back on the reins, stopping Gray Wolf a good distance from the fierce warrior.

The bay walked forward, guided by his master's knees. Yellow Hawk stretched his arms wide. His face mocking, he flicked his fingers, motioning Two Feathers to come and shoot.

The bay stopped. Two Feathers raised his rifle and sighted down the barrel. He centered on the line where the yellow and black paint met in the middle of his uncle's muscular chest. He sucked in a slow breath, held it, and squeezed the trigger. He missed! How? How'd he miss? He pulled his gaze from where the hole should've been and focused on the man's face. He watched the lips say, "You are not Comanche. You cannot kill your enemy." Yellow Hawk turned his back and raced away with the warriors and five head of cattle.

Two Feathers rounded up the remaining cattle and drove them toward the herd. He walked Gray Wolf back to the campsite, stripped off the saddle, and rubbed him down with what remaining dried grass he could find. When Gray Wolf cooled, he took him to the river to drink. Only then did he allow himself to think. *What happened? I had a clear shot. Why'd my shot go wide? I didn't move the barrel. How'd that happen?* He closed his eyes, and there, in the darkness, was Yellow Hawk, his arms wide, mocking him as always. His words, *"You are not Comanche"* pounded in his head over and over like war drums.

Gray Wolf lifted his dripping muzzle. Two Feathers led him to the campfire, where he found Curtis stretched out on a blanket. With the point of a long narrow knife, Cookie was working on the wound high on the man's shoulder just below the collarbone. The trail boss wasn't moving. Blood soaked the blanket beneath him. Will and Rory knelt across from Cookie and kept the blood wiped away from the wound.

When Will shot him a questioning glance, Two Feathers shook his head. "No, I did not get him."

With a grunt from Cookie, a low moan from the unconscious Curtis, and a gush of blood, the arrowhead slid into Cookie's bloody fingers.

Two Feathers walked back to his saddle. Digging around in the saddlebags, he found a pouch about the size of his two fists. Opening it, he dug through some smaller bags and pulled one out.

He squatted next to Curtis and felt his forehead. "No fever yet. Make tea with this ground willow bark. When he wakes, give it to him. The taste is not so good, but it will help with the pain and keep the fever down."

"I'll make the tea," said Will. He stoked what remained of the cook fire. After heating a pot of warm water, he set it next to Cookie. While the old cook washed his hands, Two Feathers pressed a folded rag onto Curtis's shoulder.

"Two Feathers?" Cookie replaced the rag with a clean towel and held it tight against the bleeding wound. "Do you think you can find some prickly pear cactus the cattle haven't trampled? I'd sure like to make a poultice for this shoulder. He's also got a nasty gash on his head where he smacked the ground. I want to be done doctoring these wounds before he wakes up and starts thrashing around."

"I will see what I can find." Two Feathers walked away from the downed man. He was glad to leave. The sight and smell of all that blood sickened him. He'd never seen so much human blood. Scrubbing his hands up and down his face, he tried to scour the image from his thoughts. He stopped. When would all this end? Maybe he should just leave Will and go back to the Comanche. Yellow Hawk might leave Will and the others alone if he went away.

Something nudged him and snuffled his buckskin shirt.

"Buck."

He scratched the long head under the forelock. *No. Even if I left, Yellow Hawk would still come for Buck.* He took the reins from around the saddle horn and led him toward the remuda where he'd left Gray Wolf.

"Come on. Will is busy with Curtis. I will take off that heavy saddle. How about we go to the river and get a drink?"

He led the buckskin along the river and found a clump of cactus within a cluster of rocks. He cut several pads while guarding himself against the sharp spines with work gloves from Will's saddlebag. Leaving Buck with Gray Wolf, he carried them to the fire, where he seared the spines from the pads. He knelt beside Cookie and split a pad open. Cookie laid half a pad against each side of the wound and bound it to Curtis' shoulder with strips of cloth.

"Will he get well?" Two Feathers remembered Weeping Woman treating wounded warriors about the same way Cookie was treating Curtis. Some of them lived, and some died. He worried about his friend.

"Oh, I think he'll be fine," Cookie said taking, a cup of hot coffee from Will. "I'm more worried about the knock on his head than I am about his shoulder." He blew in his cup to cool the black brew before he drank. "We'll know more in the morning. It will be good if he wakes up before too much longer. If he don't. . . well, we'll just have to wait and see."

Will sat next to Two Feathers near Curtis. Neither spoke for a while. Two Feathers couldn't see Will's face in the dim light of the setting sun, but his slump told him he was upset about Curtis.

"Will?"

"What?"

"It is too late to go home. We need to stay here tonight and leave in the morning."

"You're right."

"We should take Curtis with us. He needs time to heal before he can sit a horse again."

"He's not going to like staying behind while the herd goes on without him."

"I do not think it matters what he likes. He cannot ride a horse."

"He won't stay put in the supply wagon either."

At first light the following morning, Will rode Buck back to the house to get the hay wagon. By afternoon, Curtis lay in the wagon bed on a pad of blankets. Two Feathers tied Gray Wolf to the wagon with Buck and rode beside Will.

Leaving the noise and dust of the cattle behind them, Two Feathers turned around in the seat and checked on Curtis. "He is asleep."

Will clucked to the mules, and they stepped out a little faster. "What happened yesterday? I can tell you've been upset. What'd he do to you?"

"It is not what he did to me. It is what I did not do to him."

"Come on, Two Feathers." Anger put a snap to his words. "Dang it, what happened?"

"He and the Kiowas cut off about twenty head from the herd. Yellow Hawk circled away from them and toward me. He dared me, Will. He dared me to shoot him."

When Two Feathers didn't continue, Will twisted in the seat to look at him. "Well. . . did you?"

"I shot at him, but I missed."

Will stared at him. He shook his head, then slapped the mules with their reins. "You're a good shot. How'd you miss?"

"I have been thinking about that. He made no move to shoot me, only mocked me. I guess that made me miss. I heard the same thing I have always heard—I am not Comanche."

Will dropped his head and shook it. "Two Feathers, don't believe he won't harm you. Do you know what cattle he was taking from the herd? Did you see that big bunch the Kiowas rounded up?" Will threw sideways glances at his brother as his words grew louder and more curt. "The ones Curtis was trying to save when Yellow Hawk shot *him!* Do you know whose they were?" The red on Will's neck rose. "Do you know who owned the five head he did get?" Will almost shouted the last words.

Two Feathers felt sick. He hadn't thought about the stolen cattle. "They were Charlie Goodnight's."

Will stopped the wagon and faced his brother. "No, Two Feathers." He sat for a minute with his eyes closed, taking deep breaths. "Mr. Goodnight wouldn't miss the five head or even the twenty head. The stolen cattle wore the Pecos River Ranch brand. The one *YOU* worked so hard to put there. Yellow Hawk didn't want just any cattle. He wanted *YOUR* cattle. He wanted to hurt *YOU*."

The rest of the trip was dismal. Curtis moaned and stirred when the wagon bumped over the rough ground. Two Feahers slipped over the seat into the wagon bed to hold him still whenever the pain was too much. Both boys kept their rifles at hand. Two Feathers' thoughts were a jumble. Will's words circled around and around in his head, but by the time they reached the house, he knew Will was right.

Curtis was seriously sick for two days. Jake and Tony took turns with Will and Two Feathers working at the house, cutting wood for the winter, and caring for Curtis or going from one hay meadow to the next, cutting the tall grass to dry. They worked from daylight to dark. The hard work kept Two Feathers' mind too busy to dwell on Yellow Hawk.

A week later, with Jake following, Tony brought Curtis's horse from the barn and tied it to the hitching rail. Two Feathers sat on the back step next to Will.

"Tony," said Will, "talk to him. He's not strong enough for the hard ride to catch the herd. Two Feathers and I've talked to him, but he won't listen."

"What makes you think he will listen to us?" asked Jake.

"Let him go." Two Feathers pushed up from the step. "He is his own man. He knows his body and his mind. We cannot stop him." He picked up a pack of supplies and tied it behind the saddle.

Curtis walked out of the house with one arm bound tight to his chest. He mounted his horse with a grunt and an awkward swing into the saddle. His face paled with the strain.

"I thank ya, boys, for carin' for me. I'd a been a goner if you hadn't been such good nurses."

"Curtis?" Tony placed one hand on the cowboy's leg and looked up at him. "We all think you need to stay and rest a few more days. Riding is going to jar that broken collar bone something awful. A few more days won't matter to the herd."

"And," Will put his hand on the other leg, "we don't know if that knock on your head is healed."

"Boys, your concern is touchin', and I appreciate it. I promise I'll be careful, and if I get to hurtin' too bad, I'll stop. I'll tell Mr. Goodnight about how good you're doin' with the ranch and about the trouble with Yellow Hawk. Take care."

Two Feathers held the reins to keep the horse still. "My friend, do not take Yellow Hawk lightly. He is a fierce warrior. The Comanche fight for our homeland. Ride with caution."

"I'll do my best." Curtis put his hand on his bandaged shoulder and turned his horse away from the house. They watched until he disappeared into the trees across the creek, heading north toward Colorado.

Will I ever see him again? Two Feathers wondered. He watched the spot where Curtis disappeared from sight.

Leaving. . . people he cared for were always leaving, or he was leaving them. His parents left him. He left Weeping Woman and Red Wing. Pa left him and Will. Would Will leave him someday, or would he leave Will? He didn't like the hollow feeling that filled him. Scrubbing his face with his callus-hard hands, he went into the kitchen to help Will clean up the breakfast dishes. He stopped at the door to watch Tony and Jake disappear across the creek to check the hay fields.

After wiping the biscuit crumbs from the table, Will draped the wet rag on the edge of the dishpan. "If we're going to talk to the army, we need to go now. It'll soon be time to stack the hay for the winter."

Two Feathers sat in his chair at the table. How could he do this? Just the thought of soldiers made him sweat. Where were Weeping Woman and Red Wing? Were they safe in the canyon?

"Will, sit down a minute. I need to tell you something."

"Okay" said Will, suspicion clouding his face. "What is it?"

"I went by Mateo's to check on our sheep the other day. He had company. It was a brother who came from Santa Fe. When I rode up, he ran into the house and would not come out. Mateo said he told him the Comanche were raiding in Texas and in the Nations."

"We already know that. What are you thinking?"

"The Quahadi Comanche will never let the army take over the Comancheria."

"We know that, too. You've told me a lot about your people. They're strong warriors that show no fear. Our war is with Yellow Hawk, not all Comanche."

"The army's war is with all Comanche. This is the last time I will go to the fort of the white soldiers. Yellow Hawk is my enemy, but the Quahadi Comanche are my people."

"But remember, Two Feathers, so am I."

"I know. But during war, how can you be on both sides?"

Will looked at Two Feathers, then closed his eyes and braced his head on his hands. "I don't think that question has an answer."

THE ARMY

The hot days of August shifted to the cooler nights of September. Three days of hard riding with only scant meals of hardtack and jerky brought Two Feathers and Will to their regular campsite on the Gallinas River east of Las Vegas. Digging in his saddlebags, Two Feathers pulled out his coat. The chill in the late evening air made him glad he'd thrown it into his pack.

Will shrugged into his coat and picked up twigs, sticks, and branches for their fire. "I'm so hungry I could eat a bear—hair and all. I'll start some supper if you'll pull out that slab of bacon. By the time you take care of the packs and the horses, I'll have us some bacon, gravy, and biscuits."

"Will, have you ever eaten bear?" Two Feathers laughed. "I do not know about the hair, but I could eat some bear." Two Feathers stripped the packs and saddles off the horses.

"Hmmm. . . I've heard of bears around where we lived in Texas west of Fort Worth. I'm not sure I've ever seen one. No. . . I did see one."

Two Feathers watched Will standing with the biscuit dough in his hands and flour dusting the front of his coat.

"A traveling show came through long ago, and Ma and Pa took me to see it. There was a bear in a cage. It looked kind of mangy."

Two Feathers had no idea what a traveling show was, but

he was too hungry to interrupt the biscuit-making to find out. Scooping handfuls of grain into feedbags, he slipped them over the animals' ears and grinned at their eager crunching. While they ate, he collected wood for the fire. He wanted Will to have lots of hot coals to make those biscuits.

He took the horses to the river to drink when the last grain was gone from the bags. From the river, he looked back toward camp. He sniffed and picked up a faint whiff of smoke, but there was no light from the fire. Will had picked a spot among the rocks that hid the fire's small flames. He was learning to be a good Comanche.

Later, with his stomach full, Two Feathers spread his ground cover and blanket near the low burning coals in the fire ring. He stretched out, relieving muscles three days in the saddle had tightened and twisted.

Will flopped down beside him and rolled in his blanket. "We'll head for Las Vegas early and get our supplies before the town fills up."

In minutes, Will's soft snores drifted away on the crisp breeze.

Two Feathers did his best to not think of going into Las Vegas.

The next thing he knew, Will was nudging him with his foot. "Get up. I made coffee, and there's biscuits from last night."

Two Feathers rolled his buckskin shirt and moccasins and packed them away. Dressed in denim pants and a checked shirt, he stomped his feet into his cowboy boots and saddled Gray Wolf. He turned in the saddle to watch the light pink of the morning sky deepen into dark red with streaks of yellow. He remembered how much Weeping Woman liked to watch the sunrise. She would rise early to be sure to catch every bit of color in the wide sky.

Before they neared town, Two Feathers pulled Gray Wolf to a stop. Twisting his long braids together, he tucked them under his hat, tied his bandana around his neck, and turned his coat collar over his ears. He leaned toward Will, put a cocky grin on his face, and stuck out his hand.

"Howdy, Sir. My name is John Randall."

Will's face took on an official, serious look. He grabbed Two Feathers' hand, and they shook like two true gentlemen. "Glad to make your acquaintance, Mr. Randall. Ain't I met you before?"

"Maybe, but not for a good while. You met that other fella. The one that looks kinda like me."

With Will's laughter lifting his spirits, he tapped Gray Wolf, and they loped into town. The back streets were nearly empty, and they came up behind Grzelachowski's store without too many curious stares. Two Feathers loved the sights and smells inside this place of endless goods. His all-time favorite was at the end of the long counter, where the big jars of assorted candies and other delights made his mouth water just to look at them. Catching the eye of the storekeeper, he held up two handfuls of rock candy and stuffed them in his pockets. Grzelachowski's grin and wink told him the cost wouldn't appear on their bill.

Will buckled the straps on his bulging saddlebags. Before he could jump to the stirrup, the storekeeper offered his laced fingers for a boost up to the saddle on the tall buckskin. Holding onto Will's stirrup, he stopped Will's tap for Buck to walk off.

"Boys, you're going to Fort Union?" The uptick at the end of his sentence made the boys glance at each other and grin. The rise in the man's speech was a familiar sound, but today it held a sharp edge.

"Yes," answered Will. "Why?"

Two Feathers sat straight in his saddle. "Is something wrong?"

"People come into my store from all around. I've heard many stories of a band of Comanche and Kiowa raiding along the Canadian River. Their leader is called Yellow Hawk. He's evil. They say he fears nothing and believes he can't be killed. It would be best if you didn't travel near the Canadian. Finish your business at the fort and go home."

"We know of Yellow Hawk. He is why we are going to the army. We have information they need to know." Two Feathers pulled two horehound sticks from his shirt pocket and handed one to Will.

"Ride with your eyes wide open, boys." The uptick at the end of Grzelachowski's sentence was gone. His tone was flat, serious, and firm. "The devil is loose on the Llano Estacado."

After the long day passed riding the well-worn Santa Fe trail east toward Fort Union, the sun set and left only remnants of light, softly coloring the clouds. Two Feathers slid out of Gray Wolf's saddle amid a cluster of scrub juniper along a sluggish creek.

"I feel like the old men of our village whose bones pop. They walk with bent backs." He put his hands on his lower back and stretched from side to side. The pull of each muscle felt good.

Will's feet hit the ground. He groaned. Hanging onto Buck's saddle, he bent over and stretched his back and legs. He unsaddled the horses and started setting up camp.

Two Feathers stretched out on his blankets when the boys and horses finished supper and studied Will in the weak light from the glowing coals. "I have an idea. We must be close to the fort. We should go there tonight. It is cloudy, so the moon is dark."

"Why go tonight? I'm tired."

"Me too. But the soldiers cannot see us in the dark. It will be safer for me."

Will was silent for a while. "You're right. Let's go."

The boys saddled their tired horses, and Two Feathers mounted. Will didn't. He stood at Buck's head, talking to him, and stroking his forelock. "I know you're tired. So am I. But soldiers scare Two Feathers, so we have to do this tonight while it's dark, and they won't recognize he's Comanche. That way, we can start for home tomorrow." Will raised his arms high, and Buck lowered his head between them. With his chin against Will's back, the horse pulled the boy to his chest and held him there. Will's arms wrapped around the muscled neck. They stood together for several minutes. Two Feathers had seen Will hug Buck many times, but he'd never seen the horse hug Will.

Will mounted and turned to Two Feathers. "Buck said it's okay. We can go now."

They rode up to the Quartermaster's office at Fort Union an hour later and dismounted. Two Feathers pulled his hat down low over his eyes and struggled to keep calm. A few soldiers walked by, but no one paid them any attention. He followed Will into the long low-roofed adobe building. A clerk sat behind a small desk in the center of the room. A quick sweeping look around the room told Two Feathers the door they'd come in was the only way out. Long halls lined with closed doors stretched into the darkness on each side. The only light came from a lamp in one corner of a desk scattered with papers and a faint glow down one hall. A young soldier sitting in the lamp's circle of light worked at copying numbers into a big book.

"Sir," said Will. "We need to see Captain Stanaway. Can you tell me where I can find him?"

"He's still in his office." The soldier pointed down the

hall to his right without looking up. "The only one with the door open."

The clunk of their boots on the wood floor and the jingle of spurs announced their presence. Captain Stanaway looked up from his paper-covered desk.

"Well, look who's here." He stood and pulled out extra chairs from against the wall. "What can I do for you?"

Two Feathers sat sideways to see the door and the window behind the captain's chair. He looked at Will and waited for him to speak. Even though he and Captain Stanaway had settled their differences from last year at Fort Sumner, he didn't like the man's stern look and the way he barked his words.

"Do you know where Sergeant Baker is? We need to talk to him but don't know where to find him." Will's words sounded stiff and strained. He didn't like the man either.

The captain stepped to the door and hollered down the hall, "Corporal, find Sergeant Baker. I need him here."

"Yes, sir." A few seconds later, the outside door slammed.

"I'm almost finished with this report. It won't take a minute."

"Okay," said Will.

The constant bounce of Will's knee going faster and faster the longer they waited was irritating Two Feathers' nerves. He decided to slap the leg to make it stop when he heard footsteps coming down the hall.

Sergeant Baker made a crisp salute when he entered. "You need me, sir?"

Not waiting for an answer, he grabbed Will's hand, then Two Feathers'. He pumped so hard he nearly pulled them out of their chairs.

"Howdy, boys. What're you two doing here?" His head swiveled from Two Feathers to Will and back. "How'd that horse deal in Palo Duro Canyon go?"

The boys looked at each other.

"It went good." Will glanced at his brother. "We sold twenty horses to Silas Porter in Las Vegas."

"That's not why we are here," said Two Feathers.

"Well, why *are* you here?" asked Stanaway.

"It's about Yellow Hawk."

"What do you know about that renegade?" Stanaway leaned forward, his eyes boring down on the boys. "I thought you had enough of him last year."

"We need the army to capture him and put him in jail."

"Is that all?" Irritation clipped his words. "Don't you know the army has been after that Comanche for more than a year?"

"I've news for the army." Will's tone sharpened. "They haven't looked in the right places because he hangs around the Pecos River Ranch. He torments us, kills our cattle and sheep, destroys our water sources, and tries to get my horse. And tries to kill us in the process."

Encouraged by Will's words, Two Feathers spoke out. "I know we are still alive because my uncle is a poor shot."

Captain Stanaway made a frustrated huff. "I don't think he's a poor shot. He has been wreaking havoc all over eastern New Mexico Territory."

No one spoke, and Will's knee started bouncing again.

Captain Stanaway cleared his throat and straightened the papers on his desk. "Let the army take care of Yellow Hawk. They'll get him soon, I'm sure. I heard a Comanche chief was taken captive not too long ago at Fort Bascom. They captured a band of about fifteen or so warriors and their families. Maybe that was his band." He made a faint nod toward the door.

Sergeant Baker stood. "Come on, boys. Let's go water your horses and get some grub. We'll talk about this while we eat."

Two Feathers followed the sergeant and Will down the long hall. He'd been right all along about the army not helping them. He knew they didn't care about one Comanche, they wanted all the Comanche. This trip to the fort was a bad idea.

The horses at the hitching rail greeted them with a soft whinny and a gentle nuzzle, looking for something to eat. Gray Wolf's greeting lightened Two Feathers' mood somewhat.

Will scratched Buck in his favorite spots, behind his ears, and under his forelock. "You boys hungry again? You want more supper."

"Speaking of supper," said Sergeant Baker, "let's go to the mess hall before it closes for the night."

The thud of their footsteps across the plank floor of the large room turned the soldiers' heads. Some gave them a quick glance and returned to their supper. Some stared a little longer. Some stared long enough to make Two Feathers wish he were someplace else.

By the time they filled their plates and found a table near a front window, the hum of voices in the room had shrunk to a murmur that buzzed like a wasps' nest. Two Feathers watched Will. The tension on his face matched the queasy feeling in his own stomach. Sergeant Baker didn't stop talking, nor did his survey of the men in the room falter.

Halfway through their meal, the door opened and banged shut behind an officer. A lieutenant gave the room a quick but thorough scan. Every inch of the man looked starched—from his hair that stayed perfectly combed, even after removing his hat, to his shining boots—and as stiff as a skunk's upright tail.

"Boys, trouble's coming." Sergeant Baker spoke from behind his coffee cup. "Don't say anything. Just follow along."

A brisk walk that didn't threaten the crisp creases in his pants brought the officer to their table. He jerked Two Feathers' hat off. The long braids tumbled to their full length reaching the Comanche's waist. Before the lieutenant could speak, Sergeant Baker stood, saluted, and ignored his superior officer's rude behavior.

Only Will's hard squeeze and downward pressure on his arm kept Two Feathers in his seat.

"Lieutenant Dugan, I want you to meet the owners of the Pecos River Ranch from near Fort Sumner. They run horses and cattle in partnership with Charles Goodnight, one of the most respected men in the West and a personal friend of Colonel Gregg. You've heard of them in the short time you've been out West. Haven't you?"

Hearing the name of the famous cattleman and the fort commander in the same sentence caused the irate lieutenant to freeze. He choked and cleared his throat.

Will stood and offered his hand. The tight muscles in his jaws bulged. The lieutenant hesitated and glanced at Two Feathers. Shifting his look back to Will, he took the outstretched hand and gave it a limp shake.

Two Feathers thought Will might wipe his hand on his pants, but he didn't.

The mess hall door burst open again, and Captain Stanaway reached Lieutenant Dugan's side with a few long strides.

"Captain Stanaway." Sergeant Baker cut in before Dugan could speak. "I was about to tell the lieutenant of the horse deal we were discussing in your office with Mr. Will Whitaker." He nodded at Will and then at Two Feathers. "And Mr. John Randall."

"John Randall? B-but he's. . . " stuttered the flustered lieutenant.

Captain Stanaway stepped between the soldier and Two Feathers.

"Yes, we hope to have a contract with the Pecos River Ranch to provide us with horses and cattle for our campaign against the Comanche." He took Dugan by the arm and walked him toward the door. "I need you to look over some horses that came in today. You're going to need them." He threw an eye roll over his shoulder toward Sergeant Baker. "Then you can sign for them in my office." He ushered the soldier out the door before he could say a word.

Sergeant Baker watched from the window. "Stanaway has him inside. Come on before he figures out there's no contract. I don't know how the lieutenant knew you boys were here, but he sure didn't need to see Two Feathers. He's all fired up about removing the Comanche to the Nations. He thinks he's an expert on the Comanche because he read some book."

They hurried outside and mounted.

Two Feathers reached down to shake Sergeant Baker's hand. "I believe you saved me once again. Thank you."

The sergeant held Two Feathers' hand in both of his. "I think it would be good if you didn't come around the army for a while. Stay on your ranch and on the far reaches of the Llano Estacado." He let go of his hand and patted his leg." Now, go before Dugan gets away from Captain Stanaway."

"Wait a minute," said Will. "How do you know if Good-night and the Commander of Fort Union are such good friends?"

"I haven't the foggiest idea."

Will busted out laughing.

"Boys," said Baker, his tone apologetic, "I know you wanted the army to solve your problem with Yellow Hawk right now. I'm sure they will in time. And remember, the captain said he might have been captured. Stanaway usually knows what's going on because he ships supplies all over New Mexico Territory. You'll be all right."

On the ride back to camp, Two Feathers didn't speak for a long time. His thoughts tumbled around in his head, and all he felt was a deep sadness and confusion. He feared for himself and Will. He feared for the Pecos River Ranch. But most of all, he feared for Weeping Woman and Red Wing.

Their camp was a welcome sight. They stripped Buck and Gray Wolf of their saddles and watered them again. In minutes, Will had a small fire burning and coffee brewing while Two Feathers searched their packs for cold biscuits and jerky. They hadn't had time to finish the mess hall food.

"You want to know something?" asked Will.

"What?"

"I don't think Sergeant Baker and Captain Stanaway know up from slant about Yellow Hawk."

"No, I do not believe he is captured at Fort Bascom. The army will not help. He still wants us dead. And he still wants Buck."

Will stood in front of Two Feathers. He started to say something, then stopped. His shoulders drooped, pulling his head down with them. "I'm sorry I made you come."

By first light the following morning, they rode south toward the Pecos River Ranch. Two Feathers' eyes never stopped searching for any sign of danger. He didn't speak of the army. He didn't think of soldiers. He thought only of Yellow Hawk. Where was he? What would he do next? Had he attacked the ranch? Had he attacked Mateo's farm? Were Jake and Tony safe?

For two days, Two Feathers barely uttered a word. He knew Will was worried because there was no grumbling, no complaining, no wanting to stop for coffee. Stopping only to rest the horses and eat cold biscuits and jerky, they traveled from early light to nearly dark.

Mid-morning on the fourth day brought them within half a day from home. Lulled by the steady pace of Gray Wolf and the exhaustion of the long trip, Two Feathers slumped in the saddle and closed his eyes for what he planned on being only a minute. He'd no idea how long he slept when a startled yell from Will jerked him awake. Buck bolted into a full gallop. Two Feathers saw blood from an open gash running down the horse's hip. Will made a grab for the saddle horn, barely keeping his seat. Gray Wolf raced after the buckskin.

Two Feathers yanked his carbine from its boot but couldn't get a line of sight on the attacker. He leaned low over Gray Wolf's neck, the grullo keeping pace behind Will and Buck. An arrow hissed past Two Feathers' ear. Will screamed, slid off Buck, and slammed to the ground. He didn't move. Buck spun around and headed back for Will.

Yellow Hawk came straight toward the buckskin.

Knowing he couldn't save both Will and Buck, Two Feathers grabbed Buck's reins, flipped them over the saddle horn, and slapped him hard on the rump with the flat stock of his rifle.

"Home, Buck!" He bellowed with his whole being. "Go home! Run, Buck! Run!"

Buck obeyed.

Two Feathers bailed off Gray Wolf. Standing over his brother, he turned to face his uncle racing toward them on the Appaloosa, his warhorse. Raising his carbine, Two Feathers shot.

He saw Yellow Hawk's body jerk and disappear. *Did I hit him?* The spotted horse streaked past, racing after Buck with the warrior clinging to its side. The man reappeared astride his horse and screamed his war cry.

Two Feathers raised his carbine again and took aim but didn't shoot. If he missed Yellow Hawk, he might hit Buck running ahead. He'd seen his uncle ride this way before. Flat on the horse's back, the Comanche and the spotted horse ran as one being. Yellow Hawk's long black hair flew behind him, blending with the flowing black mane.

Two Feathers knew that Appaloosa, how fast he was. How could Buck make it home before the Appaloosa caught him when every pounding hoof-beat spurted blood from his wounded hip?

GONE

Yellow Hawk chased Buck over a rise, taking all sound with them. The silence they left behind made Two Feathers' ears ache. Gray Wolf raised his head and pitched his ears forward. Standing in the stirrups, Two Feathers tried to catch a last glimpse. Emptiness was all he saw. The nothingness mocked him and called him a failure. He couldn't stop Yellow Hawk. He couldn't protect Will. He couldn't save Buck.

A low groan broke the silence. Two Feathers dropped to Will's side.

"Will? Can you hear me?"

There was no response. Two Feathers yanked off his bandana and folded it to make a pad. Pressing it over the wound in the meaty part of Will's leg just below the hip socket, he tied it in place with Will's bandana. He checked Will's head and found a sizeable bulging knot above and slightly behind his right ear. Blood soaked his hair.

Two Feathers brought Gray Wolf next to Will. Knowing time was short and that a hard ride would kill Will, Two Feathers stripped the saddle from the already tired Gray Wolf. He took off his shirt, then ripped and folded it to add to the blood-soaked bandanas.

"Stand." He stroked the muscled neck. Blood seeped from Will's wound and soaked his pant leg. Two Feathers had killed enough game to know how quickly a severe wound could bleed out.

He dumped the contents of his bedroll onto the ground and wrapped Will in his blanket from head to foot as tightly as he could. Laying him across the horse's back, he mounted.

With Will cradled in his arms, he tapped the grullo into motion. Gray Wolf's gait was smooth and steady, as though he knew Will was hurt. Hoping the reduced weight of the saddle would help the horse's endurance, he turned away from the longer southern trail to the ranch. Instead, he headed west toward Mateo's.

Two Feathers held tight to Will, guiding Gray Wolf with the pressure of his legs. An hour passed. His muscles began to protest under his heavy burden's constant strain and tension. The color faded from Will's face. Two Feathers' heart screamed for him to hurry. He knew a gallop would increase the bleeding, so he held Gray Wolf to the lope. In another hour, the strain from holding Will cramped his muscles. He shifted on Gray Wolf, trying to relieve the pain.

Will's body sank even further into his arms. Two Feathers' breath stuck in his chest while his heart pounded, making his head swim. Gently, he pulled Will's head to his cheek and felt a faint wisp of air. He drew in a long slow breath that cleared his head. Sitting up straight, he pulled the muscles in his back, easing the ache.

With the sun overhead, Gray Wolf crossed the Pecos. Knowing their trip was almost over, Two Feathers dug up enough strength to make it and rode into Mateo's yard. The barking pack of dogs announced his arrival. No one yelled at them to hush. Mateo, followed by his sons, each carrying a rifle, bolted out the door. César reached up to take Will. Two Feathers wasn't sure he could relax his screaming muscles enough to let Will slide into those strong arms. Alma's calm but commanding voice issued orders to Elena and the younger girls, who held the door open for César.

Two Feathers dropped to the ground and stood on shaking legs. He stretched and flexed his muscles until he could trust them not to collapse. Mateo and Two Feathers led the tired horse toward the barn. Neither spoke. There was no need. Two Feathers saw evidence of attacks in the walls of the house and barn and in the few sheep penned in the corrals, not grazing in the fields. The corrals were empty of horses, but the barn was full. Estevan and a younger brother came from the barn with their rifles carried at the ready.

When Gray Wolf was settled, watered, and fed, Two Feathers followed Mateo to the house. Estevan and his brother returned to their guard duty at the barn. Inside, Two Feathers fell into a chair at the table and dropped his head onto his folded arms.

"Yellow Hawk shot Will and Buck. I could not take care of both, so I told Buck to go home. He took off at a hard run, but Yellow Hawk was right behind him. I do not know if he got away. I had to bring Will here. He would not have made it to the ranch."

Elena hurried past the table toward the kitchen. Two Feathers heard the pump bring up water and then the clank of the stove door after she stirred the fire. She brought him a cup and a pitcher of water with a plate of meat, beans, and cold tortillas.

"Eat," she said. "You must get your strength back."

"Elena," Alma called from behind the closed door. The girl hurried from the kitchen with a bucket of steaming water and a bundle of folded cloth bandages.

Two Feathers stirred the food around the plate and nibbled on a tortilla. "Yellow Hawk has been here?"

"Sí," said Mateo. "They attacked four days ago and have been raiding the sheep and cattle since then. They got several of our horses, so we locked the rest in the barn. We're on guard every minute of the day and night. Today is the first day they haven't attacked."

"Was anyone wounded?"

"No. By the grace of God, no." He crossed himself. "The girls aren't allowed to leave the house."

"Has he raided our ranch?"

"I don't know. We haven't heard from Jake or Tony."

Elena, carrying a bucket of bloody water, came from Will's room and stopped at the back door. César opened it a crack and scanned the area before he stepped outside.

Two Feathers grabbed his carbine and followed him. After the fight with Yellow Hawk earlier, he didn't think the man would come here. He was sure he was after Buck. But he was taking no chances. His eyes searched every shadow.

César took the bucket and threw the water on the ground. Two Feathers followed him into the house, bolting the door behind him.

Taking the bucket from her brother, Elena refilled it in the kitchen and disappeared into Will's room. Two Feathers got a quick glimpse of Will's pale, drawn face and Alma's worried one before the door closed.

Two Feathers sat at the table and shoved his barely touched plate away. He couldn't stand the thought of food. If he swallowed anything, he knew his stomach would reject it. Lacing his fingers together, he slid his hands over his head and down to the back of his neck. His head slowly sank to the table, tumbling his tangled braids onto his lap. He squeezed his arms tight against his head, hoping to force the fear for Will and Buck away. The fear wrapped itself in sadness and burrowed deep into his brain until there was no room for anything else.

A light tug on his arm brought Two Feathers to his feet. He followed César to a long room lined with cots. His friend pointed to one, and Two Feathers sank onto it.

"Cesar, my saddle and bedroll are out there. Can you get them for me?"

"Don't worry, my friend. Yellow Hawk will leave here now that Buck is loose. I'll backtrack and find your saddle and gear."

Fear lost out to exhaustion. The black void of dreamless sleep welcomed him.

Sometime during the night, the hoot of a barn owl woke Two Feathers. He sat up and looked around the room. An eerie light from the full moon left shadows in the corners. The adobe walls were lined with cots. Beside each cot was a set of hooks that held pants and shirts. A few of the cots were empty. In the cot next to him, Two Feathers recognized Estevan sleeping with his mouth wide open. On the other side was young Tomas, his gentle face even more relaxed in sleep. The boy sighed, licked his lips, smacked, and snuggled deeper into his blanket. Two Feathers decided Tomas must be dreaming of something good to eat.

Two Feathers took his carbine and slipped out of the room. He wanted to check on Will but decided to scout around outside first. When he entered the large main room of the house, Mateo struck a match and lit his pipe. He had pulled his chair into a dark corner and was watching out the window.

"I wouldn't go outside."

"Why?"

"The young boys are outside. They are afraid. They shoot first and leave the questions of who's there for me to answer."

"They are so young. Why send them out?"

"César, Estevan, and Tomas can't guard all the time. They need sleep. Young boys grow up fast in dangerous times. You and Will know that."

"Yes, I remember being a small child, but my boy days were few."

Two Feathers stood in the shadows next to Mateo's window and studied the front yard and barn in the light of the full moon—the Comanche moon—the time to strike at their enemies. Nothing moved in the yard, not even a dog. A nighthawk, showing off its acrobatic skills while catching mosquitoes, swooped between the house and barn, disappearing into shadows, then reappearing in the moon's bright glow. He told Mateo, "Yellow Hawk is not here tonight. See the nighthawk. He would not be here if there was an intruder."

"True, but I will leave my niños on guard. They will learn."

Two Feathers watched from the window for a while, wondering why the nighthawk hunted this late. Thoughts of Yellow Hawk returned. Where was he? Did he have Buck? Did Buck make it home to Jake and Tony? How would he tell Will he couldn't protect his. . . he couldn't think of a word to explain what Buck was to Will.

Yellow Hawk! Just thinking those words drained away his spirit. His uncle was stealing the good in his life. Thoughts of Weeping Woman pushed through his despair. Memories of their walks in the forests and the desert made him smile. She'd taught him so much. He remembered the words she said to him so often, *You are a good Comanche boy.*

Should he return to Weeping Woman? He missed her. He missed Red Wing. She'd always been his special friend. He knew Running Wolf would care for Weeping Woman. Two Feathers knew the man would do what Yellow Hawk failed to do.

He saw movement at the barn door. One of Mateo's boys stuck his head out, quickly looked around, and jerked it back inside. Mateo grunted. Mumbled Spanish words and a frown told Two Feathers that boy was in for a scolding. He had given away his position. If Yellow Hawk had been there, he would know where the boy was.

Two Feathers grinned at Mateo. "As you said, he will learn."

The sheep stirred. *The corral is less crowded than the last time I was here.* Yellow Hawk had harmed him and Will and their friends.

"Mateo?" Confident his uncle wasn't here tonight, he slid down the wall to sit on the floor. The old man didn't answer. His eyes focused on the barn where his two young sons stood guard. Two Feathers studied what he could see of his friend in the darkness. The man was tired, but his face was relaxed. The lines of tension and worry he expected to see weren't there. Mateo's pipe glowed red. The spicy, fragrant smoke rode away on the gentle breeze.

"The Comanche lives from the land," said Two Feathers. "We hunt for what we need. The buffalo and other animals give us a place to live, food to eat, clothes to wear, weapons, and tools." A doleful sigh escaped from Two Feathers. "But the white man's world is different. Will has taught me much about ranching. I know we have sheep and cattle. But Will kills only enough for food and sells the rest for what you call money. Then he buys what he needs in the towns. So, you have less to sell when Yellow Hawk kills your sheep and cattle. That means you get less money. And that means you cannot get the supplies you need. I am sorry I have brought this trouble to you."

"No, amigo. My family has lived here for many years. I was born in this house. So was my father. My grandfather settled here. Many times, we've defended our hacienda against the Comanche, the Kiowa, and even the Apache. We'll survive. We're a strong people." He didn't take his bloodshot eyes from the barn. "Go back to bed. We will talk in the morning."

Two Feathers rubbed his eyes. They burned and felt gritty. As he walked toward the boys' room, he stopped and cracked open Will's door. In the dim light of a low-burning candle, Will slept, pillows and rolled blankets supporting his wounded hip. Two Feathers could see the bulge of bandages under the blanket and behind Will's ear. He opened the door a little more and stuck his head in. Elena sat in a chair near the bed. She put her finger to her lips, cautioning him to be quiet. She smiled, and a little worry slipped away from Two Feathers. He returned to his bed, hoping he could sleep.

Giggles greeted him the next morning when he entered the main room to see a line of young girls, each a head taller than the one next to her, waiting for Alma to brush their tousled hair. Elena hurried past and returned with a tray holding a bowl of broth and a cup of steaming coffee. Balancing it on one hand, she opened Will's door and disappeared inside.

Two Feathers sat at the table across from Mateo and César. He looked around and didn't see Estevan or Tomas. He guessed they were already outside taking care of the animals or on guard duty while the younger boys did the morning chores.

With her hair in tight slick braids, one of the giggling girls brought him a plate of scrambled eggs, a thick slice of ham, and hot corn tortillas. Mateo slid a cup of coffee across the table. The food was good, but Two Feathers was still tired from their trip to Fort Union. The grueling ride to save Will had left the muscles of his shoulders and back aching and stiff. Worries about Will's injuries and Jake and Tony added to the strain. Had Yellow Hawk found their mustang mares? Was there still a Pecos River Ranch? He shook his head. He could do nothing for the ranch right now. Better to shove those thoughts back into a corner of his mind.

"Mateo, I need to let Gray Wolf recover. And. . . I want to stay here until I know Will is okay." Two Feathers' last words tumbled out in a rush as if he must finish them before Mateo said no. After all, it was his uncle bringing all their trouble. . . his Comanche uncle.

"Si, amigo. You're welcome here. Stay."

Pushing aside his empty plate, Two Feathers hid his relief

by sipping his coffee. That was one problem solved. Now how should he ask Mateo for help? He struggled to keep his gaze steady, but it jumped from Mateo to César and back.

The room hummed with activity. The girls worked in the kitchen or in the bedrooms. Alma lugged a pot of hot water to the back porch and scrubbed the bloody bandages she'd left soaking in cold water overnight. Estevan followed her and stood guard while she worked. Through the door, Two Feathers could see Tomas stop just inside the barn and scan the yard before stepping into the open.

Mateo was right. These were strong people who knew how to live on this rugged land. Maybe they could help him stop Yellow Hawk.

"Mateo, we need your help. Will and I cannot stop Yellow Hawk. We have tried every way we know and failed. The posse failed. And now the army has failed. They are not worried about one Comanche. They want all the Comanche. Captain Stanaway told us Yellow Hawk might have been captured at Fort Bascom, but we both know that is not true. He shot Will and probably stole Buck. How am I going to tell Will?"

César sat straight in his chair and started to speak, but a look from Mateo silenced him. He eased back in his seat.

Mateo's gaze was gentle as he studied Two Feathers' face. "Look around this house. I've many niños, little ones, medium ones, and big ones. I protect each of them and teach them to protect each other. I don't hunt Yellow Hawk. I defend against him. It would take many of us to hunt him. Who would protect my children if I left with César and Estevan?"

Two Feathers studied Mateo's face. There was understanding there and sadness, along with strength and determination. Two Feathers nodded. He knew before asking that Mateo couldn't leave his family. Even though this house was a beehive of activity, a thread of fear ran through everything and everyone. He felt it.

Mateo stood and looked down at Two Feathers. "Troubled times don't last forever. What you do in hard times is up to you. Right now, your decisions are still questions. Little by little, you'll decide their answers. Stay here until Will can ride in a wagon. Then, go home and defend *your* hacienda until *you* decide what to do."

Two Feathers watched Mateo and César go out the door together. He wondered about his own father, Tom Randall, but couldn't remember much. He'd been only five when Yellow Hawk killed him. Would he have been as wise as Mateo? What would his father want him to do? From the little he remembered and what Weeping Woman had said about him, he decided his father must have been a lot like Mateo. . . a cautious man but brave. That thought swelled inside him and made him smile.

Two Feathers slipped into Will's room the following afternoon when Alma was napping in her chair.

"Will," he whispered. "Are you awake?"

"I am now." His words were faint, his voice thin and airy.

Two Feathers tiptoed around the bed and knelt at the head of the cot. With their faces even, he smiled at Will.

"Are you okay?"

Will frowned. "I don't think so. It feels like a blacksmith is hammering in my head. If I move even a bit, my leg screams at me. Are you okay?"

Two Feathers huffed. "I am better than you."

Will grinned, then winced. "That wouldn't take much. What happened?"

"Do you remember anything?"

"No. How's Buck and Gray Wolf?" His voice was now just a whisper.

"Gray Wolf is in the barn, and everything is fine."

Will's eyes closed.

Alma tapped Two Feathers on the shoulder and whispered, "That's enough. Let him sleep."

Two Feathers avoided all but brief visits with Will for the next week. Alma threatened to ban him from the room if he told Will he didn't know where Buck was. He brushed off Will's questions about the buckskin with vague references to Gray Wolf. Alma scared him by describing the seriousness of Will's head wound, so he obeyed when she said not to upset him. She kept the room dark and said he needed quiet and rest to recover.

By the end of the week, Alma agreed to let Two Feathers and Mateo talk to Will about Buck. César helped Will out of bed. With César on one side and Two Feathers on the other, they walked him into the main room and settled him into a well-padded chair. The effort drained him. He sat shaking and pale. A drink of water and a few minutes rest restored color to his face. Two Feathers pulled a chair from the table and sat in front of him.

"Will, I have to talk to you about Buck." He forced himself to swallow the big lump in his throat.

"I've already figured out something happened to Buck. Just tell me one thing. . . is he dead?"

"No, I sent him home. He was wounded, but I do not think it was too serious." Two Feathers' words tumbled faster and faster as he hurried to get all the words out before Will exploded.

"Yellow Hawk shot at me. Then he hit you. You fell off Buck. I do not remember when it happened, but he shot Buck in the hip. I smacked your buckskin with the butt of my carbine and screamed at him to go home." Two Feathers stopped talking to take a breath. The pain on Will's face froze the rest of his words in his throat.

He stared at Will's mouth—opening and closing—trying to

form words. But no words came. Two Feathers watched Will's eyes squeeze shut. A tear slipped down his cheek.

"I tried, Will, I tried." His voice was hoarse with the strain of saying words he didn't want to say. "I could not save both you and Buck. When I last saw him, he was running strong and headed to the ranch." He didn't mention the blood.

Two Feathers looked at each face in the room, hoping someone would help him explain this to Will. But every eye was focused on Will. Tears rolled down Elena's face, and clenched teeth bulged Cesar's jaw. The room held its collective breath. . . waiting.

Will opened his eyes and sucked in air, then released it with a shuddered sigh.

"This is the second time you've saved me from Yellow Hawk. You trailed him for a week after he captured Buck and me two years ago. I owe my life to you again."

Two Feathers released the breath he didn't know he was holding. "Maybe Buck made it. Maybe he is with Jake and Tony. Maybe he will be rested and well when we get back."

"I don't think so." Will's words dropped to almost a whisper. "Buck was tired. You said he was wounded. We were still a long way from home." Two Feathers watched as Will stiffened in the chair. A red flush crawled higher and higher up his neck until it disappeared into his hairline. His voice grew stronger, louder, harder. "I know where Buck is. He's with Yellow Hawk."

Leaning forward in his chair, Two Feathers gripped Will's shoulders and squeezed. "If that is so, I promise you, Will, I will get Buck back. I promise."

"We can try. But. . . " Will paused. His voice faded back down to almost a whisper. "The Llano Estacado is a big place."

A Comanche Warrior

"Are you blind, or are you aiming for every rock or rut on this road?" Will hissed through clenched teeth.

Two Feathers glanced over his shoulder at Will bedded down on a pallet of blankets in the back of Mateo's wagon.

"Quit complaining. Alma made a soft bed back there."

Two Feathers didn't know what would be best for Will, drive a little faster and get him home sooner or take a slower pace to make the trip easier. The wagon lurched and bounced over the furrowed rock-strewn road worn into the desert between Mateo's farm and the Pecos River Ranch. Two Feathers had been over this road many times in the last three years. On horseback, it didn't matter how rough the road was. He glanced at the sun and figured they'd come about halfway. The longer it took to get there, the more nervous he got. The wagon's slow pace made him feel like a rabbit tethered to a stake and used as bait. Where was Yellow Hawk?

If he kept teasing Will, maybe he wouldn't feel the bumps or not fret about the danger they were in. "You have been lying around letting Elena treat you like a chief of the whites for the past two weeks, bringing you food, letting you lean on her when you walk, wrapping you in blankets so you do not get cold." He shook his head and turned sideways in the seat. Will's white-knuckle grip on the side of the buckboard stopped any further teasing. Two Feathers pulled back on the reins and eased the horses' pace.

The road stretched long ahead of them. Two Feathers' neck began to ache from the frequent backward turns to check on Will. He hadn't made a sound for the last hour. The wagon splashed through the creek and into the yard. Two Feathers jumped down, leaving the team to stop on its own. He scooped up his brother, carried him to the house, and eased him onto his bed.

Will's eyes fluttered and opened. "Buck?"

Two Feathers ran for the barn. He yanked on the door, but it wouldn't open.

"Jake! Tony!"

Pounding on the heavy planks, he yelled again. The horses inside nickered and stomped, kicking their stalls, frightened.

"Jake, where are you?"

No answer.

"Tony?" No sound of footsteps.

"Buck? Are you in there?" His head fell against the rough planks of the door. "*Kee*," he moaned in a hoarse whisper. "*Kee*."

The sound of horses coming into the yard jerked him around and sent him running toward the house.

Jake and Tony dismounted and took turns pounding Two Feathers on the back and shaking his hands.

"It's about time you boys got back." Jake untied Gray Wolf from the back of the wagon. "We'd decided to head to Fort Union and see what kept you two."

"I tried to get in the barn, but the door will not open." Two Feathers paced back and forth between the porch and the wagon, pulling and twisting his long braids. "Have you seen Buck? Did he come home?"

"What do you mean? He's not with you and Will?" Tony asked.

Jake picked up a blanket from the back of the wagon. "This is Mateo's wagon. What's wrong? Where's Will?"

"In the house. Wounded. I put him in bed." Two Feathers' gaze slipped to the ground. "The last I saw Buck, he was running at full gallop." His insides shrank until all that was left was an empty shell. Pain pierced him like arrows, and his words, "With Yellow Hawk racing after him," squeezed past the boulder in his throat. "I could not save them both."

Jake and Tony started for the house, but Two Feathers stopped them. "Let him sleep. The wagon ride from Mateo's was hard on him. Help me tend to these horses, and I will tell you all about it."

After the chores were done, all three headed for the house. Two Feathers sat on the edge of Will's bed. "Will, are you awake?" Jake and Tony stood behind him.

"Yes." He opened his eyes and gave the ranch hands a weak smile. Each man gave him a gentle shake. Will shifted his gaze back to his brother.

Two Feathers moved his head in one slow shake. He thought Will was pale from the trip in the wagon, but his face blanched even more, and he turned his head away. A tear pooled in the corner of his eye.

Two Feathers' worries about Will deepened one slow day after another as September ended and October arrived. For weeks, Will had refused to leave his room. He wouldn't speak except to answer direct questions that required a simple yes or no. Any other question was ignored.

Working in twos, with the third always guarding Will and the house, Two Feathers, Jake, and Tony worked the ranch. The hay was cut and stacked. They moved older cows and young heifers to the brush corral for the winter. Any straying cattle were driven closer to the ranch headquarters, and water holes were checked. The last potatoes, onions, and turnips were dug and stored with the winter squash in the root cellar.

Early one crisp mid-October morning, Will emerged from

his room, his face haggard, his eyes sunken behind dark circles. He pulled out a chair. With slow, deliberate movements, he sat across from Jake.

Tony put a plate of biscuits and eggs in front of him. "Have you decided to get your horse back? Or are you going to let Yellow Hawk have him?"

Will's fork stopped halfway to his mouth and hung there for a few seconds while he met each questioning look, then he finished the bite.

"You're right, Tony. I'll never find Buck hiding in my room in the dark. I have to get my strength back. Buck has been gone a long time. He'd have been home by now if he'd escaped from Yellow Hawk. He's not here so that Comanche got my horse. . . again."

Two Feathers put his hand on Will's shoulder. "Are you ready to ride?"

Two Feathers saw a spark in Will's eye for the first time since he'd told him Buck was gone. Was it hope or anger? He couldn't tell, and he didn't care. It was there.

After Jake and Tony left for the barn, Two Feathers sat beside Will.

"We need to talk," said Two Feathers. "We must find Yellow Hawk and Buck ourselves. There is no one to help us."

"I know."

Two Feathers struggled to hear Will's words, but he clearly heard the menace in his tone.

"You need to learn to be a Comanche."

Will started to respond, but Two Feathers cut him off.

"I know you have learned a lot. It is not enough. We will go into Comanche country. You must know how to live there."

"I'm as good with a bow and arrow as you. I can track almost as well as you. I speak Comanche. We're going into Comanche country to find Buck, not live there. What else do I need to know?"

"That is all good." Two Feathers looked out the window and watched the cold October wind blow in the treetops. *How can I tell him? How can I make him understand it is not what he does? It is how he thinks.*

"You do not think like a Comanche warrior. We will enter their land. If we come in as white men with a few Comanche skills, we will never find Yellow Hawk. The warriors will track us if we leave sign that a white man is in Comanche country. They will leave false trails, which will get us lost. If we do not find Yellow Hawk, we will not find Buck."

"I can do that. You're learning to ranch. I'll learn to be a warrior."

"Will you listen to me? Will you do what I tell you to do?"

"I need Buck back. I'll listen. I'll do what you tell me. I'll follow you anywhere."

Two Feathers studied Will's face. Even though he was pale, his skin still had the sun-browned color of tanned leather. Squinting into the distance had furrowed his eyes at the edges. They were no longer the eyes of a boy. They were the eyes of a man accustomed to the hard life on the Llano Estacado.

With a firm thump on Will's back, Two Feathers stood. "Let's go. There is work to do."

At the barn, he strapped a small pad onto Rojo and led him outside.

"Get on."

Will limped around the horse and studied the simple pad and strap. "I think I'd do better to just ride bareback."

"What will you hang onto when you slide off Rojo's side out of sight of your enemy?"

"Oh." A whoosh of breath followed.

Will stood beside Rojo. The sorrel looked back at him and the pad on his back. "Rojo," there was a hint of apprehension in his voice, "I believe we are in for some hard work."

Two Feathers was sure the horse rolled his eyes. "Get mounted. You will not learn anything standing on the ground."

The first jump landed Will in a heap in the dirt, moaning from the pain in his hip.

"Come on, Will. You can mount Buck. He is a lot taller than Rojo."

Will's answer was a groan and an outstretched hand for a pull to his feet.

On the second jump, he fared better and landed on his feet.

This time it was Two Feathers who rolled his eyes. "We do not have all day."

The third landed him on the horse's back but with a painful cost.

By the end of a long week, Will and Rojo had become used to the strange pad. It no longer slid and dumped Will off. The days were spent riding Rojo with no saddle and often no reins. Every day during the week, Two Feathers kept Will riding Rojo longer than the day before. Throughout the long nights, he delivered cool pads to Will's swollen, aching hip.

By the end of October, the air turned. Ice formed along the creek's edge in front of the house. One particularly brisk morning, Two Feathers walked into the kitchen to find Will, Tony, and Jake finishing breakfast. The coffee pot on the stove was half empty. With his plate full of the last stack of flap-jacks, he sat beside Will.

"You must be feeling better. I think Rojo needs a rest this morning. Get your bow and quiver. We will do some target practice."

"Why? I don't see the purpose of that. I shoot well enough. And I'm good with my carbine."

"Think, Will. A rifle shot can be heard for a very long

distance. We will hunt for meat. Do you want to tell every Comanche or Kiowa on the Llano Estacado where we are? And what happens in a battle if you run out of bullets? We will take our carbines and our bows and arrows."

Will sat for a few seconds, then looked up at Two Feathers. "As usual, you're right."

Before heading outside, they plucked their coats from the hooks next to the door. A stiff breeze slapped their faces and made them pull their coat collars closer around their ears.

Will stopped in the middle of the yard. "We can't shoot in this wind."

Two Feathers nocked an arrow and took a quick glance at the tuft of soft downy feathers tied to the top of the bow to gauge the direction of the wind. He shot. His arrow flew and struck a post in the corral next to the barn.

With a nod, he told Will, "Yes, we can."

As they continued to aim and shoot, Jake and Tony hung around for a few minutes to watch.

Then Tony said, "Come on, Jake. I've got guard duty, and you need to get the hay wagon ready. I don't want it to break down in the middle of winter when cattle are hungry."

Two Feathers took Will's bow. "I want your bow and quiver of arrows to become a part of your body. You must learn to run through trees, climb over rocks, and ride a horse without losing them. From now on, they will be with you every time you leave the ranch house. It is easy to shoot standing still. I will teach you to shoot while running on foot and riding at a gallop."

Taking Will's quiver, he put it behind his back. "How many arrows are in your quiver?"

"Ten."

"No. There are nine. You have lost one. If a Comanche misses his target, he will search until he finds his arrow. They are too hard to make to be careless."

Two Feathers kept Will moving all that day while shooting at the target. Every time he missed, he hunted until he found the arrow. Every time he missed, Two Feathers told him the same thing. . . "Yellow Hawk is not known for his skill with the bow, but he is better than you. If you were shooting at him, you would be dead."

By the end of the week, Two Feathers had to work hard to stay ahead of Will. Even riding at full gallop, Will hit his target more times than he missed. His skills improved quickly. But the improvement in his hip came more slowly, making Two Feathers worry. He knew he had to make a hard decision.

Heartache

Each day, they rode over the ranch checking cattle for any signs of sickness and spoke only in Comanche. Each day, they worked on tracking skills while hazing cattle that strayed away back toward home pastures. Each day, Will's impatience to begin the search for Buck grew sharper.

One morning, while checking cattle, Will complained in Comanche, "It's already December. The wind has a bite to it. I'm ready to go. If we wait too long, the weather will get worse. We won't be able to travel. I'm afraid for Buck. Is he even alive?"

Two Feathers didn't answer.

That night after supper, Two Feathers asked Tony and Jake to wait a while before they went to their quarters in the cave barn. They sat around the table sipping hot coffee and nibbling on leftover toasted cornbread sprinkled with sugar.

"If you're thinking about going after Buck, we'd better give it some serious thought. It's already cold, boys." Jake got up and stoked the fire in the stove, adding a couple of wood chunks.

"I have been thinking about that." Two Feathers slipped a quick glance at Will. "Last winter, we had some bad storms. We could have the same this winter." He watched the red on Will's neck rise. The air in the room seemed to crackle like the fire in the stove.

Silence hung like an unwanted visitor.

Will pushed his chair back and leaned against the sink. "Just say it, boys." He turned around and looked at each one. "Just say it."

"Winter's here. It isn't a good time to hunt for Buck," said Jake.

"It's not safe to be caught in a blizzard. You know that." The pain in Tony's expression mirrored Two Feathers'.

Will turned his back to the room, head drooping.

Two Feathers walked over and stood beside his brother. "You know we are right. We cannot hunt for Buck in winter. The risk is too great. We had to wait for your wound to heal. Now we must wait for spring."

Will's reflection in the window was stiff, his expression haunted. Two Feathers watched him work to stay strong, but his face crumpled and fell, taking Two Feathers' heart with it.

A few days later, winter arrived in earnest as a snowstorm dumped its heavy load for three days. Nothing was said about going after Buck. During those cold days, Will barely spoke. When he did, it was to assign jobs for the day. Hungry cattle, frozen water holes, creeks, and the lake in the brush corral kept the four ranch hands busy. On some days, one team, Jake and Tony, busted holes in the ice so the cattle could find water while Will and Two Feathers fed hay. The next day they would switch jobs. This storm was the first of many.

On a cold brisk day after the snow finally stopped falling, Two Feathers braced himself against the tall sides of the hay wagon as the team of mules plodded along. He scooped another forkful of hay and tossed it onto the ground. Cows pushed and shoved each other, trying to get a bite. The mules stopped.

"Walk on." Will hollered to the mules.

Two Feathers grabbed the wagon's side before he tumbled

out the back when the mules lunged into their harness. Draping the reins over the seat, Will joined him in the bed and threw another forkful of hay.

Two Feathers watched how Will moved and how he braced himself as the wagon lurched along the trail worn in the snow. He showed more confidence in that injured hip and didn't favor it as much. Two Feathers leaned against the side of the wagon bed. "Maybe it is a good thing we had to wait to find Buck. Maybe your hip will be even stronger than it is now."

"Gee!" yelled Will. The mules made a wide turn to the right, away from the jumbled tangle of long sharp-pointed horns twisting to reach a dry mouthful. The boys threw out more forkfuls of hay.

Will's face closed down, and his muscles tightened. "I was angry when you wouldn't go after Buck. So angry I couldn't handle it, so I buried it and pretended everything was okay. But this snowstorm has tormented my hip until I can't sleep at night because of the pain. I thought it was well, but it's not."

The wagon bounced. Will's eyes squeezed shut as pain flashed across his face.

"Haw mule!" hollered Two Feathers, then shifted his weight to keep his balance. The wagon swung to the left. Eager cows and yearlings scrambled to get their share of the hay the boys tossed on the ground.

"Walk on," yelled Will.

The faithful mules followed the worn path with a trail of hay and hungry cattle stretching behind them. With that bunch fed, Will clucked to the mules, slapped the reins on their backs, and headed the wagon toward home.

Two Feathers cocked his head to see Will's face. "I am sorry you are angry with me, but we would not have survived a winter on the Llano Estacado. We are not prepared for that. I worried we had not given your hip enough time to fully heal.

We worked it a lot, but a few hours a day is not enough for what we need to do."

"I'm not angry anymore. I know you're right."

Two Feathers twisted on the seat to look at Will. "What did you say? Do you know you rarely tell me I am right?" He laughed and gave Will's arm a playful punch. "Say it again. I want to hear it again."

Will scowled at him. "Don't push your luck." Tight lips failed to hold in the laughter.

Two Feathers sat back against the seat. He felt lighter, and the trip went a little easier.

Cold day after cold day, they fed hungry livestock. Sometimes, the bitterly cold wind burned straight through their coats and layers of clothing, wrapping its icy fingers around their limbs from fingers to shoulders and toes to hips. Two Feathers decided there weren't enough hours in the night for the heat from the fire to warm his frozen bones. The haystacks nearby dwindled. The drive to more distant stacks stretched longer with each snowstorm.

As Christmas drew close, the sun delivered its gift by shining for several days. As the temperature rose, the snow melted to slush. Tony and Jake replaced the snow skids on the hay wagon with wheels. The wagon rumbled out of the yard, one wheel squealing with every turn. The last thing Two Feathers heard before the wagon disappeared behind the house was Tony fussing at Jake. "I told you there wasn't enough grease on that wheel. Now that awful screech is going to torment me all day."

Will and Two Feathers saddled Rojo and Gray Wolf to take their turn checking the water holes.

"We better check the brush corral first," said Will. "That lake was frozen solid everywhere except the middle. We need to be sure no cattle fell through with this thaw."

Two Feathers mounted and followed Rojo south toward the brush corral. He worried about Will. He was thin, and his eyes had dark circles around them like a raccoon's. It had been several weeks since they had persuaded him to wait for spring before going after Buck. His mood hadn't changed. Every evening after supper until bedtime, he sat in the living room staring into the fire. The only thing he talked about was the ranch.

Two Feathers didn't know how to help his brother. Will spent most nights watching from the bedroom window, his rifle in his lap. He hadn't spoken Buck's name since they returned from Mateo's to the realization that Buck wasn't in the barn.

No matter how Two Feathers tried to help, Will's mood didn't improve. He decided he would have to let Will work things out on his own. The Comanche full moon would shine three more times. Then they could go after Yellow Hawk and Buck. Spring would come.

At the brush corral, Will untied the rope and swung the gate open. Two Feathers rode toward the lake and heard the cries of a calf in trouble.

"Will," he called. "Hurry. Something is wrong."

Even though he wanted to spur Gray Wolf to a gallop, Will had taught him to move up on cattle slow and easy, so they wouldn't spook and run off.

Both horses walked toward the lake. Two Feathers saw a calf down on the ice not far from the open water.

"Look."

"I see it. There's its momma." Will pointed toward a cluster of agitated cattle with one young cow at the water's edge bawling for her baby. The youngster's frantic cries and battle to stand up sent it sliding closer to the dark ice around the open water in the middle of the lake. The momma paced back and forth along the water's edge, crushing the ice along the shore. Cold black mud coated her legs to her knees, and her tail sent mud flying each time she swung it.

"I do not think you can rope the calf. It is too far out on the ice." Two Feathers' words were heavy with worry.

Will sat still on Rojo, staring at the floundering calf.

"You're right. My rope isn't long enough." He dismounted and changed into his moccasins. "The only way to get him is to go after him."

Will hung his gloves, coat, and hat on his saddle horn. "Give me your rope." He tied the loop of Two Feathers' rope around his waist and handed the rest back to his brother.

"What are you doing?" Two Feathers demanded. "You cannot go out on that ice! It is melting. You will drown."

"Calm down and be quiet. You'll spook the cattle." Will took his rope and shook out a loop. "I'm hoping the moccasins will give me better footing. When I get closer, I'll rope him. If I fall through the ice, pull me out."

"This is not a good plan, Will."

"If we don't get him, he'll push himself to the middle and fall through."

Two Feathers eased Gray Wolf forward a few steps. Sliding his feet, Will walked away from the disturbed cattle onto the ice. With each step, he tested the ice before he put his weight on it.

At roping distance, he threw his loop. To Two Feathers' surprise and relief, it settled around the calf's neck on the first throw.

The calf squalled and thrashed around, trying to get on his feet. His frenzied movements slid him even closer to the middle of the lake, pulling Will with him. Will's moccasins lost their grip on the white ice. He fell with a solid thunk.

Two Feathers heard the ice crackle and backed Gray Wolf with slow, steady steps. Will and the struggling calf slid across the ice toward the shore.

At the edge of the lake, Will scrambled onto the muddy shore. "Keep that momma off me."

Two Feathers dropped the rope and turned Gray Wolf to face the long-horned anxious momma. Keeping a worried cow from her baby was the horse's job, and Gray Wolf knew what to do. In a few minutes, the calf, on shaky legs, found her. They took off for the relative warmth of the woods.

"Come look at this."

Uneasiness in Will's voice crinkled Two Feathers forehead. "What is wrong?"

Will stood next to a fire ring burned black by the branding fires from summer and coiled his rope. He had brushed the snow away. In the ashes, held down by a small rock, was a flight feather from a hawk.

"Is it his?" asked Will.

"I do not know. It has been here a long time. But who else would leave it? The snow pushed it into the ashes."

Will tossed the rock that held it down. He picked up the feather, brushed off the ashes, and pulled it through his fingers, aligning the barbs. "You know what he's telling us, don't you?"

Two Feathers gathered broken pieces of wood and stared a fire. He ignored Will's question.

Will put on his coat and hat, then warmed his hands and feet before changing back into his socks and boots. They put out the fire and rode through the cattle, checking for any signs of sickness.

"These cattle look the best of all, Will." Two Feathers glanced at Will's stony face. He could see that the condition of their cattle wasn't on Will's mind. He watched Will smooth Yellow Hawk's feather and slip it into the inside pocket of his coat.

Two Feathers stopped Gray Wolf outside the brush corral

and waited for Will to fasten the gate. They rode toward home side by side.

"We will find Buck."

There was no answer, no change in his stiff posture.

Two Feathers pulled his horse to a stop. His tone sharpened. "Listen to me. We. . . will. . . find. . . him!"

Will's back slumped. "I can't stop thinking about what Yellow Hawk might be doing to him. Buck has never been with anyone but me. He must think I don't want him anymore."

"No matter what kind of man he is, Yellow Hawk has handled horses all his life. He knows how to treat a horse. He will not harm Buck. That would not be good and would not be accepted among the Comanche."

"Are you sure? I didn't like how Yellow Hawk treated him when he captured us at Horsehead Crossing. You remember. You were the one who rescued us."

"We got Buck away from Yellow Hawk then. But remember, Buck got away from Yellow Hawk last year and survived living alone on the Llano Estacado until he was captured by that horse trader."

"I can't help thinking about him in Yellow Hawk's hands."

"Well, would you rather Silas Porter had him?"

"No."

"Buck got over the rough treatment from that snake Porter last year when he used him for a bucking horse. Buck is strong. He will make it. He will always come to you when you whistle."

"But it's so cold. Buck is used to being in a warm barn. What if he gets sick?"

"Will, Yellow Hawk winters in Palo Duro Canyon. I am sure he took Buck there. The weather will be cold with storms, just like here. But there will be places to get out of the wind.

Do not worry. Many horses live in the canyon. Running Wolf and Weeping Woman have seen Buck before. They know he is yours. He will winter in the canyon with the rest of Yellow Hawk's herd and many Comanche horses. He will be safe."

Tired and silent, Two Feathers cast sideways glances at Will. For now, he could see at least some of Will's worries about Buck drain away. He wished he could let go of his own fears for the big horse. Where was Buck, and even if they found him, how would they ever take him back?

GET READY: WINTER 1870

The monotony of winter days wore on Two Feathers' nerves. The same chores over and over traded with long days confined to the house or the barn while the wind howled and snow fell. Two good things lightened his winter mood—there were no unshod horse tracks in all that snow, meaning no evidence of Yellow Hawk's presence, and Will's limp grew less and less. To help pass the long winter evenings, Two Feathers worked with Will to improve his Comanche. Those lessons helped pull Will out of his endless worry over Buck.

As March blew in on the wind, Two Feathers watched the clouds changing from thick gray boulders loaded with snow to billowing white hills that soared high and played hide-and-seek with the sun. The sunny days occurred more often and stayed longer, adding to the boys' eagerness to start their hunt. Two Feathers' lessons shifted from inside study to outside work on Rojo. Each day Two Feathers struggled to teach Will skills that came naturally to him but had to be taught to Will. Step by step, Will learned more of the Comanche ways.

One sunny day in late March, on their way back from checking cattle, Two Feathers stopped Gray Wolf at the mouth of a long narrow gully. Will pulled Rojo up beside him. Two Feathers explained what their lesson was going to be that day.

"You want me to do *what?*" Will stood looking up at the walls of a washed-out gully.

Two Feathers explained again. "I will lead Rojo at a gallop down this gully. You will leap off the wall and land on the horse."

Will looked up at the wall, much taller than he was. "No!"

"Yes."

"What if I miss Rojo?"

"Then you will land in the dirt. But you will not start off on Rojo. You will learn on Gray Wolf. Together we will teach Rojo."

Will bit his lip. "I've finally reached the point where I can sleep through the night without my hip jerking me awake." His gaze climbed the red wall from the rocky ground to the top, where the edge of the desert floor peeked down at him. "You want me to jump off a cliff?"

"It is not a cliff. We are in a gully."

"Can *you* do it?"

Two Feathers nodded. "Of course, I can. You've seen me do it before."

"Show me again. I'll ride Rojo. You jump onto Gray Wolf."

"Take him to the end of the gully. Start him as close to the wall as you can. When I give the signal, pop him on the rump and holler, 'Get him!'"

The brothers positioned themselves. At the signal, Will smacked Gray Wolf's hip and hollered. The horse shot down the gully, running next to the wall with Rojo and Will right behind. When Gray Wolf reached him, Two Feathers leaped off the wall. He landed on the grullo's hips but slid over the flying tail and smacked his rump on the ground.

Both horses skidded to a stop. Will caught Gray Wolf's reins and led him back to Two Feathers. He looked down at his brother sitting in the dirt with his legs sprawled and leaning back on his hands. "If that's the way a Comanche warrior does it, I don't think I want to try."

Two Feathers staggered to his feet. "I think I need to try

that again." He rubbed his behind and scrambled up the gully wall. Looking down at Will, he hollered, "Are you laughing? I better not hear one laugh from you." Not even a tiny snicker slipped from Will's lips, but his eyes roared with laughter. Will rode back to the gully entrance, leading Gray Wolf and standing in his stirrups.

By late afternoon, Two Feathers and Will limped away from the gully leading Rojo and Gray Wolf. Red dust covered all four from head to foot and hoof to head. Lagging behind Will, Two Feathers covered his grinning mouth because Will stopped every few steps to rub his backside while Rojo shook off clouds of red dust.

"You better not be laughing at me," grumbled Will.

"I am not laughing at you."

"Yes, you are."

"Well, you are a funny sight. But you and Rojo did it."

"I still don't know why I had to learn to do that."

"You never know when it might save your life. You can never know too much."

Later that night, Two Feathers awoke to see moonlight streaming in their window. The room glowed with its soft light. A nighthawk was close by. Its call sounded loud—then far away—then loud again. It was still hunting. Two Feathers slipped out of bed and sat in the shadows near the window. Maybe he would catch a glimpse of it.

The moon was bright enough for the trees along the creek to cast shadows. He watched them sweep the ground as the wind blew through the trees. He heard Will stir in his bed, then his feet hit the floor.

"Two Feathers, are you awake?" asked Will.

"Yes, I am sitting by the window. You need to speak in Comanche. You are getting better, but you still need work."

Two Feathers caught a quick movement from the corner of his eye. He turned. It was the nighthawk.

"We need to talk." Will's voice occasionally surprised Two Feathers with how deep it had become. "When Yellow Hawk shot me, where were you?"

Once again, the nighthawk sent its call into the night. Two Feathers watched it disappear into the darkness along the creek. "Gray Wolf and I were running behind you and Buck. Off to your right. There was distance between us."

"So Yellow Hawk wasn't shooting at you."

"No."

"You know he was shooting at me."

"Yes, I know."

"So, hitting Buck was an accident?"

"Yes, I told you Yellow Hawk is a master horseman. He wants Buck to raise bigger, stronger horses. But he is a bad shot."

"He knows Buck will come back to me if he's alive. So. . . that's why he wants to kill me."

"Yes, Will." Two Feathers took a deep breath. "We have known that for a while."

"But I don't understand why he wants to kill you?"

"That I do NOT know. I am not even sure Yellow Hawk is trying to kill me. He has had too many chances that have failed."

"Maybe now that he has Buck, he'll leave us alone. Maybe he thinks we won't come after him."

"No, he knows we will come." Two Feathers' voice shrank to nearly a whisper. "He will be waiting." The bed creaked as Will got up and joined him at the window.

They sat for a while in silence.

"I love Buck," Will whispered.

"I know."

"He's as important to me as Pa was."

Two Feathers sat still. *I wish Pa was here. He would know how to find Buck. He would know what to do.*

"Sometimes Buck knows what I want him to do before I even know. We think alike."

Letting Will talk about Buck was the best way Two Feathers could help him. So, he listened.

"When Yellow Hawk captured me, Buck fought him when he beat me. I'd never seen him so mad." Will rested his head on the deep adobe windowsill. "He's my brother."

"I know."

"Do you think we can find him? Can we get him back?" Again, Will's voice slipped into a whisper.

Will's pain sank into Two Feathers and became his pain as well. Two Feathers knew if he hadn't wanted Buck so much, if he hadn't told Yellow Hawk about the big buckskin, if he hadn't followed the dunnia on the cattle drive, Yellow Hawk wouldn't have captured Will and Buck three years ago. If—if—the ifs piled up inside him, stirring his anger and resentment toward Yellow Hawk until he thought he would be sick.

Two Feathers grabbed Will and pulled him from the windowsill. "I promise we will not stop until we find him. I do not care how long it takes or how far we have to go. I will find Buck." Two Feathers could faintly see his brother's face in the darkness. "Do you believe I can find him? Do you trust me?"

A smile broke through the fear and worry on Will's face. "I trust you." He returned to his bed and turned his face to the wall.

Clouds smothered the light from the moon. The shadows disappeared into the darkness. Two Feathers lifted the carbine he held in his lap and rested the barrel in the window.

At first light, he headed into the kitchen to start the fire and make coffee. Jake and Tony came up from their room next to the barn. Two Feathers waited on Will to make the biscuits. No matter how hard he tried, he couldn't make them as good as Will's.

When nothing was left on the table but crumbs and coffee cups, Jake and Tony left to start their chores.

Two Feathers asked Will to stay and talk. He filled their cups and sat down. "The growing season is here. The worst of the winter storms are over. It will soon be time for us to go to the canyon and get Buck."

"I think it's past time." Will's tone carried a sense of urgency.

"Here are some things we must do first. We need to take Rojo's horseshoes off so his hooves will toughen. I do not want to leave shoed tracks behind us. We need to hunt and jerk meat. We traveled like white men to Las Vegas, Fort Union, and even Palo Duro Canyon with an extra horse to carry our supplies. Now we need to travel like the Comanche. You will take only what you and Rojo can carry."

Two Feathers waited for Will's answer, but he just sat there staring out the window and sipped his coffee. He took another sip, then a third. "Did you hear me, Will?" Two Feathers prodded. "It's time to go after Buck!"

"Yes, I heard you. But I'm wondering about something." He took a sip.

"What?"

"Why'd we do all this? Yellow Hawk knows I'm not Comanche."

"We will search for Buck on the Llano Estacado and Palo Duro Canyon. That is the stronghold of the Comanche. We could start today making camp every night and never see anyone. But that does not mean we would not be seen. Who do you think is out there?"

"Yellow Hawk."

"Who else?"

"Running Wolf's band could leave the canyon and be out there."

"Yes, they will do that. Who else?"

"Maybe other Comanche bands. And. . . " His words faded away.

"There are many Comanche that do not know us. Seeing boot tracks of the white man and his shod horses would bring them straight to us. Also, the Kiowa, maybe the Apache, and sometimes the Cheyenne come down from the North. There are the Comancheros, and what about white men like Badger? Remember him? Do you want someone like him following your trail? He even tracked you to Santa Fe and tried to kill you. We would not be talking now if Captain Stanaway had not saved you."

Will pulled a lock of his hair from behind his ear. Two Feathers watched him twist it around and through his fingers. When had he started doing that? Then it came to him—it started after Will learned Buck was gone and his hair had grown long and curly. He'd begun this habit in the evenings when he isolated himself in the living room and agonized over losing Buck. Two Feathers continued to wait. He knew not to push Will when he had to make a hard decision.

Will let go of his hair and stood. "Okay, I see your point. But understand one thing—Rojo's a good horse. He will learn to be a Comanche horse. But. . . when we get Buck back. . . he and I will be the best Comanche on the Llano Estacado."

Two Feathers sighed in relief and grinned. "We will be the best."

With their decision made, the weeks passed in a whirlwind of activity. Will now showed a dogged determination. Two Feathers could barely keep up with him. They hunted, then jerked the meat and tanned the hides, which provided several pairs of thigh-high moccasins, shirts, breechcloths, pants, and pouches for their supplies.

At first light on a fresh April morning, they finished packing. Two Feathers tied off the last pouches of hardtack and corn dodgers Will had made the day before. Will kept going back in the house to get one more thing he might need and push it into the already stuffed bags.

Finally, the boys mounted at least an hour after they intended to leave. With Jake standing beside him, Tony stopped them with a hand on Two Feathers' leg. "Be careful. I know you've been to Palo Duro Canyon before and made it back. But this time is different. You're riding after a man who's tried to kill you and Will."

"I know."

"Two Feathers..." Tony's gaze pleaded with Two Feathers. "Come back with Will. A few weeks of learning Comanche ways won't make him one. Bring him home."

Two Feathers nodded, his throat too tight to speak.

Will's words came out a little hoarse. "Take care of things here. I don't know when we will be back."

Soberly, they shook hands all around. Then, with strained faces, Tony and Jake stepped back.

With a tap of Two Feathers' heels, Gray Wolf headed out of the ranch yard and across the creek. Will followed on Rojo. Neither spoke. The sense of adventure Two Feathers often felt when starting on a trip was missing. Instead, he was filled with questions and worries—how would he do this? To protect Will, he had to make him think like a Comanche. What if he hadn't taught Will enough of the Comanche way? What if Will was wounded again. . . or Gray Wolf. . . or Rojo. . . or himself? What if Yellow Hawk found them first? The what ifs swirled around in his head again, making him dizzy.

As if guessing his thoughts, Will rode up beside him with his I-can-lick-the-world attitude. When Will decided to do something, he didn't quit until it was done. He popped Two Feathers on the leg. "Hey, brother, we can do this. I've been to a Comanche camp before and survived. I can do it again."

Two Feathers rolled his eyes.

They crossed the Pecos and rode past the campsite where Curtis had bedded Goodnight's cattle on their drive north to Colorado. Two Feathers' gaze swept over the area where Yellow Hawk had attacked, taking away his adventurous mood. His face was troubled.

"Will, are you sure you want to do this? Are you sure you want to go to Palo Duro Canyon? It is not too late to change our minds."

"I have no choice. Buck's there so, I'm going."

Two Feathers stiffened his own resolve. "Sooner or later, we will find him."

Before nightfall, they stopped their horses some distance from a much-used campsite Two Feathers had found while on his vision quest the year before. Will stayed with the horses while Two Feathers scouted the area to be sure the site wasn't in use. Fresh tracks of a large jackrabbit covered by those of a coyote dotted the reddish sandy ground around the blackened rocks of a fire ring. Two Feathers wondered if the coyote had enjoyed rabbit for dinner.

In the jumble of rocks above the campsite, he found something else he'd located the year before. The three stone-lined basins built by long-dead warriors were full of run-off water from the rocks above. Several bees lined the muddy edge of the basins. He let them drink their fill before shooing them away, remembering how their presence had shown him this watering hole and saved his life. He drank the cold clear goodness.

A low bird call told Will to bring in the horses. "Will, the basins are full. I will water the horses while you cook." The horses clamored up the rocks behind Two Feathers.

"Cook? What am I supposed to cook? We're on starvation rations."

Two Feathers' laughter trickled like water down through the rocks. "You will figure it out."

After the horses drank, Two Feathers brought them down from the rocks and hobbled them. Will's look questioned why. "I spotted horse tracks up there but no shoed prints. Wild horses watered here not long ago. I do not want Gray Wolf and Rojo running off."

Will gave him a handful of corn dodgers and a cup of broth loaded with chunks of softened jerky. "Here, enjoy. When we get home, I'll find something to make a pie out of and eat the whole thing myself."

"You are not going to share?"

"No, I don't think I will." He grinned at Two Feathers. "Not bringing a packhorse loaded with supplies was your idea, not mine."

At dusk, Two Feathers sniffed the wind and studied the low-hanging dark cloud bank moving slowly in their direction. "I think we will be wet before morning. I spotted a washed-out place under the rock ledge near the first catch basin. It should keep us dry if the rain is not too hard."

"We can take turns sleeping. You have first watch." Will tossed a big grin over his shoulder and climbed into the small cut-out space.

Two Feathers sat by the dying coals in the fire ring. He thought about the last time he was in this place. With a stick, he poked under the bush where he'd found an unexpected can of beans. Maybe he would find another. How good they'd tasted after four days with no food or water. But, this time, he had no luck. He grinned—no luck and no beans. His stomach growled. Maybe he shouldn't have been so strict and let Will bring something tastier than jerky and corn dodgers.

With the clouds covering the moon, it was hard to gage the passage of time. He jerked awake and realized he had dozed off. A quick glance toward Gray Wolf and Rojo, both sleeping standing up, assured him all was well. A fat cold raindrop landed on the side of his forehead and trickled down his cheek. Then another hit him. . . and another. He wrapped the firewood he'd collected in his blanket, then crawled into the cut-out with the sleeping Will. He fit by pulling his legs against his chest and shoving the firewood behind him. The slow rainfall sped up as the hours passed.

First light found Two Feathers lying on Will's warm, dry blanket under the cut-out listening to Will move around while warming up their jerky soup. The rain had stopped, leaving the air fresh and clean.

Will called to him. "Are you going to stay in bed all day? The sun's coming up. And I need my coffee you wouldn't let me bring."

By afternoon, they reached the mesa where Two Feathers had waited for his puha during his vision quest. On the fourth day of his ordeal, his spirit animal, a red-tailed hawk, fought with an eagle over a rabbit it had killed. In the fight, the hawk dropped it for him to eat. He hoped the hawk would come to him today as a sign that he was doing the right thing in bringing Will.

After scouting the mesa's base for a trail the horses could follow, Two Feathers reached the top with Will and Rojo right behind him. The mesa was smaller than Two Feathers remembered. Its walls were red and scarred with ridges and gashes from centuries of storms and wind. The top was covered with red dirt and scattered clusters of juniper trees whose wind-twisted branches looked like the arms of the elderly reaching toward the sun. Two Feathers set up camp in a cluster of scrub cedar and juniper trees. Will built a small fire so the tree's branches would scatter the smoke enough to not be seen.

After another meal of jerky and corn dodgers, they sat back from the mesa's edge and watched the last trace of pink and yellow fade from the clouds the wind pushed toward them. Will pulled his knees up to his chest and wrapped his arms around them. "The wind has picked up. I'm going back to the fire."

"Wait, look over there." Two Feathers stretched his arm toward the Northeast.

"What?"

"I saw a speck of light."

Will squinted. "I don't see anything. Maybe it was a star."

"No, Will. It was on the ground. Like a campfire."

"I don't see it."

Two Feathers followed Will back to their fire. "It is gone. But think about what that means—someone is out there."

QUANAH

Two Feathers stood under the juniper tree facing east and watched the sun pull itself off the horizon. He smoothed the tangles out of his hair, parted it, and pulled one side slick against his head. While his fingers worked the tight braid, he spotted a hawk flight feather dangling from the tip of a juniper branch and another on the ground. It must have been quite a scramble for the bird to lose two big feathers. He picked them up and gently pulled them through his fingers, first one, then the other. They were perfect—neither broken nor bent nor tattered.

He stepped to the mesa's edge and let the wind, colder today than yesterday, sweep his loose hair away from his face. "Thank you, red-tailed hawk, my puha, for the gift of your feathers. Thank you for this place. You led me into manhood here. I come to you, puha, asking you to take us to Buck. I ask your blessing on our search. I ask for your protection and your guidance." He shaded his eyes from the sun's glare and searched the sky, but it was empty.

When he returned to camp, Will had everything packed and the horses ready.

"You found new feathers." He handed Two Feathers Gray Wolf's reins. "They're longer. I'm glad you found new ones. The others were getting a little worn looking."

Two Feathers tied the feathers in his braids and followed

Will and Rojo off the mesa. They headed northeast in the direction of the brief flicker of light he'd spotted the night before. The wind had shifted overnight and now blew from the north. Two Feathers kept it blowing against his left shoulder to maintain their northeasterly direction. He hoped the wind wouldn't wipe out any tracks from whoever had built that fire. Were they friends or enemies? He wanted that answer before he caught up with them.

The long day riding into the cold wind with few stops and skimpy meals wearied boys and horses alike. Late in the afternoon, they started looking for a place to camp. They followed a faint trail hoping it would bring them to water. As they rode, the sparse scattering of tall, white clouds with lead-gray bottoms grew thicker as the day advanced until the sky was the color of gray bullets.

Will tapped his heels on Rojo's flank and caught up beside Two Feathers. "Do you know where we are?"

"We are on the Staked Plains."

Will rubbed his red ears. "Okay, but where? How close are we to the Canyon?"

"I have no idea."

Will's head dropped so fast his chin bounced off his chest. He rode that way for several minutes, then lifted his head just enough to cock it sideways at his brother. His eyes made Two Feathers think of a prairie dog easing his head out of his hole so his eyes could investigate something suspicious.

"Will, that is why I made you work so hard making all that jerky and corn dodgers. I did not know how long we would be out here."

Will's chin flopped back down on his chest. He said nothing else.

The trail rounded a knoll and led them up a low swell toward an old juniper tree. A Comanche warrior, a few years older than Two Feathers, leaned against the twisted trunk. Startled, Two Feathers stopped Gray Wolf. Will stopped Rojo a little behind him. Two Feathers eased Gray Wolf toward the man. The warrior, like Two Feathers, was considerably taller than most Comanche. Strength showed in his muscled arms and legs. It showed in the way he stood, like a stout oak. His face held dignity and confidence. He stared at them with gray eyes that missed nothing.

"I am Two Feathers. This is my brother, Tall Horse. We seek shelter from the cold and water for our horses."

The man stepped away from the tree and moved toward them with a mountain lion's smooth, gliding step. Two Feathers felt the weight of his gaze as those eyes, so much like his own, studied every inch of him and then shifted to Will. Two Feathers held his breath, hoping Will would stay steady and not waver. Will sat straight on Rojo, held the horse still, and matched the warrior's stern gaze. But Two Feathers wasn't sure he was breathing.

The tiniest of smiles flicked across the warrior's mouth. He motioned them to follow him down the hill into a large round buffalo wallow that slanted toward a tumble of large rocks. A good-sized pool of water had collected there. With the knoll acting as a windbreak, the camp was sheltered. Two Feathers welcomed the relief from the constant wind. Four warriors sat near a small fire that gave off almost no smoke. They watched as he and Will stripped their weary horses' supplies and saddles.

Will leaned close to Two Feathers. "Who is that?" His whisper came out in a gush. "I've never seen such a big and scary Comanche. He'd make two of Yellow Hawk. And those men—they know I am not Comanche."

"I believe that is Quanah of the Quahadi Comanche. I've never met him, but I've heard about him."

"Did you know he would be here?"

Two Feathers' head swung in a slow arch toward Will. "What? How would I know that? I followed a game trail hoping it would lead us to water."

Will shuddered. The horses followed them to the pool, with Quanah and the four warriors watching every move they made. Their stares stretched the few minutes it took the horses to drink into what seemed like forever.

After hobbling the horses, Two Feathers and Will settled around the fire. Quanah offered the boys some of the rabbit simmering in a small beat-up pot that had seen many fires. Two Feathers added some jerky to their concoction. Will handed the Comanche sitting nearest him a handful of hardtack from their pack. The night was quiet. None of the four Comanche men spoke. Quanah slipped away into the dark. Soon, the warriors rolled into their blankets.

Two Feathers stayed with Will after he stretched out and was relieved when he heard his brother's slow, even breathing. He slipped away from the fire and found Quanah, where his shadow blended into the darkness under a slight overhang. Sitting beside him, he looked out over the vast expanse of the Comancheria in silence.

A feeling of loss came over Two Feathers. A heavy sadness he couldn't explain settled over him. "Quanah? What is going to happen to the Comanche and to me?"

In the darkness, he felt rather than saw the young Quanah turn to him and study him for a long time. But he didn't answer.

Two Feathers dropped his voice to barely above a whisper. He knew sound carried a long way. There'd been enough surprises for one night.

"I have seen the Navajo at Fort Sumner. I have seen the life go out of their eyes. I have seen them defeated by the white man. The soldiers brought them to the reservation, but white men far away crushed them when the promised food never came. The water was bad. They farmed, but the crops would not grow. Their spirits cursed the land. They could not live in that place, so many of them died. Will that happen to the Comanche?"

For a long time, the tall Comanche said nothing, and Two Feathers decided he wasn't going to answer. When Quanah did speak, Two Feathers was surprised at his words.

"I have heard of you. You are half Comanche and half white as I am. I have heard you left the Comanche to live with the whites."

"My uncle, Yellow Hawk, killed my white father. Soldiers killed my mother. Weeping Woman, my aunt, is all I have left. My uncle is my enemy and wants me dead. He has tried many times to kill me. His aim is not good." Two Feathers heard a muffled chuckle from the tall warrior.

A lone star found a break in the clouds and shone its tiny light through the darkness. All it did was make Two Feathers feel more lost in the emptiness around him.

"I live with the whites to learn of my father's people. I found family here—a second father. But Yellow Hawk also killed him, leaving me with no man to teach me. Here, I have a brother, so I am not alone. But I have not left the Comanche. In my heart, I will always be Comanche."

Silence settled around them again. Two Feathers waited on the older man to speak.

"My family also was killed. My brother and I were left alone." Quanah's voice was gentle. "That is a frightening thing."

A bird chirped out its sharp cry as though startled from

sleep. Both listened for other sounds in the night but heard only the soft swoosh of the wind.

"Two Feathers, only you can decide the path your life will take. Choose what you think is best. The clash between you and Yellow Hawk is within your family. I cannot tell you how to live or what to do with your uncle. That is to be settled by family."

"I know of Yellow Hawk." Quanah's voice hardened. "And his claim on the dunnia of your white brother. Yellow Hawk is a good warrior, a fierce fighter who wins many battles. A warrior the Comanche need in our war with the soldiers. But he changed. He left his band and his family. His people refused him as chief. Now, he rides alone. Many people fear him. Both Comanche and Kiowa have felt the pains of death at his hands. He takes what is not his to take. His desire for the dunnia of the white boy has twisted his mind. He captured the horse many times, but the spirits told him the horse was not for him. Each time the horse gets away and returns to your brother. The Comanche have heard of this. Yellow Hawk has become feared by all the people."

A measure of relief passed over Two Feathers like a fresh breeze. Finally, someone understood his difficulties. Just sitting beside the tall Comanche gave him a feeling of power. He took a deep breath and hoped he would have enough courage to face the days ahead.

Quanah stood. "It is late. We need sleep. We will let our horses guard the night."

Two Feathers followed the man toward the bed of coals that remained from the fire. He welcomed the warmth of his blanket.

Quanah's low words brushed over him on a wisp of smoke from the darkness. "How you deal with Yellow Hawk will shape the warrior you will become. Will you run, or will you fight?" The big man stepped away from Two Feathers and faded into the darkness.

Two Feathers didn't think he would sleep because his mind was full of Quanah's words. But his body was weary, pulling him into the nothingness of sleep. A stick snapped. Two Feathers' eyes opened, but he didn't move. Listening, he heard Will's soft snoring. He sat up on one elbow. In the dim light of early morning, the warriors were packing camp and loading supplies on their horses. Two Feathers leaped to his feet. Quanah smiled at him.

"Are you leaving?" asked Two Feathers.

When the man didn't answer, Two Feathers nudged Will with his foot. "Get up. Quanah is leaving." Will scrambled up, and they rolled their bedding.

Quanah left the boys and took his horse to the pool. Two Feathers and Will removed Gray Wolf's and Rojo's hobbles and followed him. The tall Comanche stood beside Will while their horses drank.

"I have seen the dunnia. A stallion fit for a chief."

Will smiled at him. "That is what Two Feathers tells me. When did you see him?" His excitement made him switch to English. "Where was he?"

Two Feathers squeezed his arm. "Slow down. You need to speak Comanche." Two Feathers felt pride that Will was learning the Comanche language so well.

Quanah studied Will for a quick moment. "Yellow Hawk had him in Palo Duro Canyon before winter set in."

The grin on Will's face lightened some of Two Feathers' worries. But the smile faded as Quanah continued.

"Yellow Hawk will never let you have him. There are other good horses. You should let this one go and find another."

Two Feathers jerked his head to see Will's reaction. He was ready to jump on Will if he exploded at Quanah.

Will didn't move. He stood there while Rojo drank. His gaze traveled up to the tall man's eyes and stopped there. "I'll die first."

The hard gray eyes softened, and the older man squeezed his shoulder. "You will make a strong warrior."

Nearly a week of riding daylight to dusk, of Will's constant asking where they were, and of his own fears of running out of water made Two Feathers' head ache. The worry of not knowing where Yellow Hawk was made the muscles in his back feel like ropes pulled tight enough to hum in the wind. By the end of the week, he was tired, thirsty, hungry, and covered with grit that itched and made his skin raw.

Remembering Quanah's words lifted his spirits. Knowing someone besides Will and himself who suffered from the loss of family and growing up without parents melted away some of the emptiness inside him. He wished he could have talked with Quanah again. Instead, on the last morning in camp, Two Feathers had stood alone at the spot where they had shared their stories the night before. He had watched Quanah ride south, scouting for campsites farther from the whites.

The days slipped behind them, and the land slowly changed. The flat desert floor became more broken. Two Feathers found a trail winding through shallow rocky gullies and ravines with ragged, orange walls spotted with scrub trees. The trail deepened the farther north they traveled.

They had made it to canyon country. Who would they find first—Buck, Yellow Hawk, or neither?

WHERE'S BUCK?

The trail led to the rim of Palo Duro Canyon. The vast abyss spread before them as far as they could see with its tall red and white striped walls, flat-topped mesas, and deep green valleys. Two Feathers searched for a way to the bottom and the sweet water that flowed there.

But before he found a trail, the sun disappeared behind the far canyon rim pulling darkness behind it. Slipping off Gray Wolf, Two Feathers watched the shadows in the canyon stretch long until the fading light erased every trace of them.

"Well," said Will. "You did it. You found the canyon without getting lost. Are we going to find a way down tonight?" Rojo shied away from the dark hole before them. Will rubbed his neck and cooed soothing sounds to quiet the nervous horse.

Two Feathers rolled his eyes. "Do you think that is a good idea?"

"Kee! No." Will answered in Comanche. "I do not."

Backing away from the rim, Two Feathers found a secluded campsite in a cluster of boulders with a clear center area of loose sand trapped there in some past storm. They brushed the horses with some tufts of grass they found. Then poured what little water they had onto their bandanas and wiped out their horses' mouths, saving enough for each of them to have a couple of sips. Two Feathers and Will shared hardtack and corn dodgers and the last of the jerky.

Will flipped his blanket to unroll it and spread it on the soft sand. "Tonight, I'll dream of tall golden biscuits and hot black coffee."

The last swallow of water didn't carry the bite of hardtack down Two Feathers' dry throat. He worked up enough spit to make it go down. "You know what I want?"

"What?"

"Bacon. Lots and lots of bacon stuffed in a handful of your biscuits."

Will huffed and settled under his blanket. "Go to sleep, Two Feathers, and dream about biscuits. That's as close as you'll get to one out here."

The following morning, they rode the rim for several miles before they found a wide trail that took them down to the river along a more gradual decline than their last time at the canyon. The trail was covered with animal tracks going to and from the rim. None were fresh. The river ran full, turning the water a muddy red from the sand it picked up.

"Two Feathers, maybe we can find a stream with clearer water. I'm not thirsty enough to drink *that*." Will jerked his thumb sideways toward the red river. Rojo and Gray Wolf didn't seem to care what color the water was. They drank their fill.

Two Feathers' thirst made the muddy water look better and better the longer they rode. After riding a few miles, the canyon walls opened, widening the floor. Off to their right, Will pointed out a cluster of scrub trees mixed with willows that veered off from the river. In its midst, Two Feathers found a trickle of water that tumbled off the canyon wall and over a series of sandstone slabs to the canyon floor. The clear, sweet water rippled as it made its way to the river. Small pools formed in the low places. From the wide bands of damp sand around each pool, Two Feathers figured they would dry up soon. He bellied down next to Will on the rocky sand and drank his fill. When they stood, Gray Wolf and Rojo lifted their heads and stepped back from the pool. Droplets of water rained from their muzzles. Both boys filled their water pouches.

"I don't know about you, Two Feathers, but I'm about done in. I want to find Buck as soon as possible, but we're tired. So are Gray Wolf and Rojo. Let's make camp."

Two Feathers scanned the area and decided it was as safe a place to rest as anywhere else. "There is a deadfall for fuel and trees for cover. We can camp here for today. You find grass for Gray Wolf and Rojo. I will hunt for food."

Later that night, Two Feathers awoke but stayed still. The sky was black, with clouds covering the moon. Not even a star offered its weak light. The noise of the water trickling down the stream made him listen more closely. The remaining meat from the turkey he'd killed hung safely in a pouch away from predators. Maybe a fox trying to get the meat had awakened him.

He settled deeper into his blanket, but sleep wouldn't come. The fact that Yellow Hawk hadn't attacked them surprised him. The man must know they would head for the canyon. Two Feathers decided he should be relieved, but he wasn't.

The wind blew from upriver. He heard it rustle through the trees. He could barely see the movement of the willow branches as the clouds scudded across the sky, admitting only small patches of light.

He heard a splash—then another—and another. Gray Wolf and Rojo lifted their heads, their ears pricked forward. Leaving Will to keep the horses quiet, Two Feathers made his way out of camp and down to the river. Staying behind the rocks and boulders, he moved far enough upriver to get a clear view. Or as clear as the clouds would permit.

Horses—mustangs—walked to the water's edge and drank.

Two Feathers heard the soft splashes of their steps more than saw them. Moving shapes, darker than the night around them, milled along the river's edge, fading in and out of the black night like spirits in a dream. Even though he knew what they were, the sight made him shiver. He caught his breath and watched for a while. Not able to see anything definite, he slipped back to camp where he found Will waiting.

"It was a herd of mustangs coming to drink," Two Feathers said. "I could not see them, only shadows."

"Do you think Buck was with them? The wind's coming from upriver, so there'd be no scent to catch. He wouldn't know I'm here."

"I do not know. I did not see anything that looked like Buck. It was too dark. We will check the tracks in the morning."

By daylight, Two Feathers and Will studied the ground along the riverbank, finding old tracks from the many past trips to water and new ones from last night.

"Can you find anything that tells us about Buck?" Will stepped away from the water's edge and moved farther from the river. Two Feathers didn't answer.

Will leaned closer to the ground. "Two Feathers, come see this."

"First, come see what I found." Two Feathers stood and waited for Will.

Two Feathers pointed to a track in the sand—a hoof print that showed a broken piece of a horseshoe was attached to the hoof.

Will looked up at Two Feathers. "That's the same track I saw." A smile spread over his face and spilled out into his voice. "It has to be Buck. None of the other tracks showed a shod hoof."

Jumping to his feet, he grabbed Two Feathers by the shoulders and shook him. "He's alive! Yellow Hawk didn't kill him.

He got away again. He's alive." In his excitement, he slipped back into English.

"Wait a minute, Will." The caution in Two Feathers' voice slowed Will's celebration. "We need to think about this. Just because we found a print of a shod horse does not mean it is Buck. The Comanche take many horses from the whites. It could be one of them."

Will stood with his hands on his hips. "You're right." He heaved a big breath. "Okay. . . you're right." Will followed Two Feathers back to camp.

After a breakfast of hardtack with turkey left from the night before, Will sat across from Two Feathers, sipping a cup of water. "I'm sure Buck's here. Even if that track isn't his, he can get away from Yellow Hawk. He's done it before."

"I think you are right," said Two Feathers. "I do not think that track is his. But, if he got loose, Yellow Hawk would hunt him."

Will's gaze turned toward the river. "The tracks weren't clear, and I'm not sure they were big enough."

"I thought about that." Two Feathers gaze followed Will's to the river. "The track you found was not as fresh as the one I found, so they were not made at the same time."

Will's face sagged. "That means we still don't know if Yellow Hawk has Buck or if he has escaped."

"No, we do not." Two Feathers sat still for a while and let Will think. "Remember, Will, those tracks mean that wild horses travel through here often. There is more than one herd."

Will nodded, hope shining from his eyes again. "We know he's here because Quanah told me he saw him." Will shook out his bedroll, rolled it, and stuck it under his arm. "Let's go find him."

After mounting Rojo, Will turned to Two Feathers. "We'll

split up. I'll go upriver, and you go downriver. We'll meet back here tonight."

Still standing on the ground, Two Feathers looked up at Will. "You are the one that made the rule to never go anywhere alone. You refused to break it when we went to Fort Union. Why break it now?"

"We can cover more ground if we separate. Maybe we'll find Buck quicker."

"That is possible, but are you sure you want to do this? We do not know where Yellow Hawk is. I do not like this plan." Two Feathers' words bounced off Will's stiff stubbornness like arrows from a shield. He spoke louder and with more force. "Searching alone is too dangerous. This is not good."

Will's words raced from his mouth as if Two Feathers had never spoken. "I don't think Buck's with Yellow Hawk anymore. I know how Buck thinks. I know what he'll do. Yellow Hawk can't hold him."

Even though Will was calm and sure of himself as he rode off, Two Feathers wasn't. He watched Will until he disappeared, his worries in a whirl and his anger swelling. *When will he ever learn to listen? He forgets everything sensible when Buck is in danger.*

"Will. Do not leave. Wait!" He watched him go. He grabbed every fist-sized rock within reach and slammed them into the river, stopping only when he could not find any more. IF the mustangs had turned upriver and IF there had been any tracks to lead them to Buck, Will had ruined them. Two Feathers' anger seeped out into the water puddled at his feet. Staring at the empty canyon wouldn't bring Will back or find Buck. If Will wanted to split up, he'd no choice but to let him go. But he didn't like it, not one bit.

Two Feathers finished packing their camp, rolled the pouch with the leftover turkey into his bedroll, and headed downriver. The shallow muddy water flowed at a good pace and had long since washed away any tracks the mustangs had left in the riverbed.

After three hours of riding, Two Feathers came to a flat meadow of about fifty acres that spread away from the river on the far side. He crossed over. In the abundant grass, he found old horse droppings and fresh ones. He found an area where horses had rolled in the grass to scratch away any elusive itch. He rode through the meadow studying the tracks but saw none that could've been Buck's. Mustangs were smaller than Buck and left a smaller hoof print. Twice he found the track with the broken bit of horseshoe. Like the others, it was too small to be Buck's.

Convinced Buck wasn't with this band of mustangs and worried about Will, he continued downriver. Maybe he would find more tracks. He crossed back over the river at the far end of the meadow. After an hour, a mesa rising to a height almost reaching the canyon rim blocked his progress. Rusty red walls rose from the water's edge in jagged columns. Horizontal bands of white rock, like painted stripes, showed near the top. At the mesa's base, where it curved away from the river, stood a good-sized grove of cottonwood trees with sumac and willows that hugged the fractured wall.

Turning away from the river, he found a game trail show-ing mustang tracks in the sand from the river's edge through the trees. He lost them in the jumble of red boulders and slabs of yellow sandstone tumbled in heaps as though some giant whirling storm had hurled them off the mesa top.

Two Feathers shaded his eyes with his hand and searched higher up for a glimpse of the trail. Although he couldn't see it, he thought it must be there. But the sun told him it was time to return. He headed Gray Wolf back upriver, knowing Will would worry if he returned and didn't find him in camp.

Their campsite was as he'd left it that morning. The sun was low. Streaks of light pink and yellow clouds stretched across the western sky. In the time it took to water and stake Gray Wolf on some grass and slice off a chunk of turkey breast, he began to worry about Will. He reassured himself that Will couldn't get lost. All he had to do was follow the river back to camp.

Two Feathers watched the color in the sky spread and reach across the horizon. He waited with increasing concern while it faded away.

Where's Will?

Searching

Throughout the night, when Will failed to return to camp, Two Feathers' worries alternated with guilt at letting his brother go off alone. He lay on his bedroll, staring at the high canyon walls as the clouds drifted past the moon. Its light faded in and out as if chasing but never catching the shadows that appeared and disappeared throughout the endless hours. Finally, his frustration gave way to exhaustion. Two Feathers slept during the few remaining hours of darkness before the first hint of morning found him saddled and heading upriver.

Rojo's tracks from his trimmed hooves on top of the mustangs' ragged ones were easy to follow. Two Feathers moved at a steady pace all morning.

By early afternoon, after munching on the turkey, he moved at a more cautious pace. The last thing he wanted to do was stumble into Yellow Hawk's camp.

The canyon narrowed, and the scrub trees became thicker. Two Feathers stayed in the water to hide his tracks. When rocks were available, he dismounted and searched away from the river, leaving nothing behind for Yellow Hawk to find. He approached each curve, each grove of cottonwoods, and every cluster of short willows as though they held danger.

A small trickle of water seeped through the underbrush and blended with the flat red sandy bank at the river's edge. The sand was smudged. Two Feathers slipped off Gray Wolf and staked him in a small clearing to graze. He took his carbine and followed the trickle a good distance, stopping often to listen. The faint sound of water rolling over the rocks in the tiny stream was all he heard. No flutter of birds in the trees. No rustle of small animals in the brush. No wind whispering through the treetops. It was too quiet. He lowered himself to the ground, lay still, and listened harder.

The ground ahead of him was sprinkled with twigs, dead leaves, and small stones. Two Feathers pushed himself to his feet and stepped on a flat rock in the stream. Planning the placement of each step, he moved forward, making no sound. A slight breeze brushed his face. He sniffed. A skunk had passed during the night. The small creek slid around a sand-filled tangle of tree roots draped over a low embankment. He eased around the obstruction to see into the clearing. What he saw tied to a tree at the edge of a clearing stopped him cold. He held his breath until the shock passed. It was Will. Two Feathers searched the deepest shadows for Yellow Hawk but saw no hint of the man.

Two Feathers eased himself back behind the embankment and studied the terrain between him and Will. He spotted a series of willow trees whose draping branches provided cover to the outer branches of the large oak tree where Will was tied. Two Feathers slowly worked through the willows, stopping in the underbrush beneath the thick oak branches. He watched Will, hoping for some sign of life. He was battered, beaten, bruised. His head hung over. Dried blood caked what he could see of Will's face.

There was no evidence Buck had been here—and no evidence of Yellow Hawk, except for Will's wounds. He inched forward out from the underbrush.

He stopped. "Will." His call was faint. He didn't know if Will could hear him and hoped Yellow Hawk couldn't. "Will."

Will's head swung from side to side the tiniest bit. Fresh blood streaked his face.

Two Feathers flattened himself even more into the dirt. Will was alive! The relief almost overwhelmed him. He rested his head in the crook of his elbow, took a full breath, and eased it out through his mouth. He lifted his head enough to see his brother.

Will's head was up. For a tiny second, with the one eye that wasn't swollen shut, he made eye contact but didn't beckon Two Feathers to come. His head continued its slow upward movement and stopped. Two Feathers waited. Was Yellow Hawk waiting for him to rush to Will? He knew Will wanted him to stay away. Why?

Will's eyes stayed focused on the branches high over his head.

Two Feathers gripped his carbine and rolled over. The tip of an animal's long tail twitched. A pair of greenish-yellow eyes stared down at him over a gaping mouth showing sharp fangs.

A mountain lion, muscles rolling under the tawny hide, rose from a stout branch of the oak tree. He launched himself with a low rumbling growl that instantly froze Two Feathers to the ground. An arrow hissed overhead and pierced the cat's neck, choking off its growl. Two Feathers rolled. The lion slammed into the ground where he'd lain. Writhing and spewing blood from its neck, it struck at the arrow in its throat.

Two Feathers swung the carbine and aimed at. . . nothing. He waited.

Yellow Hawk stepped from behind a juniper's weathered, contorted trunk. The Comanche raised his bow in his clenched fist and pointed the tip at Two Feathers. His eyes held Two Feathers' in their steely grip. The bow dropped, and he nodded.

Two Feathers' fingers locked on the trigger. But he couldn't pull it. He heard Yellow Hawk running through the undergrowth.

A low gurgle pulled his attention back to the lion. It was dead. Yellow Hawk's arrow had ripped through the animal, spilling a puddle of blood under it. He hurried to untie Will. "Did you see Buck? How did Yellow Hawk find you?"

Will studied Two Feathers' face. "What just happened? Did Yellow Hawk save your life?"

Two Feathers removed the ropes and helped Will to his feet.

"We need to wash this blood off. I do not like you being cougar bait."

"He didn't intend me for cougar bait. I was Buck bait."

With Will leaning heavily on his shoulders, Two Feathers walked him down to the river and cleaned his wounds.

"He beat you pretty good, Will." A catch in Two Feathers' throat made him cough. "What happened?"

"He wanted me to whistle for Buck, but I refused. Each time we stopped, he tried to make me whistle. When I didn't, he'd hit me again. I got in several pretty good licks, but that man's all muscle and outweighs me by about fifty pounds. I didn't do much damage."

Two Feathers left Will resting beside the river and collected fuel for a small fire. He stayed away long enough for his anger to ease off. Every time he looked at Will, tears wet his eyes. He wiped them away when cutting small strips of bark from a willow tree whose draping branches hid him from Will's view. While warming some water in a cup, he dropped in the bark and brewed willow tea. The bitter taste puckered Will's face. After one sip, he refused to drink anymore.

"If you do not drink this, I will have Gray Wolf trot back to camp. Do you want your sore ribs bouncing around for the next few hours?"

Will sat on the riverbank holding a poultice of cold, wet leaves and mud on his swollen eye. He glared at his brother with the other. "Are you sure you aren't trying to poison me?" he retorted in Comanche.

"If you think back far enough, I bet you will remember your mother giving you this when you got sick. I know my mother did." He knelt and removed the poultice.

Will grunted, sipped the bitter brew, and slowly gnawed on a leftover turkey leg Two Feathers handed him from his pouch. "Well, at least Yellow Hawk doesn't have Buck. We know that for sure." A slow grin pulled at Will's lips, but it morphed into a grimace. He laid his hand against his reddish-purple cheek.

"I—I do not know what's so funny." Guilt wormed its way from its corner in Two Feathers' mind, guilt for all that had happened to Will and his own family. No matter how often people said that what his uncle did wasn't his fault, that he couldn't control what Yellow Hawk did, thoughts of the man always made him sick. There was no understanding Yellow Hawk. Why had he shot the cougar? Why had he left them alive? Nothing made any sense.

As if reading his thoughts, Will commented, "Yellow Hawk talks to himself all the time. Out loud." Will shifted into Co-manche. "You taught me enough that I understood everything he said." Taking a small bite, he held his cheek and chewed with his eyes squeezed shut. He sipped the tea. "It hurts so bad to chew. I can't tell if Yellow Hawk knocked any of my teeth loose. It hurts to wiggle my tongue around." He closed his eyes again and sipped his tea.

"What did Yellow Hawk say about Buck?"

"He would mumble about the 'dunnia' and pace back and forth. He said something about the spirits not wanting him to have the stallion. That he wasn't a chief and couldn't have him, so that's why Buck keeps getting away. He blames you that he's not a chief anymore."

"Me? How did I do that?"

"Who knows? But I know one thing—teaching Buck to untie knots is the smartest thing I ever did. If he can get his teeth on a knot, he will worry it until he pulls it loose. There's no give-up to him."

Returning to the oak tree, Two Feathers searched around it in widening circles. He found where Yellow Hawk had waited and where his horse was tied. But no sign of Buck or Rojo.

He went back to Will. "You ready to go?"

"Can't we stay here?"

"No. Buck is not here, but Yellow Hawk knows we are. We cannot wait here to find out what he will do next. You can make it."

Two Feathers boosted Will onto Gray Wolf and mounted behind him. The horse made it plain he didn't like carrying double. After humping his back, prancing in circles, and stomping his feet, a few soothing words from Two Feathers calmed him somewhat. They headed downriver. "Where is Rojo?"

Will spoke through clenched teeth, his breath coming in short, sharp gasps. "Yellow Hawk took him away last night when he left me tied to that tree."

"When did the lion show up?"

"I spotted him shortly before you arrived. I was afraid to move and was sure wishing you'd hurry."

"How did you know I was coming? I was mad that you didn't listen to me. What if I decided not to come after you?"

Will shifted his position. "I knew better."

A soft snort and a slight smile accompanied Two Feathers' reply. "That lion must have eaten not too long ago, or he'd have eaten you."

Wrapping his arms around his brother, Two Feathers eased

him back. "Lean on me. Try to relax. Gray Wolf will dump us off if you do not stop squirming." Their shadows grew longer in front of them, and then faded away taking any color in the western sky with them.

Reaching camp in the waning light, Two Feathers slid off Gray Wolf's rump and caught Will as he fell. He laid him on the ground, lit a small fire, and brewed more willow bark tea. Holding Will's head in his lap, he forced him to drink it. Three times in the night, when Will's moans returned, he made him drink more tea and sat with him until he slept again.

While Will recovered during the next two days, Two Feathers searched for several miles around their camp for signs of Buck or any mustang tracks. His senses, however, focused on Yellow Hawk. He never stopped fearing what his uncle might do next. He sniffed the wind for even the tiniest wisp of smoke or the smell of broiled meat. He studied the ground for any disturbance showing someone had moved over the area. He watched how the grass lay or waved in the wind. He looked in the trees for broken branches or bruised leaves. He studied the animal trails for any sudden shift in the direction of the tracks. Since they'd been in the canyon, the water in the river had cleared somewhat. He studied its flow, watching for changes in color or the amount of debris floating by. He found nothing. By the end of the second day, he deci-ded he and Will had camped long enough in that place.

Two feathers shot a deer with his bow and jerked the meat while he waited for Will to heal enough to travel. The night before they set out, he gave Will a cup of broth with softened jerky and studied the bruises on his face. They were a dark bluish purple. Will could open his swollen eye to a small slit, showing a bright red eyeball. They'd decided his ribs weren't broken, but the skin over them was a dark purple.

"Do you think you can ride?"

Will shot him a doubtful glance and moaned.

Two Feathers grinned. "So, do you think Buck is just going walk into camp and give you a big sloppy kiss? Is that how you plan on finding him?"

Will lay still for a few minutes. "I wouldn't be surprised if he did that very thing. He's a smart horse." He groaned and sat up.

Two Feathers studied him with both hands on his hips. "I am not a medicine man. I will not take care of you forever."

A slight grin wiggled at the corners of Will's lips. "I'll be ready to ride by morning. I'm sure Yellow Hawk's still in the canyon because he knows Buck's here." The little grin faded away. "Two Feathers, Buck has been running free with wild horses for a long time. Do you think he has forgotten me? Do you think he will want to come back home with me?"

Two Feathers looked at Will as if he'd gone loco, "Yes. Will. He will come with you. Horses do not forget. But first, we have to find him before Yellow Hawk does. And that will not be easy."

THE MESA

By late the following morning, Two Feathers wanted to dump Will in the river. Each time his brother slid off Gray Wolf's rump to search for Buck's tracks—tracks he didn't find—Two Feathers rubbed the back of his neck until it started to burn. The sun would soon shine overhead, and they'd made limited progress up the canyon. Rounding a wide sweeping bend in the river, Two Feathers spotted the distant mesa he'd seen a few days earlier rising from the canyon floor. Before he could point it out, Will again slipped off Gray Wolf and raced to the river's edge.

Two Feathers sat on the horse, waiting. He cocked his drooped head sideways to watch his brother hobble along the river's sandy bank. "Gray Wolf, kick him the next time he slides off your rump to look for tracks that are not there. One more bruise will not make much difference." Gray Wolf huffed.

A grove of cottonwood trees near the river offered shade from the hot summer sun for their lunch with plenty of grass for Gray Wolf. Sweat trickled down Two Feathers' neck. It tickled. Swiping at it, he stripped the saddle from the tired horse and staked him close enough to the river to drink. With a few sticks and dried grass, Two Feathers built a fire. He warmed cups of water and soaked venison he'd jerked while waiting on Will to recover.

Will walked up and eased himself onto the ground across the fire from his brother. "This isn't getting us anywhere."

"I know. We need to get on high ground. Remember when we came here before and trapped the mustangs? That is what Running Wolf did. He went to the canyon rim so he could see far. Then he was able to spot the herd."

"Maybe we need to do that."

"I know where to go. When we split up the other day, I found the perfect spot. There is a mesa that rises from the edge of the river. It has a dry, rocky creek bed that winds to the top. I did not go up, but I did see tracks."

"Buck's?"

"No, mustangs. The river makes a wide bend around the mesa wall. From the top, we should be able to see a long way in both directions."

"What if we don't see anything? Then what'll we do?"

Two Feathers looked at Will, then at the river, following its winding course down the canyon until it disappeared around a bend. "I do not know. I guess we will have to wait until we see something."

They sat side by side in silence. The sounds of the river lapping against the bank, splashing over rocks, whispered secrets too low for Two Feathers to hear as it flowed past on its way to someplace he might never go.

"I think I know." The frank tone of Will's words pulled Two Feathers from his thoughts. He studied Will's face. The purple bruises now held a yellow tint around the edges. He thought about Will's courage, loyalty, and the many times Yellow Hawk beat or shot him. Will never stopped searching for Buck. He never stopped coming.

Two Feathers decided to stop thinking that because they were in Comanche country, he was the chief of their band of two. Believe in Will. Trust him. *Will would find me if I were lost instead of Buck*. After a moment, Two Feathers asked, "What do you know?"

"I know we need to stop being bait."

"What does that mean?" Puzzled, Two Feathers looked at Will.

"For three years, Yellow Hawk has battled against us. Each time he takes Buck—we go after him. He attacks—we defend ourselves. He attacks our friends—we go to the army for help. Everywhere we are. . . Buck is there. Yellow Hawk stays close to us because we're the bait that brings Buck close to him."

"That is true. But what do we do? We cannot keep Buck without fighting Yellow Hawk."

"You told me earlier you didn't like me being cougar bait. So, we stop being the bait and become the hunter." Will's words ended in a matter-of-fact tone.

"What are you thinking?"

He flashed a cocky grin. "We'll stop *looking* for Buck and start *hunting* Yellow Hawk." He grabbed their cups, gave them a swipe with his bandana, and stuffed them away. "Let's go. We're wasting time."

An hour of steady riding brought them to their old camp. "Look at those tracks." Two Feathers pointed to the ground. "There are Rojo's and an unshod mustang." He barked a hard laugh. "Well, well, Yellow Hawk certainly left us a message. His moccasin tracks are everywhere."

"I guess he wanted to be sure we didn't miss that he was here," said Will. "He's trying to keep us rattled and afraid."

Two Feathers walked around studying the scattered tracks. "He is telling me I am not Comanche, and I cannot track." He kicked the ground as he walked, smearing all the tracks. "I am getting tired of hearing that." He stopped and looked at Will. "You were right earlier. I do not want to be the bait for Buck. I want to be the hunter."

They followed the tracks at a fast pace. After about half an hour, Two Feathers stopped. "Will, we need to slow down. Yellow Hawk is making this too easy. I do not like it."

The boys slid off Gray Wolf and walked along the river, following fresh tracks in the red sand. The tracks veered into the water and disappeared. Following the river's edge, Two Feathers stayed several yards back from where the water lapped the sand and studied the ground, finding nothing. Will caught up, and they searched the riverbank. The tracks didn't reappear.

"Where'd they go?" Will waded into the water but found nothing. Up ahead, three flat sandstone rocks lay half-buried in the wet sand. He stepped out of the water onto the first slab. When he reached the third, he called out, "Two Feathers, come look at this."

"Did you find his tracks?"

"No, but he left us another message."

Two Feathers stepped out of the water onto the slab. He stared at a handful of sticks, broken into different lengths, some with one end charred black. They lay in what looked like a random cluster on the slab. But after he squatted on his heels to take a closer look, a quick breath brought him to his feet. The charred black ends of the sticks made the legs and tail of a crude horse. On each side lay the broken figure of a man.

"I wish he'd come up with a new message," said Will. "I'm getting tired of this one. Your uncle's a sick man."

"Yes, that is true." Two Feathers swung his foot and blasted the sticks into the water. He glared at them as the current carried them away. He stood that way for a minute pulling his anger back into its corner in his mind. If he didn't pack it tight enough, someday it would explode, and he would kill Yellow Hawk. The thought scared him. Sucking deep breaths in through his nose and out his mouth cooled him.

"Look, Will." Two Feathers pointed downriver. "The river is getting more narrow and the water deeper. It is moving faster and washing away any tracks. Yellow Hawk does not want us to know where he is going."

Will searched the surrounding brush. "I don't see anything that isn't supposed to be here."

Two Feathers stood staring upriver. "When we get to the mesa, we can stay in one place for a while and watch from high ground. And not find any more of Yellow Hawk's messages." He shaded his eyes from the sun and scanned the canyon rim. "When you do *not* see Yellow Hawk, that is the time to worry."

Gray Wolf began to tire as the afternoon passed. The boys slid off and walked beside the grullo to relieve him of the load he'd carried all day. They came to the mesa as dusk spread shadows among the boulders scattered along the base like the remains of some violent earth eruption. The last of the sun's rays lit its red walls. The river hugged its base. Shadows hid the narrow strip of sandy bank, making it look like the wall rose straight from the water. No vegetation broke the illusion of the red pillars stretching to their towering heights and scraping the bottoms of the low gray clouds that scudded overhead.

Two Feathers took Gray Wolf to the river to drink and brushed him thoroughly with dried grass. Staking him in a cluster of piñons and junipers to graze, he gathered fuel for a small fire.

"I'll go set a snare," said Will. "We'll eat something besides jerky tonight."

When he returned, Will sat their cups on a rock at the edge of the flame. "I wish we had coffee instead of jerky broth. Do you think a fire's a good idea? It could tell Yellow Hawk where we are."

"Yellow Hawk already knows. He does not need to see our fire. He is waiting for us to find Buck. We talk about hunting Yellow Hawk. But the truth is, we are all three hunters."

Will sat silent for a few minutes. "You're right. We're hunting the same things, each other and Buck." He leaned against a boulder. "So, we'll come together no matter what."

"Tomorrow, we will camp on the mesa top where Yellow Hawk cannot get to us and watch for Buck. We have seen many mustang tracks. I am sure Buck is with a herd, and maybe he will come by here."

"I hope so." Will went to check his snare.

Two Feathers heard a mockingbird whistle and trill from across the river. He tried to figure out which cottonwood tree held the warbler with its melodious assortment of songs. He stretched out on the ground and rested his head on a rock. He closed his eyes and listened to the rustle and rattle in the undergrowth as day hunters settled in for the night and night hunters came out for breakfast.

Soon, a rabbit, skewered on a green stick, grilled over red coals, and hot rocks from the fire warmed the cornpone they dunked in a cup of broth. For the first time in a while, their stomachs stopped growling.

The following morning, Two Feathers lay in that hazy state between sleep and wakefulness but stayed warm in his blanket. Thick clouds allowed only a thin line of pale light to make its way upriver from the east. It brought a slight breeze with it. The weak light outlined the trees of the canyon floor. The splash of water and the snuffle of horses pushing against each other when they came around the base of the mesa wall woke Two Feathers.

"Will?" His voice stayed within the foggy confines of their rocky nest.

"I hear them." Will slipped from his blankets and, hugging

the ground, inched his way around the large boulders that separated them from the riverbank. Two Feathers followed. Blurred shapes moved in and out of their line of sight. The mustangs were upwind, so the animals were unaware of their presence. The boys dared not move or make the slightest sound. Even a hint of alarm would alert the horses' keen senses, and they would be gone. Before returning to camp, they waited until all the mustangs passed out of sight.

"Buck wasn't with them." Will turned his back to Two Feathers and busied himself packing.

"I know. This is the second herd of mustangs we've seen in two days. We'll find him."

Two Feathers helped Will as he packed up camp. With Gray Wolf carrying the supplies and full water bags, they started up the rocky creek bed lined on both sides with dark sienna walls that rose like giant stairsteps to the mesa top. The dry watercourse was filled with gray rocks, some as small as a man's fist, others large boulders.

Two Feathers coaxed Gray Wolf up the trail. His hooves couldn't gain traction, and he balked. Two Feathers turned him around when he refused to go any farther. They all clambered back down, rocks rolling and tumbling behind them. At the bottom, Gray Wolf was the only one still on his feet.

Will sat with his legs splayed out. "Well, that didn't work."

Two Feathers shook the dust out of his braids and surveyed how they'd come down. "A man could make it, but no horse could. Those rocks are too loose."

"What're we going to do? We can't leave Gray Wolf down here. Yellow Hawk would get him for sure. We couldn't walk home, so we'd never leave this canyon."

Since there was no panic in Will's voice, Two Feathers decided to ignore his last statement.

Leading Gray Wolf, Two Feathers followed the river. Will

limped beside them, rubbing his hip. Rounding the mesa wall, they found a strip of sand with old mustang tracks along the water's edge. The sandy bank widened, but the tracks hugged the wall. Farther down, the river swerved away from the mesa, leaving a wide sandy beach littered with large rocks and a few good-sized boulders. Will found tracks leading to a split where two pillars, the outside one jutting farther out than the inside one, made a hidden gateway. Inside, the floor was covered with tracks where the mustangs traveled to and from the mesa top. The trail wound up the mesa, enclosed between tall columns like a high-walled hall.

Will dropped to his knees, his fingers skittering over the tracks in the sand. He stood, stumbled a few more steps, and collapsed to his knees again. "He's here. Look at this. He's here."

Two Feathers dropped Gray Wolf's reins and slid to the ground beside him. "What? What is it?"

"Buck! It's Buck."

"Are you sure?"

"Look." Will spread his fingers wide open and placed his hand inside a large hoof print against the wall. "My hand fits perfectly. I've been doing this since I was seven when Pa put the first pair of shoes on Buck. Here's one going up." He scurried up the trail on hands and knees, scouring the sand for another track. "Here's one coming down. It's him. He's here."

Two Feathers leaned against the rough wall. It'd been a long time since he'd seen a grin that big on Will's face.

Will sat beside him. "All we do now is wait. He'll come to us."

"And. . . avoid Yellow Hawk."

Keeping Vigil

Leading Gray Wolf, Two Feathers entered the opening in the wall. Will followed him up the steep mesa trail. They couldn't see far ahead, so Two Feathers pulled his carbine from his saddle boot. Will nocked an arrow in Two Feathers' bow. The narrow trail held a thick layer of red sand covered with mustang tracks, along with elk and deer, some going up and some coming down. High walls rose on both sides. Switchback turns led them up the side of the mesa. At the third sharp turn, the path widened. The outside wall had crumbled, tumbling rocks to the ground below. The trail followed the open shelf, which widened the farther they traveled. Stepping to the edge, the rocks and boulders he'd seen earlier spread out where the river pulled away from the mesa base and looked small from the ledge. The height made him queasy.

Will caught up with Two Feathers before the trail flattened into the wide shelf. Walking silently, side by side with Gray Wolf keeping pace behind them, Two Feathers held tight to his carbine. They could see where the trail ended at the mesa top. A large boulder sat against the wall, causing the trail to swing around and toward the open edge. A lone juniper tree, its thick trunk and limbs twisted with swirling ridges, jutted at an angle off the trail's edge with half its limbs hanging below the shelf. Its few green branches seemed to float in the air, its roots clinging precariously to the rocky ground beside the trail.

Rounding the boulder, Two Feathers waited for his brother to catch up. As he turned to speak to Will, Gray Wolf exhaled a loud grunt and jumped ahead. Slamming into both boys, he knocked Will off the edge. Will disappeared without a sound. Two Feathers hit the ground, striking his shoulder on a rock, and dropped his carbine. Leaping over the stunned Comanche, Gray Wolf raced up the trail and disappeared.

Yellow Hawk stepped out from the trail. The boy grabbed his gun and shot before the rifle butt touched him. The gun slammed into his collarbone, making his shot ping off the wall. Yellow Hawk disappeared back down the trail. Two Feathers rolled into a ball, pain stabbed through his shoulder. The echo of the shot faded down the canyon. But the sound of Yellow Hawk's voice, held by the walls of the mesa trail, was loud and clear.

"Hear me, son of a white man. You killed my sister. I killed your brother. You cannot live up here. There is no water. You are trapped. The dunnia is mine." The sound of running footsteps faded down the trail.

Stunned, Two Feathers gasped. His heart pounded like war drums. Blood roared in his ears when "*WILL!*" exploded from his lips. He scrambled on his belly to the juniper tree and looked over the edge. There was Will—alive—but hanging with both arms wrapped around a thick lower limb, his clenched fists white with the strain. Blood smeared his face, and his mouth was wide open. His legs swung over the tumbled boulders and river far below. As their eyes met, Will's squeezed shut. His mouth clamped into a tight grimace.

The long distance down the mesa wall to the canyon floor made Two Feathers' heart jump. *Oh, Will, do not let go!* The words screamed so loud in his head he thought he'd said them out loud.

"Get me up. I can't hang here much longer. Get me up!"

The pleading in Will's voice stopped Two Feathers' panic. He wrapped his right arm around the old juniper's fat root and gripped it with all his strength. The left one he stretched toward Will. "Grab my hand."

"I can't reach it."

"Yes, you can. Hang by one arm and grab my hand quick. Do not look down. Do you hear me? Do. . . Not. . . Look. . . Down!"

Will let go with one hand but grabbed the limb again when his body swung away from the tree.

"Wait a minute. Hang on." Two Feathers searched the wall above Will's feet, willing himself not to look at the river so far below. He took a deep breath and steadied his voice. "Will, above your left foot is a rock that sticks out several inches. Pull your foot up and step on it. Push yourself up far enough to grab my hand. Steady yourself on the tree."

Will's leg swung against the wall. His foot searched for the step and scraped off small rocks that pinged and clattered to the bottom.

Two Feathers refused to consider how long it took them to hit the rocks below. "Easy, Will!" he barked. "It is a little higher, closer to you."

Will's boot caught the rock. With his eyes locked on Two Feathers', he pushed himself up, let go with one hand, and grabbed.

Will's weight pulled the muscles in Two Feathers' arm, his sore shoulder, and back until he thought they would rip loose. He held onto the root with everything he had, but Will's weight slid him closer to the ledge. Scrambling back, he tightened his grip even more on the root, dug the toes of his moccasins into the dirt, and pulled. His stressed shoulder and bruised collarbone screamed their protest.

Sand, dirt, and pebbles broke loose as, grunting and

straining, Two Feathers pulled Will back over the edge. Together, they scrambled across the trail and collapsed in a heap against the mesa wall. Breathing in ragged gasps, they sat without talking. Two Feathers kept his carbine in his shaking hand and pointed back down the trail.

Finally, Will spoke, "Are you hurt?" He turned Two Feathers' head sideways. "Do you know your head's bleeding?"

"It is?" He rubbed his head. "There is a big knot back there."

"What happened to Gray Wolf? Why'd he jump like that?"

"Yellow Hawk somehow snuck up the trail behind us and either shot him with an arrow or hit him with a sharp rock. That is the only reason Gray Wolf would jump like that. I do not know why we did not hear Yellow Hawk coming."

Two Feathers didn't want to get up, but he did. His wobbly legs didn't want to cooperate, but they did. "Come on. I need to check on Gray Wolf." He picked up the bow, quiver, and scattered arrows and handed them to Will. "This time, I will not fuss because you dropped the bow."

Will's smile was a little off center, and his hand rattled the arrows as he stuffed them into the quiver.

The shelf opened wider as they walked up the path. At the trailhead, they walked out onto a broad flat meadow. Two Feathers stopped and swept his gaze over the lush space. He spotted Gray Wolf grazing on the rich grass.

Will stood beside him. "This has to be at least twenty acres."

A sheer rock wall reaching up to the canyon rim made the meadow's back boundary. The sight of it brought a smile to Two Feathers' face. "Looks like there is only one way up here. That will make it easier to guard against Yellow Hawk."

"That's true."

"But. . . Yellow Hawk could be waiting below at the trail entrance."

"That's also true. But. . . this is the best way to find Buck, and that's why we're here."

Walking farther out onto the meadow, Two Feathers ran his hand through the tall grama and buffalo grasses that waved in the wind. Large patches of prickly pear, dotted with red and yellow blooms, grew among clusters of boulders worn smooth by the sand that blew down from the canyon rim above them. Yucca plants showed off their tall spires of white blossoms.

"This is why we saw so many horse tracks on the trail up." He knelt on the ground. "Look, Will. There are all kinds of prints here. I see deer, even elk."

Will settled in behind a large boulder at the trailhead. "I'll stand watch first. Hand me your carbine. Yellow Hawk has mine and my ammunition."

Two Feathers nodded and walked toward the grullo. "Hey, boy. You all right?"

Gray Wolf came to the Comanche, grass hanging from his mouth. Wrapping his arms around the grullo's neck, Two Feathers leaned against him, breathing in the familiar smell of his horse. He stood there, the time running by unnoticed. Gray Wolf shifted his weight and swung his tail at flies. Two Fea-thers stepped back and ran his hand over the horse's rump, disturbing the flies gathered on a shallow gash oozing with blood.

"He shot you!" Looking at the sticky red smeared on his hand, Two Feathers sucked in air. "He shot an arrow at you."

He picked up Gray Wolf's trailing reins. "Come on. We need to set up camp and clean that cut." A tall, wide-spreading mesquite tree with low branches sweeping the ground looked like a good spot. Heading that way, he pulled a handful of grass and cleaned the blood from his hand, or at least most of it.

In the shade of the old tree, he unsaddled Gray Wolf. Digging in his bedroll, he found a bandana and wet it from the water bag. After cleaning the wound, he scraped the jelly-like insides from a prickly pear pad and spread it over the cut.

"That's the best I can do right now. There is plenty of cactus here, so you should heal right up. Knocking Will off the ledge is not your fault. Yellow Hawk caused that."

Before heading to Will, he stroked the horse and scratched him in his favorite spots. He remembered Yellow Hawk saying his mother wanted him to have a good strong horse. She wanted his uncle to give him one. Well, he had a horse like his mother wanted, but it was given to him by a white man. Mr. Goodnight was a man he'd learned to admire almost as much as he admired Running Wolf. He remembered that day three years ago when he watched Mr. Goodnight ride Gray Wolf off a cliff and into a ravine. He'd been certain both man and horse had been killed. But here he stood, his own Gray Wolf. He was a strong horse then and a strong horse now. "My uncle shot you. I am certain he aimed at me, but he shot you. I am sorry for that."

Gray Wolf ambled away, grazing on the abundant grass. Two Feathers rinsed the bandana and joined Will at the trailhead. "Here, clean your face. There is so much blood I cannot tell where you are cut." He sat beside Will and leaned against the boulder. "He shot my horse! My uncle, my mother's brother who taught me to ride, shot my horse with his arrow."

Will made no answer. The only sound was the click when Will chambered a round in the carbine.

Two Feathers closed his eyes. His chin dropped. He forgot to breathe until his body made him suck in a long breath. "How could he do that?"

Will's fixed gaze never left the trailhead. "Haven't you been looking for the answer to that question since you found out he killed your father?"

Two Feathers made no answer. He scrubbed at the pain in his head and watched Gray Wolf pull on mesquite leaves.

With Will on guard, Two Feathers explored the meadow. He found a dry creek bed near the mesquite tree and followed it to the rim. He realized it was the rocky creek bed they'd tried to come up earlier that day. From this angle, he could see they would never have made it. A man could climb up, but it would be a scramble. A horse had no chance.

Two Feathers took his turn at guard duty behind the boulder near the head of the mesa trail. He told Will about the dry creek bed and watched his brother search the ground for Buck's tracks. Will spent the rest of the afternoon sitting on a boulder at the mesa's edge, watching the river below in both directions.

The day turned warm, making Two Feathers sleepy. Sweat running down his back tickled, keeping him awake. Tall towers of dark clouds gathered in the northwest. The wind pushed them together through the afternoon, turning the sky a brooding dark gray. By dusk, thunder rumbled in the distance. The wind increased in speed, bringing the booming thunder louder and closer.

Two Feathers didn't like the feel of the air. Abandoning his guard post, he yelled for Will to come. They hurried to pack up camp. Not wanting to shelter between the walls of the trail because of Yellow Hawk, they stashed their goods on the leeward side of a cluster of large boulders away from the mesquite tree. At the first flash of lightning, Gray Wolf pulled on his reins, wanting to run before the storm. Two Feathers held tight and tried to calm the animal. Huge raindrops announced the coming downpour with a splat on the rocks. Soon, the few turned into a deluge. They couldn't see more than a few feet ahead, and the mesquite tree where they'd camped disappeared.

The boys huddled under Two Feathers' ground cloth, trying in vain to ward off at least some of the pounding rain. A streak of lightning fired itself from the clouds in a jagged line and struck the mesquite with such force the explosion split it in half and knocked both boys to the ground. Gray Wolf screamed, jerked free of Two Feathers' grip, and galloped into the storm. Thunder followed immediately. Its deafening boom shook the ground. Two Feathers tried to jump up and go after Gray Wolf, but Will grabbed him and wrestled him to the ground. Two Feathers watched his lips move as he yelled, but the storm drowned out all other sounds.

Two Feathers' eyes saw black spots from the flashes of lightning. His ears rang from the booming thunder that rumbled away. The rain stayed, making a wet, cold, and miserable night. He and Will huddled together between two boulders, trying to wrap the soaking wet saddle blanket around themselves and hold the wind-blown ground cloth over their heads. The wind had a different plan, lifting one corner to let in the rain, then another. When the storm tired of tormenting them, it moved on. Two Feathers fell into an exhausted sleep.

The warm sun on his face and Gray Wolf pushing his sore shoulder woke him. Grabbing his rope, he fashioned a hackamore and slipped it over the horse's head. Looking around, he saw the mesquite tree. It hadn't split in half as they thought, but the top limbs lay scattered on the ground. Two Feathers decided it wasn't the first time lightning had struck that old tree. Tying Gray Wolf to the stub of a limb, he spotted Will sitting on his boulder, watching for Buck.

After building a small fire and heating cups of broth for Will and himself, he took up his guard duty at the trailhead. After a while, the sun dried his clothes. He worked the tangles from his hair, braided it, and secured his hawk feathers, now bedraggled from the storm. Somewhere he'd have to get new feathers.

He knew Buck would eventually return to this meadow with the mustangs following him. Just when that would be worried him. They were low on supplies. With only one horse, they couldn't stay here long. They'd have to go to Las Vegas and get supplies or find Weeping Woman in Running Wolf's band.

Weeping Woman—he wanted so much for her and Red Wing to come live on the Pecos River Ranch. They would be safe there. He would keep them safe from the reservation in the Nations. When they found Buck, he would talk to her. Maybe she would come. If she came, so would Red Wing. Maybe Yellow Hawk wouldn't harm them anymore and leave Buck alone once Weeping Woman lived with them. He thought about that all morning while he watched the trail. He couldn't convince himself, no matter how hard he tried, to believe things could work out so well.

Noon came and went. Will didn't leave the boulder. By mid-afternoon, Two Feathers headed to Will's lookout to swap guard duties. Before he got there, Will leaped to his feet. "Two Feathers, hurry. Come look."

Will grabbed his outstretched hand and pulled him up onto the boulder. He was hopping around so much Two Feathers thought they would both fall off. Will pointed upriver. "See those horses?" His voice shook, making his words come out in a squawk. "Look behind the mustangs. See him? Do you see him?"

There, moving behind a herd of about fifteen mustangs, was Buck. They watched as he lifted his head high and sniffed the air. He stood still. The wind rippled his long black mane and tail. "Look at him." Will shook Two Feathers, nearly tumbling them off the boulder. "Just look at him. He looks wonderful. He's strong and healthy." Without taking his gaze off the stallion, he inhaled and blew out three huge breaths of air. "You found him, Two Feathers, you found him." He swallowed several times, sniffed, then wrapped his arms around Two

Feathers and hugged hard. The "thank you" Two Feathers heard was hoarse and choked.

They watched as Buck nipped at a lagging mare and moved the herd forward.

Will started to put his finger to his lips but stopped. "If I whistle, it will alert Yellow Hawk that Buck's nearby. What if he catches him before I do?"

"It is like I told you yesterday. Yellow Hawk is below, so he already knows Buck is here. I am sure he is waiting below to drive the herd up the trail. He can block the entrance. The mustangs and Buck will be trapped up here. If we let this chance pass, there is no telling how long until we find him again."

By then, Buck had driven the herd closer to the opening in the mesa wall.

Will put his fingers to his lips. The shrill whistle filled the canyon.

Buck stopped, his neck arched, his head lifted high. He pranced in a circle, whipping his tail.

Will moved close to the edge of the mesa and whistled again.

"Buck!" he yelled with all the force he could muster.

The buckskin held still, his head high, and focused on the mesa.

Once again, Will put his fingers to his lips and blasted the loudest whistle he'd ever made.

Confused at the strange sound, the lead mare, a blue roan, pranced and sidestepped in a nervous dance. She watched Buck, who nipped at the mares and young colts driving them ahead. The mare raced before the herd. When they reached the break in the canyon wall, she turned them up the trail as though she'd done it many times before. She knew there was good grazing up there.

Two Feathers stopped Will from racing to the trailhead, held him under the mesquite tree, and waited. They heard the clatter of the mustangs' hooves when they reached the rock ledge where Will had fallen. Two Feathers tightened his grip on Will so he wouldn't rush out into the path of the wild herd. He knew that if Will jumped out too soon, the horses would panic and bolt back down the trail, driving Buck away. They needed to be on the far side of the mesa top before he let Will step out from cover and approach Buck.

"Easy, Will. Not yet. . . Not yet. . . Do not run. Walk slow. Let Buck see who you are. Go slow, Will."

He gave Will a shake. "Are you listening to me?"

"Yes, I hear you. I understand."

Two Feathers gasped as Buck burst out from the trail. His tangled mane swirled around his head, and his long tail brushed the ground. Last night's rain had washed his coat clean, and though shaggy, it shimmered bright golden in the sunlight. His ears stood straight up and turned nearly in a circle. His head moved from side to side as he searched the meadow.

Two Feathers released Will. "Go to him, Will. Go."

Will walked out into the open meadow toward the big stallion that had run wild for nearly a year.

Lifting his head, Buck sniffed the air.

"Hey, big boy. Remember me?"

Buck stopped. His eyes focused on the boy who'd been his companion for the five years of his life. He nickered and trotted to Will.

Relief spread a smile across Two Feathers' face. Gray Wolf pranced and tugged on the rope, wanting to go to Buck.

"Easy, boy. Give them some time." Two Feather didn't take his gaze off Will and Buck.

Will raised his arms straight up. Buck lowered his head between them the way he'd done all his life and rested his head on Will's shoulder. Will wrapped his arms around the muscled neck, buried his face in the knotted ratty mane, and hung on. After a minute, he stepped back. Buck nuzzled Will's joy-filled face, his lips gently rubbing the boy. Will's laughter drifted easy and relaxed on the breeze.

Two Feathers watched for several minutes, grinning until his cheeks ached. The grullo pranced and shook his head, wanting to greet his friend. It was a struggle to hold his hand on Gray Wolf's muzzle to keep him quiet.

"Will, Gray Wolf wants to say hello. I am letting him loose."

Will waved at them to come on. Gray Wolf trotted to Buck with a welcoming nicker. They touched noses and breathed in each other's breath, then gently nipped at one another. Buck laid his neck over Gray Wolf's back. After a short time, the friends traded places.

"How about a cup of broth?" Two Feathers called out and stoked the fire.

Buck and Gray Wolf followed Will to the campsite. Will dug into their almost empty sack of supplies and pulled out a corn dodger for each horse. While Buck chewed his, Will rubbed his hands over the muscled body. Two Feathers waited for him to find the long scar Yellow Hawk's arrow left on Buck's hip. He could see it from where he stood. There were other scars on his body that hadn't been there before. Buck had fought to win his herd. Will rubbed his hands over each one. His fingers searched under the long mane and down each leg. He checked his hooves and moved to his hip.

Two Feathers took a few steps toward Will, then waited.

Will's hands and eyes found the long scar at the same time, and he froze. Two Feathers walked closer but remained silent. It was thick and raised. The golden hair covered part of it.

Will's fingers slid gently along the ridge that bulged through the horse's coat. He leaned his head against Buck's hindquarters, one hand resting on the scar and the other on his own scar. They stood together for several minutes. Two Feathers returned to the fire and left Will and Buck alone. After a while, Will joined him. Neither spoke about the scar. They watched the herd across the meadow as they sipped their broth.

Two Feathers liked what he saw. Some excellent mares stood out in the bunch. The lead mare, the blue roan, paced around the others and kept them bunched. She never stopped moving. Two Feathers knew the man smell meant danger to her. She stayed alert, ready to bolt at Buck's command.

She stopped. Her loud snort carried over the meadow. She sniffed the air, her ears pricked up and forward, her eyes focused on the trailhead—watching. The herd milled in confused circles and stirred up a cloud of dust.

Buck bolted and raced toward his herd.

Both boys dropped their cups. Two Feathers grabbed his carbine and handed Gray Wolf's rope to Will. "No matter what, don't let him loose. He will follow Buck." He raced to the boulder, took aim at the trailhead, and waited.

TROUBLE ON THE MESA

"Two Feathers!" Yellow Hawk called out. "No Comanche would get trapped like this. You are a coward!" A menacing laughter rumbled from the trail opening. The sound sent a shiver over Two Feathers.

The mare bolted, running the herd away from new danger. She and Buck kept them bunched against the canyon wall at the back of the mesa, trapped by the loud noises and the smell of man.

Yellow Hawk fired a shot. The bullet pinged off the boulder sending tiny slivers that stung Two Feathers' cheek and sent his heart into a mad race. Waiting, he peered around the base of the boulder. A brief glimpse of Yellow Hawk flashed, and he squeezed the trigger. The bullet struck the wall. Two Feathers huffed and checked his ammunition. *I'm no better a shot than he is.*

The Comanche warrior laughed. Two Feathers didn't recognize the sound. It was different from before, more low-pitched, then rose to a squeal. He'd never heard such a foreboding sound from Yellow Hawk. Two Feathers thought for a minute and realized he'd never heard him laugh, a chuckle now and then, but not happy laughter.

"Yellow Hawk." Two Feathers spoke just loudly enough for the man to hear him. "Stop! This is not a good fight. There is nothing here for you."

"The dunnia will be mine. I will once again be a chief. You cannot stop me. You will have no water, no food. I will not let you go down to the water below. You will see it, but not drink it."

Again, Two Feathers heard the weird laughter.

Bullets slammed into the boulder, spraying tiny rock shards all over Two Feathers. He shifted further behind the stone. A trickle ran down his forehead. Thinking it was sweat, he swiped at it, leaving a red streak on his palm and tiny rock shards. Blood! His blood! He closed his eyes and buried his face in the crook of his elbow. The last thin thread of hope that Yellow Hawk would accept him as family shredded. He wanted to leave here, go far away, and never see Yellow Hawk again.

Another bullet slammed into the boulder. Two Feathers waited. Would he fire again? Jerking his head up, he took a quick look at the trailhead. He could no longer see Yellow Hawk. Two Feathers glanced toward the mesquite and spotted Gray Wolf safely tied behind the tree. But where was Will? He squirmed between two large rocks to get a better look and caught a quick glimpse of him on his belly, making his way up the creek bed. What was he doing?

Again, Two Feathers counted his bullets and groaned. He knew Will's carbine was also low on ammunition, so Yellow Hawk would hoard his. Two Feathers' quiver held six arrows. How many did Yellow Hawk's have? He had no idea.

He searched again for Will, spotting him in the creek bed, working his way through the runoff from last night's rain toward the back of the mesa. Where was he going? Another shot popped from the trail. Two Feathers sprawled back on the ground. The whining ricochet of his answering shot sent Yellow Hawk scrambling deeper into the cover of the canyon walls. Two Feathers heard the rattle of rocks falling off the shelf at the juniper tree.

Two Feathers threw a worried look toward his brother. Stopping near a muddy offshoot of the creek, Will popped up, looked toward the mustangs, then dropped back to his belly.

What's Will planning?

Covered in mud, Will wiggled through the offshoot and disappeared behind a huge red boulder balanced on a sandstone base. The top had settled at an angle with the back end nearly to the ground. The front of the rock nearest the runoff was eight to ten feet off the ground.

Two Feathers looked back and forth from the trailhead to the creek. He didn't want to let Yellow Hawk out but needed to know what Will was doing. If Will climbed on that rock, he would be in the open—in a direct line of fire from Yellow Hawk.

And that's what Will did. Two Feathers' heart banged inside his chest like a trapped animal. He blasted the trail opening with a barrage of shots hoping his ammunition would hold out. Yellow Hawk, trapped inside, held his fire.

Will scrambled up the slanted rock to its highest point and bellied down. At his whistle, Buck came from the back of the mesa at a racing gallop, his black mane and tail flying behind him like winged death. *No, Buck. No!* Two Feathers silently pleaded. *"Do not come."*

Will stood, his bow across his back, arrows in his hand. Two Feathers' heart leaped. *No, Will, do not jump,* ripped through his head. He clamped his mouth shut before the words exploded from his throat and broke Will's focus. Buck wasn't trained to take a jumping rider. He turned and fired shot after shot toward the trailhead to hold Yellow Hawk back.

At a gallop, Buck circled the leaning boulder and disappeared behind it. And then—Will jumped. Two Feathers held his breath. A shot exploded from the trail opening and pinged off the rock where Will had stood. Two Feathers couldn't breathe. Where was Will? Was he dead? Was he lying crumpled and broken on the ground?

Buck bolted out from behind the boulder. Turning back toward the far end of the mesa top, he ran toward the roan mare. There was no one on his back.

"Will?" screamed Two Feathers, his head buzzing like a swarm of poked bees. Yellow Hawk stepped into the open and raised Will's carbine. Two Feathers yanked up his and, in a panic, blasted the trail opening. Yellow Hawk stepped behind cover. Two Feathers shot without stopping until he had no bullets left, holding his uncle away from Will.

Before the buckskin reached the herd, Will popped up from his horse's far side and settled himself astride the running stallion. Two Feathers' knees weakened, and he dropped to the ground. Yellow Hawk's return fire sprayed the cluster of rocks sending bullets whining over his head. The barrage stopped suddenly.

Buck and Will raced along the back of the mesa, driving the mustangs along the East rim. The noise and commotion made the roan mare panic. Leading the herd, she galloped for the trail leading off the mesa about a quarter of a mile away. The herd followed.

Two Feathers nocked an arrow and aimed at the trail opening. *Drop off Buck's side, Will.* The pounding of horses' hooves came closer. *Slide down, Will. Slide down!* By now, he could smell their dust in the wind. He waited for the blast of bullets to erupt. It didn't come.

When the herd entered the trailhead at full gallop, Will turned Buck away from the rim and rode up to Two Feathers. "What happened to Yellow Hawk? I didn't see him. Do you think the mustangs drove him down?"

Two Feathers stepped from his nest in the boulders still holding his bow and arrow. He leaned against the big buckskin, hoping his legs would hold him up. "He stopped shooting. He had to have run down the trail ahead of the horses. I hope he is gone. I am out of ammunition. I think he is, too."

"I had to get him off the mesa." Will slid down from Buck. "He had you pinned down. He was going to kill you this time. We can get down from here. I have Buck now. We could get Weeping Woman and Red Wing and go home."

They watched the trailhead for several minutes. Seeing nothing, they walked toward the mesquite tree to get Gray Wolf, who was stripping leaves from every branch within the limited reach of his tied reins. The grullo stopped in mid-chew and watched them come. Turning toward the opening where the herd disappeared, he lifted his head and sniffed the breeze. Will untied him and scratched behind his ears and under his forelock. The horse continued his chewing.

"Come on, ol' boy. Let's pack up and get off this mesa. I need a big drink of water. How about you?" Leading Gray Wolf and with a tight grip on Buck's mane, he and the horses walked across the open mesa.

Eyes on the ground, Two Feathers searched for arrows, either his or his uncle's. He spotted one and bent to pick it up. When he stood, Yellow Hawk stepped out of the trailhead with his bow in hand. With each stride, he ate up the distance between him and Will like a snarling wolf moving in for the kill. Will stood frozen in the open as though he were a deer alerted to danger.

Without thinking, Two Feathers nocked his arrow and pulled the string to his cheek in one fluid movement. He watched Yellow Hawk's bow rise and the taut sinew string stretch until the arrow was centered on Will's chest. Two Feathers sent his arrow ripping through the air, singing its death song. He watched it strike his uncle's neck sending the warrior's arrow off course. It clipped Will's arm, embedding in a limb of the mesquite tree behind him.

Frozen in place, Two Feathers felt blank. There was no

sound, no air, no thought in his head. Unable to move, he stared at the shape in the dirt.

Then, a weight slammed into him, smacking him to the ground. It pressed him into the red dirt, covering him. He couldn't move. He lay there, motionless, and watched a red ant scurry away.

A moment later, he was flipped onto his back. Hands searched his chest, arms, legs. Finding no wound, Will shook him, grabbed his head, and turned his face toward his. "Two Feathers?" He shook his shoulders. "Two Feathers, are you hurt?"

Will's words made their way through the fog that enveloped Two Feathers. His eyes focused on his brother's face. "Is he dead? Did I kill him?"

Will helped him sit up. "I think so. He hasn't moved."

"Will, he would have killed you. He was coming too close. This time he would not miss."

"I know. He had me dead center. I could see the tip of the arrowhead. You knocked him down, and he still clipped my arm. You saved my life. . . again!"

"Go check. Go see if he is. . . If he is. . . "

Will stood still, his wounded arm stiff against his body. He turned his head toward the shape on the ground. "Uhh, I'm not going over there."

Shaken, Two Feathers moved one leg, then the other, before he could stand. Will reached out to steady him. "Breathe, Two Feathers. Stand still for a minute." The boys leaned against each other, neither taking a step.

Two Feathers noticed his left fingers ached. He looked at them. Surprised to see white knuckles gripping his bow, he stretched them out, feeling the pull of each tendon. The bow dropped to the ground. He looked at it as though he didn't know where it came from, then picked it up.

"Come on." Will nudged Two Feathers' elbow. "We need to check on him."

Still not moving, the boys stood and stared at the figure on the ground. It seemed so far away, as though they'd come upon a strange sight never seen before. Without thinking, Two Feathers took the last arrow from his quiver, nocked it, and held the bow ready. The mesa top was quiet. Nothing moved. The clouds overhead held steady in the rich blue sky. Their whole world was holding its breath. Together, side by side, they took one step. . . and watched. Then a second step. . . and watched.

When there was only one step left, they stopped. Two Feathers wondered if he should feel something. All he felt was empty. He looked at the man lying in the dirt. His face was turned toward him, and his eyes were open. What had he seen in those eyes? Anger. Hate. Indifference. Sorrow. Sometimes there was something he couldn't name, sometimes it was evil, and sometimes, very briefly, he saw tolerance or maybe affection. But there was never enough for him to hang on to.

Dark red dirt, stained almost black surrounded the man. . . where'd the stains come from? He'd watched deer, and other large animals die, but they weren't people. He couldn't pull his gaze from this man. He waited for him to stand and be angry he'd let the horses stampede or taunt him by saying he did woman's work or insult him by saying he was not Comanche. But the man on the ground didn't get up. He was dead.

The box inside Two Feathers' mind that held his years-long pain from Yellow Hawk's hatred cracked. He felt a trickle seep out of it and out of him. He looked at the stains around Yellow Hawk, expecting to see the trickle, like water seeping into dry red dirt, join the stains darkening the ground under his uncle.

What have I done?

TRUTH

Will stood beside Two Feathers, still holding Gray Wolf's reins. Buck backed away, not liking the man on the ground. "We can load him on Gray Wolf to take him down. I'll pack up our stuff first."

"Wait, Will. Leave one blanket to wrap him in. I will make him ready. We can bury him here."

"Are you sure? Don't you want to take him to Weeping Woman?"

"No. I will tell her where he is and bring her here if she wants to come."

Will sat still, watching his brother. "Two Feathers, I. . . Umm. . . I'm trying to think of something good about him for you to remember, but I just can't. I'm sorry."

"I do not want to remember him. Yellow Hawk was a strong Comanche warrior, but that was not enough. He was not a good man. And worst of all, he did not care for his family."

Will took the water pouches down to the river to fill them. When he returned, they prepared Yellow Hawk in the Comache way. Two Feathers washed the body covered in scars. He ran his hand over their rough ridges. Yellow Hawk *had* been a strong, respected warrior who'd fought in many battles for the Comanche against the Apache and Arapaho. And in battles against Mexicans and Whites. He remembered sitting in Running Wolf's lap around campfires when he was small and listening to stories told of Yellow Hawk's bravery and courage, of his success in battle. He wondered if Yellow Hawk was really such a bad shot. Why did he always miss him but not Will? What had happened to him?

Two Feathers ran his fingers through the long black hair, smoothing out the tangles. Gray hairs were scattered all through the black. He'd never thought of his uncle as growing old. He parted the man's hair and braided it tight. He looked at the hawk feathers the man had worn. Two Feathers tried to smooth them out, but many barbs were missing.

He studied them for a while, then glanced at Will. "I remember when I was little, my hair was thicker, lighter, and longer than any other boys my age. My mother was proud of my hair. The wind would blow it over my face. I could not see and would laugh and run away from her. It was a game we played. One day, while playing that game, I smacked into a tree and bloodied my nose. Yellow Hawk picked me up and washed my face. He pulled my long hair into two braids, took two robin tail feathers from a pouch on his belt, and tied one into each braid. He set me down in my mother's lap and told her, "This boy will be called Two Feathers." My hair was always braided after that with a feather in each one, just like Yellow Hawk's."

He pulled at the barbs again, trying to straighten them and fill in the empty gaps. Will picked up one and worked on it.

"My mother told me that story every time my braids came loose. She would warn me, 'Never let Yellow Hawk see your hair untidy.'"

Two Feathers ran his fingers over the tattered feathers, then threw them down. He looked at Will. "I forgot all about that. It was a long time ago." He removed his red-tailed hawk feathers from his slick tight braids and worked the shafts into his uncle's hair.

They dressed him, then wrapped Yellow Hawk's body in the blanket and tied it with what rope they had. Searching the ground toward the trailhead, they found his bow, quiver, and several arrows. Will found his carbine, which Yellow Hawk had taken.

A large slab of sandstone formed the bottom of a cutout in the canyon wall at the back of the mesa. It jutted out several feet to make a shelf. They put Yellow Hawk on the slab as far back against the wall as they could and faced him toward the rising sun. His knife was in his scabbard, and his bow, quiver, and arrows lay at his side. Working together through the afternoon, they carried rocks to cover him with layers deep enough to keep the varmints away.

The boys sat in the shade of the canyon wall towering over them. Two Feathers stretched the sore muscles in his back. Blisters puffed up on the calluses on his hands. He poked at them. Taking turns drinking from a water pouch, they watched Buck and Gray Wolf grazing together.

"Two Feathers," Will leaned back and closed his eyes. "We need to tell either the army or the sheriff what happened here."

"And Running Wolf."

"I've been thinking about it. When we start home, I'll stay until we get the herd trail broke. Then, I'll go to Las Vegas and tell Sheriff Crook. He can tell the army, then I'll catch up before you've gone too far."

Two Feathers did not answer. Will opened one eye. The Comanche was asleep.

The following morning, Will packed up their meager supplies, and they came down off the mesa. Will and Buck drove the mustangs behind Two Feathers on Gray Wolf. The boys came across Rojo's hoof prints and tracked him upriver. They found him grazing on thick grass in the holding pen where Running Wolf had held the mustangs they took to Las

Vegas. With the blue roan mare leading the herd and Gray Wolf pushing from behind, they passed through the gate. Will counted fifteen horses, mostly mares with a few young stallions. Two Feathers wrestled the gate shut.

After several days, the horses no longer spooked when the boys entered the pen. One afternoon, Two Feathers sat beside Will in the shade of cottonwoods along the creek that meandered its way through the holding pen.

"Will, I need to tell Weeping Woman what happened."

"Yes, you do. I'll stay here with our mustangs. You find Running Wolf's camp. Talk to her and bring her back here." A grin spread across his face, and with a chuckle, he added, "And don't forget Red Wing."

Two Feathers ignored the jab. "I may be gone a long time."

"I'll wait."

The confident tone in Will's answer pleased Two Feathers. Never before had Will been willing to wait alone in the canyon without Two Feathers. He grinned. *"Will might become a Comanche after all."*

After searching for two days, Two Feathers rode into Running Wolf's camp. Red Wing saw him coming and ran to him. He reached for her hand and swung her up behind him on Gray Wolf just as he'd swung her up onto Old Pony when they were children. She wrapped her arms around his waist and hugged him. Gray Wolf didn't seem to object to carrying Red Wing.

"I have been so afraid for you. I missed you. Yellow Hawk was here days ago to see Weeping Woman. I do not know what he said, but she will not speak. She does not often come out of her teepee."

"Where is Weeping Woman? I have much to tell her."

"There." Red Wing pointed to a teepee at the edge of a line of willows along the creek. "She will be happy to see you."

Stopping Gray Wolf in front of the teepee, Two Feathers dismounted. "Take Gray Wolf to the creek for water. I will talk to you after I see Weeping Woman. We have much to talk about."

Red Wing grinned. "Yes, we do."

The light inside the teepee was dim. At first, he didn't see her beside the small fire. She was scraping dried corn kernels from their cobs.

"Weeping Woman."

She looked up and gasped. Scrambling stiffly to her feet, she threw her arms around his neck.

"Two Feathers." His name came out in a quiet sob.

She hugged him as though she would never let go.

Grasping her hands, he stepped back to see her better. He chuckled. "I come to see you, and you nearly choke me. What kind of a greeting is that?" He wiped the tears streaming down her face.

She pushed his hands away. A smile straightened her slumped shoulders and lit her eyes, which sparkled in the firelight.

"Come, sit down." She grabbed a pouch hanging from one of the poles and broke off a hunk of pemmican. "Eat. I always keep your favorite waiting for when you come."

He took a bite. The sweet flavor flooded him with memories. When he did something good or if Yellow Hawk scolded him, Weeping Woman always slipped him a hunk of his favorite treat. It made him feel safe and loved.

"I have persimmon tea." She filled a tin cup to the brim. Careful to not spill a drop, she handed it to him.

He grinned and sipped the warm brew. "You spoil me." *How can I tell her that her husband's dead? That I killed him.* He choked slightly on the tea.

A small sob escaped. She seemed to shrink into a smaller version of herself.

Two Feathers put down his cup and picked up her hands. "What is it? What makes you so sad when I have come?"

"Yellow Hawk. He told me he would end your life. He told me that is the only way he could bring back Morning Dove."

"What? My mother has been dead for a long time. She cannot come back."

"He is twisted. He makes no sense. But he is dangerous."

How can I tell her this? Where are the words? He took a deep breath, shook away his doubts, and decided to tell her exactly how it happened. "You do not need to fear your husband anymore. Yellow Hawk is dead."

She stiffened. Her gaze bored all the way into his heart. Unable to hold her eyes, he looked away. When he forced his look to return, her gaze shifted outside the open flap of the tee-pee. *Will she walk out? Will she turn her back and leave me?*

"Did you kill him?" The question, whispered as faint as a hummingbird's breath, landed with a heavy thud in Two Feathers' stomach. He shifted away from her and fed a few small sticks to the fire that didn't need them.

"Yes." He took his tin cup from a smooth stone in the fire ring and lifted it to take a sip. Tea drops splashed and sizzled on the hot rocks. "I buried him with his bow and arrows and all he had with him that I could find."

She studied his face, stroked one cheek, then put her arms once again around his neck and hugged him close. "Go tell Running Wolf and Red Wing."

Two Feathers realized he was holding his breath and let it out in a slow stream. Relief flowed through him, making him go limp. His eyes blurred, and he buried his face in her neck. Comfort, as always, flowed from her into him. He let go, and this time, she wiped the tears from his face. "Go." She gave him a gentle push.

Two Feathers ran to the creek where Red Wing waited. He

found her giving Gray Wolf a bath by dipping a large gourd into the water and pouring it over the horse. The dirt and grit were gone, leaving the horse's gray coat shining like Two Feathers hadn't seen in a long time.

"Whose horse is this, and where is Gray Wolf?" laughed Two Feathers. "Bring that handsome horse out of the creek. I will help get the tangles out of his tail and mane."

Red Wing led the grullo onto the bank and put on her moccasins. "I do not know who owns this horse, but he needs to learn to take better care of it," she teased. "Maybe he needs someone to help him."

Two Feathers' smile faded from his face. He picked up a strand of the horse's tail and started working out the tangles. "Red Wing, I have something to tell you." While his hands work-ed, his gaze stayed away from her eyes. He took a deep breath and started talking. "I killed Yellow Hawk. . . "

They talked through the long afternoon. He told her the whole story of Yellow Hawk's stalking him and Will and of Yellow Hawk trying to capture Buck. At dusk, she left him for a few minutes, and when she returned, she brought two red-tailed hawk tail feathers and tied them in Gray Wolf's mane behind an ear.

"I found these long ago and saved them for you. Gray Wolf is a fine horse. Old Pony would be proud you have him."

"Red Wing, we have been friends since we were old enough to know each other. You always stood beside me. Thank you for caring for Weeping Woman. I want her to come live with me." Somehow, one of his braids appeared in his hand, and he twisted it between his fingers. He couldn't keep his feet still. He began to sweat. "Will you come, too? I am not ready for a wife. You are not ready to have a husband, but will you be Weeping Woman's daughter until we are ready? When that time comes, I will speak to your father."

Her head was down, and he couldn't see her face. He waited for her to say something.

"I will give him as many horses as you want," Two Feathers' pleading tone dropped to almost a whisper.

A tiny sob hiccupped from her. She raised her head. The most beautiful smile he'd ever seen was on her face. She threw her arms around his chest and squeezed hard enough to stop his breath.

Two Feathers, with Gray Wolf following, walked through the Comanche village, holding his head high with pride. Red Wing walked beside him to the teepee of Running Wolf, her father.

Weeping Woman stayed inside her teepee for the next two days. She mourned the loss of her husband in the Comanche way. She cut her hair, cut the skin on her arms and legs, cried aloud, and sang sad songs. On the third day, she walked down to the river and sat there all day. Before dark, she washed in the clear water and cleaned her wounds. Holding her head high, her jagged, cropped hair slick with water, she walked back to the village.

Two Feathers followed her inside her teepee. He sat beside her and held her hand. "I need answers. Yellow Hawk is gone. Tell me why he hated me so much, and we will speak his name no more."

She looked away and wouldn't meet his gaze. He put his hand on the side of her face and gently pulled her head around until she had to look at him. "Tell me, Weeping Woman. Tell me the truth."

Morning Dove

Weeping Woman took his hands away from her face and pulled them to her chest. "There is no need to speak of these things. Yellow Hawk is dead."

"Weeping Woman, I *need* to know the truth. You told me part of mother's story before, but not all of it. What happened when Yellow Hawk returned and learned Morning Dove had married a white man?"

Even in the dim light of the teepee, Two Feathers could see a change come over her. Weeping Woman's eyes lost their far-away look, her face tensed, and the crinkles hardened. Her body stiffened. He slid closer.

The words spit from her mouth. "It was terrible. Yellow Hawk almost killed his father because he allowed such a marriage. The men pulled him off. He took Running Wolf with him and found Morning Dove at their cabin on the Red River. He tried to take her back. He tried to drag her back. But she would not go. She told him she loved John Randall. She stayed." Weeping Woman breathed out a low sigh. Her head sank. "She left us all."

The fire burned down to a small bed of coals. Even though the air was warm, her words chilled him. Adding more fuel, he stirred the coals, and the flames sent heat toward them. He picked up Weeping Woman's cold hands and rubbed her fingers to warm them. She didn't seem to notice.

"In Yellow Hawk's mind," Weeping Woman's eyes glazed over as though she'd slipped back in time, "she betrayed him by marrying a white man. She defiled herself. She was no longer Comanche. When the time came for you to be born, John Randall brought her back to us. You were born here in the canyon. For a long time, Yellow Hawk would not look at you. He would not touch you."

"Why?" *What was wrong with me? Was I so awful?*

"Because your father was white. Every time they visited, Yellow Hawk would leave and return only when John Randall was gone. I think he planned to kill her husband and force Morning Dove to return, but you were born. Every time he looked at you, he saw only the white. To him, you were not Comanche."

Two Feathers rolled his eyes. "He told me many times. But he named me. Why did he do that if he thought I was not Comanche?"

"He also named his sister Morning Dove. It was not his place to do, but he did it anyway. It was not his place to name you, but he did it anyway."

Two Feathers dropped his head into his hands. *I am so confused. What am I supposed to do now?* A deep ache settled in his throat. He sat that way for a long time, unable to admit that he knew this—that he'd always known it. Weeping Woman sat silent.

When he looked at her, she was watching him. Her smile was back. He swallowed several times and dug at his eyes with the heels of his hands. His voice husky, he asked, "Why was this never spoken about?"

"He would not allow it."

"What do you mean?"

"After the Day of Death, when Yellow Hawk returned from hunting, he found your mother dead and your father in mourning. Rage consumed him. Yellow Hawk killed your father on that day."

"I remember the Day of Death. I thought the soldiers killed my father. The sound of the guns and the screams were in my dreams for many years. I did not know the truth until the day Yellow Hawk tried to choke me to death, and I left his camp."

Weeping Woman gripped his hand. "Yellow Hawk would not allow her name to be spoken. No one could tell you about her. As the years passed, his rage grew. I became afraid to even think of her. When you were a baby and cried for your mother, he would put you outside our teepee and leave you there. The women would come get you. When he left, I would bring you back. He was the chief of our village and a hard man. Many people feared him."

"Why am I still alive? He had many chances to kill me."

She smiled at him. "Because he loved you. You are his sister's child." She stroked his cheek.

"What?" Her words roared through his head. He could find no sense in them. "There was no love for me in him. He hated everything about me."

"You have your mother's face. When he looked at you, he saw her. Sometimes, Two Feathers, love and hate walk hand in hand."

A memory slipped from the locked box in his mind. He remembered being small and sitting at the edge of a river watching the minnows swimming in the shallow water. A frog hopped from rock to rock. Trying to follow it, he slipped on a flat mossy slab under the rushing water and fell. The current sent him tumbling down the river. Strong hands scooped him from the water. Coughing and sputtering, he wrapped his little arms around Yellow Hawk's neck and hung on with all his strength. He felt the gentle pats on his back and his soothing sing-song words as his uncle carried him to his mother. He remembered Yellow Hawk scolded her for not watching him better. Where had that Yellow Hawk gone? That Yellow Hawk was like a wisp of wind, leaving only a faint memory behind.

Confusion overwhelmed him. *Hate. Love. How was I to know? What did Yellow Hawk want from me?* Suddenly, he was cold. Cold as though he had no blood. *Maybe there's no answer. Maybe I need to let it go.*

Weeping Woman fed sticks into the fire and warmed water in a tin cup. Taking crumbled leaves from a pouch, she dropped them in the simmering water. She handed him a small pemmican bar. The aroma of mint filled the teepee.

A feeling of deep sadness squeezed Two Feathers until he could barely breathe. Why had he stayed away from Weeping Woman? He'd turned his back on her because of his hate and fear of Yellow Hawk. Never again! Never again would he stay away.

He looked at the pemmican in his hand and the hot tea in his cup and he remembered all the cups of tea, all the pemmican, all the tears they washed away. They sat in silence while he ate.

"You want to know something funny?"

She took his hand in hers. "What?"

"When I go to the white man's town, the people there don't see me as half white. They only see a Comanche."

He left his hand in hers, and she gripped it tightly. "You are what you make yourself to be. Do not let others decide who you are."

"But I am two people fighting a war that neither one wins."

She placed one hand on his cheek. "That is not true. You are Two Feathers, a fine Comanche man."

Her words wrapped around him like a warm blanket and

brought him peace. The box in the corner of his mind was still full, but a little empty space was opening.

Two Feathers rose and stepped through the flap of the teepee into a bright warm morning. He wished Will was here to help him sort out the jumbled thoughts in his head. Thoughts of Will shifted his thinking from Yellow Hawk to the Pecos River Ranch and Pa, Will's father. He'd taken Two Feathers into their family without questions, not caring who he was, Comanche or White, but *what* he was, a boy worthy of care. Weeping Woman's words could have come from Pa's lips, "You are what you make yourself to be." He would no longer keep his two worlds separate. They'd come together with Yellow Hawk's death. His mother had chosen to live in two worlds, and he would follow her. The box in the corner of his mind opened all the way. It felt good, and he didn't think he would need it anymore.

He took Gray Wolf to the river. While the horse drank, he wondered how he would persuade Weeping Woman to come live with him on the ranch. After all, he was her only family. However, she'd never known any other life but her life with the Comanche, and all her friends were here.

He didn't worry about Red Wing coming. He knew she would go anywhere he went. That thought made his heart race and spread a smile across his face. His cheeks grew warm, and a little chuckle slipped out. He glanced around to be sure no one heard it.

He looked back at Weeping Woman's teepee standing apart from the others. It was time to ask her. He couldn't put it off any longer. Gray Wolf followed him to Weeping Woman's teepee, where he secured the horse to a tree branch. He stepped inside and sat down across from his aunt. "I want you and Red Wing to come with me."

"Where are we going?"

"I want you and Red Wing to come to my land and live there. I will help you pack, and we can bring everything to my land."

"Why?" Her voice rose with a hint of panic. "Your enemy is gone. There is no danger for you or your brother." She twisted her hands, rubbing first one and then the other. "Come live with the Comanche."

Two Feathers stood and walked around the sides of the teepee, running his hands over the bags and baskets that hung from the support poles. Many of them he remembered. One held pemmican, another held herbs she would give him when he'd had a runny nose. On the large floor was a roll of deer skin he knew held the knives and tools she used to clean and prepare hides. Another roll held smaller tools she used to make his moccasins and shirts.

How could he make her understand her life as she'd always known it was ending? The thought lay heavy across his shoulders like the weight of a buffalo hide. He sat back down across from her.

"It is not as simple as it used to be. I have a story to tell you. You know of the Navajo in the western canyon country. The soldiers took them from their homeland to the Pecos River at Fort Sumner, many days south of here. Old ones and small children died on the long walk." Her eyes closed. She turned her face away from Two Feathers.

"The soldiers said they had to live on the reservation with their enemy, the Apache. They told them they could grow food, have cattle, and live their days there. But the land was cursed with salt. The water was bitter. No food would grow. The Navajo starved. If they left the reservation to hunt food for their families, the soldiers came and took them back."

Her face hardened, and she squeezed her eyes tighter.

"I met a Navajo girl named Na-es-cha at Fort Sumner. I

watched her stand in line with her mother to get food. They were given only a small bag of flour—no meat. Their bones stuck out under their skin. I watched men that had once been strong warriors, but now they walked with no spirit. Their eyes held no life."

Two Feathers paused and studied Weeping Woman, who sat in silence. Did she believe him? Did she realize the Comanche might face the same fate as the Navajo?

When she finally looked up at him, her eyes scolded him for his words. "That will not happen to the Comanche. We are warriors. We are part of this land. We live in it, and it lives in us. They cannot take that away."

"Come with me." He took her hand and pulled her to her feet. "Come outside." He led her to the river and turned her in a slow circle. "Look. See the walls rise high above us. See the trees, the grass. See the river that gives us life. See this place that we share with all living things. Very soon, it will not be ours. Soon, we Comanche will be forced to leave this place and never live here again." He waited, letting his words sink into her mind. "I speak the truth." His voice sank to a whisper, "I have seen it happen."

"How can that be? Why do you say these things?" Her words were clipped, her voice shaky.

"The white man has already taken some of the Comanche to the reservation in the Nations. Soon, they will come here, and we will have to go."

"We will fight. The Comanche are strong warriors."

"Yes, we are. But we are few. The whites are many. We will kill some of the whites. But more will come. White soldiers with guns will kill many Comanche. Soon, there will be no more of us to fight. They will not stop coming, and we will die."

He stopped talking and waited for his words to sink in. Weeping Woman staggered as though his words had knocked her off center. She rocked from foot to foot with her arms squeezed around her as if holding her life together. The fresh grief slashes lay red and raw, scattered between old scars like ridges on her arms. The marks had been there since Two Feathers had known her. Why hadn't he noticed them before?

Red Wing walked up and stood next to Two Feathers. Weeping Woman beamed at the young girl. She took her hand and then picked up Two Feathers'. She held them both as tears rolled down her face. "You will not stay, and you are taking Red Wing."

"I have a place for you and Red Wing." Two Feathers took a step toward Weeping Woman and gently squeezed her hand. "We will be Comanche, but we must also learn the ways of the whites. I have done this and have learned to make their ways mine. I can ride out on the Llano Estacado and know I am Comanche. I have food to eat and a warm place to sleep. I have family. I do not want to see the light go out of your eyes like it has for the Navajo."

Weeping Woman studied their faces until Two Feathers pulled his hand loose and stepped back.

Stepping forward, she picked up his hand again. "I will think about your words and talk to Running Wolf and the old men. I will decide what to do."

Two Feathers tried once more, putting all his love for her into his words. "You are called Weeping Woman because you have lost so much. Your husband is dead. Your children are dead. Your mother and father, sisters and brothers are all dead. Your arms are covered with scars of the dead. I am alive. You are the only mother I know. Come live with me."

PALO DURO MUSTANGS

On a warm sunny morning a week later, Two Feathers swung the gate of the holding pen wide open and tied it to a tree. He mounted Gray Wolf and sat with Will in the gap, watching the mustangs grazing in the meadow. "Look at them, Will. What a sight! I have always wanted my own herd, and this is it." Buck, his long black mane and tail rippling in the breeze, watched from a small hill in the center of the meadow. "With your Buck standing at stud, the Pecos River Ranch will raise some fine horses."

Will threw his head back and laughed. "I wish you could see your face. You look as proud as a hen with her first chick."

Their laughter washed over Two Feathers, filling him with confidence. "It is time to go. Tell Buck to head them up the trail."

Will stood in his stirrups and hollered. "Buck." He raised one arm and circled it over his head. "Bring 'em out!"

Buck drove his herd of Palo Duro mustangs, led by the blue roan mare, out the gate and upriver toward the trail to the canyon rim. Water exploded under their hooves and sparkled with rainbows in the morning light. Two Feathers bunched the horses and slowed them to a walk. He followed them up the steep trail from the canyon's confining red walls to the Llano Estacado covered in blue-gray sagebrush. It was as if the vastness of the open high desert stretched the muscles of his eyes as he looked across the land with nothing to stop how far he could see.

He rode up next to Will. "Buck and the lead mare make our job easy. These horses are going to take themselves across these Staked Plains." He loosened his water pouch from the saddle horn and took a quick swig. "I am hungry. When we get back to the ranch, I want a big plate of biscuits smothered with bacon and gravy."

"Too bad. There's nothing to eat until we make camp tonight except jerky."

Two Feathers shook his head. "No jerky for me. I am tired of jerky." Two Feathers studied the mustangs. "Look at Buck. I have never seen him look so proud. He struts along behind the herd like a big ol' Tom turkey."

Will grinned. "Kinda like that hen with one chick."

Two Feathers chuckled. "Yep, kind of like that." He rode away from the herd to watch Weeping Woman riding a short, stocky horse with a stubby mane and tail and spots scattered over his white rump. The horse had scrambled up the canyon trail like a mountain goat. She led a second horse pulling a loaded travois. Two Feathers couldn't understand how she'd packed that travois so it didn't fall apart on the steep trail. She'd finally agreed to come after he'd promised to take her to Running Wolf's camp whenever she wanted. Head high and eyes straight ahead, she rode with her back stiff as though the tiniest bend would shatter her.

Off to the west of Weeping Woman, away from the wilder mustangs, Red Wing drove the two women's herd of horses, leading a packhorse loaded with more of their belongings. She was strong and moved as though she was part of the horse. He'd been right. It didn't take much to persuade Red Wing to come along. He promised to give her father several strong ponies when the time was right, and here she was. Red Wing helped him convince Weeping Woman. The girl had refused to leave her family unless the older woman agreed to come.

Pulling his bandana from his pocket, Two Feathers wiped his face and tied it around his neck—cowboy style. "In a few days, we will be back at the Pecos River Ranch."

"I'm ready," said Will. "It feels like we've been gone forever. But we must do one more thing before this is over."

Two Feathers rode easy in the saddle. He smiled. "I know. Sheriff Crook."

They moved the herd at a slow pace, letting the horses graze as they went along. Several times Buck managed to find water. A week of travel brought them to the Gallinas River, where they made camp. Weeping Woman and Red Wing filled the water pouches, washed, and spread blankets over bushes to dry.

The following morning, Will and Two Feathers changed out of their buckskin clothes and into jeans, shirts, and boots. Two Feathers tucked his braids under his hat. Weeping Woman walked up and studied him. She shook her head, reached up, and took off his hat, letting the long brown braids fall to his waist. She fastened a hawk feather into each one.

"Remember what I told you." She tugged a braid. "You are a good Comanche man." Cocking her head to one side, she patted his plaid shirt, "And a good white man. Do not forget that."

Will's grin stretched across his face. Weeping Woman removed his hat, and his curly, sandy hair tumbled to his shoulders. She reached over and twisted a curl around one finger. "Soon, Tall Horse, you will have Comanche braids."

Cowboys again, they started the herd south toward the Pecos River Ranch. Will left Buck to help Weeping Woman and Red Wing with the horses and rode Rojo. The two cowboys turned away from their herd and headed west toward Las Vegas.

An hour later, they rode down Main Street, crowded with wagons and buggies of many shapes and sizes pulled by either horses or mules. The boys drew the usual stares and curious looks. Two Feathers sat tall in the saddle, eyes straight ahead. They dismounted in front of the sheriff's office, and the hard clomp of their boots on the boardwalk sounded loud in the morning sunlight. On the door, they found a note saying the sheriff was at the cafe.

Dodging wagons and horses, they crossed to the boardwalk on the other side of the wide street. The bell over the cafe door rang as they entered. Two Feathers savored the aroma of bacon and biscuits, ignoring the curious looks. Spotting Sheriff Crook at a corner table across the room, they headed toward him. The sheriff nearly knocked his chair over in his eagerness to greet the boys.

"Well, look who's here. I'm mighty glad to see you." He grabbed their hands tight and squeezed so hard Two Feathers worried he would not be able to hold his fork. "Sit down, sit down. Knowing you two boys, you're about half starved. How about breakfast?" Not waiting for an answer, he hollered across the room. "Mary Pearl, bring these horse wranglers platters of bacon, biscuits and gravy, eggs, and whatever else you've got." He sat back down. "And coffee, bring us a whole pot of coffee."

Two Feathers and Will followed Sheriff Crook to his office an hour later with their belt buckles pinching their stomachs. Once settled in his chair, his tone became serious. "Now that we're alone, tell me what happened. You're about as thin as toothpicks and shaggy as rangy mules in the dead of winter. Where have you been?"

Two Feathers and Will took turns telling all that happened over the last several months, Will being shot, losing Buck, the long winter, their decision to cross the Llano Estacado alone, finding Yellow Hawk in Palo Duro Canyon, Will's capture, the fight on the mesa top... and finally, Two Feathers killing Yellow Hawk to save Will's life. When they were done, Sheriff Crook eased back in his chair and sat in silence so long Two Feathers began to fear what he would say.

"That's quite a story." The sheriff choked on his words, walked to the window, and stared outside for a while. "I'm amazed you're still alive." He whipped a half-clean hand-kerchief from his back pocket and blew his nose. Facing the boys again, he returned to his chair. "Sergeant Baker should be coming into town from Fort Union in the next few weeks. I'll report your story to him. He can tell the fort commander."

They stood to leave. "Thank you, Sheriff. We will be return-ing soon for more supplies." Two Feathers offered his hand along with a smile. The man grabbed it in both of his and shook it gently. "You do that, son."

"And maybe to sell more horses to ol' Silas Porter." A grin-ning Will also shook the man's hand. They mounted Rojo and Gray Wolf and headed south.

A few hours riding at a steady lope brought them to the herd. Two Feathers watched Weeping Woman sitting easy in the saddle as though she'd been born there. He wondered how many miles she'd traveled pulling a travois. He was relieved to see the beginnings of a change in her. Maybe she'd accepted the differences going with him would bring. All her life, she'd been on the move. Would she adjust to staying in one place? He hoped she would learn to accept ranch life. He felt certain it would make her life easier. He hoped it would make her happier. He shifted his look to Red Wing and smiled. He liked watching her ride. She was as good on a horse as he was. He couldn't imagine a future without her.

He remembered that day three, almost four years ago, when he'd run away from Yellow Hawk. And now, he was together again with Weeping Woman and Red Wing, two of the people he loved most. He was taking them to the Pecos River Ranch. His throat clenched so tight he could barely breathe. He stopped Gray Wolf and sat still. Closing his eyes, he made a fervent promise to them: *I will do my best to make a safe place for you*. Will and his Pa had offered him a safe place. He'd never felt like he didn't belong with them.

He watched as Red Wing kept her herd moving at a steady pace. New feelings welled up inside him. He decided one of those feelings was family—his growing family. Joy and affection came with family and a sense of responsibility—that one scared him. How was he going to care for them? He wished he could talk to someone older, like Pa or Running Wolf. In a panic, his gaze skipped back and forth between these two new members of his ranch family, finally settling on Weeping Woman. As always, she calmed him. She wasn't just a rock to lean on—she was a boulder.

Two Feathers turned his eyes south toward home. There was that word—home. He thought about it. It felt different from any other time he'd used it. There was no worry, no fear that home was only a dream that could blow away with the wind. There was love in the word. It felt solid. He liked the weight of it and rolled it over in his mind.

He and Will would make a home for Weeping Woman, for Red Wing, and for their Palo Duro mustangs—a loving home.

— The End —

ABOUT ALICE V. BROCK

 Alice V. Brock learned to love Western books as a child when her father brought home a Louis L'Amour paperback and she fell in love with the cowboys galloping through those pages. Mr. L'Amour's books brought the West alive to her. The history of Texas and New Mexico are full of stories of those times. Her wish is to bring them alive for kids of today.

Her chance to see cowboys in action came when she married and moved to her husband's family ranch in Iola, Texas. Now, she and her son operate the ranch with the assistance of her two granddaughters, AKA The Tumbleweed Club. These two cowgirls keep things lively on the Brock Ranch.

The first book in the award winning Will and Buck Series, *River of Cattle* and the second book, *Mystery on the Pecos* have both earned Western Fictioneer's Peacemaker Awards and Will Rogers Medallion Awards.

The Will & Buck Series can be purchased at www.Pen-L.com, on the web, or by request at your favorite bookseller.

DON'T MISS THE REST OF THE WILL & BUCK SERIES BY ALICE V. BROCK!

– BOOK 1 –
THE RIVER OF CATTLE

**Winner of the
Western Fictioneers Winner Best Western
YA/Children's Fiction, 2017
and
Will Rogers Medallion Finalist for
Younger Readers, 2017**

Will Whitaker's eleventh summer is one thrill after another.

A cattle drive with a famous Texas Ranger, a Comanche trying to steal his horse, a buffalo stampede, thirst-maddened cattle crossing eighty miles of alkali desert to a dangerous ford on the Pecos River—it's almost more than Will can endure. He gets to work as a drover, riding his best friend Buck, a big buckskin stallion, until he is captured by a vicious Comanche war chief. And only his worst enemy can rescue him.

Two Feathers—half white, half Comanche—runs away from his tribe when he learns his uncle killed his white father. He sees Will's horse and knows he is destined to have him, this great warrior's horse. Camping alone and following the winding River of Cattle across the High Plains of West Texas, he tries again and again to take him. Will foils him every time, but Two Feathers comes too close and is captured by the drovers.

The two boys, both fighting the grief of their mother's deaths, both without a true home, face death and danger separately, but eventually they must learn acceptance of each other's differences or their mutual mistrust could lead them to disaster on the brutal Texas-New Mexico frontier.

Will they become brothers or mortal enemies?

"A compelling and triumphant introduction to the colorful bygone era of cattle drives. Alice Brock entertainingly weaves fact and fiction into a dual tale of high drama, where diversity and friendship must meet head-on to determine who survives."

– Tim Lewis, Director of the Writing Academy at West Texas A&M University, author of *Forever Friday*

Dear Readers,
If you enjoyed this book enough to review it for Goodreads, B&N, or Amazon.com, I'd appreciate it!
Thanks, Alice

Find more great reads at
Pen-L.com

www.ingramcontent.com/pod-product-compliance
Lightning Source LLC
Chambersburg PA
CBHW021500240626
47154CB00002B/457

* 9 7 8 1 6 8 3 1 3 2 5 1 6 *